Pirate Spirit

THE ADVENTURES OF ANNE BONNEY

A NOVEL

JEFFERY S. WILLIAMS

iUniverse Star
New York Lincoln Shanghai

PIRATE SPIRIT

THE ADVENTURES OF ANNE BONNEY

iUniverse Star
an iUniverse, Inc. imprint

iUniverse books may be ordered through booksellers or by contacting:

iUniverse
2021 Pine Lake Road, Suite 100
Lincoln, NE 68512
www.iuniverse.com
1-800-Authors (1-800-288-4677)

ISBN: 978-1-58348-467-8 (pbk)
ISBN: 978-0-595-89364-5 (ebk)

Printed in the United States of America

To Katherine
My Anne Bonney,
My piratess of the high seas,
You have plundered my heart and soul.

To Calvin
My son,
My first mate,
You have made my life's voyage an adventure.

ACKNOWLEDGEMENTS

I am indebted to my wife, Katherine.

Without her, I could never have finished this novel. Her gentle yet consistent prodding encouraged me to reignite the fires of my muse, reunite with my daemon, spread my literary wings and dramatize Anne Bonney's story—for the sake of our family's legacy. As we worked closely together on this book, she helped me to better understand the mysterious, romantic ways and whims of the feminine spirit.

Call it a genuinely absurd venture for a man to consider writing from a woman's point of view, but I embraced the challenge, and thankfully had the sense to enlist my wife to help me in this odyssey. Her intuition and discernment into the human psyche are a continual source of amazement for me, and the insights she plumbed from the historical records on Anne Bonney and Mary Reade proved an indispensable element in the writing of this novel. It has been an unforgettable experience I will always treasure.

Truly a "wise and understanding wife is from the Lord."

You are beside me always, my bride, my wife, the love of my life.

Many thanks are in order to my mother Diane Williams and my mother-in-law Rosalie Gilcrest for their careful proofreading, and to Renée Schwetzer for her many helpful observations.

I also want to express my appreciation to the editors at iUniverse for their assistance.

In researching the materials for this work, credit needs to be given to the following books and authors: *A General History of the Robberies and Murders of the Most Notorious Pirates* by Daniel Defoe, *The Pirates Own Book* by Marine Research Society, *The Pirate Trial of Anne Bonney and Mary Read* by Tamara

Eastman and Constance Bond, *The History of Pirates* by Angus Konstam and *Under the Black Flag* by David Cordingly.

AUTHOR'S NOTE

Anne Bonney's story is a truly remarkable one. From the turmoil of her early life in Ireland, to her teen rebellion in the New World, to her spirited two-year odyssey among Caribbean pirates, her experience with all its amazing coincidences is well documented. Anne Bonney, and her friend Mary Reade, are the best-known female pirates during the Golden Age of Piracy in the early 1700s, and reinforce the adage "truth is stranger than fiction." Even Daniel Defoe in his seminal work *A General History of the Robberies and Murders of the Most Notorious Pirates*, grants the reader "may be tempted to think the whole story no better than a novel or romance."

While the many sources on Anne Bonney make for an intriguing read, there are too many holes for a full-length, detailed biography. Her story captured my imagination, so I decided a historical novel was a worthy undertaking. While I remained true to all the recorded documentation, the novelist in me had to surmise and create her reflections and dialogues and fill in a few gaps of her life. Most of the principal characters—William McCormac, Peg Brannan, James Bonney, Mary Reade, Woodes Rodgers, Calico Jack Rackham and much of his pirate crew—were all real people. Other than Edward Brannan, the other characters play minor roles, which helped dramatize the plot and flesh out the themes.

The end of the novel is based on one of the theories historians have posited about Anne Bonney, since there exists no records of her death or release from prison in Jamaica after 1721. No one knows the rest of her story. What I have created here I hope is a tribute to her piratical and prodigal experiences.

CHAPTER I

I could hear my mother calling for me, but I ignored her. I was building a sodden cave, and I did not want to be interrupted. As I wedged sticks together to make supports and crossbeams for my cave, I heard her voice drawing closer. She rounded the corner of our cottage and found me near a cluster of hawthorn.

"Oh, Anne, you're a fine kettle of fish. Your clothes are filthy, your hair is a rat's nest, and you smell like the bog. You act more like a boy every day."

I went on with my construction.

"Your father is coming today. He has something very important to tell us," she said.

I saw my father once a week, and even then, our meetings were brief. I could not recall my father ever having weighty news to share with the family. I looked up at my mother. She wore a white, flowing dress. The light of the sun shimmered on her wavy red hair, giving her an angelic appearance. She smiled at me.

"He said all things would be new."

"What things?" I asked.

"We'll find out soon enough, but first we have to get ready for his arrival."

After enduring an afternoon of my mother scrubbing, dressing, and primping me, my father finally arrived. My Uncle Edward, who was one of his servants and my mother's older brother, drove his carriage. Uncle Edward drove my father from his mansion in Cork to our little cottage in the country. I knew Father would not tell us the news right away. My parents would first have a drink of sherry and exchange pleasantries. As we finished our meal of black pudding, mackerel rolls, and colcannon, my father arose from the table, adjusted his wig, and straightened his waistcoat.

"We are going to the New World," he said.

Those words sounded within my depths. They were my deliverance. I would gladly depart my Irish homeland for the hope of new possibilities.

Even though King George's reign had unified England with Scotland, my father said Ireland would never be at peace with the British, and he would never be at peace with his wife back at his mansion. He habitually grumbled that between the Parliaments, the Protestants, and the peasants that infested our land, was it any wonder Ireland reeked like a steaming, rotting swamp?

As I listened to him, I determined never to return to my green and stormy homeland. Though I was only eleven at the time, the insults, the fights, and the cruelties I had endured from hypocrites had forever soured any loyalty I may have once felt for Ireland.

"Anne, how do you feel about sailing across the ocean to a new land?" my father asked.

I reached out and took his hand, and I thanked him repeatedly for the chance to explore the unknown rather than to make the best of a bleak existence. Why stand and fight for an ounce of dignity and decency when I could walk away and gain pounds of adventure, freedom, and opportunity?

I knew the supposed security of Cork, where my life would be dictated by the expectations of others, would slowly suffocate the spirit and life out of me. Give me the New World. Give me new adventures. Give me hope.

"We will depart in about a fortnight," my mother said shortly after my father left for the evening. She ran a brush through my long and ever-tangled red hair. "Your father and I will first marry, and then we will set sail for the Carolinas—and a new life."

I listened in a stupor, blinking at each new fact that would change my future. In a few days, my mother, Peg Brannan, would become Mrs. William McCormac, married into wealth and respect. No longer would she be my father's fired chambermaid or a wanton seductress who had ruined his marriage. And I would no longer be the illegitimate product of an advancing nobleman's lust.

"But what of Father's wife?" I asked, grimacing at each stroke of the brush. My mother paused. In the mirror, I could see her smile droop to a frown, unsettled by my pointed question. I wondered whether I was in store for a scolding.

"He will issue her a certificate of annulment. Then he will be free to marry me in the Americas, which is allowed in the eyes of our compassionate Lord."

"But I heard in church that it is a sin to divorce," I said.

"Annul, not divorce. Besides, your father protests against such ridiculously strict rules that the Church burdens us with. He claims men, not God, designed such rules. We will become Protestants in the Americas, where religious freedom is a God-ordained right. Now, Anne, enough of this idle prattle, and you will attend to your studies until we leave."

"But why?" I whined. "If I'm to leave this country, I would rather stay at home and help you and Uncle Edward prepare for our journey. I hate the school."

She patted my head. "It is your father's will. You will obey."

I knew it certainly was not my father's decree; she was using his authority to keep me out of the house so I wouldn't broach any more difficult subjects. My mother's avoidance of certain conversations always angered me. I never understood why she refused to answer some of my questions. She would rather keep things under lock and key than discuss them openly.

It was her simple yet comely character, which would ultimately prove her bane in life. She had little education and had worked as a maid all of her life. She accepted her station without much reflection and had learned to take orders, never questioning authority. This approach to life had served her well in keeping her employment and preventing many mishaps, until the day my father persuaded her to sleep with him. I can only imagine my mother's simple thoughts as this unfaithful man satisfied his passions with her body. When he had finished, he ordered her not to speak a word of it to anyone, especially to his aristocratic wife of a mere year, Catherine.

For the next few months he tumbled her nearly every day in various rooms of his mansion, evidently finding her compliance more satisfying than his wife's frigidity. Predictably, my mother sought him out one day to inform him of the wages of his sin: me.

The scandal seeped through the walls and down the stairs and eventually spread to the public square of Kinsale. Edward told me my father caught hellfire from his wife, his in-laws, his parents, and the priest. He garnered his only support from sympathetic fellow lawyers and investors at the pubs, who offered him a wink and a pat on the shoulder.

He steered clear of the places where his character was attacked and spent most of his time on the successful aspects of his life, namely practicing law and making money. In truth, he had inherited a great estate from his father, but he possessed the Midas touch when it came to maintaining and bolstering his wealth. He fired my mother but then quickly and quietly set her up in a cottage with my Uncle Edward. Edward may have been older and wiser, but he often needed moral support and financial help due to his taste for liquor and his occasional episodes of public drunkenness.

On certain days of the week, my father would visit our cottage, couple with my mother, eat dinner, and then travel back to his mansion at a late hour, choosing to sleep in the solitude and solace of his study.

By the time I was born, my father had set up this weekly rendezvous with my mother and had managed to assuage the embittered feelings of betrayal at home. His wife had decided to accept her place as the spouse of a philanderer as long as she could enjoy the delicacies of preferment—as Edward once said to me, "Men only go bad once they get rich, while women only get rich once they go bad."

I always knew which nights Father would visit. Mother would wash, perfume, and prepare her long red hair throughout the day. I would watch her apply nuances of color to her pallid, smooth face. If I asked a question about my father, her emerald eyes seemed to flash and widen, and her pursed lips would break into a half-smile—ever careful to keep her mouth closed, since her front teeth slanted to the left. I adored her smile because it seemed to raise her cheekbones and make her eyes sparkle, eyes that I imagined contained mysteries and secrets. She was tall, slender, and small-breasted, with Rubenesque hips, as I once heard Father say about her under his breath. She walked with a gentle sway I tried to imitate but could never match. While I may have shared some of my mother's features, I did not possess her alluring style, which obviously hypnotized my father.

When my Da, as I sometimes called him, would arrive at our home, I always wished our brief moments together would last longer. He would give me a quick hug and a swift pat on the head, and then quickly turn to Mother and embrace her warmly. He had piercing blue eyes, a distinct crease down the middle of his forehead, and an enormous frame. When he removed his wig, I admired his blond hair, and his dark suits were always clean and well brushed.

At the time, I thought him honorable for owning up to his responsibilities, standing his ground under the societal pressures, and possessing so great a love for my mother and me. I longed to feel closer to him.

A few years later, I would come to understand that he was merely looking out for his own best interests and refining his hypocrisy (a twisted condition I would sadly recognize in my own decisions until I finally came to my senses, like a prodigal soul).

Chapter II

The thought of crossing the Atlantic Ocean and seeing the New World engulfed me into a heightened state of emotion, which was tempered only by my mother's directive that I still attend to my education for the last few days as well as face one last visit with my "noble" stepmother. I loathed my schoolmaster, though I had come to appreciate the education I received, both from books as well as experience. And he did manage to instill in me an interest in and an appreciation for the stories and poetry of the Holy Bible and other works of literature.

Concerning my stepmother, my father gave her the task of teaching me proper etiquette. Once a week, Mother dressed me properly and Edward escorted me to the mansion, where my father decided it right and proper that his misbegotten daughter be taught manners befitting an aristocrat.

I despised both of them though I could now say they no longer made me distraught.

The morning after we learned of our imminent departure, I cradled my books under my arm, whispered a prayer, and walked to school with Edward along a cobbled street, buttressed by hedgerows. Beyond the hedgerows, forests of pine and greensward, wet with dew, glistened in the sun.

Edward was the most wonderful man alive, and I secretly hoped I would someday marry him. Though he was older than my father, I thought of him as handsome and distinguished with his salt-and-pepper hair. He had a rugged face with a moon-shaped scar on his left cheek. Once I asked him about his old wound. He told me a saucy tale about earning it in a tavern fight. Above all, I admired his strength—the huge loads of wood he would carry to the house, or the heavy axe he could wield so effortlessly.

Sometimes I would purposely fall and claim I had twisted an ankle and could not walk. I loved it when he lifted me into his arms, and I would rest my head against his chest and smell his scent: an aroma of brawn and vigor, of wood shavings and rum. He told me amazing stories of knights, soldiers, highwaymen, and pirates. He explained the reasons behind our customs and patiently answered all my questions, except a few he claimed I was too young to know about. He gave me guidance I seldom followed, but most of all he listened to me.

He was my guardian, my protector, my mentor. In retrospect, I would say Edward taught me more than my real father about how a father could be: formidable, wise, compassionate, and loving. Whenever Edward sternly corrected me, he followed it with an embrace. Sometimes when we walked, he would gently cusp his hand around the back of my neck. I loved the warmth and security.

As we walked to school, I enjoyed looking at the herds of sheep, cattle, and occasionally deer that grazed in the grassy, rocky fields. We passed farmers piling the shale that surfaced after each growing season. Others worked on tilling the ground in preparation for sugar beets and grains, mostly for the breweries come spring. "The Irish must have their ale," Edward often said with a smile. The bells of Shandon Steeple in St. Anne Church, where I was baptized as an infant, rang. The school was located in the center of Cork. Father told me education would prove a vital asset to freedom and security, especially for a woman of high birth, so I must be schooled in the classics, science, history, music, and arithmetic. He finagled it so I could attend with the students of blue blood whose parents were not wealthy enough to supply them with a governess. It did not matter; I hated the school and everyone who attended it, but I still had to go.

After wishing Edward a fine day and climbing the steps of the school, I recalled my first painful days here nearly two years ago, how I overcame fear, and how I had planned to turn the tables on my enemies before I sailed for the New World.

* * * *

The first day I attended the school they called me an illegitimate, a bastard, a whore's daughter, a harlot's whelp. Their insults stung, and I cried most the morning, feeling utterly alone. I begged my mother not to send me back, but she announced that my father had paid a great deal of money to provide me a suitable education and that I should respond with gratitude. Most girls with my background never received an education. Ignore their rude comments, she said. For the next two months I tried to bury myself in the books while I endured their abuses and cruelties. During our walks back and forth to school, Edward listened to me loyally and gave me sage advice, sprinkled with the Scripture and experience. He spoke of honesty, dignity, discipline, and tolerance. But one day, about a year ago, his counsel changed me forever.

As we strolled along a field, a large hound bolted out into our path from a row of cornstalks. I trembled at the sight of his curled lips, immense teeth, and raised hackles. When Edward shouted and stepped toward the dog, I turned and ran. The dog shot past Edward, chased me down, and leaped on my back. I lay on my side, covering my eyes with my hands and screaming. I felt his teeth pierce my cheek, and then he began to shake me violently. Pain erupted in my head. I felt myself fainting. In moments, though, Edward grabbed the dog and repeatedly stabbed the hound in the belly with a knife he had pulled from his pocket. The dog released his grip and howled. It struggled for a few minutes but then became still and silent. Edward ripped off his shirt and pressed it against my face, gathered me up into his arms, and began running. The fresh stabs of agony were horrible, but resting in his arms and seeing his frantic-yet-sure face comforted me. Tears streamed down Edward's cheeks, but I knew all would be well. He was like a guardian angel sent directly from God to shield me from harm and to care for me.

The doctor told me I was fortunate to be alive. I rested in bed for several days, biting my lips against the pain until they, too, bled. I slipped in and out of nightmare-filled sleep, struggling with fever. Edward never seemed to leave the room. The poor man looked terribly guilty and apologized to me many times. He cleaned my wounds and fed me soup. Sometimes he would read to me from the Bible. Other times he would regale me with funny poems from a book by Geoffrey Chaucer called *The Canterbury Tales* or from La Fontaine's *Fables*. I kept thanking him and reassuring him that I harbored no bitterness, only appreciation for his presence.

The day came to pull off the bandage and let me look at myself in the mirror. I am not sure what I had expected, but the oval scar on my cheek shocked me. First I looked to my mother, but she just looked away without a word. Tears brimmed in my eyes. I turned to Edward, expecting him to flinch at my hideous face.

"I am grotesque! I look like a monster," I sobbed, hoping someone would disagree with my words.

My mother did not reply.

But then Edward did an amazing thing. He stepped toward my bed, knelt beside me, and kissed my scar. He smiled and said, "I think it's unique and mysterious and bewitching."

I studied his intense eyes, searching for insincerity. The tone of his voice sounded genuine, but I had learned from my mother and father that people look away when they lie, especially if I held my gaze on them. Edward's eyes never shifted from mine. I smiled back and reached out to hug him.

"Even better. A smile makes it even better. Ah, Anne, those eyes, that voice, and now that cheek—you will intoxicate a man, and will no doubt have suitors lining up some day." He gave me his vintage wink. So I winked back.

"Oh, and now a bit of the minx. Careful, you're still a bit young for such allure."

When the time came to return to my schooling, I told Edward I did not want to go back, and then he gave me advice I would never forget.

"The dog attacked you because he sensed your weakness and fear."

"But I'm only ten," I said.

"Age has little to do with being a mark. Victims come in every size and shape."

He went on to explain that standing tall and strong in the face of mistreatment would change the way animals perceive you. "And there are animals everywhere you turn in this world," he said. "You must decide if you will be a martyr or a master to them."

He bent toward me. "Now listen. If you ever have to fight a man or beast bigger than yourself, remember this: go for the eyes."

"The eyes?"

"The eyes are the most vulnerable part of any animal. Press your thumbs into the eyes with all your might, and your attacker will let go and run from you."

I lay in bed and thought about his words, and about my mother and father and the choices they had made in their lives. I looked at the angry scar on the side of my face, a permanent reminder of the ambush and my cowering. I clenched my fists, closed my eyes, and vowed not to quietly accept the role of victim any longer.

It wasn't long after that fateful day that I returned to school. A few days later I lashed out and hit a girl in the face with my book for excluding me from a game with the other girls. Blood spouted from her nose. She screamed and ran to the schoolmaster. I received a thrashing on the behind with a paddle, but I learned an important lesson. The girls now feared me, and with fear came a kind of respect and force I had never before realized. Edward questioned whether I had not lost the balance between strength and civility, but there was no returning to the place I had been.

The boys still harassed me, though, especially Peter, an older, larger boy. During recreation, he badgered me most. "Your mother is a filthy strumpet. When is she teaching you the old trade?"

This event set my mind toward my next challenge. If I fought Peter, would the boys leave me alone as well? I sat in class and planned. It was during a history lesson, and the schoolmaster spoke of Irish blood boiling at all injustice and refusing to accept defeat against the tyranny of any nation. My schoolmaster noted with pride the many times Ireland had been a thorn in the side of conquering nations. He reminded us that Irish had pushed the Vikings and the Normans, from our homeland. Britain's extraction would soon follow. And Ireland, he said, also had a rich history in arts and academics. The Book of Kells, the Catholic monasteries, and the miracles of St. Patrick—all were sources of Irish pride.

As I sat in my seat and vacantly listened to the schoolmaster, I found myself inspired by Irish defiance in spite of my preoccupation. I figured if I caught Peter by surprise, he would fall and I could cudgel him a few more times so that he would never forget me.

For the next couple days I practiced using a sturdy oak branch to smack a head-shaped rock off a high stump. Edward inquired about what I was doing, but I refused to answer. I chose the day and hid my branch inside a cluster of bushes where Peter and his friends walked by during our free time. Instead of nervousness, I felt supremely confident, prepared to hurt him and then stand up to the consequences. I did not hope to win the fight, merely to create mutual respect and a treaty of sorts. I wanted to show him and his friends that though they were larger and outnumbered me, I could still rise up and prove my mettle. I dashed to the bushes and lay in wait.

Peter led the pack, bragging about some feat he had accomplished. Gripping the branch in my hands, I leapt from the bushes and stared at him without a word. He stopped and looked at me with a sneer. He smiled and started to speak, but I did not let him. I swung with all my strength, bashing him squarely in the face with the branch. He went down, holding his hands to his nose. Blood trickled through his fingers. His friends stood shocked. I did not wait for a reaction. I pounded him again and again on his chest and legs with my branch, and when he rolled over, I gave him two blows to the back before his friends grabbed me and yanked the branch from my grasp. One grabbed my hair and started to drag me away, and another cuffed me once across the cheek. Then the schoolmaster intervened.

He pulled me into his room. His grip on my arm frightened and thrilled me. He pushed me against a desk and pulled out a switch from behind a bookcase. "You wicked child. You've been nothing but trouble, and now I'll make you regret the day you were born. God smote Sodom and Gomorrah for their wickedness, and that is what you deserve."

He started whipping me, aiming for my bare calves, punctuating each snap with Scripture. "Spare the rod, spoil the child. I will do what your mother and father are too weak to do."

I had envisioned this moment. I had made an oath to show no emotion and mask any indication that the stinging switch hurt at all. I predicted that it would anger the schoolmaster more but that my silence would begin to spook him. He relented after the twelfth stroke. I turned and stared at him without a word. I could see his discomfort over my long gaze and I formulated a new principle: silence in violence and violence in silence. It left my enemies adrift with uncertainty.

Finally he spoke, but more out of insecurity than authority. "I am going to see to it that you never return, you little trollop. Illegitimate children should have no right to the privilege of education," he proclaimed. "I will be speaking with your father."

I held my stare and said nothing. He finally turned and walked away.

That night my father made a special trip to our house. He demanded Mother give me an unforgettable thrashing. Edward later told me my father used his money and influence to pay off Peter's parents and settle the issue with the schoolmaster. Edward said I should apologize to my father and thank him for mediating. But something inside me made me think that my father had acted less for my sake and more for his own so I said nothing. My mother did not have the heart or stomach for severe punishment. After a couple light swats, she hugged me, cried, and apologized for the life she had arranged for me.

Peter didn't return to school for ten days. I heard from others that I had broken his nose, and purple black bruises had welled up around his eyes. I cherished my handiwork. When he did return, he confronted me right in class while I was seated at my desk. He loomed over me with a clenched fist while the schoolmaster watched.

"I will flay you in the yard and make you plead for mercy," he whispered. He waved his fist in front of my nose. "You may be a lass, but I will beat you like the dog you are."

The class snickered and awaited my fearful response with anticipation.

I smiled and leered around the room, staring at whoever looked at me until they turned away. I felt a power emanating from within me. I simply felt undaunted and even indifferent to the next upheaval I would face.

"No," I said, staring into Peter's eyes. "You will leave me alone or you will regret it."

A vein in Peter's forehead pulsated and his jaw set for action.

I shrugged and said, "As you wish."

Since he stood over me, I balled my fist and punched him right between the legs. He doubled over, holding himself. He made an easy mark, so I smacked him across the nose with my book. Blood gushed afresh from his nose, and the schoolmaster ran to him. I stood up and declared to the class, "I do not fear any of you!"

The schoolmaster balked at the thought of whipping me that day. I suppose my unswerving defiance unnerved him, so he took a different tack. Instead, he railed at Peter for trying to incite a fight, for stooping to the uncivilized and untamed aggressions of an illegitimate child. That proved to be the end of the fighting. My cunning plan had propelled me up to a pedestal, and no one wanted to challenge me. I had learned another valuable lesson: most people do not have the stomach for direct confrontation. Most so fear the penalty that comes with the crime they are goaded into backing down. Courage was the ability to face the aftermath. But for me, whippings did not deter me in the least. I felt I had experienced about the worst and emerged stronger.

I thought of the stories Edward read to me: David and Goliath, the Walls of Jericho, and Daniel and his lion's den. Had God been with me? I could not be sure, since I recalled Edward speaking of "turning the other cheek" but I thanked Him nonetheless for the independence and control I suddenly tasted. It was sweet and exhilarating. Edward seemed a bit shook and at a loss for words by the events that had transpired. But I could see in his face as I told the story that he was pleased at seeing this new fortitude within me.

* * * *

I climbed the stairs, opened the door, and found my seat at the back of the class. A peat stove simmered at the front of the room, but because I was deemed unruly, I had to sit where the heat barely reached. It also made it difficult to hear the lessons, but I did not care. I spent much of my time drawing pictures or reading what I wished. My favorite books were the straight-faced, shock-laced writings of Jonathon Swift. I loved his *A Tale of a Tub* and his irreverent and sarcastic jabs at Parliament and commerce, particularly his *A Modest Proposal.* I suppose

Cork would have been a bit more peaceful if my mother had sold me at the age of one. When the schoolmaster assigned arithmetic, I ignored him and read verse from the poet John Dryden. He roamed the room, commenting on student progress while I scanned the pages for a couplet or quatrain to memorize. The rhythm and rhyme of poetry pleased me. I reveled in a line by La Fontaine, "It's doubly sweet to deceive a deceiver." But then I came upon an epigram that seemed delivered directly to me from the hand of providence: "Great wits are sure to madness near allied/And thin partitions do their bounds divide."

"Anne, why are you not working on mathematics?"

I looked up at the schoolmaster. "Because I am traveling over the ocean to the New World in two days."

He furrowed his brow and blinked. "Your imagination is burgeoning, my child."

"No, it is not. My father is leaving this cruel place and taking us with him, and I am glad I will never have to see any of your faces as long as I live. You may all rot here for all I care."

"Anne, we will not tolerate your impudence!" shouted the schoolmaster.

I stood up and pointed at him. "I hate you and your whole class of snobs. A pox and a plague on all your families. You will no longer torment me with your bloody judgments!"

The schoolmaster took a step backward, stunned by my outburst. He then raised his hand to strike me, but I leapt back, cursed the class, and flew for the door. No one pursued me. It felt fine to burn this bridge and watch it fall—ashes to ashes and dust to dust.

CHAPTER III

Once outside, I decided it would be best to postpone the surefire reprimand I knew I would get at home. Rather, I decided to explore Cork one last time before my family's departure. I purchased two apples from a woman selling fruit and set off along the open streets. I saw the familiar contrast from richly dressed nobles riding in carriages to destitute laborers in rags rummaging among the garbage heaps. I drifted past the harbor docks and watched fishermen unload and clean their catch of haddock, cod, and herring. Pelicans and gulls flapped about in a frenzy, searching for offal or an overlooked fish. Merchants hawked a variety of fish, as well as cockles, mollusks, and prawns. Next I wandered past the smelly breweries, where workers shoveled loads of oat and barley into wagons for malting. People mostly ignored me and I savored the feeling of invisibility, something I would strive for much more in later years. My ability to go unnoticed allowed me free reign to observe and learn.

I walked past Cork Harbor and reached the Lee River, which flowed through the town. Father once took my mother and I picnicking in a marshy valley beside the river, where Edward helped me catch a huge catfish. Mother and I picked heather and fern and decorated our hair and clothes. It had been a beautiful afternoon without a cloud in the sky. I wondered what the Carolinas of the New World would be like.

As I wandered aimlessly, I passed St. Finbarr's Monastery. St. Patrick may have miraculously driven all serpents off Ireland, but St. Finbarr had tracked down and killed the last dragon on the island. Strains of Celtic songs floated through the walls. Occasionally I had seen the robed monks begging for alms in the streets, crawling on their knees in prayer, and even flagellating themselves with leather straps.

As I walked along I heard a storyteller earning his keep by telling the love story of Tristan and Isolde to those who would listen so I stopped. Tristan, he said, was a great knight from King Arthur's Camelot court. He sought to right wrongs in Ireland. After slaying a dragon that was persecuting Ireland, he fulfilled his mission by escorting the Irish Princess Isolde to England to marry his uncle, King Mark of Cornwall. On the journey to England, Tristan and Isolde partook of, by accident, a love potion prepared by the queen for her daughter and the King, creating an imperishable bond of love between them. When King Mark discovered what had occurred, he became inflamed with jealousy. The king captured the couple and ordered Tristan burned at the stake. But Tristan escaped by leaping into the ocean from a chapel perched along the cliffs. He swam to shore and rescued Isolde from a band of lepers the King used to guard her. They hid in the forest of Morrois for several months before being captured again. Weary of their persecuted life, they agreed to separate. Isolde married the King, and ironically, Tristan married another Isolde, Isolde of the White Hands, daughter of a duke.

But the love potion proved too strong. Wounded by a poisoned weapon in a battle, Tristan sent a message for his true love. If she agreed to come across the channel to Ireland, the ship on which she had embarked should fly a white sail. If she would not come, the ship should fly a black sail. Tristan's wife discovered the secret. In jealousy, when she saw the vessel approach on the horizon, she told Tristan it had raised a black sail. A heartbroken Tristan turned his face to the wall and slowly died. When Isolde arrived and saw she was too late to save her true love, she embraced the corpse of Tristan. She died in his arms, unable to survive the power of the potion. After they were buried side by side, a miracle occurred, the storyteller said. Two trees grew out of their graves and intertwined their branches so that their love would never be put asunder.

As I listened to the storyteller, I prayed that I, too, would be inseparably linked to my one true love, and that whatever adventures I had to face, I would ultimately save or be saved by the man of my dreams. I prayed our love would endure like that of Isolde and Tristan.

I left the storyteller as he begged for coins and started toward Blarney Castle. It had earned its name through trickery and flattery. Now, as others did, I came to kiss the stone to inherit eloquence and craftiness. But I stopped when, I heard the echo of familiar laughter. I followed the sound and reached a dark hovel where fire licked at the darkness. I peered in and saw two forms drinking and laughing over a seamy tale.

"Edward?" I called.

A figure loomed toward me. He came into the sunlight, squinting at me. "Anne? For goodness' sake, what are you doing here?"

"I quit school and I'm exploring the town one last time," I said proudly.

"Exploring? You're liable to have your throat cut, or worse. The vermin here would rob you blind in a minute. Come in with me and I'll escort you home."

Edward took my hand as we entered the blacksmith's shed. Whenever my mother and father went out, I relished having Edward watch me. Besides being my rescuer, he sometimes told wonderfully forbidden tales. Sometimes he spoke of the sadness of losing his wife and then he would drink too much ale. He would forget my age and tell me wickedly funny and suspenseful stories about duels and tortures and scandalous trysts, stories of highwaymen and pirates. I never tired of Edward. When he lost consciousness, sometimes I would stare at his wrinkled face, the drooping bags under his eyes, and the gnarled nose he had broken in a pub scrap. I often touched the scar and watched its color change when I applied pressure to it. I would hold his big, lumpy hands, kiss him on the scar, and blow gently in his ear. It never failed that Edward would smile, delighting in some experience from another place and time.

Edward guided me into the darkness and lifted me onto a stool.

"Wot 'ave we 'ere? A wee lil' street urchin?" said a voice.

"Robert, my lad, this lovely, bonny lass is Anne McCormac, my master's little product of an illicit affair," he said formally. "This is why I am leaving Ireland. Anne, I hope you will understand my celebrating and my sadness at leaving my homeland."

At the time, I did not often understand Edward's words, but his pleasant brogue always put me at ease. John the blacksmith bowed and smiled. "Mi lair is yer lair. Just watch the conflagration. It's living and hostile, been known to reach out 'n nip ye in the bum." He laughed drunkenly.

I was soon forgotten, sitting on a stool in the shadows and enjoying the show. Edward wandered around the shop, casually glancing at the tools and devices on cluttered tables. "You have a fine array of clysters here." Edward's tone made me laugh, for his face was serious but his voice was forever tinged with irony, much as I would imagine Jonathon Swift's to be. "I read that Martin Luther once said," Edward coughed and laughed, struggling to finish his words, "that in the act of administering the clyster, the doctor is like a mother to her child."

John shook his head and walked over to another table. He held up a contraption shaped like a hoop with a connecting bar of sloped iron and cleats.

"Ah, the chastity belt. The great insurer of fidelity." Edward saluted and accepted it from John. "Come hither, Anne."

I stood up, unaware at the time of the contraption's purpose. Edward held it up to me. "Someday, Anne, you might wear one to keep you faithful."

"Aye, but we smiths 'ave our price," piped in John. "I've been known to make an extra key in mi day for the right price."

"Calls to mind the ditty—" Edward said, his voice a singsong, "More love a mother than a father shows: He thinks this is his son; she only knows."

"Which is why I keep getting orders for these contraptions," the blacksmith said.

They drank a bit more and proceeded to show me all manner of torture devices blacksmiths were commissioned to create: a set of weights for pressing, pinchers to cut body parts, and branding irons. The blacksmith belched and said he was not unlike the Italian artisans Michelangelo, Leonardo, or Donatello. They had been commissioned, he said, to bolster and preserve the Church. He was paid to protect the nobles.

"No mincing words: without you the whole bloody system would cave in," said Edward.

I had many questions about each device, which prompted Edward to place a brank around my face and muzzle my mouth. "This is for chatty shrews that ask too many questions. And if this fails, we can always duck you. Wait," Edward raised a hand, "another ditty from Old England: 'A spaniel, a woman, and a hickory tree/The more you beat them, the better they be."

They laughed, but I did not mind because I was receiving a glimpse into matters I knew were forbidden at my age.

I roamed over toward a stack of swords. I lifted one up and swung it, enjoying the swishing sound it made as it cut the air.

"I like these," I said.

"We got a regular cutthroat here, 'ave we?" said John.

"Aye, a pirate princess," Edward added. He tied a glove to a piece of twine, tied it to a rafter, and let it hang in midair. "Have at it—in one slice, Anne."

I hefted the sword to my right, and then screeched like a banshee and swung with all my strength. The twine split and the glove pitched across the room right into the blacksmith's fire. He dished it out quickly.

"Zounds, most excellent," Edward said with a smirk. "Now I better take that off your lethal hands before you slay every ne'er-do-well in Cork."

The sun cantered at the bottom of the horizon, and Edward led me home. I pleaded with him to keep my secret about quitting school. He winked. I loved Edward.

At home, I mentioned a few of the stories Edward told me. My mother bristled at first, but then patted my head and said, "Edward is a storyteller and a coxcomb, who must have cadged a few too many pints of ale today. I daresay little that comes from his lips when they are liquor laden is true. Remember, Anne, every person in the world has feet of clay that Satan uses to tempt us and the Lord uses to train us."

"What are yours and Father's?" I asked.

My mother grimaced. "It's God's business, not yours, to identify the Achilles' heels we all possess. But I do know one of yours must be an insatiable curiosity."

CHAPTER IV

That night I noticed my mother looked particularly graceful and beautiful. My father had sent a hairdresser to prim her hair, make up her face, and fit her with a regal, low-cut velvet gown, which emphasized her delicate bodice. The dress flowed to the floor with ruched and French lace folds. My father brought her a glittering brooch, necklace, and dangles to make her all the more inviting, though she also wished to wear a cross, as always. I never heard her complain or question the morality of being my father's mistress; she anticipated instead the time she would become his lawfully wedded bride. I suppose she was grateful to have a home, a daughter, and such nice things. I do not know whether she considered being an object of my father's passion a true pleasure or merely an obligation to gain security.

My father arrived peacocking a classic periwig and a vermilion waistcoat with gold buttons and charcoal breeches. His hat was gaudy and plumed with exotic feathers. The gold chains, emerald rings, and stockings with silver-buckled pumps he wore were staple items to express his vanity. Later, I would decide his exterior attempted to shield his interior cowardice. For a lawyer who thrived on confrontation in court matters, he seemed to fly from any and all conflicts with the women in his life.

He seemed agitated by all the details that needed wrapping up before we left. My mother tried to calm him with a drink. I slipped outside to the carriage to tell Edward how happy I felt that he was traveling with us.

He smiled. "I will never be put asunder from my little Anne. Who would protect you?"

Edward was my only friend so I had no one to say good-byes to. The only wall left to climb was a last visit with my stepmother, the spurned wife who had always treated me cruelly whenever I had to visit. While my parents went to a social gathering I spent the evening with my uncle. He read to me limericks and then we made some up. Edward's was best:

> There once was a lady named Banker
> Who slept while the ship lay at anchor.
> She awoke in dismay
> When she heard a mate say:
> "Now hoist up the top sheet and spanker."

However distracting Edward's company proved, I felt unhinged by the visit I had to pay to my stepmother the next day. I recalled the last time I had visited her, still galled by the sting in my cheeks.

After my mother's hairdresser had dressed and groomed me, Edward drove me by carriage to the McCormac mansion. When I entered, I stared at the gold and scarlet furnishings, the marble statuary and the portraits of family members. I listened numbly while my stepmother showed me the eighteen rooms. Among them were the entertainment room, library, dining room, billiard room, arbor, swimming room, smoking room, and bathhouse. Each room was decorated in a theme, she said. My father's smoking room reflected artifacts from China with its rugs and wall hangings. His den celebrated the Dark Continent, filled with carved ivory, pagan idols, and various skins stretched across the walls. The other rooms revealed a more feminine approach.

My father's wife was an easy woman to abhor; her civility was just a ruse to shred me. In church I learned that Sarah accepted the custom of Abraham lying with the maid, Hagar. But once Hagar was pregnant, Sarah had turned wrathful. Eventually Hagar bore Ishmael and fled to Arabia to escape Sarah's anger. I often wondered about my destiny.

My stepmother would constantly chide me at supper, pointing out my infractions in using utensils, napkins, and language. She discussed hygiene, puberty, menstruation, and virginity. "You would do well to remember my words, though it is like casting pearls before swine," she once said.

She always spoke to me with an iron smile and a biting tongue. I have heard the tongue is the only tool that sharpens with use. Her tongue could eloquently slice me to ribbons. I simply was no match for her. Her barbed words reduced me to tears every time, and when I wept, she would remind me of my lowly, illegitimate birthright, my unhealthy constitution, and my weakness for emotion. She would talk to me of the sirens in Greek mythology and compare them to my mother, who had lured my father to sin and entrapped him in the coils of immorality. She would discuss the Inquisition and the burning of witches, and then explain how my mother and I should be torched because corrupt blood coursed through our veins. "Harlots breed harlots. You should be stamped out to prevent the ruination of Christians," she said at another time. Insults slithered from her smiling mouth with grace and etiquette. Once I screamed at her, but I looked like an uncontrolled, hot-tempered girl. She rewarded my behavior with a stinging slap across the cheek.

"Now, turn the other cheek to me. Now!"

I did and she backhanded me, cutting me with her diamond ring.

"You must grow accustomed to this treatment. Your superiors will always mistreat you because they are stronger and wiser. Your lot in life is a vale of tears, a test of your meekness and your worthiness. The only way you will inherit the kingdom of God is to remember that weakness and wickedness are your destiny and repent of your sins every day of your pathetic life."

Edward put me to bed and I lay there wondering what would occur during my last encounter with my stepmother. But when I awoke the next morning, I felt the motion of the sea. My mother greeted me with fine news: we had left by stealth in the middle of the night. I was grateful to be reprieved from a last visit with my stepmother and to be experiencing the adventures of the sea. I later discovered that my father had feared confronting his wife again, so he had liquidated all his accounts and slipped out of Ireland before she could take measures against him. I had fantasized about slapping my stepmother at the end of the evening, but I wasn't certain I had the nerve. Thus I gloried in my father's escape, though later it would add fodder to my belief that he was spineless.

CHAPTER V

I arose to the sound of a flute and the splash of waves against the hull. I dressed and climbed the stairs to the deck. Ireland was but a shrinking dot on the horizon and I felt my hopes soar for a new beginning. I thanked the good Lord for a whole new world—a merciful second chance and an act of grace. The power and mystery of the sea enthralled me. I sat for hours straddling the edge of the bowsprit, watching the hull thread through the blue foamy swells, feeling the blast of salty spray against my face, sucking in the briny breezes that filled the sheets, and listening to the rippling halyards tauten and quiver under the gale winds. At night I discovered that the ship created a phosphorescent wake that glimmered in the moonlight.

I imagined about all that might lie beneath the surface of the ocean, all the varied life teeming amidst a world unexplored by humanity. The seamen occasionally told me wild tales of sea monsters that rose from the depths to destroy ships and capture virgins, saying that King Triton favored lithe, red-haired lasses. I was introduced to whales, which broke the surface of the water, raising their flukes and firing blasts of mist into the air. I shivered with thrill when pods of porpoises frolicked about the ship with acrobatic flips and fearless leaps and dives just in front of the bow. I could spend an hour at a time just watching the wild directions they darted. The swirling, lifting current mesmerized me into dreaming of fanciful stories of lovely mermaids.

I pestered the grizzled crew with questions about the Carolinas. Between their bits and pieces and my father's readings, I learned that the Carolinas were similar to Ireland—plenty of rain and pine, though thriving with many kinds of wildlife

I had never seen. My father said Charles Towne, like Cork, was also surrounded by waterways, and the landscape was a mix of marshy areas and fertile cropland.

"It's a good settlement with a few Irish," my father said with a proud tone. "They rebel against British tyranny even over here."

"Forever a burl in their britches. Bloody fine Irish form," Edward remarked.

I did not understand my father's words, but I swelled with pride nevertheless for the pioneering Irish.

During the voyage, I earned the nickname "Pistol Red," a reference to my long, flaming hair, which forever whipped about my face and shoulders from the winds. The "pistol" also illustrated my interest in firearms and my hot temper.

"Now boys," Edward said to the crewmen. "That's a name befitting a pirate, not a banshee like my Anne."

That set off a round of laughter. I must confess I grew impatient about everything as the voyage went on; if I asked a question and the answer was not forthcoming or was clearly altered to account for my tender ears, I ranted and roiled against everyone, to the amusement of the mariners, using salvos of filthy epithets I learned from them. Edward had spoiled me with glimpses into hidden matters of adulthood. I believe the seamen, busy caulking the seams, holystoning the mildew from the decks, or repairing the ratlines and hawses, rather enjoyed my torrential displays, baiting me by saying things like, "I cannot tell you that; you're just a wee bonny lass, Pistol Red." I would then berate them with a stream of oaths, and then bolt away, their laughter reverberating in my ears.

I found hiding places and eavesdropped on the sailors. In this way I learned much about life in the New World. The seaman described the noble, painted savages who populated the Carolinas, spoke unusual languages, practiced heathen rituals, and attacked settlers without notice, using bows and arrows, spears, tomahawks, and guns. Some were easily enslaved, but others were barbaric. I also learned about African slaves, who were brought to the Americas to work the plantations, but who sometimes revolted and killed their masters with the very tools they were forced to work with. And then there were the roving pirates, who were beholden to no nation, sea-robbers who roamed the oceans in search of ships to attack and plunder. I learned how they raised a black flag displaying a skull and crossbones to inflict terror and how they brutalized their victims for pleasure.

"They have all sold their souls to Satan," a sailor rasped, and then turned and grinned at me. I had not fooled them with that hiding place.

It all sounded incredibly fascinating and frightful, though I felt safe and secure in Edward's presence. During the voyage, Edward rescued me twice from perils. The first occurred midway through our voyage. One day I asked one of the sailors named O'Shaugnessy a question about the ship. He smiled and directed me to the hawser lines at the stern of the ship, hinting that I might hear an interesting yarn. I followed him innocently, never considering the potential danger. The moment we were alone, however, he grabbed me by the arms and tried to kiss me. I wriggled in his iron grip and swung my head back and forth. I could smell his rancid breath and feel his rough whiskers scratch my face. I screamed over the sound of the waves and winds, but he mashed his right hand over my mouth. Sinking my teeth into the palm of his hand, I immediately tasted his salty blood. He grunted and I could see fire well into his eyes. He pushed me back and back-handed me. I fell to the deck. I saw a wicked and hideous smile spread across his face as he reached for me.

Then, just above O'Shaugnessy, I saw my guardian angel: Edward. The vein in the middle of his forehead bulged and his eyes squinted with rage. It seemed as though O'Shaugnessy was launched into the air and flung across the deck. I watched Edward leap on the man and pound him with his fists. Each crunch made me flinch. Edward then pulled O'Shaugnessy up and pinned him against one of the masts, his hand clasped around the man's neck, his knife held against his chin. I thought of the dog and secretly hoped he would gut this man, too, for daring to harm me.

"If I ever see you so much as look at her, I will slit you from navel to neck. Do I make myself clear?" Edward whispered each word.

O'Shaugnessy struggled to breathe, but nodded. Edward released him. As O'Shaugnessy bent over to catch his breath, Edward suddenly kicked him between the legs. The man groaned and fell to the deck, his breath a scraping rasp.

"That should help you keep your filthy hands to yourself," Edward said. He put away his knife and rushed over to me. "Anne, are you all right? Did he harm you in any way?"

I hugged Edward and started to cry into his shoulder. He gathered me into his arms and carried me to our cabin.

"I fought back. I promise. I did not give up. Do you believe me?" I asked frantically.

"Shh, Anne, calm down. It is okay. You did well and I am very proud of you."

His affirming words reduced me to a mess of blubbering tears. I had never realized how much I longed for his approval. It filled me with a love I had never felt for my mother or my father. And only two days later Edward would have to save me again.

This time I was perched on my usual spot—the bowsprit. I so luxuriated in the warm sun and cool breezes that I grew drowsy and must have fallen asleep. I awoke to the freezing shock of the ocean and turbulent swell of the current. I flailed to stay above the waves and shout for help, but each time I opened my mouth it filled with icy saltwater. My clothes seemed to be pulling me under. Within moments I saw the main hull of the vessel drift past me and saw the lights of the ship getting smaller and dimmer. I knew I wouldn't last much longer, but the thought of death in this way didn't seem too horrifying. It would be peaceful. I let my arms and legs relax, let the current have its way.

Just then I saw the stern lift over a swell, and I glimpsed a figure diving overboard and swimming toward me. Of course it was Edward. He held me above the wash of the breakers and reassured me while I watched several sailors lower a longboat and row their way toward us. My fear was gone, and I actually enjoyed the turbulent force of the ocean around me while I rested secure in Edward's arms. I did not say so, but I was disappointed that the rescue boat arrived so swiftly. I loved the raw energy and the endless sweep of the Atlantic.

"What am I going to do with you, Anne? You are so prone to danger."

"This is the third time you have saved my life, Edward," I said with pride. "You are my angel, Michael."

Much to Edward's relief, the remainder of our journey went without incident, but two other experiences made lasting impressions on me. One day as I played in a pinnace, I overheard a loud commotion. I peered over the edge and watched a sailor as he was tethered to the mast and his shirt was stripped off his back. The captain accused him of an "act of larceny" and ordered him flogged methodically with a cat-o'-nine-tails. The man grunted and winced after each stroke. I gazed with horror and lurid interest at the bleeding lacerations that crisscrossed the sailor's back. It looked agonizing. Finally the whipping was finished and the sailor cut down. He plunged to the deck and curled up into a ball. Everyone turned and walked away, leaving him alone. I asked Edward what he had done to deserve such punishment.

"He stole a potato from the galley."

"Is that all? He was probably hungry," I said.

"He probably was, Anne, but the rules on ships are very strict and the punishments severe."

"But why?"

Edward considered. "I am not sure, but they always have been. I suppose it discourages mutiny."

"And pirates?"

"In truth, it probably contributes to piracy. Despair either destroys a man, or it makes men desperate and deadly."

At the time, I didn't understand.

The other experience involved my mother and father. A few days into our voyage, my mother started to change. The open sea, with its huge swells, made her pale and shaky. She holed up in our cabin and seemed persistently seasick. Almost every morning my father would order me out of our cabin, but I would press my ear against the door and listen to him explain to my mother the things expected of the wife of a blueblood nobleman, as well as the demands that awaited her in Charles Towne. I would then hear the rhythmic sound of coupling, something I had once peeked in on out of curiosity. After he was done, he would start to leave and I would dash up on deck. He would find me and tell me to attend to my mother's needs.

"She is feeling poorly and you always brighten her day," he would say.

"But I don't want to stay in the cabin. I like it better up here."

"Anne, your mother needs you. If you don't spend time with her, she will only get more ill."

"Where are you going?"

He scowled. I could tell he was ready to reprimand me, but then his face calmed. "I have important matters of commerce to discuss with the other gentlemen onboard. It is vital to our livelihood in Charles Towne."

I followed him one morning to find him playing cards and drinking with some men. They laughed a great deal. There were a couple women who served the men. I saw that they were constantly touching and teasing the women, and the women did not seem to mind in the least.

Out of a sense of guilt I spent many hours cooped up in Mother's cabin, reading passages of her favorite Scriptures and trying to be supportive, but each day my mother grew weaker and I became more impatient. One day I decided her illness was nothing but weakness, her inability to rise above this new challenge in our lives. Her lack of courage frustrated me, and her neediness irritated me.

On this day I headed back to the cabin, hoping to persuade her to at least leave her bed and take in some fresh air, but as I entered the room, I knew my hope was like a mirage. She lay on the bed, feverish and vacant, her eyes staring without focus at the wall. She looked dehydrated, and her skin had a deathly pallor. "Only a few more days," I said. "The ocean is beautiful. Wouldn't you like to come out and see? The fresh air might do you well."

My mother attempted to smile. She raised a jittery hand. "Not just now. Perhaps in a little while, Anne."

I wanted to leave, but my inner tribunal compelled me to offer service. I forced myself to say, "Would you like me to read to you?"

"Yes, please."

I picked up the Bible on the table and sat beside her. She loved to read and memorize the Scripture, and had even taught me to read by it and assigned me passages to learn by heart.

"Could you tell me of other places where the sea is described in the Bible?" I asked.

I had already read the Book of Jonah and Chapter 27 of the Book of Acts. I loved these passages because I found descriptions of the sea in their pages. It was my mother who had taught me to appreciate the Bible and showed me these passages.

"Psalm 42, I believe," she said.

My mother often said I had a lilting and sonorous voice, and that when I read, my soft, Irish accent lulled the listener. My lips made even dense writing sound poetic. Though her weakness frustrated me, her compliments warmed my heart and battered my conscience for thinking ill of her. I scanned the Psalm until I came to these words: "Deep calls to deep at the sound of Thy waterfalls. All Thy breakers and all Thy waves have rolled over me. The Lord will command His loving-kindness in the daytime; and His song will be with me in the night, a prayer to the God of my life." I fell in love with the words immediately and decided to memorize them by heart.

"That's beautiful, Mother. It reminds me of my fall into the ocean and Edward saving me. And it also reminds me of Jonah's journey to the bottom of the sea," I said and quoted, "'To be cast into the deep, in the midst of the seas, and the floods encompassed about me...even to the soul.'"

My mother tilted her head, smiled, and touched my face with a clammy hand. "You are adventuresome, Anne. A fine attribute for a man, but it is a rare and dangerous one for so young a girl."

She had lost much weight and her eyes were rheumy. I worried she wouldn't make it to the New World, but I did not know what to do. I finished the Psalm and noticed my mother had dropped off to sleep. This made me happy. I was anxious to leave, and now my mother would not notice my absence. I shut the Bible and slipped out to survey our ship cresting the foamy combers, sliding into the breach of the sea and catching the fresh trade winds as they filled the sheets.

I found Edward sharpening a dagger on a piece of whetstone. "Hello, Anne."

"Edward, what is wrong with my mother?"

He sighed and scraped the blade across the stone.

"Edward?"

"I heard you. The trip is gnawing away at her."

"But then why not me as well?"

Edward wiped at his nose with his sleeve. "Anne, you have gone through the fire. The strength you have learned and earned is now engrained in your blood so that you can face nearly any trial. Your mother has been sheltered, and I worry that this change is too demanding for her."

"But why?"

"Dread is a powerful emotion. She has been a maid all her life, and now she will be expected to organize the domestic affairs of a large house and oversee the duties of house-slaves and servants. She will need to entertain other aristocrats and not embarrass her husband. She has never exerted authority over anyone. I am worried that your father's expectations are too high. We will have to help her," he said.

"I promise I will, Edward," I said and then walked away, brooding over the course my mother's health was taking.

CHAPTER VI

Toward the end of our passage, I set myself to learning about sailing, pestering the crew with incessant questions, parroting their maritime vocabulary. The navigator, a burly old man with a crinkled white beard, took me under his wing. He seemed pleased to explain to me the use of nautical maps, binnacles, sextants, and compasses. He explained how to sound for fathoms, predict leagues, judge knots, and navigate by the stars. He was patient with my questions, and I have to admit there was plenty I did not understand. He helped me memorize the parts of our schooner, and under his tutelage I grew familiar with many nautical commands—"Raise the anchor," "loose the rudder bans," "hoist the mainsail," "luff to the wind," "tack to portside," and many more.

I treasured the sea—the creamy salt breezes, the snap of the sails in the wind, the sizzle of foam as the hull cut a swath in the ocean, the rise and fall of the swells, and the creak and groan of the ship's timbers. There was purity and beauty, and a power and mystery, in the waters I cherished. Humanity's attempts to conquer the ocean were tomfoolery, I decided, for at every moment death surrounded us. Enveloped in this power, I began to think more of God. I had heard in church that all people are accountable to believe in God merely because of his creation. As our little ship struggled against the tides and rose and fell on the swells, I could see how creation attested to its creator, and I found my creator wonderfully powerful and majestically artistic. I felt so small and insignificant among the wild winds and turbulent waves, or when I gazed upon the starry host in the night skies.

One morning I arose and realized as I dressed that our ship had anchored. Our ship swayed gently. On deck I was greeted by a bustling harbor. The captain had slipped into the bay under cover of night to avoid any roving pirate ships that may have hovered near the opening.

I leaned over the railing and watched with fascination and exhilaration as the longboats ferried passengers to the docks. I could see Charles Towne bustling with commerce and labor. Several schooners and sloops lay moored in the harbor. The pungent odor of rotting fish filled my nostrils. A multitude of crying gulls and veering pelicans fought over scraps the fishermen flung into the bay as they cleaned their catch. It was all so new and I reveled in each moment.

I saw my first African slaves and noble savages loading and unloading barrels, hogsheads, demijohns, and crates. Some rattled leg chains. Their appearances tempered my excitement with sadness. Edward pointed out the gibbets attached to hanging posts, which held skeletons covered in tatters of clothing, the recipients of justice and a reminder for those who considered a life of crime. I remembered once seeing a decaying arm nailed against a wall in Kinsale—another clear message that breaking the law could lead to severe consequences.

My father arranged passage to shore and rented a stately room in Charles Towne's best inn for the next few weeks. He planned to purchase a tobacco and rice plantation with slaves who were already experienced. I learned from Edward that Father had successfully sold off lands and tucked away a cache of funds before spiriting out of Ireland. Now he had all he needed to buy an already profitable plantation—lock, stock, and barrel.

I spent a good deal of time taking care of my mother, who still needed her bed rest but who managed to steal time gazing out the window, observing the ways of colonial America. Frequent auctions of Indians and Africans were staged. Normally the slaves were stripped naked to display the strength of their muscles for labor, or the youthfulness of their bodies for reproduction. Some were manacled and defiant looking, their bodies scarred from past whippings. Others appeared downtrodden and resolved to lifelong slavery. I lamented this sight. It reminded me too much of Ireland. How could birth dictate one's station in life? No amount of education seemed to make a difference. I found myself praying for these people, though I was confused when I asked my father about slavery because he said it was all part of God's plan for "the Sons of Ham." It would be many years later before I came to see that people twisted the Bible to justify prejudice and greed. I was more proud of those who refused to be broken. They might carry scars, but their faces shone with courage.

One day I observed a woman dressed in loose, colorful clothing leaning against a building beckoning the men that passed. I watched wide-eyed as one man stopped and ushered the lady into the alley. From my vantage, I saw the entire act. Now while I had seen my parents on one occasion, this display reminded me of the mating practices of animals. It seemed men were so needy, while the women I had observed thus far were merely indifferent. To this woman, it appeared merely a nuisance of everyday life that had to be dealt with quickly and unemotionally, like a purging of the bowels. The man's expression was wholly distracted, and then contented. The woman looked bored but in control.

Not more than an hour later, though, I saw the woman dragged to the stocks in the square by uniformed men. The officials ripped away the back of her dress. One man called to the passing people to witness the punishment of a prostitute, while another soldier began to methodically whip the woman. As she screamed, a crowd encircled her and jeered and threw things at her. Tears brimmed in my eyes at the merciless beating she endured. She underwent a shocking change before me. She now looked so humiliated and helpless. I cried to my father, who walked over to the window and watched the scene stoically. The whipping tore bleeding slashes across her back until she lost consciousness, hanging limply in the stocks. The official then coiled his whip, and the crowd melted away into the street.

"Why did they beat her so badly, Father?"

"She is a harlot. They are beating her as a deterrent to other women who commit adultery with other wives' husbands."

"But why only her? I saw her with men. What about their punishment?"

My father smiled and patted my shoulder. "Samuel Butler said it well: 'The souls of women are so small, that some believe they've none at all.'" The gesture ignited my blood.

"It's unjust," I snapped. "Men do what they wish and women are punished for it? It is damnable."

My father glared down at me, his face a scowl. "I would be careful of your tongue, my daughter, for it could bring you much pain in the future. Remember your station, your gender, and your age." He then walked out of the room.

The officials left the prostitute tied to the post all day. I felt drawn to the window throughout the afternoon, wishing I could help her in some way. I wondered if perhaps she had died, but eventually she emerged from her stupor and pleaded for water and a covering. Passersby either ignored her or mocked her. She sobbed with such despair that it seemed she had probably lost much more than blood that afternoon—her dignity and her soul. I believed dignity could be regained, but I was not so sure a soul could. I learned something new that day: for women, the punishment for wrongdoings was more shameful and painful than for men. I never wanted to be in that woman's position, dependent on the caprice of men and enslaved by their whims.

The scene sparked another thought I had never considered. My mother could have been tied to that post while my father sat in ease in his drawing room. I started to tremble. Seeing a letter opener on the sideboard, I snatched it up and looked around the room. There was a small pillow resting on a settee. I stalked over to it, gritted my teeth, and started to stab and slash at it, ripping it open and exposing the stuffing. My rage finally spent, I dropped the weapon, closed my eyes, and held my breath as long as I could. I exhaled and pressed my palms against my temples. I could feel myself start to relax.

I glanced in the mirror. The light from the window to my left and the shadows in the room to my right cast an unusual aura on me. Half my face was illumined and the other half darkened, with my scar adding a spectral effect. I remembered that I had once asked Edward about the impulses I had toward violence.

"You have a civil war within you," he said. "We all do. Each of us has to learn a way to control it. And sometimes we need the other half."

"Why?"

"To protect ourselves and to rescue the ones we love."

The coming months proved fascinating and sorrowful. We moved into a respectable mansion that overlooked an enormous tobacco and rice plantation. I enjoyed walking among the long rows of tobacco plants while the slaves hoed, raked, and tilled, but the weather tested my patience at times with its humidity. Ireland was cool, breezy, and rainy, and though Carolina had its rains, I found myself sweating terribly and feeling forever sticky under my dresses. There wasn't much relief, either. A cool bath was a fine escape, but the minute I emerged from the lovely water and began to dry myself, the stickiness returned with a vengeance. The bugs annoyed me equally, constantly buzzing in my ears and leaving itchy bumps on my skin that I scratched until they bled.

Father's control of the slaves astounded me. I had never seen him so brutal, so pitiless. He brandished a bullwhip wherever he went on the plantation, and frequently meted out lashings for the smallest of offenses. He became a terror to the slaves.

"I need to remind them who is in charge here," he would tell me. "My scourge delivers a message. Pain is the best way to make a point with them."

My father encouraged me to exercise my dominance over the slaves. He asked Edward to teach me how to use a whip, a cane, and a gun. Though I learned the use of each weapon, I hesitated at baptizing them on the slaves. I felt too sorry for them.

Mother's illness grew increasingly worse. She had weakened to the point of routine confinement to bed, and I once again felt pressured to visit and read to her for long hours. I had grown to despise these times even more, because in my heart I viewed my mother as a resigned slave, accepting without fight her disintegrating health. She seemed to lose her will to live, jettisoning all her hopes and dreams of the future. I wanted to rail at her for giving up and demand that she cease imagining her illness, but I could see that she resided in bedlam and was too far gone now to be saved. So I kept my mouth shut, distanced my emotions from her, and prepared for her death.

To escape the oppression of the house, I would take long walks among the palmetto forests with Edward. We learned the names of trees–willow, palmetto, cypress, live oak, loblolly pine, and myrtle. Most of the trees were festooned with moss and populated with lively birds. We would see deer, raccoon, fox, and wildcat. Edward occasionally shot wild turkeys and rabbits. Along the inlets and estuaries, I hunted for frogs, and we angled for catfish. I savored those times with Edward. Whenever we neared the house again, though, I felt the brooding dread return.

For the next few months my mother seldom strayed from her bed. My father avoided her, as well, spending his time in town or on the plantation. Rumors filtered to me that he had been visiting prostitutes in Charles Towne as well as coupling with a young slave who was now pregnant with his child. I decided that Father lacked something, eluding his problems by satisfying his passing lusts.

He called for a doctor who bled a pint of blood from and administered a purgative to my mother. When this procedure showed no positive effect, he repeated the process of bleeding and purging. She grew listless, and the doctor shook his head and said, "If we had started sooner, I could have saved her."

I will never forget her last day. I was sitting beside her, wondering whether she might offer me some final insight, some token of meaning to cherish in my heart. But she only said good-bye and drifted off. I felt betrayed by her and robbed of what few memories I had of her. Those last months had obliterated her goodness in my eyes. I once thought she was so beautiful and charming, but now as I scrambled to learn something from the pieces of her life, I only unearthed a person of compliant sorrow, of unquestioning obedience, and of too much weakness to adapt to her new life. My father sat in a chair at the back of the room and smoked his clay pipe. He had as little to say as my mother. I could not tell whether he was plunged into an abyss of grief or whether he was stoically thinking about his next step.

I was thirteen and my mother had just died. I needed someone to try to console me. I walked out of the room and flung myself on my bed, cursing God for my loss, questioning his goodness, and demanding to know why I had to endure this loss.

It was Edward who came in and held me. He said asking God the reasons behind life's struggles was like asking why there was a rut in the lane. "You don't stop and ask why," he said, gently rubbing my back and shoulders. "You simply maneuver around it. Everyone would think you daft for questioning its purpose. Wisdom lies in the choices we make in the face of tragedy and trial."

"What about my father?" I whispered through a teary voice.

"Perhaps he is in shock," replied Edward. "Or perhaps his mind is on other pursuits."

Edward's voice was strange. I sensed an edge of anger. Later that day I saw my father slip into the slaves' quarters and stay well into the night.

I went to my room and found a note on my pillow in Edward's handwriting. It was a portion of poetry from Shakespeare:

> There is a tide in the affairs of men
> Which taken at the flood, leads on to fortune
> Omitted, all the voyage of their life
> Is bound in shadows and in miseries
> On such a full sea are we now afloat
> And we must take the current when it serves
> Or lose our ventures—

I folded the note and placed it in a special box I kept on my sideboard. I fell asleep trying to imagine what life would entail now that Mother was gone. The last year had not offered much in my relationship with her, but her death felt like the tearing down of a support I could turn to in confusing times. During the funeral, I did not pay attention to the parson's words. My father stood without emotion. Edward wept. At the end, he embraced the coffin, told her he would miss her deeply, promised to watch out for me, and prayed for a safe and restful passage to heaven. I did not cry for my mother. I cried for Edward.

Life without my mother fell into a routine. My father, who had hired a governess to continue my education when we first arrived in Charles Towne, now employed her full-time to assist me in the duties of the home and prepare me for social occasions so that I did not embarrass the family name. Edward remained invaluable to our family, helping me order food, set up schedules, train slaves, and manage their needs. Nearly three years passed, and the drudgery and doldrums of the domestic work bored me terribly and enveloped me in restlessness. I did not know what I wanted. I only knew if running a household was to be my station, my heart would have to be skewered to numbness. I was now sixteen and was reaching a breaking point.

I hate to confess this, but though I treated them generally well, one slave so burrowed under my skin that she moved me to violent behavior. She sluggardly avoided work in every instance and assailed me with diverse reasons why she could not complete the most menial of tasks. I believe she must have thought she could take advantage of my youthfulness. One day I entered the kitchen to find her shirking her duties.

"Maggie, this simply will not do," I said, my hands on my hips. "I expect these wash bins scoured spotless from now on."

"Yes, ma'am," she said.

As I turned I caught her lips mimicking my words. My emotions curdled. I clenched my teeth. "What did you say? Are you forgetting I have the power to have you horsewhipped?"

She was a large woman in her thirties, her face fleshy and wrinkled, her eyes sprinkled with cataracts. She stared at me and said only, "Yes, ma'am."

But there was a tinge of sarcasm in her voice that spun me out of control. I snatched up a knife and thrust at her, slitting her arm. She cursed me. Without uttering a word I slashed at her again, shredding part of her dress. She stared at the bleeding slice with a look of shock, and then her eyes drilled into me.

My head pounded with rage. I moved toward her, the knife upraised.

She ran out the back and disappeared around the corner of the house. Edward stepped into the doorway. "No arguing she's a weasel," he said, "but your temper is ill-placed. That would have been more appropriate for your father."

My first impulse was to curse and swear at Edward, but my thoughts felt murky, so I sighed instead, sat in a chair, and put my hands to my face. He squeezed my shoulders. "I do not believe this is the life for you. This life will make you homely and hopeless before your years," he said.

I nodded. I wanted so much more than life in Charles Towne had to offer.

Chapter VII

Besides the constant grind of domesticity, there was also the interminable schedule of church services, piano lessons, and petty social affairs. I bristled over my father's demand that I learn womanly arts of entertainment—particularly piano and dance. I purposely performed poorly so that my father would despair of my ever mastering them. Another frustration of mine was that we took no trips to interesting locales. I had heard of New York and Boston and Williamsburg, and I whined and begged for my father to take us to visit them, but he absorbed himself in commerce, politics, and law instead. He had no time for such excursions, he said.

Edward and my governess Rebecca persisted in developing my intelligence, though more often than not I kicked against their goads. I can say, however, that I found much pleasure in the books that gathered dust in my father's library. Though it is a tired old saying, that books can take your mind to every imaginable time and place, I must admit that the characters and settings gave me escape from my impatience with the routines of life. I adored Christopher Marlowe's *Doctor Faustus* and William Shakespeare's *Taming of the Shrew, Antony and Cleopatra,* and *Twelfth Night.* The poetry of John Milton, Ben Jonson, and John Donne, and Cervantes' *Don Quixote* proved sound distractions as well. For humor, I thought Moliere's *Tartuffe* and *Don Juan* wickedly funny.

Halfway through my sixteenth year, I began to learn about courtship. Each day after bathing I spent time observing what my mother said would be some of the last brushstrokes the good Lord made on my body, seeing the growing similarities to my mother's figure. My breasts had become spare and symmetrical like hers, but I was taller and stronger. My legs and arms had a firmer, more solid quality. I did not believe my face was very attractive, especially with the discolored scar, but I did like my emerald eyes. Standing before the mirror naked, even I could admit that my long red hair and my taut body were stunning and desirable, and I seemed to possess my father's disarming smile and an occasional gift for wit.

And so suitors came to call. I was at a very marriageable and fertile age—with a wealthy father to boot. Indeed, I enjoyed playing the coquette to my suitors, teasing them with the subtle affection and suggestiveness I read about in books. I recall finding forbidden copies of Aristophanes' *Lysistrata* and William Wycherley's *The Country Wife* among my father's books and devouring their frank depictions of carnal knowledge and the power women held over their men. I acted the flirt, letting my various suitors hold my hand, embrace me, and even offer a lingering kiss while I pressed against them. If they pushed for more, I would calmly push them away and send them off full of yearning and frustration. It was a game I wickedly enjoyed.

During this time my father informed me of a gala to be held in Charles Towne. All the noble families throughout the South would attend, particularly the eligible men of my age. Edward told me Father had contributed significant funds to make the occasion a grand one. A week before the ball, my father took me to Charles Towne and set me up in suitable lodgings. He made arrangements to have me fitted for a new frock and to have my hair spruced up and my makeup perfectly applied. There were a few social events leading up to the party, and there was much talk of merchant vessels arriving with the latest fashions and delicacies from Europe, but then a pirate ungraciously interrupted our aristocratic delights.

His name was Blackbeard, and he had the audacity to blockade the mouth of the Charles Towne port and pillage every ship that attempted to enter or exit. It was the only topic of conversation. My father decried the governor for being too impotent to stop Blackbeard's two ships from putting a stranglehold on a town of more than 10,000 citizens. After robbing eight vessels, he had sufficiently brought all shipping to a standstill, which meant our gala would have to be delayed.

A dozen schooners remained moored in the harbor. Fresh goods destined for Europe rotted on the docks. Messengers were sent on horseback to Virginia, where it was hoped men-of-war would be fitted out to contend with this hooligan. I heard that Blackbeard was seeking a ransom before he would consider setting prisoners free and leaving to freeboot some other coast. He required an unspecified amount of funds and a chest of medicines with a physician. Heated debates erupted all over town, but the merchants ultimately felt forced to accept Blackbeard's demands.

While the leading citizens gathered the ransom, a delegation oared out to Blackbeard's schooner, *The Queen Anne's Revenge.* The cutter returned to shore with a few pirates. While two of the pirates looked roughshod in their ragged and unmatched clothes, the third pirate dressed with style, like a dandy, wearing a calico waistcoat, black breeches, buckled shoes, and a plumed hat. From my room, I watched him swagger through town. I found it amusing that thousands of people looked upon him with candid hatred, and yet he smiled and greeted every person he passed with courtesy. The effrontery of it all amazed me—that one man's strength could choke an entire town and that he and his crew could so brazenly break the law and terrorize people without fear of punishment. I found these pirates remarkable, and I coveted their bravery and their freedom to live on the open water. I made inquiries and learned that the well-groomed pirate was Jack Rackham, quartermaster to Captain Charles Vane, a consort of Blackbeard's armada. Shortly after the bribe was made, Blackbeard and his ships left Charles Towne harbor, but the memory of him remained.

I returned to the plantation and its domestic demands. Something about Blackbeard's brashness prompted me to be more daring and devious with my suitors. I ratcheted my seductive play to bolder levels, feeling empowered to the point of invincibility. I fault the books for failing to warn me that I could lose this game to a predator who ignored the rules. Simply put, I nearly lost my virginity to a rapist.

Frederick Jones was a tall, handsome man. He rode his white horse with style and confidence. His parents owned a much larger plantation south of ours, where the soil was more fertile and the hills rolling. He spoke with grace but also persuasion. He was nearly ten years my senior, and I learned an invaluable lesson from him: professional appearance and good training do not necessarily indicate moral character. Someone's faith may reside in their mouths but never reach their actions or the portals of their heart. After lemonade and cakes, we strolled around the plantation. We had just come to the end of a row and were entering a cluster of palmetto. Frederick spoke of the news in Charles Towne, and I began playing the coquette, teasing him and leaning against him.

He stopped speaking and pulled me against him. He pressed his lips to mine roughly and grasped the front of my dress. I pushed against his shoulders but his grip tightened.

"Stop, Frederick!" I yelled, swinging my head back and forth to avoid his mouth.

I felt his right hand begin to reach under my dress so I raked my nails across his cheek. He winced, pulled away, and then reared back and bashed me in the nose. Pain flooded my head and I felt my legs weaken. I tasted blood as it dripped over my lips. I crumpled to the ground on my knees. I suddenly felt a hard slap from his open palm, which knocked me flat on my back, my head spinning and reeling like I was in a dream world.

"No more games, Anne. You're mine now," he said, grabbing at the bodice of my dress, lifting my head and torso off the ground. He backhanded me soundly, the force of the blow knocking me backward, tearing open the front of my dress, exposing me. I lay there stunned and struggling to catch my breath, watching him unbuckle his belt and pants, his face sweaty, determined, lustful.

I turned my head away, not wanting to look. My vision focused on a half dozen slaves peering through the palmetto fronds at us. Why weren't they helping me? I tried to call to them, but my voice was a dry rasp. I reached out with a pleading hand, but realized they couldn't help. How could they stand up against a white slave owner? Any interference would bring certain death. Perhaps they were grateful that finally a European was getting such punishment for once instead of their women. But I saw more than their pathetic faces, the beaten droop of their shoulders, and their scarred and helpless hands; I saw people broken by the strong, cowed for the rest of their existence. I thought of my compliant mother wasting away under the domination and expectations of my father. I thought of my stepmother's words, of Edward's advice, and of the dog that had forever scarred my cheek. Was this my lot as well? To be a violated woman, ruined by a brutal man? Not without a fight.

But I knew I could not fight him unless, like I had done with Peter, I could get a clean first shot. So I steeled my emotions, controlled my fear, and suddenly smiled at him; forcing my voice to sound seductive, I whispered, "Finally."

Frederick was just starting to pull down his pants, but he hesitated at the sound of my voice.

"Finally," I said. "I have finally found a strong man who isn't afraid to show what he really wants."

Frederick stood there, staring into my eyes in disbelief, doubtful of my words and the tone of my voice.

I lowered my voice, trying to make it even more sultry and seductive. I wiped my mouth on the sleeve of my dress and raised my trembling arms to welcome an embrace. "You do not need to take me. Come to me. I want you to have all of me: more than you've ever imagined."

His expression remained surprised, but the distrust vanished. Then he grinned. "So that was your game, Anne. I had a feeling you'd want this." Men are easily fooled.

He kneeled and began to lean toward me. I considered trying to kick him in "the one-eyed pirate," as Edward had once called it, but I knew I had only one chance. A better plan came to my mind. As he leaned over me, I gently took his face in my hands, parted my lips, and started to close my eyes. I could feel his body relax. Then I stiffened my thumbs. Just as he was about to kiss me, I squeezed hard against his temples so I wouldn't lose my grip and jabbed my thumbs into his eyes. He lurched backward and shouted, but I held on like a vice. He grabbed my wrists and wrenched himself free of my grip. He moaned and heaved as he tried to soothe his eyes with the tips of his fingers. I leaped up and started to run, but then I saw one of the slaves holding a shovel.

In my own blind rage, I screamed, "Bring that here right now or I will have you flayed!"

The man rushed forward, and I yanked the shovel out of his hands and rushed back to Frederick, who was still kneeling on the ground and crying out for help. I raised the shovel over my head and brought it down with all my strength. The blow knocked him over. He curled into the fetal position, protecting his head. Over and over, I beat him on the back and legs. I had murder in my heart. With each swing, I raved and cursed him.

"No man will ever violate me!" I screamed. "I will decide when, where, and who will have my maidenhead!" I struck him again. "Burn in hell! May demons sodomize you for eternity!"

I beat him to unconsciousness. I was about to toss the shovel aside, but then a lurid thought crossed my mind. I turned the shovel around and delivered a swift jab between his legs with the handle. Then I stepped back and looked down at the shredded and bloody condition of my dress. Drops of my own blood dotted my exposed chest. Later, I would learn that the Africans had shared this account, and now feared me even more.

I covered myself and turned to the slaves. "Drag this pile of manure back to his family."

I limped home, still clinging to the shovel and wary of a counterattack. My head throbbed and my face felt puffy and tender. I bathed and stood in front of the mirror naked, arms akimbo. My face was ruddy, and my scar darker. I felt strong and proud and vindicated. I had confronted a beast and beaten him with my wits. I wondered what God thought about me? What did He have in store for me? What was I to learn about the world of men? I thanked Him for helping me overcome this danger.

I did not foresee my father's response, though. I had assumed he would champion my cause, trumpet the weak versus strong, praise my victory, and broadside the ignoble character of Frederick. But I suppose all daughters have their moments or lifetimes of denial concerning their fathers. They are mere men with frailties and contradictions. My father the lawyer seemed more concerned about his standing in Charles Towne than the health and welfare of his only daughter.

"You almost killed him! He will be bedridden for months. The family plans to press charges and have you flogged and jailed. His mother wants you pressed like a witch!" My father yelled as I sat like an obedient daughter on a divan. My nose and mouth were still swollen and bruised, throbbing with stinging pain. "I do not know what I am going to do. This will cost me a great deal. If your mother had—"

I could listen to no more. I stood and yelled. "Father, he nearly raped me!"

"Because you are a harlot! I have seen you shamelessly seduce—"

"Seduce? Father, look at my face! You should charge him with assault. Have him jailed. Defend my honor—our family honor!"

My father raised his hands in defense. "Anne, these are powerful people. We have to get along with them or they will ruin me…us."

"My father is a Jephthah, not a Jacob."

He grimaced. "What in hell are you talking about?"

"The Scripture I learned in the church that you made me attend, Father. Perhaps you should have gone, too. Jephthah sacrificed his virgin daughter for success, but Jacob avenged the rape of his daughter. He killed the man and his entire family, and when the neighbors complained, Jacob said, 'My daughter will not be treated like a harlot.' God did not reprimand Jacob, and yet I believe you would rather I had been more agreeable toward Frederick."

"Anne, I have half a mind to horsewhip you for your insolence."

Anger seemed to flood my veins, filling me with such a rage that I wished to attack him right there. I suddenly took a step toward my father. His eyes widened and he backed up a pace.

I pointed at him. "Careful what you consider, my father. You would not want to end up like my suitor. Obviously I can take care of myself."

He started to raise his hand, but frowned and dropped it. The defeat in his eyes reminded me of my former schoolmaster. "I have to make restitution for your temper again, lest we all be imprisoned and cast out of house and home!" he shouted. "Someone has to be responsible! And the doggerel from that vile tongue of yours taxes my patience!" He started out of the house.

"You fly from every battle, Father!" I yelled after him.

I stormed downstairs and found Edward standing beside the door. He nodded. "Your father cannot see it, but let me commend your courage. Look at you: you're beautiful and so strong." He reached out and took me in his arms. A flush of emotion overwhelmed me. Edward's tenderness melted my rage, and I started to weep. He patted my back. "I'm so sorry I wasn't there, Anne. I wish I could be everywhere for you."

My body convulsed as I wept. Edward released his embrace and cupped my face in his hands. "Ah, Anne, you are a truly unique woman. Most smart women have to accomplish their purposes through flattery and lies. But you, you can beat a man with your fists. I am proud of how you fought. And let me say, he was a much better mark for punishment than a slave."

I smiled as he dabbed at my tears with a handkerchief. "Thank you, Edward. I wish you were my father."

He smiled. "Well, how about I just keep treating you as my prized and precious daughter?"

His words brought more tears to my eyes. "Edward, are there any honorable men in this world?"

He sighed and looked off into the distance. "God surrounds us, but seldom does it pierce our armor-plated souls. Men resist the truth, refusing to love and honor women as God designed. Instead, we treat women like our cattle and expect them to submit to our rules to make ourselves feel powerful. Pathetic."

"So there are none?" I asked.

"Finding a good man is difficult, and unfortunately I've seen many women go blind and forget what they're searching for in a man. My advice is to forget the mysterious and flashy and dangerous. They may seem adventurous, but they offer no stability. Look for loyalty, honesty, respect, modesty, and reverence for the Lord; those qualities may not always be thrilling and romantic, but they are the best for marriage and a family," he said.

I nodded.

He rested his hand on the back of my head. "And you won't find them by the little games others seem so fond of playing."

I looked down, suddenly ashamed of myself.

Edward lifted my chin and met my eyes. "I love you, Anne. You'll find your way."

I asked Edward to saddle my horse for I planned to ride into Charles Towne for a while. I did not want to be home when my father returned from his "mission of restitution."

Chapter VIII

It was in Charles Towne that afternoon that my life was forever changed by two important experiences. Witnessing the hanging of a pirate captain and three of his crew was the first.

I had hobbled my horse when I noticed a large crowd gathering. At first I thought it was another public humiliation of an adulterer—a woman, of course. The authorities never seemed to find and punish the man. Whenever I saw such scenes I thought of the story from the Gospels, where the Pharisees brought a woman caught in adultery before Jesus, testing him to discredit him, and Jesus drew in the sand, silent before the accusers. And then those immortal words came from his lips: "Let him who is without sin cast the first stone." The Pharisees dropped their stones and walked away. That always seemed to be the part of the story that parsons would preach upon, but I have often thought about the woman. I imagine her standing, disgraced and humiliated, her clothes torn, her hair tangled, and her face streaked with dust and tears. She must have been wondering whether the stones would strike her at any moment, wondering why she had been singled out when so many men and women in Jerusalem had committed the same sin. When the men began to leave, she probably did not presume to speak, nor did she feel free to leave. I wonder whether I would have hurled insults at the men for their hypocrisy. She remained before the Righteous Judge of the Universe, the Savior of the World, even as he continued to write on the ground.

Then Jesus stood up and said: "Woman, where are they? Did no one condemn you?"

What went through her mind? Guilt? Shame? Fear? Shock? Anger? Would she be freed from one accuser only to be condemned by another? She said, "No one, Lord."

"Neither do I condemn you; go your way, and from now on sin no more." Those were quite possibly the last words she ever heard Jesus say. Certainly she was not perfect the rest of her life, but did she ever commit adultery again? Could the mercy and compassion of God truly change a person?

I made my way through the jeering crowd and then saw four pirates awaiting execution, nooses snug around their necks. The captain blubbered over and over that he was not guilty, but the other three stood on the gallows grim-faced and defiant. The audience crowed and threw rotten fruit and handfuls of packed muck at them so their faces were covered with filth. As I listened to the public prosecutor recite their crimes and misdeeds and the subsequent judgment of death by hanging on "this day of our Lord, November 18, 1718," a young man strode up beside me—the second event that would alter my life's course.

"That is Major Stede Bonnet. They say he conspired with Blackbeard," the man said. "They say he was once a decorated officer who took to piracy to escape his nagging harridan of a wife."

I smiled and glanced at him. "Like the proverb: 'Better to live in a desert land, than with a contentious and vexing woman.'"

"Well said." He smiled. "And better to live in a corner of a roof, than in a house shared with a contentious woman."

I looked at his aqua blue eyes, and observed his slightly bent nose, his youthful-yet-rugged jaw sprinkled with a stubbly beard. "You know your Scripture."

"Especially when it comes to termagants, I suppose. One more," he winked, "such a rich trove of wisdom in the Book of Proverbs: 'the contentions of a wife are a constant dripping.'"

I decided on a Scriptural parry for the sake of balance. "'Husbands, live with your wives in an understanding way…and grant her honor as a fellow heir of the grace of life so that your prayers may not be hindered.'" I gestured toward Bonnet. "It appears he's at the end of his prayers."

"I cannot argue with that, so are about thirty of his crew members," he said, redirecting his eyes to the four men at the gallows.

He could not have been five years my senior, nor an inch taller than me. Ruddy complexioned with sandy, pork chop sideburns, he wore his hair in a disheveled tail.

"On the other hand, going to the gallows is one way to escape a shrewish wife," I added.

The man sighed. "Aye, but a real pirate would rather blow himself to bloody hell, pardon the language, and commit his soul to the deep than be hanged up in the sun, drying stiff and pecked by the gulls, like Captain Kidd."

I liked the defiance in what he said. He was not a wealthy man. His shirt and breeches were worn, but clean. His stockings were frayed, and his buckled shoes creased and tarnished.

"My name is James Bonney. I am a free rogue in search of a ship. No prey, no pay—only a cut of the spoils." He bowed to me.

I introduced myself and glanced back at Bonnet, who was straining against the rope. He looked frail, old, and afraid, muttering an inaudible prayer or plea. "His wife must have been quite a wench."

"A real Jezebel. He is probably the only pirate to buy a ship and fit it out at his own expense. Everyone else steals them. His ship was the *Revenge*, and he plundered a few sloops along the Carolinas for a couple years before they finally captured him," said Bonney.

"Please, have mercy. I didn't hurt anyone. Blackbeard made me do it...I am a privateer for Britain. I don't belong with these men," Bonnet cried. He was met with another barrage of feces and mud from the crowd. He choked and gagged.

Suddenly, one of the other pirates spoke. "Yes, I am a pirate and proud of it. I don't deny anything you've charged me with except that I ever served under this Capt. Bonnet." His voiced was strained because of the stiff rope, but he spoke without fear—pure, unfettered tenacity.

"I have lived my life in freedom, not beholden to a King to dictate my life." He seemed to spit each word at the crowd. "You are the slaves, fighting over the table scraps that spill from the nobles' plates. You are nothing but a pack of mangy dogs and hen-hearted idiots, imprisoned by their oppressive, hypocritical rules. I have lived free and I will die free. It is you who are to be pitied."

I found his words frightful and inspiring. I glanced around to see how others were responding. A few women dressed in habits started to cry, folding their hands in prayer for the men's souls. The men listened stoically but watched with curiosity. I turned to James, who was smiling and nodding with each phrase the pirate uttered.

A moment later the man's speech was cut short. The chutes were released and Bonnet and others jerked and dangled on the ends of the hemp nooses. I stared for a long time in silence as they died, the pirate's words still resounding in my ears. As I watched the life seep out of them, I wondered what people would say about them now. I wished that Bonnet had been as brave and dignified in the face of death as his crew. I tried to picture how I would behave locked in a dungeon, awaiting the hangman's loop, facing my last breaths. It seemed a good test of one's character.

I turned to James. "Major Bonnet was not a brave pirate, then, not like that other man. Are you brave?"

He blinked and smiled. "May I purchase you an ale?"

In a smoky tavern, Bonney began to tell me of the earliest recorded history of the sweet trade: piracy. He called it the "third oldest profession, next to prostitution and medicine."

I found myself more intoxicated by Bonney's vivid portrayal of the first sea wolves of the Mediterranean than by the ale we drank. Those ancient pirates sacked hundreds of towns along the Roman Main before the time of Christ; they even captured the Roman Emperor Julius Caesar and held him prisoner for nearly a day, demanding a ransom. It is written, Bonney said, that during his imprisonment, Caesar taunted the pirates, claiming he would capture every one and watch them be crucified. The pirates mocked Caesar. When the ransom was paid and Caesar was set free, he ordered a fleet to pursue the pirates and bring them back to Rome. The pirates were brought before Caesar. He reminded them of his promise, and then had all of them crucified. It was a sobering tale of the brief whims of pirate pride.

We ordered a supper and James talked about the Vikings, who had terrorized England and Ireland, carrying off the fairest women to be their brides. The Barbary corsairs plied their trade along North Africa, the most famous of them being Barbarossa, "Red Beard."

"He was a sadist who enjoyed watching his captives tortured. He liked to invent new torture methods," said Bonney. "Legend says that after his death he had to be buried several times because his bones would not lie quiet in the ground." Bonney shrugged his shoulders. "Pirates do have their superstitions."

As I listened to his stories, I felt my emotions stirring. I may have been raised to express revulsion for the things he spoke fondly of, but I wanted to hear more from this man rife with pirate history, lost mores, and forbidden attitudes. I found his words easy on my ears. I was drawn to his sure and articulate voice, his strong jaw, and his smooth lips. His forearms and hands were no strangers to labor. I asked, "Mr. Bonney, how is it you know so much about pirates?"

"Well, I must confess I am reading a book: *Bucaniers of America* by A. O. Exquemelin. I find it fascinating. I feel I should be prepared before entering my station as a marauder."

It seemed a bit naïve to learn piracy from a book, but I enjoyed Bonney's descriptions. I learned about the Chinese pirate Cheng, who plundered merchant ships along the China coast with a battalion of junks. His fatal flaw? He proved too vain for his own good, accepting an invitation from the Emperor to share a meal in the royal court. "He came without arms and left without his head."

European pirates had gone so far as to create a pirate nation called Libertatia on the island of Madagascar. "I suppose it was a rogue utopia—shared wealth and limited laws—but it's been mostly wiped out now. They killed each other over who would rule. Greed, pride, and lust for power—every man seems to have his bane," said Bonney.

"And what is yours, Mr. Bonney?"

He hesitated, a bit startled by my question.

"Ah, might it be a weakness for simply not perceiving your own inward blemishes?"

He looked wounded.

"Certainly if you learn nothing from these piratical imperfections, might you not be doomed to repeat them?"

His jaw tautened and then he leaned forward, staring at me unwaveringly in the eye. "Miss McCormac, yes, I have my lion's share of personal weakness and spiritual deformity, one being a wariness to share those openly at such an early stage in a relationship with so enchanting a woman. Might not you be a *belle dame sans merci*—poised to ensnare me with a kiss?"

There was moment of silence between us. His last words prompted me to hold my breath for a spell and I found his eyes hypnotic. I forced a calm smile. The moment passed when the owner brought us bowls of soup with bread. I turned to a safer subject.

"Do tell me more about pirates."

He went on to describe probably the most well-known pirate-buccaneer captain, Sir Henry Morgan—commissioned a privateer by England to swarm the West Indies and capture Spanish galleons. He had more than 2,000 men and 40 ships at his beck and call, and he sacked the richest Spanish city, Panama.

"The beautiful part of his trade was that it was legal. He eventually retired and died in his bed—a rarity for pirates."

I stared into those blue eyes, luminous and fiery. The raw energy in his voice and his stories of untamed men enamored me. "Why do they turn to piracy when they will almost certainly die at the gallows or be lost at sea?"

"The spirit of adventure and the despair of broken dreams. Some crave excitement. Others are jobless men with nothing to lose. To work honestly on a ship means grueling hours, poor pay, food rations, and severe discipline."

I thought of the man I had seen scourged on the ship as we sailed to the New World.

"They are quickly flogged for the smallest slights; some are chained and forced to eat roaches and mice alive. Others are hanged from yardarms or towed from the stern. And then there is pressing, flaying, branding, stoning, thumbscrews, and the rack; sailors are just dumb, driven mules. That's a goad to get out if there ever was one," said Bonney. "We hate authority, and that is essential to being a pirate. So we declare war on the entire world and live indebted to no man or god."

His hands were callused and large, and he gesticulated as he spoke. His voice had a gravelly quality, poetic in a stark sort of way. I watched the movement of his lips as he spoke, absorbed by both his stories and the way he told them.

"Take Captain Kidd," Bonney said, taking a drink. "For years people say he was an honest seaman, living on a pittance. Then King George commissioned him as a privateer to capture picaroons in the Indian Ocean. Well, the privateer life was a poor life, too, so Kidd finally turned to piracy and sweet prizes."

"What happened to him?" I asked.

"His crew of scullions mutinied, so Kidd returned to England, hoping for clemency. He was caught, tried, and executed soon after." Bonney chuckled and took another gulp. "A parson urged him to repent, but he was too drunk to listen. The rope broke the first time and he had to be strung up again. Afterward they tarred his body and hung it in chains for years, just swinging in the wind."

I thought about the turbulent Atlantic during my passage a few years ago. Its raw energy and its endless sweep had lured me to cherish it. A life at sea indeed seemed adventurous. I imagined fearless pirates, battling all hypocritical nations and living a truly free life. Ideas rose and fell in my head like a lilting melody. I did not want to say farewell to James Bonney that night, so I promised to return the following day for a second visit.

"My ship leaves for New Providence in a fortnight and two days, Anne. I long for our next visit."

Darkness had fallen by the time I rode my horse home. I felt wild, full of pluck, almost wishing for the chance to confront an armed brigand or breech-clouted Indian on the road and give them a tang of gunpowder and a taste of steel. Predictably, Father was already in bed when I arrived home.

I dreamed of James Bonney, the aspiring pirate, who could perhaps release me from the toil of this tobacco plantation, the parade of dull suitors, and my controlling father. Could he take me face to face with the greatest adventures this life had to offer—sailing the seas and fighting for treasures?

In bed I thrashed and fidgeted, boiling at the thought of marrying, giving birth, raising children, and running a household, relegated to a conventional life. That path seemed well worn and strewn with desperation and resignation. I despised the idea of forever bending to my husband's every whim and fancy, existing for his good pleasure and the endless needs of my children. Only mundane servitude awaited me if I stayed in Charles Towne—my own gallows and noose. No. I would not watch my dreams dissolve away as my soul slipped into shrinking, squirming sedation.

Where were the surprises, the unknowns, the experiences to explore? I chose to be the huntress rather than the prey. When dawn appeared, I arose, bathed, and dressed hurriedly. At breakfast Father said nothing of our argument. His silence only angered me more. I told him I was going for a ride. Edward saddled my horse and I ventured back to town to find James, the aspiring pirate.

CHAPTER IX

I spent the entire next day walking with James Bonney. He once again bewitched me with his talk of the ocean and piracy. In his voice I could almost hear the swells of the ocean, the combers crashing against the hulls, and the scream of the wind in the rigging. Near the close of the day we held hands, and I do not believe I had ever been so happy. He proved to be a refined gentleman, though he was so low on funds that I purchased our meal. He asked me about my scar. After I told him the story of the dog, my mind and tongue loosened. I shared the stories of Peter and my school rebellion as well as my fight with Frederick. He just sat there quietly, staring at me. I was beginning to think I shouldn't have told him. But then he reached out and took my hands in his. "Anne, you are truly amazing."

I blushed, savoring his words of admiration.

By the end of the day, he asked to kiss me. His request made me blush and I could not look at him, but I pined for sincere affection. I raised my head. He slowly slid one arm around my waist. His other hand gently caressed my hair. Our eyes met, and I gave my lips to him. A kiss never tasted so sweet.

We strolled along the beach and found two domed boulders to sit on. We spoke over the sound of the waves, talking about our families. I discovered our lives were not so different. His family was also Irish and owned a plantation, but he could no longer endure his parents' high expectations and had chosen to relieve himself of their presence and authority. Though he was penniless, he would make a good livelihood and at the same time experience the greatest of voyages.

"The Irish do make fine pirates. Have you heard of Red Legs Greaves?"

I leaned forward. "No. Tell me."

"In the 1670s he accidentally climbed onboard a pirate ship to escape a cruel master. Well, he challenged the pirate captain to a duel and ran him through with a borrowed cutlass. Instead of cutting his throat, the crew elected him captain. He was a typical Irishman—subservient to none, taking the helm." James spoke with passion and pride.

"But he was a noble pirate, which is what I aspire to be," James said.

"Noble?"

"He was the Robin Hood of the seas. He never robbed the poor or mistreated his prisoners. If one of his crew attacked a woman or tortured a passenger, he had him either marooned or keelhauled. He attacked and looted the wealthy only to help the impoverished. He captured an island and made his utopia there for years. But one of his crew played the Judas and he was imprisoned, tried, and sentenced to hang in Jamaica. However, the Good Lord was watching over him because an earthquake of biblical proportions destroyed the prison and he escaped. He was later granted a pardon and lived out his days a respectable and well-regarded man. He was truly a noble pirate, which I aspire to as well."

We spent a great deal of time together over the next two weeks, and our conversations shifted from the history of pirates to talk of our future together. Leaving and cleaving to James sounded like the beginning of all my dreams coming true. We could marry and set sail together, free from our parents and parliament, savoring the sea and our blossoming love and awaiting one grand adventure after another.

I am not sure how, but my father caught wind of James. Two days before our secret marriage and departure, my father confronted me while we ate breakfast. He demanded I stop seeing the "penniless hellion bent on my daughter's destruction."

"Father, he is an honorable man," I protested.

"No, he is an indentured servant with five years to serve. He is on the run and is wanted as a fugitive of the law in Maryland."

"That is a lie, Father. You are saying that just because I don't fancy one of your suitors—like the rapist!"

My father narrowed his eyebrows and sipped his tea. "Entertaining this rascal is beneath your class, Anne. Perhaps I will make further inquiry. Is that what you wish for him?"

I folded my napkin, trying to control my fury. My eyes fell upon the tobacco fields thriving in the Carolina sun and humidity. I watched the slaves laboring. I knew he had enough power and influence to have James arrested, whether what he said was the truth about him or not. All my father's claims and threats jolted me, but I refused to listen, and blocked the questions about his background out of my mind, not believing what my father had said.

I knew I must change tactics; further argument would only make matters worse. So I conjured the role of obedient daughter and began to shed crocodile tears.

"Oh, Father, I didn't realize...has he lied to me all this time? How could he be so cruel?" I lowered my face.

My father grew sympathetic and patted my shoulder. "I know, dear, it must hurt, and I hate to be the bearer of bad tidings, but it is better to know the truth now than later."

I rushed to my room under the guise of despair and plotted my next course.

Later I would discover that it was Edward who had told my father. I did not blame him too much for I knew he was only trying to protect me, but I could not see reality clearly. I was nearly eighteen, and my beloved would depart in two days. Letting such an opportunity pass by would be nothing less than emotional death. I could not hesitate or all would be lost. "There's only this life," I kept saying to myself.

I decided to sneak out late at night to elope with James, sail to New Providence, and live in the lap of new hope. I crept into the horse stable and began to saddle my mare when I heard Edward whisper to me.

"Anne, I think this a jester's move. Marriage is too big a decision to make in so scant a number of days."

I felt tears come to my eyes. I ran to him and embraced him. He was my true father, and I longed for his blessing. "Oh, Edward, but he is all I dream for, and he is leaving. I cannot let him go. I am suffocating here."

"I know, but fools rush in...What about your father? What about me?"

I could feel the pain in his voice. I thought about his loyalty and love. He had always protected and comforted me, instructed me with wisdom and humor. I was on the brink of staying when Edward suddenly whispered, "And we must take the current when it serves—"

I said the last phrase with him: "or lose our ventures."

Edward held me at arm's length, staring into my tear-smeared face. "Well, my daughter, the course of true love never did run smooth. Follow your ventures. Don't settle for a lukewarm existence that will only decay your mind. Go."

I hugged him again and felt him choke tears on my shoulder. I held him tight, and then he abruptly pulled away, raked a sleeve across his eyes, and finished saddling my horse.

"I will never forget you, Edward. I will write."

"Spur on; your lover waits. Godspeed."

I rode into the night, thanking God for so fine a man, a benchmark to compare to my future partner. I felt tears rolling down my cheeks and dripping off my chin. It broke my heart to leave Edward, but I was spurred on by youthful longing and untamed abandon. My beloved would steal me away and carry me to places of beauty. I knocked at the door of his room, and when he opened he greeted me with a humble iron band and a long, hungry kiss. We found a Methodist minister and paid him a pittance, and he married us within the hourglass. I know James felt ashamed of his poverty, but I assured him we would soon be as wealthy as Red Legs and as noble as Robin Hood and King Arthur. We stopped at a merchant's shop and sold my jewelry.

We returned to our shabby room, ready to consummate our marriage on a vermin-infested bed, and I was filled with nervousness at the thought of willingly offering myself to him. James' love of poetry calmed me and made our lovemaking natural and free, an exchange of our passions for one another.

We sat on the bed fully clothed, and James opened the Bible to the Song of Solomon: "Rise up, my love, my beautiful one, and come away," he read.

I smiled. He handed the Bible to me. I was touched by the idea of using the holy tome to help us come together in one flesh.

I scanned the chapter and read: "'Let him kiss with the kisses of his mouth—for your love is better than wine...Therefore the virgins love you. Lead me away!'"

James leaned over and slowly kissed me. I embraced him. Over my shoulder he continued to read, but my attention was lost in his strength and the warmth of his body against mine. I began to kiss his neck and blow in his ear, which kept interrupting his reading. "'...Your mouth is lovely...Your breasts are like two fawns...You have ravished my heart with one look of your eyes...' Enough Scripture for now," he said.

He raised his hands to my face, nudged my head upward, and kissed me deeply. "'Put me like a seal over your heart for love is as strong as death.'"

I looked into James' eyes, searching for the strength and virtue I sought in a man. I believed it shone in his eyes. I whispered, "I want to give myself to you."

By candlelight, James began to run his hands over my body. He closed his eyes and seemed to delight over every part of me. I could feel myself giving in to this moment, and my body shivered with his touch. As he undid the first button of my lace corset, our desire burst into fire, and we tore at each other's clothes with frenzy. As he pushed away the last of my petticoats and pulled off his pants,

James suddenly stood up. He reached for my hand and pulled me up. I moved to hug him, but he stepped back and with only the sound of a ticking clock, we looked upon each other's naked bodies. I felt exposed and yet surprisingly safe and comfortable. He stood before me, aroused. He stepped forward and gathered me into his arms, twirled once playfully, and then rested me on the bed. Our bodies one, we rested afterward in each other's arms. It was a night full of mesmerizing words and uninhibited passion.

The next morning, James returned with breakfast and word that Father had sent for the magistrates to arrest James and send him back to Maryland and to find me and return me home. James and I packed up what little we owned, a risible sight, and we boarded a merchant schooner headed for Jamaica, which would make a brief stop in New Providence. I used much of what I had saved and sold to secure a berth for the passage. From there we would ascertain a way to reach New Providence. The schooner unmoored and hoisted its sails, and we cruised out of the harbor—and I escaped the grip of my father.

We were at sea for a month, and it was bliss. The sea and my man romanced me. To James I recited the proverb: "'There are three things which are too wonderful for me, yes four which I do not understand: the way of any eagle in the air, the way of a snake on a rock, the way of ship in the midst of the sea, and the way of a man with a virgin.'"

"But Anne, you're no longer a virgin," James said. He tickled my ribs.

"And you're not an eagle, but we're on the sea," I put my arm around him and felt his warmth.

"What about the snake and rock?"

I arched my brow, took his hand, and led him to our cabin for another dose of our rapture.

He regaled me with more tales of pirate battles, plundered ships, and buried treasure. The tides and currents, the wind furling the sails, the briny spray of seawater, the frothy waves as the ship sliced the crests, the fluking whales and playful porpoises, the gulls and pelicans arcing in their flights—it all fed my soul. The ocean called to me like a siren, made me love more deeply its unforgiving power and raw beauty. I saw myself once again as an eleven-year-old, tingling at the adventure and aching for fresh experiences.

Still, in the quiet times, I was ill at ease milling along the deck and taking stock of my decisions. I had cut the ties between my father and me, and though I basked in the joy of my new life with James, I missed Edward tremendously and regretted the finality of my move. I hoped, too, that time and distance would pale the harsh memories I had of my father.

One night I could not sleep. I felt loneliness and depression sweep over my soul. Finally, I climbed out of my hammock and walked onto the deck. The blackness of the night left me full of longing, though for what I was not sure. On a whim, I decided to try something I had never done in the dark: climb the ratlines and rigging from one spar to the next, resting only for a spell on the crosstrees until I reached the top of the mast. With the gentle swell of the currents and the blasts of wind, I nearly lost my grip three times. If I had not caught myself each time, it certainly would have meant a fall to the death. But I was driven on by a desire to stand above it all: the ship, the sea, and my life.

When I reached the crow's nest, the sun was just starting to break the horizon. I felt my heart lurch in my chest at the sight of the brilliant hues of yellow, red, and green, and I closed my eyes and exhilarated in the caresses of the wind on my face. I looked down and saw a couple sailors, who looked like rodents scurrying around the deck. I glanced upward at the wind-streaked clouds and felt a dizzying hypnosis gazing at the expanse of sky. "...This brave o'erhanging firmament, this majestical roof fretted with golden fire," as Hamlet said.

It was a transcendent moment, like I was communing in the presence of the Almighty, straining to hear his still-small voice. The rising sun colliding with the clouds made them seem as if they were afire, and staring at them made me wonder for a moment how Moses might have felt when he witnessed the burning bush. I took deep breaths as if to drink in every ounce of this marvelous moment, to store it up and lock it away for times when I would need it. For the first time in a long time, I prayed with a clear and attentive mind. I thanked God for the beauties of His creation. I believe it was a moment of God's grace that kept me from sleep and compelled me to climb to the top of the mast.

As I looked back down I saw James roaming the deck in search of me. I asked the Lord to help me understand the misgivings in my heart, fearing my quick decisions were foolish but hoping they would prove as wise as they were romantic to me.

I took one more deep breath before descending. I thanked God again for this experience, one I could return to in my mind when life suddenly turned gruesome and confusing.

Chapter X

If Dante had seen the island of New Providence, he might have created another level of hell. Within one day all my dreams cascaded into a stinking cesspool of doubt, dread, and disappointment. The sight of the island from a distance—with its palms, its skylines of multicolored hues, and its crystal-clear waters—thrilled me. Up close, though, Nassau Harbor was more fitting for swine than humans. Dirty, cheap, stinking, and violent, it reeked of vice, rot, and human waste. And yet I had heard it said that when a pirate slept, he dreamed not of heaven but of New Providence, where no government ruled and a pirate was free to live as he wished.

I stood on the white, sandy shore observing the dilapidated buildings and the ragged and diseased people while James attempted to procure lodgings. To my left I saw merchants hawking spices, trinkets, silks, lamps, and all manner of seafood. I listened to their curse-laden haggling. Women in worn dresses stood at tables shelling peas, cleaning fish, prying open crustaceans, and chopping coconuts. People thronged the area, some buying, others panhandling. Shrill and bawdy oaths emanated from two makeshift booths. Wealthy merchants walked through town, often with slaves trundling handbarrows behind them or carrying umbrellas and fans above their masters' heads.

African and Indian slaves, both male and female, stood on the auction block like sheep destined for slaughter. The destitution etched on their faces saddened and nauseated me. The weasel-like auctioneer carelessly stripped and fondled the women and made lewd innuendos while he took bids. How could these people be so beaten as to relinquish their humanity and be treated like dogs? I pitied and despised them. Why not die fighting?

James returned and told me that the only lodging to be found on the island was a tent made from worn-out sails. Even the few wattle huts were occupied. Next to our tent a harlot entertained pirates for pay day and night. A bit farther down the path, pirates spent the night gambling. Fights and duels seemed to break out constantly. Screams of pain and taunting epithets and curses filled the air. It was not uncommon to find a bloody body not far from our tent in the morning. It would be removed, but the splotches of blood left on the sand and sails testified to the meager worth of humanity.

James' nervous manner also unsettled me, especially when pirates catcalled me and made vulgar propositions. I would look at my husband curiously when he acted as if he had not heard these profane suggestions. I saw fear flickering in his eyes and I felt ashamed and upset that James did not take a stand and defend my honor. I kept these thoughts in my heart and steeled myself against my own fears, carrying a large knife with me wherever I went. James may have been revealing a yellow stripe, but in this dangerous place I would remember Edward's words and never leave myself a helpless target. Nonetheless I felt anxious. I was overwhelmed by the sheer number of pirates—their deft skills with knife, sword, and gun, and their disregard for life.

In our tent at night, I would ask my husband searching questions over the din outside.

"James, what are we going to do? We have no money and no prospects."

"I never said this would be simple. I suppose you miss your ruby slippers, velvet chairs, and Persian rugs?"

"No, I do not."

James tried to strike a devil-may-care stance, but it was ankle deep. "Granted, it has taken more time than I first thought. But we will find a ship to join, and we'll sail away to freedom and adventure," he reassured me. "We will be real pirates, not like these rascals who give piracy a bad name."

I sat on our straw mattress, which was populated with fleas and chiggers, and looked down at the sand and sighed. I could hear the prostitute starting up her trade again in the tent next to us. "This isn't anything like I imagined. I cannot envision that being on a pirate ship will be any better. The men here are barbarians and the women whores."

He knelt down in front of me and grasped my shoulders. His eyes looked straight into mine. "Anne, I promise you everything is going to be all right. Don't worry."

I could see right through him, with his shifting eyes and his wavering voice. He did not know what to do. We slept that night in each other's arms, not in a passionate embrace, but in a huddled state, flinching at the violent sounds and musket shots that echoed in the humid night.

I awoke late in the night, needing to relieve myself. I peered out the flaps of the tent. A semblance of peace had finally descended on the island. I stepped around the tent and blinked at a thousand sparkling lights that flitted about in the night air, vanished momentarily, and then reignited and plashed about again. It took me back to Charles Towne and a time after a heavy shower when Edward had led me outside to see the fireflies. It was a beautiful respite from what passed as humanity here. The contrasts here were unsettling. The soft white sands, the palms shifting in the sea breezes, and the crystal blue waters all fell in sharp relief to the grotesque behavior of humans.

The next morning I received a second shot to my crumbling confidence. While James went searching for some manner of work, I followed some women to the reefs, where they hitched up their skirts and gathered conch and mollusks as well as an occasional lobster or crab. I managed to slip in with them, and they taught me how to fish the tidewaters. I listened to their talk of freebooters, and I was surprised to discover there were hundreds of people scattered throughout the Bahamas, some settlers with families, and some pirates and prostitutes. These women were part of a settlement that had been established years ago before the pirates selected it as a lair to lay low from the roving British man-of-wars. The shallow bay was best suited to sloops and was precarious to the hulls of larger ships. As the pirates came, they brought a great deal of money and goods into the area, but they also brought lawlessness.

"And how many of you sail on the pirate ships?" I asked.

There was a pause among the women as they slowly turned toward me. Only the foamy wash of the waves, sizzling on the sand and rocks, filled the air with its sound. Then the women began to laugh and tease each other.

"Women pirates! Now there's an idea too long in coming," shouted one of the women. The others responded with a fresh round of giggles.

I felt heat rise to my face even as I attempted to join in the laughter.

"Listen, my lass," a woman named Annabelle lisped through a hair lip and few teeth. "Women on a pirate ship would serve one and only one purpose, and it wouldn't include cooking or cleaning. Besides, women onboard a ship—it's plain bad luck."

Annabelle was probably twice my age; she was stout and her face was furrowed and cragged by years of sun and wind. I don't know whether she had ever been a mother, but she possessed that maternal, nurturing spirit. She took an interest in me, which I appreciated. Over the next couple days, I met her at the tidewaters and confided in her about everything. She nodded and chuckled occasionally at my story, which sometimes sent her into a spasm of coughs. When I finished, she patted me on the back and said, "Where did you hear this swill? I am afraid your dreams about pirate life are wrong in just about every possible way."

After leaving the shore, I wandered through the well-trod paths of New Providence. I felt blood rush to my ears after my talk with Annabelle. It felt like I was under water; all sound muffled in my ears. Despair engulfed me. I whispered a prayer, confessing my foolish haste and pleading for protection. As I headed back to the tent I felt no peace—trapped and confused.

One day James entered the tent with a smile on his face. "I have finally found good employment, work that will tide us over until we find a suitable crew to join."

"What kind of employment?"

"Profitable work." He pulled from a canvas sack a gammon of bacon and a leg of mutton along with potatoes and carrots. "Tonight we celebrate. And soon we will leave this tent and lodge in more proper quarters."

I looked at the food with confusion. "How? What is your job?"

"I am employed by Governor Woodes Rodgers. He governs all these islands, though he is presently stationed on Jamaica."

"But there is no magistrate here. What are your duties?"

"I am to keep him abreast of the activities on this island."

The position sounded respectable enough, but something about it left me unsettled. Call it intuition. I had to grant that no well-known pirates were harbored in Nassau Bay at the time, which did not offer us much prospect. This work could carry us until we could find a ship. He also pulled from the sack a brace of pistols with powder and balls, as well as a pair of cutlasses. He was so pleased with this boon I hesitated to bring up what the women had said about pirates. I started to but he barreled me over with the news that he had to sail to Jamaica soon to meet with officials and make plans to improve order on the island.

"And now it is time to celebrate!"

That afternoon we hiked to a secluded area near a beautiful waterfall and practiced our shooting and swordplay. At first I slashed at clumps of stephanotis and bamboo. I tried to shear away my haunting concerns and cradle my hopes and happy memories of James in the front of my mind.

After working up a sweat, we shed our clothes, vaulted into the pool of water below us, and swam beneath the falls. I loved to watch how the cataracts of water hurtled off the shale pinnacle and burst into a plume of mist that licked my face. I traced single sparking rivulets on their descent into the pool. A circular rainbow formed within the mist. No pot of gold there, I thought. I dove under the water and peered into the murky depths, sighting a school of tropical fish finning against the current with arrowy movements. There was even a place underneath the falls where we found a hollowed-out, water-smoothed rock we could lie against and luxuriate in the refreshing spray and undulating current. I felt a renewed tenderness for my husband, and with the day's last light illuminating us through the cascading water, we made love on a pile of bulrushes in the shadow of the falls. A partial peace had returned. I found myself again turning to God in thanks for this sanctuary from the ugliness of New Providence.

CHAPTER XI

The next morning James set out early to prepare for his trip to Jamaica. Even though we had ample food, I felt restless so I joined the women at the tide pools. There were only a few ladies out that day, and because I did not know them well, I wandered along the shore aimlessly, searching for pretty shells.

Just as I plucked a shell from the sand, I saw a man out of the corner of my eye approaching me with deliberateness. I sensed potential danger. We had been on the island only six days now, but already I had learned to stick close to large groups of people. There had been numerous remarks that made me feel that a brigand would make a move soon, though. As he neared me, I unsheathed my knife and pointed it at him without a word. With my free hand I beckoned him, trying to bolster my courage. He also said nothing. He merely drew his knife and began to circle me, leering at me with a knowing smile. He feinted right and slashed, but I shifted to his other side.

"The next one will send you south of this world," I whispered, fighting to control my voice.

His eyes were cold; his gritty, brooding expression revealed a violent lust, as if he had smoldered over this plan for quite a while and now nothing would make him swerve from his intent.

He stuck out his tongue and wriggled it at me. "I could come back with me mates, or ye could make it easier on yerself."

"Don't be a fool," a woman shouted from behind me. I recognized Annabelle's voice. "Not unless you want soldiers landing here and tracking you down."

The man's eyes bounced toward Annabelle who emerged out of some foliage onto the beach. "She's the wife of the new spy?"

"That's right, sweet," Annabelle returned. "Better for all of us that you find another victim to slake your thirst."

He cursed and spat, battling between reason and desire. "We'll settle this matter another time. And soon." He winked, backed up, and then trudged off the beach.

I stood there trying to calm my breathing. I wasn't sure I could have fought him off. I turned to Annabelle and I began to ponder her words as my fear receded. Pirate snitch? A rat?

"The only thing that saved you is your man working for the governor," Annabelle said. "It'll keep you safe—for a while. But I don't know for how long because you're too pretty for this hellhole. You better push off while wind is at your back."

I clenched my fists and ground my teeth.

"Now, Anne, before you flay your spouse, remember he likely did this for your safety. He doesn't have the skill to protect you."

"He has lied to me from the first day I met him," I said.

"Did he have any other choice?"

"Just what do you mean by that?"

"Well, just look at your lissome self. You're a catch with a high price. Your expectations demand a pack of lies to keep you happy," Annabelle said. "You even deceive yourself; you're full of contradictions, and a bit spoiled, too."

I looked down at my left hand and realized I had been tightly squeezing a sharp shell. I flung it into the surf. "I know somebody back in Charles Towne who would have been perfect for you—brutal honesty and wise advice. Thank you, Annabelle, for helping me."

As I walked back to our tent, my head was a whirlpool of rage over my new understanding of my husband. Annabelle had stirred a gale in my brain. I wanted to be cruel to James, but I also felt sympathy for his predicament. Just before I reached our tent, though, I heard cannon fire. I gazed out at the ocean and saw three shallow-hulled sloops entering the harbor. I heard excited calls saying that Blackbeard had arrived. Curiosity slowed my swirling emotions. I wanted to see him—see the legendary pirate who had blockaded Charles Towne. I sat in the tent, peeking out, trying to catch a glimpse of Blackbeard and straining to hear any news. When James showed up an hour later, I decided to set my anger aside for now.

I tried to sound pleasant, saying, "James, Blackbeard is on the island! Perhaps he is the answer to our problems?"

James looked at me with a nervous hesitation.

"Can we go see him?"

"Perhaps I can."

"But can I just sit in the back of the tavern and see what he looks like?"

"Anne, it might be dangerous. He is notorious for his unpredictable fits."

I pleaded and pouted, even making a promise I had no intention of keeping, until he agreed to escort me through New Providence until we found Blackbeard.

We found him sitting in the corner of a tavern with a young woman and four other men, who all looked like captains. I sat down with James and observed Blackbeard out of the corner of my eye. He wore only black, though his long beard was braided with ribbons of crimson, blue, and gold. At the end of two ribbons, he had fixed two smoldering wicks, which eerily illuminated his scarred face. His massive body filled his chair and seemed to ooze over it. His bull neck, thick forearms, and huge hands were darkened, creased, and scarred from a life on the sea. His laugh boomed across the room.

He leaned over and asked the woman a question. I discovered later that she was his new bride of a few days. The woman looked down and shook her head, and Blackbeard suddenly grabbed her hair, pulled her head up, and slapped her across the face. She fell out of her chair and sprawled on the floor.

I recognized one of the men with Blackbeard: it was the stylish man who had strolled the streets on Charles Towne during the blockade, Jack Rackham. He was as handsome as I remembered him, and still a dandy pirate, clad in brushed, gaudy calico, silver-buckled shoes, and a fine hat with a plume. He flinched at Blackbeard's violence against the woman; meanwhile Blackbeard let loose a raucous laugh and kicked her in the backside as she arose, catapulting her a few feet forward, where she tumbled against a stool. The gentleman arose and reached out to the sobbing woman.

"Leave her be, Jack," Blackbeard grunted. "Lived all her life with a silver spoon in her mouth. Time to blood let some of that blueblood. Get up, you slut, before I sell you as a whore."

The man hesitated. I wondered whether he might defend the woman, perhaps challenge Blackbeard to a duel and rescue her, but he merely forced a smile, bowed royally to Blackbeard, and sat back down. I could still tell it bothered him to see the woman abused in such a manner. He had a fine smile and a refined demeanor, and sitting next to Blackbeard, he looked like a noble beside a brute. Rackham's every move seemed deliberately cultured. When he spoke it was with eloquence and wit. I saw a gold chain dangling from a front pocket of his waistcoat. At one point he fished out a gold watch fob and checked the timepiece.

With trembling hands, the woman crawled into her chair and wiped away the tears from her face and the blood on her lips. James told me later that the woman was Blackbeard's fourteenth wife and had been forced into marriage as a negotiation to end hostilities in a Florida harbor. It was Blackbeard's custom after the ceremony to take each wife to his ship with great fanfare, only to brutally and repeatedly rape her and then offer her to each of his crewmembers. Word was that most of his wives had died, many by their own hand, though a few had managed to escape. As I sat there drinking rum, I felt my notions about the pirate life congealing in my mind, a stew of horror and fascination.

That night I asked James about the well-dressed man who sat next to Blackbeard.

"His name is Calico Jack Rackham, quartermaster. He used to sail with Blackbeard, but Blackbeard ordered him to serve under Captain Charles Vane. I understand he fancies himself a gentleman pirate and noble rogue," James said. "The other two were Captain Vane and Captain Howell Davis."

"What is this? A pirate captain reunion?"

James smirked. "A unique circumstance, indeed."

Two days later, Blackbeard, Vane, and Davis raised the anchors of their sloops, hoisted their sails, and left under cover of night. Ironically, a pair of British man-of-wars appeared in the bay one day later. Both remained at the mouth and sent in a couple cutters. The ships were too large to navigate the harbor without endangering their hulls. When the cutters came ashore. James went down to meet the officers.

The time had come for our talk.

I would never see Blackbeard, Vane, or Davis again, but I found myself thinking frequently, though absently, about Calico Jack Rackham.

Chapter V

That night James and I had a huge fight. I knew he had sent word to the governor, alerting him of the pirates. I attacked my husband on every front—his cowardly work, his questionable character, his embarrassing reputation, and his lying tongue.

"People laugh behind your back. They think you are an imbecile who doesn't have what it takes to be a pirate. James, you've deceived me from the beginning; you're an escaped indentured servant, a coward who claims he is a pirate," I ranted, screaming words impulsively, without thought of their damage to our relationship. "I am ashamed I stooped to marry you. You are a toothless, spineless rat with no pirate blood in you!"

"How dare you talk to me that way!" He shouted, moving toward me with an upraised hand, poised to strike.

I held my position, prepared for the assault. "If you try, I will beat you worse than your worthless reputation."

My words halted him. He kicked the mattress, cursed, and stormed out of the tent, but I pursued him outside. I wanted him to fight me or at least be honest with me. If he had admitted his shortcomings, I very well may have forgiven him and planned a more practical course for our lives.

"You gutless puppy. You are too yellow to stand up even to me! You wouldn't even make it as a cabin boy, cleaning up after pirates."

The venom of my words shocked me. As I stood outside our tents fuming, I ignored the laughter and proposals two nearby pirates made for me to visit their beds and meet real men. I cursed them and went back inside my tent, lay on my bed, and sobbed. After a time, my tears were lulled away by the sound of the surf crashing on the shore. I thought about the stories of wild and intrepid characters who had made the sea their life and cursed the world's rules. They accepted unpredictable storms, dogs of war, and fiery battles undaunted. I may not have liked Blackbeard and his barbarity, but I knew there had to be other pirates like Red Legs who had a moral code and a clear sense of their mission.

Over the din of a quarrel outside, I considered the pathetic place I found myself in. My marriage and life here were not much different than what I had left behind in Carolina. All my life I had witnessed human frailty, in my mother, my father, the slaves, and now in my weak-kneed informant of a husband. I had not married to better my fortune but to jettison the constraints yoked upon me. Where were the heroes of the Bible and the epics? The Moseses, Davids, and Elijahs? The King Arthurs, Robin Hoods, and Rolands?

I then tried to recall the valor and honor of women. Cleopatra? Sheba? Then I thought of Joan of Arc, leading an army to victory. How had she done it? God must have been with her up until she was betrayed, imprisoned, and burned at the stake. He had protected her because of her devotion and uprightness. I could claim neither. Since landing on the island I had fallen away from reading the Scripture, much less praying, but instead of regretting my hasty choices and meteoric judgments, I felt a surge of rebellion. Right then, kneeling and confessing my sins seemed weak, a ritual I had learned from my mother as a child. My adult blood roiled with wrath.

I washed my face and combed my hair. I looked at my face in the mirror, and then at my dress and frowned. It drew attention to my femininity, a telltale sign of feebleness. It made me a target to be violated and was an invitation to harlotry on this island of hellcats. I wandered around the tent. Joan of Arc had worn armor. Her clothing matched her interior power. If I walked three steps outside I would hear rude remarks and crude proposals. My eyes fell on James' clothing. I reached over and held up his pants and a shirt and wondered. I pulled off my dress, wrapped cloth tightly around my upper body to flatten my breasts, which were still more spare than prominent. I put on the pants and shirt and donned a hat, and then put a pistol and cutlass inside my belt. I stared into the mirror. I grabbed a burlap sack and rubbed my cheeks raw. I flexed my muscles and formed a scowl. The scar from the dog bite so many years ago looked redder, angrier. I made gravelly, hoarse sounds with my voice. My face still had an effeminate quality, and my frame was slender and emaciated looking, but I decided my garb had transformed me well enough to pass through the dim taverns and dark streets.

I breathed deeply, then imitated the walk of a man out the door and into the road, and then walked back. No one said a word to me. I felt bold. I stepped out again and headed for a tavern. On the way I passed what some might call a public square. I let my fingers pass over the rough edges of a wooden rack and then the flogging post. I remembered once seeing a soldier in Charles Towne who had deserted being given the Moses Law—forty stripes save one on the bare back with a cat-o'-nine-tails. His back had been a bloody mush after the whipping was over. I smirked, realizing if I were caught I would likely face a similar sentence.

I entered a tavern, set down a coin on the bar, and ordered, in my best guttural grunt, a bowl of punch. The barkeeper responded by wordlessly taking the silver and pouring me rum. I kept my head low and listened to the stories around me. I tested my voice by interjecting an occasional stunted word. It was a seamy place, filled with debauchery. I watched female servers manhandled, and I sat in amazement and disgust when a woman fell into the lap of a pirate and let him grope her. I made mental notes whenever a pirate was pointed out.

Most were dirty, drunken, and disheveled. I stayed only a few minutes, but as I walked back to my tent I felt a surge of strength flow through me. I spent the rest of the night practicing feint, parry, and thrust with my sword and throwing a knife at a tent post. Just after I changed clothes and slipped between the sheets, James stumbled in quite inebriated. I pretended to be asleep. As he lay beside me snoring, I felt my resentment mushroom. I remembered how my father had often turned to alcohol to avert uncomfortable conversations with my mother. I shifted my body to the edge of the mattress and curled my body up and wrapped my arms around my knees. I felt very much alone.

CHAPTER XIII

The next morning neither of us brought up the fight. James groaned about a headache while I prepared a simple breakfast of salted pork, sweet biscuits, and coconut. We talked about our trip to Jamaica and then he left for the morning. We simply avoided awkward conversation, preferring to tiptoe around our problems. I thought of Edward's rhyming rejoinder whenever I had asked him why he had never remarried: "Needles and pins, needles and pins/When a man marries, his trouble begins."

Two months passed this way. James continued drinking, and I continued donning his clothing and venturing into town, taking bigger risks each night. During the day I practiced with the sword. I knew if I were caught dressed as a man, it could likely mean rape or even death. Even my husband's position and influence might not protect me. Such a discovery could very well send a few drunken pirates over the edge of caution. Meanwhile, as promised, James secured lodgings above a tavern. We spent a few days moving and setting up house. It was during this time that some of the raw wounds from that night seemed to callous into numb scars. I knew our rift was not healing, though, but still festering in our hearts.

It was during this fragile period that my uncertain destiny crossed with another lost soul's turbulent course. Captain Calico Jack Rackham returned to Nassau Island, this time without Blackbeard, Vane, or Davis. His sloop entered the harbor with great fanfare; he even had some of his men playing the pipe, fiddle, and drum. He swaggered ashore in a grand, vain manner, but I noticed how other men made way for him. My curiosity was reignited. That night when James went out, I decked myself out in his clothing and found Jack Rackham in a tavern. I watched him order cakes and ale and regale the men and women around him with stories of prizes his crew had taken on the high seas. When asked about Blackbeard and Vane, Rackham rattled off the old saying: "Am I my brother's keeper?"

I overheard him speak of his crew careening and refitting his tired vessel, the *Vanity*, in New Providence and, in the meantime, trading their plunder and looking forward to some much deserved rest and pleasure. He anticipated receiving a pardon and commission from Governor Rodgers as a privateer against the Spanish.

He said the word was that for the time being Britain had abandoned its quest to stamp out piracy in the West Indies because tensions with Spain had been resurrected to a fever pitch. It had been reported that a new Spanish governor for the Bahamas had been named and an invasion force of galleons with soldiers was being sent to seize the islands and wrest control from Britain. Governor Rodgers was fighting tooth and nail to retain his position, and New Providence and the pirates were too difficult to control now that the Spanish were complicating matters. For now, Rackham said, he would bide his time and carouse with his hearties and the lassies. The men laughed. Perhaps it was my imagination, but it seemed like Rackham kept glancing my way during the evening. I kept my head down and my shoulders slouched, but I could sense his gaze.

Finally, I left my drink unfinished and returned to our room, my mind turning over the visage and vagaries of Rackham. As I opened the door I was greeted with a shock: James was sitting on the bed staring at me.

"Where have you been? Why are you wearing my clothes?"

I paused, debating what tack to take. I decided to stick with sarcasm, a gift women can use as readily as seduction. I had learned that few men could stand tall under the tongue of a spirited woman.

"In the taverns, boozing with cutthroats and carousing with rapscallions, trying to understand what men call 'manhood.'"

James grimaced. "Anne, if they had suspected, you could have been arrested or, worse, raped."

"Not with this," I said, displaying my cutlass and pistol. "These are now my security and protection."

"You're being foolish." He shook his head and sighed. "And taking absurd risks."

"Yes," I said. "I was a fool, and I am sorry for being blind, but no more."

James stared at me for a moment. "What are you saying?"

I stepped up to my husband, leering into his eyes. He stepped back slightly, and I pulled out my cutlass and let it rest against his chest. "I am sorry I so foolishly married you, but I will not let that stop me from making something of my life. I may be surrounded by cowardice, but I will not settle on it." I tapped the blade against his chest.

James took a deep breath. "Anne, you must be drunk. You are talking strangely. Settle down and think logically. I know you don't like my job..."

"Playing the Judas? Why, I pay homage to it."

James hesitated, looking down. "This place is not as we thought it would be. All this cruelty and corruption—it sickens me. I do not want to live like a crazed, drunken pirate. I want to make a legitimate living I can be proud of. Invest in a life that will be meaningful. Settle down and raise a family."

I laughed cynically. "Your drinking is fogging your brain." I removed my hat and sat down on the bed. I listened with half an ear while he explained his work for the governor, how he was looking for ways to solve the many problems on the island. I felt bored, but it did sound respectful, and my heart softened somewhat for my husband. He still sounded hen-hearted, but he was taking an honest appraisal of his limitations—a naïf with scruples. I ended up giving myself to him that night out of pity, but in the darkness of our room, next to each other in bed, my thoughts skipped waywardly to Rackham.

The next morning, after James left to snoop and rat, I put my husband's clothes back on. I felt aggressive and confident in them, and I ventured back to the taverns. I found Rackham seated with some of his men. I sat within earshot and overheard them discussing James, who had been identified as the newest lackey for Governor Rodgers. He was the brunt of jokes, my husband—an imbecilic, bumbling spy. One man suggested killing him, but Rackham shook his head. "Easier to keep an eye on a buffoon than kill him. We can feed him false information, but we also need him to obtain our pardons and privateer commissions."

My husband was not enough a concern to be considered a target by the pirates, I thought. My disgust with James nauseated me to the point that I considered teaching him a lesson myself. As I considered a punishment I could inflict on him for shaming me, Rackham sauntered over and sat beside me at the bar, ordering another shot of rum. I was taken aback but I pretended to ignore him.

He spoke to me in a low tone. "I am a little confused and intrigued. I know you are the informant's wife. So I wonder: are you gathering bits for him, or are you dressed as a man for other reasons?"

Fear crept into my stomach. I didn't know what to say.

"You have no need to be afraid of me. Your secret, for me, is treasure at the bottom of the sea," he said. "But tell me, why dress like a swine when you're as beautiful as a baroness?"

I withdrew into my tough shell. "That's none of your bloody business." I swallowed the rest of my drink, relishing the burn down the back of my throat.

"Another for my saucy mate," Rackham shouted to the bartender and slapped me hard on the back. Then he resumed his near whisper. "This garb simply does not do service or justice to the finery God blessed you with. You are obviously not looking for a man...perhaps a woman? No, but you are looking for something?"

I turned to him and for the first time observed Rackham's dark, lined face and irisless eyes up close. His hair, cleaned and combed, lay over his broad shoulders, his mustache and beard were well trimmed, and his face was freshly shaven. He smelled masculine yet it was mingled with the scent of something else. He obviously took pride in his appearance. I noted that his clothing was laundered and brushed. Under his jacket he brandished a brace of four pistols and a coral-handled cutlass.

"Yes, I am searching for something."

He leaned toward me and whispered. "Pray tell, what is it, my lovely lady, my sphinx?"

"I don't know, but I will know when I find it."

He smiled with an air of cool control. "I must confess that I am utterly bored with my crew and the men and women on this piratical paradise. They are mostly beasts without education or refinement. It is lamentable that the women here are easy, sleazy, and...disease-y."

He smiled at his forced rhyme. "You, on the other hand, seem intelligent and literate and blessed with an exquisite form. If you would amuse me for an hour and tell me about yourself, I will give you my word of honor to listen just to hear the purity of good English and a noble colleen's view," he said, sweeping his arm across the expanse of the room, "of this sewer of sin, this quagmire of bacchanalian revelry."

I was beginning to be won over by this man. I longed to share my colliding thoughts with someone who truly cared to listen, and Rackham stood before me with an attentive air and handsome face. We took a seat in the back of the tavern.

"I must first ask...how did you know? My disguise has fooled everyone else."

Rackham shrugged his shoulders, grinned and winked. "I am a connoisseur of the feminine aura, a cognoscente of women's manner and style. I noticed you the first night I was here with Blackbeard. I memorized your mystique." He glanced toward the ceiling, searching for elegant words. "You are as captivating as a countess and delightful as a duchess."

I rolled my eyes. My interest started waning.

He leaned forward. "I even sense the very vibrations of your heart—fully woman, and yet there's a dash of the wild and wanton. Am I wrong?"

I held my breath, trying to conceal the warmth reddening my cheeks. I sipped at my drink and began to share my story. He kept his word, fixing his eyes upon mine, nodding and smirking at some of my youthful antics, politely interrupting me on occasion to ask for more detail, particularly concerning Edward's devotion and about the time I nearly beat Frederick Jones to death with a shovel. When I spoke of my affinity for the untamed wonders of the sea, he joined me and poetically described the pleasure he took in hearing the release of the anchor and its shuddering splash, the snapping of the sheets catching a southeasterly breeze, the pregnant calm before the onslaught of a tropical storm, and the lament of the timbers straining among the wind and the wash of the current. At one point I shut my eyes as I imagined the visions he sketched.

Rackham told me about the more notorious pirates who frequented the island, such as Captain Edward Low, known for hacking off the ears off his victims, Simon Peter style, to help them remember him and become more devout to Christ. There was Bartholomew Roberts, or Black Bart, who drank only tea, allowed no gambling or women onboard his vessel, and loved crimson waistcoats trimmed with a gray Vandyke, hats with vermilion plumes, and an array of gold chains, diamond crosses, and watch fobs. The ladies giggled over him because for all his showy array, temperance and morality, he was actually a known sodomite. He told me about Congdon Condent, John Gow, Benjamin Hornigold, and Nathaniel North. I learned the pirates all mocked and spurned Rodgers, once a pirate and privateer himself, who now tried to legitimize himself. He clung to a semblance of power from his post in Jamaica, but his magistrates were corrupt, accepting money under the table to ignore the pirate activity that prevailed around them.

When Rackham spoke of the sea, the genesis of his privateering, and his descent into piracy, I experienced afresh the enchantment that had drawn me to my husband. Like James, he was poetic and well read, not a simpleton or ruffian. But his grace and good manners, fused with his tough exterior, lured me. As promised, Rackham acted like a gentlemen during our conversation, and when we finished he merely patted me on the shoulder, letting his hand linger there just long enough to make me remember it.

I returned to my room and switched back to my dress. I scrubbed some clothing in a basin behind the tavern. Later Annabelle stopped by. I asked her about Rackham.

"He has the grist for captaining a pirate ship and a passion for women. He is a favorite among the lassies, but he's not a marrying man," she said.

My hesitancy was overshadowed by a sense of challenge. I had so much coquettish confidence, I reflected for hours on the prospect of taming this Rackham and making a one-woman man out of him. I can only shake my head now over my slender perspective on men with roaming eyes. I locked these adulterous thoughts in the innermost recesses of my soul. I did not speak a word of Rackham to my husband.

The following day I made a decision that set me on a new course. James reminded me of our trip to Jamaica. I politely declined. I told him I wanted to reflect on the past months and some time in solitude was what I needed. Melancholy filled his eyes and sorrow tinged his voice. How simple it is to hurt those who love us.

"Whatever you need, Anne. I will be here," he said.

His response frustrated and infuriated me. His pretense of sensitivity made me want to scream. Fight for me! Find your backbone! Be a man! But I only thanked him for his understanding.

* * * *

The next day I saw him off. I stood on the shore loyally watching until the schooner, boldly flying the Union Jack, left the bay. All the while my thoughts flowed like a juggernaut toward Rackham. I shoved aside all the passages of Scripture I knew and determined to pursue a course of adventure.

I hurriedly returned home, donned my husband's clothing, and explored Nassau in search of Rackham. I found him in a tavern seated at a table alone, reading a book of poetry. He beckoned me to sit and reached out to shake my hand. He deposited into my hand a small fabric bag, tied with gold ribbon. I eyed him with uncertainty.

"A trifle to thank you for indulging me with your enchanting company. Please, open it."

I glanced around the tavern, and then quietly opened the gift. My shock must have shown on my face, because Rackham chuckled. Inside there was a necklace studded with rubies and emeralds.

"I request the honor of seeing those jewels grace your neck the next time you show yourself in attire becoming to your gender," he said and let his hand glide across my arm and squeeze my wrist. It was a quick gesture, unnoticed by those in the pub, but I shivered at his touch.

"Aye, for such a beautiful lady, being adorned as a queen with those jewels will serve you well."

I tilted my head. "That's not quite possible on so primitive an island, don't you think?"

Rackham winked. "Since the first day I saw you in Nassau, I've admired you from afar. I have acquired embellishments to make you more fetching—French lace and Chinese silk, dangles, gewgaws, and brooches. Yes, those belong on your elegant frame, which could 'launch a thousand ships.'"

The next few days Rackham lavished me with more jewelry and garish baubles, which I hid in the corner of my closet. Sometimes I would wear the jewels and look at myself in the mirror. I delighted in their sparkling beauty. One day we took a stroll around the island and Rackham showed me a sea cave, claiming it was a perfect place to bury ill-gotten treasure. We also took up some pistol and musket practice. Rackham complimented me on my shooting.

He also taught me strategies of fighting with a cutlass and knife. He struck a fencing stance and beckoned me, saying, "Give me your worst, wench." He stuck out his tongue. That set me off. I launched my attack, trying to cut him. During our duel, he smacked me three times across my bottom with the flat part of his sword. His swordsmanship enthralled and enraged me. I finally cursed, threw down my sword, and swore at him. I realized that when James and I had practiced with swords, we had done so in silly ignorance. He picked up my sword and began to teach me footwork and how to feint, parry, and thrust. Later that day, Rackham asked if I would come to his sloop tomorrow. I knew his meaning and hesitated to answer.

"Are we coy, Anne? Shall I woo thee with poetry so thou mayest swoon?" He smiled and quoted: 'A hundred years should go to praise/Thine eyes and on thy forehead gaze,/Two hundred to adore each breast,/But thirty thousand to the rest.'"

I looked away. A pang of guilt grabbed me as I thought about James and our first night together. Rackham quoted a few more lines, these from Shakespeare, staring squarely into my eyes. I controlled my trembling, a sensual abandon dancing in my body. I only have this life, I said to myself at this moment. Live it to the hilt and regrets will prove paltry few. My desires triggered a tingling and swelling in my secret parts. I chose not to give him a direct answer, struggling with my clouding passions and clear morality.

"It is a painfully short life with so few pleasures, Anne," Rackham said. "I daresay we deny ourselves so much in the name of honor we lose grip on what happiness truly is."

"Aye," I said, "but our decisions to indulge in the passing pleasures of sin can forever destroy the good and deep things that may last our whole lives."

"Marvelously stated. You are a woman of letters, a rare find in these parts, even the entire world. And such is lust—a heaven that leads men to hell."

As we walked back, I pondered my choice. Was my future with James or Jack? There was much to admire about James. He was educated, upright, and responsible, but doubtful, subservient, and cringing. I stewed over a vision of children, routine, and complacency. I then considered Rackham and the taboos against being with him. I cannot pretend to know why I always seemed inclined to defy and rebel against social expectations. It never actually made me happier, but it did stimulate me and bolster my sense of strength. Thus curiosity and desire raised their flags over my marriage vows. As we departed, Rackham handed me one more gift a beautiful gown of silk and lace. White with burgundy and ginger trims, it was snug in the bodice and waist to accentuate my body, but regal and flowing to the floor.

The next morning I bathed, perfumed, and powdered. I put up my hair, dressed in my gown, and adorned myself with the sparkling necklace. I found Rackham waiting for me in the street. He escorted me to his longboat and rowed me to his sloop, which he ordered emptied, offering his crew enough money for a good bout of revelry.

He did not just tumble me, but his passion was certainly urgent, even a bit rough at times. It was nothing like the clumsy and apologetic and yet tender times I had shared with James. Rackham took control of our lovemaking with the confidence of much experience. I took a docile role. I sensed after our first time that there would indeed be more to come.

We coupled three times that afternoon. After each time he praised me with honeyed words, saying that the touch of my body so enraptured him, it made him yearn for more. I was flattered he found me so desirable, and I loved the feel of his strong, clean body against mine. His rich scent, his passionate kiss, his expressive face, and his groans of euphoria filled me with pride that I could please him so well.

"Oh, Anne, it is delicious fornicating the day away with you. You are the elixir of life, liberty, and addiction," he said. "And I love the way your eyes light up when I reach for you." He reached out and touched the scar on my face.

I expected him to ask the story behind it, but instead he caressed my scar and said, "It makes you more mysterious, and even more alluring." I looked into his eyes and smiled.

Later in the day Rackham dropped me off at the shore with a kiss and the promise of a rendezvous the next day. I returned to my room full of elation, but after an hour the stillness of the room made me lonely. Suddenly the import of my infidelity seemed to draw the walls in around me. I changed back into male clothing and decided to hike to the waterfall James and I had discovered. I needed to consider the direction my life was turning. I wondered whether I was merely another act of fornication in a long line of women for Rackham, or whether I had filled him with such pleasure that I would become foremost in his mind. While I pined to the point of mania for greater escapades with Rackham, guilt snuck up and tempered my exhilaration. I sought distraction, cloaking myself in the past, shearing away the haunting memories and cradling the fond ones.

I began climbing a coral outcropping that towered above Nassau. In the distance I heard pistols discharge and the coarse cheers of men. I tried to shuck off the chaos below me and enjoy the tropical breezes and vast silences of nature. I clambered over a tier of sharp rocks and reached what I considered my special place—a hidden waterfall above the one James and I had frolicked in. Rivulets of water hurtled off a pinnacle. I watched individual drops glitter as they fell and disappeared into the pool of water below. I breathed deeply of the misty air. After awhile I slid down the piles of crumbling rock, grasping bulrushes to stabilize my descent.

The fresh water, rippling in widening circles, invited me. I peeled off my clothes and vaulted off a mossy rock into the pool. Swimming underwater, I peered through the murky depths and saw fish darting into the shadows. The pool dissolved my cares momentarily. It was in these solitary times I considered God most often. I had made a significant choice, and I was not sure how it would turn out. Among the grandeur of creation, the faces of my mother, my father, my husband, and Edward haunted me with their accusing eyes. On the other side was the smiling Rackham, beckoning me to come join him, though to what and where I had no idea.

I sunned myself on a rock and wondered what advice Edward would offer me. I started to ask God for wisdom, but stopped because my conscience throttled me. This made me want to rebel rather than to repent. My father would have had no room to talk, and my mother seemed beyond my concerns. I left feeling rebellious and proud, yet miserable. I knew a serious conflict awaited me, but I did not care. I wanted more of Rackham.

For the next five days I visited Rackham's cabin. Then word came that my husband, the lackey of Woodes Rodgers, had returned.

CHAPTER XIV

I was lounging on the bed in my room, reading from a volume Rackham had given me: *The Thousand and One Arabian Nights.* What piqued my interest most was the story behind the book. A sultan of Persia had discovered his wife's unfaithfulness so he had her executed. Then he began marrying a new woman each night but having her killed the very next morning, believing each would one day betray him just as his first wife had. After a couple of months the number of available women was rapidly disappearing. The sultan's eyes fell upon Scheherazade. Her family became deeply upset, assuming it would be the last day they would see her, but she assured them she had a plan.

That night, in the sultan's palace, Scheherazade told her husband an engaging story. Just as she reached the most scintillating part, she stopped and told him she would finish the story the next day. The sultan threatened her, but she said unless he let her live, he would never know how the story ended. The sultan agreed. The next day, however, she continued the story and stopped at an equally intriguing part, which bought her another day of breath. This continued for one thousand and one nights, but by then the sultan had fallen so in love with her that they remained married for the rest of their lives.

As I turned a page, James threw the door open and stomped into the room. "You whore!"

I looked up from my book. "That would be tramp. He seduced me, nor did he have to pay." I yawned as if bored and returned to reading the book.

James leaped forward and bashed me in the nose so hard I felt a sudden ringing in my head. I had never seen James violent. Fear and rage swirled in me. He grabbed my hair, lifted my head up and raised his hand to slap me. I thrust out my legs and pushed against his knees. He fell backward off the bed. I leaped on top of him and beat at his head with a flurry of slaps and punches. He grabbed my wrists and held them tightly. I spat in his face. He pushed me away and reached for a knife on the chest of drawers.

I shuffled backward as he crawled toward me, pointing his knife. "You are my wife, Anne. I will not let you make a mockery of me."

"Too late for that. The whole island scoffs at you!"

The door of our room swung open and Rackham stood in the doorway, pistols drawn, smiling in his smug way. "A fine and timely entrance. Ahoy, permission to board. I would put down that blade, laddybuck, if you know what's best for your constitution."

James set the knife down, trembling with fury and fear before Rackham.

"Good form, mate. Now, I know you have reason for resentment. I have breached your holy vow of matrimony and soiled the purity of your marriage bed, but I have a business proposition for you. I will pay you handsomely for an annulment."

"A what?"

"I will pay you for Anne's freedom—a ransom of sort, if you will."

I wonder whether I should not have been vexed by Rackham's gall, but in truth I reddened at the gesture, viewing it as a strange and paradoxical honor that had been bestowed upon me. I must have left an impression, my imprint outweighing the myriad other women he had bedded but never wed. Rackham must have been enamored with me, indeed. I do not think Rackham wanted to kill James, but he was prepared to. The steadiness in his tanned face and the power of his hands, which had caressed me only hours earlier, filled me with even greater ardor for Rackham. On the other hand, my husband's perspiring face and shallow breathing repulsed me.

"You whoremonger. Sell my wife? I would kill her first," snapped James.

"Not the answer I preferred to hear." Rackham fired his pistol, striking James in the thigh. My husband screamed and writhed on the floor, holding his wound. "You simply do not have the mettle to please your wife. She will be coming with me, and we will leave Nassau after my ship's been repaired. And you may continue your spying, sponge of Rodgers, puppet of Britain."

I looked at James, feeling a strange detachment, as if he had never been my husband. He gasped for air and held the oozing wound. Lying there in a gathering puddle of blood, he seemed an object of pity, a symbol of brokenness. My upbringing told me to curse Rackham and tend to my husband's wounds, but everything else in me longed for Rackham's courageous company and stimulating touch. I told myself that James' lies and his sickening frailty proved he was a charlatan through and through, selling me a bill of rotten goods.

I stood up. "James, I will be taking my leave of you. I am sorry for your pain, but I cannot remain here under this masquerade of a marriage. You lack spine. You disgust me. And your lying tongue should be cut out."

He said nothing. I turned to Rackham, whose eyes seemed to penetrate my soul, communicating a new level of devotion, an embodiment of unswerving liberation.

"Anne, will you come away with me?" Rackham's voice was not a demand, but rather a poem, even a prayer. He reached out his hand to me.

I took his hand and we started out of the room.

"Thank you for your hospitality," Rackham said.

James yelled, "You filthy whore! You are the Judas, and a Jezebel!"

"Don't forget Delilah!" I quipped.

We walked hand in hand down to a waiting longboat. Two crewmen oared us back to Rackham's sloop. We climbed a rope ladder and went to his cabin. I stood in the room and Rackham embraced me, and then slowly, wordlessly lifted me into his arms and took me to his bed. The danger of the past hour triggered unrestrained lust. Rackham taught me two new words: fellatio and cunnilingus. It was the right moment and I found the experience unabashedly pleasurable. Whatever conscience I once possessed about adultery had been shipwrecked and jettisoned. The forbidden nature of our actions proved wickedly fun.

That night over a meal Rackham recounted his own history in the sweet trade, starting from navigator under Blackbeard to quartermaster under Vane, and finally becoming a captain through mutiny. He talked of the fat prizes he and his crew had plundered.

He had grown up in Wales. His father was a mariner and had taught him the trade at an early age. His mother tutored him in mathematics and English. He had worked on many ships in various capacities, but apprenticed as a navigator on a British privateer, which roamed American waters in search of pirates and French.

"It was a formidable education. Life was hard, the food was poor, and the wages were piddling. When we captured a French vessel, I saw that life for them was no better," Rackham said, sipping a glass of port.

While he talked of his life, I studied the features of his face. He was easy to look upon, and I liked the way his eyes flashed when he spoke of seafaring.

"Once we caught a pirate schooner unawares and took it. As we searched the vessel and talked with the pirates, I began to secretly envy them. They had better things. They had their own rules, and almost everything was put to a vote—majority rule. Yes, it was criminal, but it looked sweet," he said.

I looked around Rackham's cabin. He had chests of fine clothes; an assortment of liquors, silverware, goblets, and candlesticks; a good bed with soft linens; and a library.

"One day while harboring in New York, I jumped ship. New York was full of pirates, and I found a crew to put in with." He laughed. "Our first prize was a vessel loaded with convicts headed for the West Indies. We acted as thieves of mercy and set them free. Some joined our enterprise."

Rackham explained that a squall off the coast of the Carolinas had left their sloop foundering, so they were forced to abandon it and oared in longboats to Bath.

"We were anxious to find a new sloop and return to the seas, but then our fortunes collided with Blackbeard's."

Rackham smiled nostalgically. "He made us a grand offer: to consort with his liberated nation on *The Queen Anne's Revenge*, the oceans being the boundaries of his kingdom and all other countries being his mortal adversaries."

I poured more port from a decanter into our goblets. "He seems like a fascinating man."

"He was a dangerous man with cruel mind. He had fiery, crazy eyes. He was a natural leader. He navigated marvelously, managed his wealth skillfully, and fought ruthlessly. He was amazing."

"So you accepted his proposal?" I asked.

Rackham stood up and began to change his shirt. "Blackbeard had three ships, the largest was an impressive sight—forty cannon. It was an opportunity I could not let pass. Then he told us his audacious enterprise: he wanted to blockade Charles Towne Harbor."

"I remember vividly. I was there when it happened."

"We had Charles Towne in a stranglehold. They had ships floundering in the bay and stores of goods rotting on the docks. We cut trade off completely," Rackham said.

"You ruined my father's gala. It was supposed to be my coming out ball," I said. I threw a piece of cork at him.

"My deepest apologies, milady," Rackham said, chuckling. "The best part was when Blackbeard had the pluck to kidnap some citizens and demand medicines. He picked me to go ashore to collect the ransom. He thought I had diplomatic flair."

Rackham's laughter grew into a frenzy. He daubed at tears and tried to catch his breath. "You cannot imagine the pleasure I took in walking the streets, greeting the lovely lassies, boldly entering taverns and enjoying all the drinks and food I wished without charge, residing in a fine room. And oh, the looks the people gave me. I do not believe I have ever been so hated in my life. It was a charmed moment I will likely never experience again."

"I remember seeing you."

"Really?"

"Even then I thought you were handsome," I said. I reached out and squeezed his right hand.

Rackham went on to describe some of Blackbeard's unusual customs. One day he was in his cabin playing cards with some of his crew. Suddenly, he blew out the tapers, drew his pistols, and shot blindly in the dark. He relit the tapers to discover two wounded.

"Were they plotting a mutiny?" I asked.

"No. Blackbeard said if he didn't kill one of his crew now and then, they would forget who he was."

I frowned, confused by the logic.

"I know, I know," he said. "Another time he was so drunk he challenged his crew to make a hell and see who could stand it the longest. So they sealed the hatches, set brimstone and sulfur on fire in the hold, and tried to outlast each other. Blackbeard beat them all."

"He was insane," I said.

"The crew thought he was the devil himself." Rackham grew somber and stared at the ceiling above me.

"What's wrong, Jack?"

"Anne, all dreams must run their course."

Rackham went to a hutch and pulled out a newspaper and began to read an account of Blackbeard's last fight. Of late, Blackbeard had been plundering the coast of the Carolinas. He was hiding out in the Ocracoke inlet of the Carolinas, selling his pillaged loot and enjoying the spoils with nightly carousals. Though the Carolina governor was too weak to stop him, the Virginia governor was not. Alexander Spotswood, weary of hearing about Blackbeard's notorious exploits, dispatched two sloops, commanded by Lt. Robert Maynard, to ferret out Blackbeard and arrest or kill him.

"Call it destiny," Rackham said. He set the news account down. "Captain Vane had our sloop out in the open water when Maynard's sloops entered the inlet. If we had been there, this would have been a different story." He picked up the paper and began to read again.

"After Maynard hailed and engaged him, Blackbeard raised a glass, toasted Maynard's force as it approached, and said: 'Damnation seize my soul if I give you quarter, or take any from you.' Blackbeard fired a broadside and damaged one of Maynard's sloops, killing several of his men. Maynard sent longboats ahead to row toward Blackbeard. He decimated those, too."

Rackham looked up from the paper. "Bloody fine tactics. Blackbeard was a master. You would think Maynard would have raised the white flag, but he was a warmonger. He never gave in. He just played it smart and let Blackbeard make the next mistake."

The newspaper account described how Blackbeard, figuring he had Maynard on the run, ordered his men to attack Maynard's sloop. They threw grenades just before they boarded her, but Maynard's men were hiding below deck. Blackbeard's men swung across and planned to cut them to pieces, but Maynard's men came out of hiding and swarmed them.

Rackham set down the paper again, shifted his plate aside, and rested his elbows on the table. "I love the sound of swords clashing as men fight for their lives. It's an art no artist has been able to capture truly on canvas."

"What happened next?"

He smiled. "I practically know this story word for word. As the pirates and soldiers fought to the death, Maynard sought out Blackbeard. But like a coward, Maynard shot with his pistol first. A foolish act if you ask me, since that would've only made Blackbeard madder."

I leaned forward and nodded.

"Blackbeard broke Maynard's sword, knocked him to the deck, and went in for the kill. But one of Maynard's men slashed Blackbeard from behind and saved his captain. Blackbeard cut him down. When he turned back around, Maynard's crew emptied their guns on Blackbeard.

"The bastard was still standing. Maynard and Blackbeard crossed swords again for a spell, but Blackbeard finally fell. The newspaper claimed he had five gun shot wounds and twenty sword strokes in him. Maynard lost an arm, but Blackbeard lost his head. They decapitated him and hung his head on the bowsprit of their sloop."

"What happened to the rest of the crew?" I asked.

"All arrested and later executed. They scuttled *The Queen Anne's Revenge*. The news account said that Blackbeard had even received a warning from a fisherman earlier that morning, but he laughed it off. Another story of hubris."

Rackham finished his drink and stretched, but then seemed to remember something. "One more thing. One of the crew asked Blackbeard, just in case anything should happen, where he had buried his treasure." He returned to the paper and quoted: "'Nobody but I and the devil know where it is, and the longest to live will take it all.'" He grinned and shook his head. "I bet Blackbeard is giving Old Scratch a run for his money in the Lake of Fire."

He placed a hand on his forehead. "I wish I had been there. I might have saved him."

"Why couldn't you help him?"

Rackham blinked, seeming to flinch at my tone. "Anne, I told you the tide was ebbing. We could not maneuver into the inlet. Destiny."

"But couldn't you have taken longboats up the inlet?"

He waved me off. "All we heard was Blackbeard's broadside. We figured he had the upper hand. At any rate, he was never one to need help."

"Yes, but when you saw Lt. Maynard's sloop come out of the inlet and saw Blackbeard's head hanging from the prow, surely then you attacked them?" Something in the recesses of my heart stirred with doubt.

Rackham wiped his mouth with a napkin and slowly set it on the table. "Just what are you insinuating, Anne?"

I looked into his eyes and recognized I was teetering on a precipice. What lay on the other side was a mystery. I started sculling the conversation backward. "Nothing at all. I was...just eager to hear more about your dangerous, piratical exploits on the high seas. They are so alluring." I smiled, wet my lips and tilted my head.

It achieved the desired result. Rackham's face softened again. "Actually, we gave chase, but Maynard's sloop was swifter.

"Some good pirates were lost that day—some to the noose and others to Davy Jones' Locker in a hail of gunfire. Anne, join me in a toast to Captain Edward Teach, the great Blackbeard. He fought bravely and died proudly, and his wives are eternally grateful."

Chapter XV

The next morning Rackham greeted me in bed with a cup of tea and a volume of poetry: *The Rubaiyat.* He had an admirable library for a pirate: the Holy Bible, St. Augustine's *Confessions, Medea, Lysistrata, The Prose Edda, The Niebelungleid, Beowulf, The Divine Comedy,* and Exquemelin's *Bucaniers of America.* He also pointed out Basil Ringbone's *The Adventures of Bartholomew Sharpe,* a biography of a privateer turned pirate, describing his acts of piracy to his capture to his acquittal, and finally his murder by pirates in the South Seas. I liked that Rackham was a well-read man who educated himself from the imagination, wit, and wisdom of the masters.

I had been rolling back and forth all night, thinking about James and wondering what lay in store for me with Rackham. It appeared that for now I had charted a new course in unfamiliar waters. As I blew on my tea and nibbled at a hard roll, I kept glancing at Rackham while he quietly stirred his tea. He looked up and smiled at me, but then stopped his stirring.

"What haunts your soul this morning?"

"Jack, what are your intentions toward me?"

He set down the cup and smoothed his mustache and beard. "Yes, there you rest in my bed—deflowered in more ways than one." He winked. "You certainly have chosen a slippery, precarious path, one very well fraught with peril if prudence is not practiced."

I felt a knot forming in my stomach. "Poetically put, Jack. But I am serious."

He raised a hand as if to ask for time to explain. "Today, you are my sole interest, but I can't predict what our future holds." He leaned over and sipped at his tea. "My crew and I are still waiting on your husband's employer. We have received assurances that Rodgers has pardons and licenses for privateering earmarked for us. But every day that passes makes us more restless for action."

I fingered the edge of my cup, trying to quash the thoughts racing through my mind. "When can you expect a reply?"

Rackham stood up, locked his hands behind his back, and strolled around the cabin. He paused at the window. "The *Vanity* should be refitted in a couple more weeks. Pardons or not, we're sailing. My crew is itching for new battles and fresh prizes. I know how to keep them happy. That's why they voted Vane out and me in."

I stood up and walked up beside him, resting a hand on his shoulder. I spoke boldly. "I want to go with you."

Rackham raised his brows, tilted his head, and chuckled. He reached over and squeezed my hand. "Anne, women have not been allowed on pirate ships for awhile, unless for brief spells as ransoms or tramps who service the crew."

"But I would carry my own load. You've seen me shoot and swordfight."

"There are no female pirates."

"I wouldn't be a woman. You've seen my disguise. No one knew."

"I knew."

"You knew before. And you have," I let my hand caress gently down his velvet waistcoat, "a roving eye and a sensitive nose."

"Touché. Anne, I know of islands where I could set you up. Then I could visit you a few times a year."

I clenched my hands. Apparently I hadn't left as strong an impression as I had hoped. I imagined the scene: living out my youth in a thatched hut on a secluded and primitive island, always waiting for my pirate to return for a few precious days—reduced to the status of one of Rackham's many mistresses. I had not foreseen this twist with Rackham.

A fight over gambling broke out on deck. Threats and insults bristled in the air. Rackham stuck two braces of pistols in his belt and stepped out of his quarters. I watched him from the open door. Two of Rackham's crew had drawn swords and started fighting, cursing each other and promising no mercy. They parried and riposted each other's thrusts. One feinted left and then slashed with a wild roundhouse and quicksilver slit the neck of the other. The pirate hesitated, dropped his sword, and grasped at his bleeding throat. He fell to his knees, gasping for breath, trying to staunch the crimson flow. Finally he slumped to the deck. The victor finished the business, running the dying man through with his cutlass and spitting on his body.

"We do not cotton to cheatin', do we, Rack?" he said.

But these were his last words. A pair of pistol blasts erupted, and two balls whistled into the man's back. He arched and tried to grab at the spots from behind. He folded to his knees, his breath scraping, his eyes wide, and flopped over onto the deck.

"Muttonhead killed me shipmate," a man holding two smoking guns grumbled. He dropped his pistols, drew his sword, and backed up, poised for any retaliation from the others.

I felt oddly calm as these events unfolded. I had grown so accustomed to gunshots and swordfights on New Providence that they did not startle me.

Rackham stepped from around his crew and pulled out his pistols. "And you never shoot a fellow pirate in the back on my ship." He pulled the triggers and the lead balls punctured the avenging pirate's chest. He dropped his sword and fell backward. Rackham placed the guns in his belt and grabbed the other two loaded ones, surveying the rest of his crew. No one stirred. He put back his pistols. "Damn it to bloody hell. Three crew. That will probably put us back further. Fetherston, have these knaves dumped overboard."

Rackham returned to the cabin and observed my steely reaction. "Are you prepared for such hellion matters?"

"Life is short for fools." I winked. "Only the wise and strong thrive and survive."

Rackham shook his head and smiled. "Don't know whether you are a vixen or a hellcat."

"I might add nymph to that."

"Could not agree more."

There was a knock. I kept myself in the shadows of the room as Rackham opened the door and Fetherston, the navigator, handed him a note. Fetherston had sallow skin and a gaunt face with sharp cheekbones that seemed ready to burst out of his face. His nose was bent to the left, and his brown beard grew in patchy tufts resembling hog bristles.

"Rumor has it that your lady's husband has issued criminal charges to Rodgers against her. I believe that's an ultimatum—"

"Thank you, Fetherston. That will be all."

"She's bad luck, Rack. We got to get her off this ship."

"I don't believe I stuttered. I said that will be all."

Fetherston frowned and stalked away. Rackham read the letter.

"What does it say?"

"Basically, either you repent and return to your husband, or the authorities will arrest you, put you in stocks for public disgrace, and then have you stripped and whipped as an adulteress."

I blinked in disbelief. For the first time I felt panic.

Rackham grinned. "That Rodgers, always the hypocritical puritan, trying to uphold moral laws he never follows."

"Can Rodgers do this?" I asked. Any control I had over my voice was lost.

"I'm afraid so, Anne."

I grabbed Rackham's arm. "I will not go back to that leech, that whimpering whelp—"

Rackham chuckled. "Such suppression of emotion does not befit your high-born station."

"Jack, what are we going to do?"

"Me? I am probably just as wanted as you, the horny cuckolder of Rodger's shamed pirate informer. Our options are few. The pleasures of our sin seem to be passing more swiftly than we thought possible."

"We will fight them."

"We? How quickly you assume allegiance in the face of a formidable foe. Anne, let me clarify something for you. When a British man-of-war enters the harbor, it is best to run away and live to fight another day."

I glanced out at the harbor with desperation. There were a few fishing boats and three worn-out sloops being refitted, one careened on its side while workers scraped the exposed hull of barnacles and repaired the worm-eaten timbers. Then I spotted a slight movement on the horizon. A single mast, with sheets flush to the wind, cut a swath through the water toward the harbor.

"What ship is that?"

Rackham pulled a spyglass out of his breast pocket and surveyed it. "A merchant sloop—looks swift and new. He's got mounted guns for protection. Now I see it. It's John Haman's sloop, the *William*. He's a commissioned privateer under Rodgers. I hear he has pillaged several Spaniard vessels. The motto goes 'There goes John Haman; catch him if you can.'"

I watched the sloop threading swiftly through the water. "Perfect. Let's take it over and leave."

Rackham turned to me. "Avast, milady. Easier said than done. We don't know the number of crew she has, nor the firepower she possesses. My ship and crew aren't ready to sail over and broadside it. I am down to nine pirates."

I remembered Edward's words for me before I left Charles Towne. I quoted: "'There is a tide in the affairs of men, which taken at the flood leads on to fortune.'"

Rackham raised his eyes to ceiling, straining to remember. "'And we must take the current when it serves or lose our ventures' I do love a well-read woman who can quote. So bewitching and alluring." He paused and meandered thoughtfully around his cabin, stopping to gaze upon Haman's sloop for spell. "Shall we seize the day?"

I stood beside him, sensing the need to be quiet. I have found silence and stillness allows for introspection, providing people with their own persuasion and motivation.

He stopped at a shelf of books, selected a volume, and turned its pages. He quoted: "'Ah, Faustus, now hast thou but one bore hour to live and then you must be damned perpetually.' Damned fine stuff to live by."

It was my move if I hoped to be more than a mistress on a lonely island. "Perhaps I could assist in retrieving the necessary information to plot our plan?"

"Anything is possible if the will and skill are available."

"Then I will do it."

"Dare I ask how?"

I arched a brow and smiled suggestively. "I will weave my web and ensnare him."

"Anne, I would not have you prostitute yourself."

"No concern there. I will play Judith of the Old Testament. I will promise much to Captain Haman, let him believe he will make sport of me, and return with his head in a sack—metaphorically speaking."

"Oh, to be a fly on the wall," Rackham said.

We planned our strategy through the day. I was surprised to see Rackham blow hot and cold on the scheme. It took sweetly dripping flattery and seduction to finally convince Rackham of the soundness of our plan—not just taking Haman's vessel, but letting me try to fit in on Rackham's ship. I even quoted Lady Macbeth's "unsex me here" and I assured him the risk would be all mine. He would have the added benefit of a nubile female to visit him in his cabin late at night, rather than enduring long days at sea without. Rackham's ego and libido alleviated all his concerns, blinding him to the dangers. After all, I suppose he had everything to gain and virtually nothing to lose. Would he try to defend me if I was discovered? Or would he play deaf and dumb and let the wolves have at me?

"What name will you go by? I must practice it," he said.

I thought a moment. "Edward O'Malley Brannon."

"Suitable."

"He is the finest man I've ever known. I would be honored to borrow it for awhile."

"I would like to hear more about him sometime. But did you know there once was a Irish colleen pirate named Grace O'Malley?"

"No, who was she?"

"It was in the 1500s she led a crew that plundered English ships. They called her 'Grace of the Cropped Hair.' It is all in Exquemelin's work. She pirated for nearly twenty-five years. She was a ruthless, notorious pirate. She started out as a fisherwoman, but found the sweet trade more to their liking. She ruled a fleet of galleys, terrorized English waters, and eventually received a pardon from Queen Elizabeth I so her vessels could harass the French. She had quite a run for a pirate."

"I love her already. I wish to read more about her soon."

As it grew dark, Rackham and I got into a longboat, and he rowed me to shore. I dressed in my finest apparel, compliments of Rackham, made up my hair, and prepared myself for my role. Rackham shadowed me at a distance while I introduced myself to Haman's quartermaster, one of the first to reach land in a cutter from the sloop. Within an hourglass I had joined him on a trip back to Haman's vessel. As I glanced back, I knew Rackham was seething with jealousy as I leaned my body next to the quartermaster and whispered promises of pleasure in his ear.

Simple to the point of boring is how I would describe my encounter with John Haman. Bright eyes, a constant smile and a quiet tongue were all I really needed to offer. He took those qualities as a signal to boast much and drink much. Men are dreadfully boring when drunken braggarts. I asked him to lie on the bed and close his eyes. One well-directed blow to the temple with an empty bottle finished the episode.

A couple of hours later, I sculled myself back to shore in the same cutter. Rackham spotted me, dashed into the surf, and pulled the boat in.

"What happened?" he said.

"I have a sack full of what we need to take that sloop."

"Did you have to lie with him?"

"Only had to lie to him. Wine is the great equalizer between men and women. Got him drunk, clubbed him, tied him up, and cut his purse to boot. Many pieces of eight in here."

We heard a shout of alarm and saw mariners scrambling around the deck of Haman's ship, climbing down the ladder to a pinnance and preparing to come to shore.

"They will be searching for me. This would be a perfect time."

The time had come to disguise myself again for my protection against both Haman's and Rackham's crew. We found a vacant tent, where I changed. Now in loose male garb, I wrapped a kerchief around my neck, smeared my face with soot and sand, and crammed my hair under my hat.

Rackham shook his head. "Still a damned fine-looking youth."

"Can't help myself," I drawled.

Rackham and I rowed back to his sloop. He introduced me as a youthful Irishman named O'Malley who was hot for a sloop and handy with a gun and cutlass. The crew eyed me with suspicion but not hostility. As Rackham laid out the plan we had hatched and gave the crew assignments, I assessed the pirates. Their clothes were dirty and shabby. Most were barefoot. All of them had some identifying quality—earrings, tattoos, scars, or missing limbs. But all carried swords, knives, and guns. Rackham completed his orders, and the pirates set about gathering their belongings, weapons, and ammunition; Rackham's navigational instruments; the ship's log, journals, and books; and chests of clothes that we loaded into the longboats. As we pulled away, Rackham tipped his hat to his vessel.

"May the currents be kind and your next captain be a gentleman to you, milady," he said, tears brimming his eyes. "Perhaps our voyages will cross once again."

I was oddly touched.

Rackham ordered one of the crew, Harwood, a brazen character with a tarred stump for a right hand, a nasty dagger scar on his cheek, and a shuffling gait, to oar ashore and cave-in the hulls of the Haman's cutters while his men searched the island for me; he would meet us back at Haman's sloop. Harwood picked another man to join him.

Clouds shrouded the moon and stars and a misty rain began to fall. Under cover of night, Rackham, I, and eight others took three longboats, loaded to the gunnels, to the bow of the Haman's sloop.

Before Rackham could say anything, I decided it best to prove myself here and now, so I grabbed the hawser line to lead the assault. I stuck a knife between my teeth and started climbing the rope to the bowsprit. I peered over the edge and saw two watchmen holding empty bottles and nodding off. I crawled over the rail, sleek as a feline, lowered myself onto the deck, tiptoed to the men, lifted two pistols from my trousers, and laid them against the backs of their heads.

"Make a sound and I will blow your brains out," I whispered in a gritty voice.

They froze and relinquished their weapons. I whistled and the rest of Rackham's crew snaked over the side. It turned out there were only three other crewmen onboard, not including the cook and four galley slaves, all of whom

Rackham planned to retain. We tethered the five crewmen, stuffed their mouths with cloth, lowered them by pulley into a cutter, and left them to founder until morning. I watched with pride as Rackham's crew moved into action, unloading the longboats, casting off the moorings, raising the anchor, falling to the halyards, hoisting the sails, and slipping silently out of the harbor past the other ships rocking at their cables. Once beyond the sandbars and reefs, Rackham ordered all sails set and the wind carried the sloop out to the open sea. The crew let loose proud huzzahs. One member named Howell pulled out his fiddle and began to play a cheery tune. As I coiled a line, I looked out into the darkness, searching for the horizon.

The rain stopped and the clouds parted, revealing brilliant, glimmering stars. I gazed at the Southern Cross for a while.

My first thought was, "All things new."

CHAPTER XVI

That night I slept in a hammock in the hold near the rest of the crew. I spoke to George Fetherston and the quartermaster Richard Corner briefly, and then went to my hammock. But I stayed awake for the next couple of hours, watching and listening. I overheard two other pirates, Carty and Dobbin, recount to Harwood, who had been destroying Haman's cutters while we attacked the vessel, how I had waylaid the guards and set the theft of the sloop in motion.

I pulsed with pride when I heard them speak of me in agreeable terms. "He is young but savvy," Carty said. "Rackham said we'll have to train him, but he's got what it takes—no powder monkey or holystoning rat."

I listened with rapt interest as the pirates talked of matters aboard the ship. They spoke of the promise of future prizes, their favorite weapons, and their ailments and aches, and proudly compared their scars from past battle.

"Haman must be blowing a fuse," Carty said.

"Duped him good. It be sweet to pirate a privateer," Harwood said.

They laughed and released a howl. "Rackham had a right savvy plan," Dobbin added. "And a bloody good show to thumb our nose at Rodgers. He can kiss our crotchety arses."

Their talk shifted to the rum they had swilled and the Delilahs they had thrilled, and how fond they were to discover a pair of six-toed cats stowed away on the sloop to keep the rat and vermin population down. Howell picked up the fiddle again and played somber melodies this time, which did seem to fit our victory. The air in the hold was stifling and I perspired heavily; I was grateful when one of the crew threw open the portholes to let in the tropical breeze, driving away the sweaty stench of the men. I finally slumbered, assured I had passed at least this day as one of the men.

The next morning I arose early, found a hiding spot in the bilge, and cut my hair. Dark and isolated, it would be a good spot to deal with my feminine matters in the future. I scratched my face a bit with a holystone, took a deep breath, and emerged from the bowels of the sloop. Most of the pirates sat around the deck and breakfasted on dried fish and stale biscuits. Rackham strode onto the quarter-deck in full dress and called for the crew. I felt Rackham's eyes fall on me for a long moment, but none of the pirates seemed to take notice.

"Fellow rogues, Rodgers made us wait for pardons and licenses far too long. I daresay he would rather we rot in Nassau. So we begin a new enterprise without his blessing. We declare war on the entire world. Our motto shall be 'a merry life and a short one!'"

The crew raised their fists and cheered raucously.

"Consider the wonders of this sweet trade," he shouted with bravado, "spying a ship and giving chase, hoisting the Jolly Roger and drawing to its flank, shouting mayhem and bloodlust, shivering the timbers with a broadside, terrorizing the crew, and leaving the bones and brains of the undaunted few flooding the scuppers. Quarter only for the weak-kneed and law-abiding, the jolly sound of doubloons, guineas, and pieces of eight, a safe haven in harbor, and a willing Delilah in your hammock, and at the end of it all we swing and sundry in the wind, or we join Davy Jones at the bottom of the sea."

A chorus of laughter and whistles rose from the men. I felt proud of Rackham's poetic vision of the pirate's life. I swelled with pride and verve.

"Join me, men, for a new beginning, an adventurous life to pass the rest of our days on this spinning globe!" Rackham unsheathed a knife and impaled a document against the main mast. "I have the ship's articles to sign if you wish to share in our humble and ignoble endeavor."

The pirates lined up to sign the contract. I bathed in the defiance of Rackham's irreverent speech and the admiration he inspired in his fellow rogues.

"We'll need a new Jolly Roger. I have a design in mind, but I will need our best tailor, and today we change the name of this sloop to *Sweet Anne's Revenge*." Rackham cast a slight glance my way.

That triggered applause and cackles. "Aye, Captain, was she a hot, wild tumble worthy of your appetite?"

"Fetherston can vouch for her beauty, aye?"

Fetherston raised a flagon of rum. "A wanton beauty who's probably getting a cruel taste of the cat-o'-nine-tails upon the rack as we speak. Took your pleasure then took your leave, aye, Rack?"

"I am incorrigible." Rackham smiled. "But her memory be sweet and lasting. She purred like a kitten, scratched like a cat, and then mewed for more."

The pirates gave a hearty shout. I joined them but secretly marveled at the egos of men.

"I also think it good form to venerate Blackbeard with this sloop. So, me fellow pirates, who will make our flag?"

I raised my hand and spoke in my trained voice. "I have skill in thread and needle for sheets and flags."

"Agreed. Visit my cabin for supper, and I will show you my sketches," Rackham said. "I will also have you touch up our fair maidenhead with a brush. She needs a bit of dolling up."

I reached the front of the line and stared at the garbled signatures and the commandments of the ship:

1. Every man shall obey the command. The captain shall have one full share and a half of all prizes.
2. If any man attempts to jump ship or keep any secret from the company, he shall be marooned with one bottle of powder, one bottle of water, one pistol, and shot.
3. If any man steals from the company, he shall be keelhauled.
4. The man who spreads dissension, breeds mutiny, or fights onboard will receive forty stripes, save one, or a keelhauling.
5. The man who fires an arm, smokes tobacco, or lights a candle or lantern in the hold will suffer the same punishment.
6. The man who fails to keep his weapons clean and fit for engagements, or who neglects his duty in battle, shall be cut off from his share and suffer a punishment that pleases the captain and crew.
7. If any man loses a finger during battle, he shall receive 400 pieces of eight or the equivalent in booty, and double that amount for a lost limb.
8. If any man steals or defrauds another man, he will be marooned.

9. If any man has a grievance against another, a straight fight will be set up to settle the conflict. Any man taking vengeance without conferring first with the captain will be marooned.
10. Any man proved a coward or drunk during a time of engagement shall lose his share and receive forty stripes, save one.
11. Every man has a vote. Majority rule will determine the prizes we chase, battles we fight, and who will be captain and quartermaster.

"Swear a blood oath on the Good Book before you sign," Rackham said.

The crew shouted a loud cheer and stepped up to the mast. Each member swore his oath and signed the articles without question or complaint. I followed suit, pledging in my huskiest voice my allegiance to Captain Jack Rackham and the ship's crew. He winked at me and I moistened my lips.

"We'll chart a course for the Berry Islands and see what prizes may be won along the way," said Rackham to his crew.

I was hot for my first battle. Over the next week, I sharpened my cutlass and double-checked the powder charges on my brace of pistols. I practiced flinging marlinespikes at targets with the crew. I practiced heaving the grappling irons as well as dropping the leads to check fathoms. My muscles started to harden and I pushed myself a bit further each day, climbing the ratlines and yards, learning to swing and release from a line to board another vessel. Working on the masts, I learned to balance myself at heights and untangle sheets and lines with adept speed. At times I would still myself and enjoy the wind in my face as I worked high above the deck.

One of the gunners, Dobbin, instructed me in the art of loading, aiming, and firing one of the eight cannons and two swivel guns the sloop was fitted with. I learned that after packing powder, wadding, and shot, one must take care to secure the cannon before lighting the fuse.

"The recoil could lop off yer bleeding hand or crush yer leg," he said.

Dobbin showed me how to skim cannonballs off the water, and how he sometimes used handfuls of shrapnel and balls linked with chain to take out the rigging on another ship.

In the evenings, I often asked the two friendliest pirates, Harwood and Fetherston, more about navigating by the stars. They pointed out the constellations, and even told me a few of the mythical stories about them. This close to the equator, we could see almost all of them through the course of a year. Nautical maps, the sextant, the binnacle and compass, and the astrolabe—all became familiar to me once again. Recalling stories of larger pirate ships and crews, I asked them why our crew seemed comparatively small.

"That's Rackham's angle," Harwood said, taking a swig from a flask. "He likes his ships sleek and swift as quicksilver to strike terror fast and speed away. Our crew may be few, but he handpicks us to leave lasting impressions."

He offered me the flask. I took a gulp, felt a burn in my throat, and coughed. He slapped me on the back and chuckled. "That'll put hair on yer chest, boy."

One day the winds died and the current seemed to slow. I asked Rackham about this abrupt change. He shrugged his shoulders and said, "We are at the mercy of Triton. We'll make the best of it."

During this lull I began to paint. From the block and tackle, Fetherston and Harwood lowered me over the foredeck gunwale and I touched up the masthead, a forlorn-faced wench with ample cleavage and a flowing red frock and white petticoat. I spent much of the day repainting the woman and savoring the sounds of the sea. I watched pelicans dive into shoals of fish, saw seal swim by, and looked down into the clear blue waters to spy sea turtles and colorful fish darting in and out of coral reefs. Later that day I worked on the sloop's escutcheon, painting over *William* and taking pleasure in renaming the vessel after me.

By day I played the pirate, by night the paramour. Slipping quietly out of my hammock past the snoring men, I snuck to Rackham's quarters each night for a tryst. He was usually impatiently waiting for me, trying to distract himself by reading a tome from his library. When I would arrive, he would beam and shift in his bed, making the sheets hiss, and the muscles of his arms and chest would contract, showing off his strong physique.

The first night I came to him, he reached into a hutch beside the bed for another book, one offering erotic instructions and drawings on the art of coupling. At first I shied at the explicit language, but as I watched Rackham's lips and peered at the sketches, I gave myself over. There was no restraint in our lovemaking that night. "A lather of lust," Rackham called it. Our energy together seemed boundless, and it wasn't until early morning that I took leave of his bed and tiptoed back to my hammock. I had not forgotten my husband or my holy vow, but it was flattering to be the essence of Rackham's insatiable desire as well as the inspiration for his reading. The forbidden and dangerous manner of our rendezvous danced in my head during the day, and I ached for the night, which would bring his touch to my body again.

Someone must have noticed because I overheard rumors of us, but no one seemed to care. In fact the pirates seemed to have a mixture of pride and empathy. The gossip only humanized the captain, Rackham's physical needs being so demanding that he needed to turn to a youth. I snickered to myself as the pirates discussed how he steered from both the port and starboard sides when it came to satisfying his ravenous appetite.

But all this talk led to the inevitable: the test. I dreaded and yearned for it at the same time. The thought of losing my first scrap, the discovery of my gender, and the very real possibility of a gang assault petrified me, but the prospect of turning the tables on my first nemesis and proving my cutthroat capability with flourish stirred my blood.

At the end of our first week at sea I was laboring in the hold, holystoning a portion of the timbers. I hummed a tune and scraped at the mildew and slime. Rats skittered across the planks and gnawed at the stores of food. I saw one of the cats poise to strike, its tailed jerking about. He pounced on the rat and played with his prey awhile before killing and consuming it.

I was isolated in the shadows and could hear the banter of the men topside. Howell was working on the other side of hold, whistling one of his songs. Suddenly, from behind, someone grabbed me around the neck and slapped an arm around my torso, very near my flattened breasts. He whispered into my ear. "Ok, powder monkey, I'm game for ye. Where will ye have it—yer bum or yer trap?"

I recognized the voice of Throckmorton. I knew him only as a quiet man who mumbled a great deal under his breath. He was not much larger than me, but I remembered he was skilled at hurling a knife.

I pulled at his arm but his grip was like a vice. A scream rose in my throat, but I held it back. I thought of Edward's words and the day I had fought a suitor among the tobacco fields and slaves. Out of my peripheral vision, I saw Howell dash up the ladder and disappear. The hatch closed.

"Now we got privacy. Don't make me cut ye," he rasped.

I felt him fumbling with my pants, trying to pull the back of them down. This gave me my chance. I cast about for my weapons, but they were too far away. My arms were pinned so I could not throw an elbow. I went limp and waited for him to work on his own breeches. He stumbled with my dead weight and gave me my chance. Freeing my right arm, I reached around and grabbed him between the legs. He grunted and loosened his grip. I tried to slip free but he tightened his hold again, one hand now around my throat, the other trying to release my clutch. I lowered my head and sank my teeth into his arm, tasting blood immediately. He shouted and pushed me away. I spun, crouched, and waited for his onslaught.

"You squeal like a sow, and stink like one, too," I rasped.

He said nothing. We circled each other in the shadows, only bits of light streaming through the cracks in tarpaulin and hatches.

"Rackham knows ye. The whole crew wonders what ye do. I'll have me a taste of ye, too," he said.

"An elegant proposal that is nearly irresistible. But I believe I will respectfully decline, but not before I castrate you."

"Ye talk more than a woman," he croaked. But I sensed, as he took a step backward, he was wavering between attacking and retreating.

I knelt and felt around, kicking at some irons. Just as I found a grappling iron, he charged. I swung upward and caught him on the chin. He reeled back and I lunged forward and swung again, feeling the iron connect solidly with his temple, knocking him to the floor. He scrambled for a defense, and I swung the point of the hook over and over, at every scuffling, sometimes connecting with his legs, and sometimes the deck. I swung harder and harder, and then the iron stuck into the wood so deep I had trouble releasing it. Throckmorton got up slowly. I could hear the sound of a knife being pulled from its sheath. Its blade glinted once in the light.

"Sodomite, I'll cut ye for resisting." His voice was hoarse and he wheezed with consumption.

"You'll have to bugger my corpse," I said.

"So be it."

He made his move, and I ducked to the floor. He sailed right over me and crashed against a pile of yards and sheets. The door to the hold opened and a wash of light rushed in. All I could see was the outline of a figure at the top. Was this help for me or for Throckmorton? In the new light I saw a marlinspike. I snatched it up and hurled it at him. It penetrated his right thigh. He let loose a yell, dropped his knife, and held his bleeding wound.

"Quarter? Quarter?" he begged.

Tough on the surface, but a coward underneath, I thought. I despised this kind of man. They picked their battles carefully, seeking out those they believed were too weak and feeble to fight back, all to strengthen the frailty within them.

I walked up to him, white ire pulsating through me. I grabbed the marlinspike and twisted. "Squeal like the stuck swine you are!"

His eyes widened and he gurgled. Sweat poured down his red face.

I picked up his knife and put it to his neck.

"This what ye were game for?" I mimicked his voice. "I stuck me spike in ye thigh, not ye bum?" I bent to his ear and whispered, "And here's a wee little secret…I am a woman, and I said no." I rammed the knife home into his throat and sliced outward and he fell forward, jerking in the throes of death. I swung about, knife drawn, ready for another opponent.

"Avast, O'Malley. Now that's quite enough carnage for today," said Rackham, his figure outlined in the shadows. "You've obviously made your point to Throckmorton, and now to the rest of the crew. You may be an upstart, but you are no easy mark. Besides, I can't afford to lose anymore of my pirates. I saw enough to vindicate you. Your honor remains intact."

He stepped down and took the knife from my shaking hand. He winked, his voice softening. "Impressive display," he whispered. "No one will bother you again."

He turned to the gathering crew climbing down the ladder. His voice grew official again. "Fetherston, have the crew deliver this carcass to the sharks. Mix a bowl of punch for Edward O'Malley. He needs one. First kill for you?"

The import of the question began to creep into my mind. "Yes," I murmured. I had ended a man's life. It had been him or me, but nonetheless I had driven a man's spirit from the earth. He had a mum and da, perhaps even siblings. I remember someone once saying that there are men who need killing. Certainly, God in heaven believed so. But I knew his pleading, shocked eyes would return to me in my still hours.

Most of the men kept a clear berth of me the rest of the day, but Harwood and Fetherston sauntered up and congratulated me.

"I never liked the man. Grumbled all the time," said Harwood.

Later that night, I snuck into Rackham's cabin and found him reading Milton's *Paradise Lost*. "'Better to reign in hell than serve in heaven,'" he quoted. He set the book down, rose, and held me for a long time.

"Were you hurt?"

"No, but why didn't you help me?"

He held my shoulders and looked into my eyes. "Anne, you know you had to prove yourself to earn their respect, though I did not count on you slaying the man."

"Their respect? Most men are spineless underneath, like Throckmorton and probably most of this crew. I could have been ravaged and killed."

Rackham walked around his cabin, staring at the ceiling. "Yes, but it was a chance I needed to take. No one will bother you anymore. I never trusted him from the first, so you did me a bit of a favor."

I stared at him dumbfounded. "But, what if it was Fetherston or Harwood or—"

Rackham came to me. "I knew it wouldn't be."

"How?" I felt myself shuddering. "Did you—"

"I set it up for your own good, Anne."

The room swirled like a whirlpool. Rackham had sent a rapist to attack me? He stood aside and made me kill him or be killed? "What if he had succeeded?"

Rackham narrowed his eyes. "I knew he wouldn't. But that's why I was there, waiting to come between you if it came to it."

"But it could have happened before you arrived!"

He pondered. "It was a calculated risk. One must gamble at times. But by handpicking the day, time, and victim, the hazard was considerably less."

"I could have been made the ship's whore!"

Rackham shook his head. "Anne, lower your voice. Now hear me. That would not, could not happen." He patted me on the back. "And now here you are, the toughest and most beautiful female pirate ever to sail the West Indies—the stuff of legends and literature."

"And Calico Jack's cabin harlot." I started for the door.

"Anne, I set this up for you to reduce the risk and element of surprise, for you to show your strength, to prove yourself to the men, and to build confidence in yourself. You even said you were bracing yourself for the time."

"Yes, but I do not like someone else playing God over my life."

"I love you, Anne. I wish to marry you. I have never said those words."

I began to turn the doorknob but stopped. The whirling in my brain contributed to my ambivalence. His explanation and sudden proposal both disgusted and moved me. I had to learn the pirate way. Wrong was made right, bad was made good, and evil was a common reality to be accepted and seldom questioned or understood. In Rackham's mind, he had acted wisely, and for my benefit. I had shown the crew, and myself, I had what it takes to handle myself in a fray. No striking the tents and scampering away from the field of battle. I could fight the good fight on a ship of cutthroats. Had not Harwood and Fetherston congratulated me—two of the best onboard? But no warning? No preparation for this brutal episode Rackham had hatched?

I released the doorknob and turned back to him. I tilted my head, did a small curtsey, and let my hands move enticingly down my breasts and around my hips. I began to unbutton my shirt. Rackham arched his brows, blinked, and approached me. He leaned to kiss me, and I grabbed him firmly between the legs and squeezed. Rackham pulled back, his eyes dilating, and he stumbled onto the bed, groaning and holding himself.

I stood over him and my finger in his face. "You conniving, raffish, scullion! I'll not be a 'calculated risk'—that smacks of the utmost, which you're far from, my lordly Jack. You want me, you deal square with me. Equal partnership. No secrets, no lies. And then I will gladly marry you, my sweet love. Are we clear?"

I threw open the door and yelled over my shoulder. "Otherwise, find a new boy!"

The crew greeted me with a bray of catcalls, whistles, and applause.

"A lover's spat? How sweet, how touching!" yelled Harwood.

I brandished my cutlass and pointed toward Harwood, livid and on edge.

"Easy, O'Malley. You raise Cain, and you may take me, but not all me shipmates. Relax. We're friends, just giving you a wee tease. Your little fracas was within earshot. No more, no less."

I sighed and sheathed my sword. "I need a drink."

"Have a bottle." Harwood tossed it to me.

I joined the men as they bet over a cockfight, occasionally stealing a glance at Rackham's cabin.

Chapter XVII

Three days passed before Rackham, under the pretense of discussing the Jolly Roger, asked me to his cabin. I was still smoldering. He offered me a glass of port. I declined. He tried chocolate. I turned away. He started to hand me a wrapped gift, but I raised a hand and shook my head.

"Anne, it was wrong of me not to warn you beforehand. Please hear me when I say my intentions were good. Will you forgive me?"

I reflected a moment. I recalled a time that Edward had said I had a talent for holding a grudge when wronged. I had learned to counterattack with a mix of silence and insults. My goal? Punishment—making the other person regret their slight. I might forgive in word, but not in my heart, and definitely not before I impaled them and roasted them over my spit. I never could get anything past Edward, though. When I tried it on him, he said, "What are you trying to do? What more do you want from me?" It made me angry because he had exposed my pettiness and bitterness.

What more did I want from Rackham now? I wanted him to feel what I felt, but I did not see how that could be done. So I forgave him in word, for now, until a more opportune time came to teach him the lesson I felt he ought to learn. I possessed an enduring memory—a curse or a blessing? I accepted the port, the chocolate, and his gift, and I demanded Throckmorton's coral-handled knife—my first bounty.

Still trying to quell my anger, I suggested we talk about the flag. Rackham seemed relieved to steer our conversation to safer waters. He sketched out some of the flags he had flown under or had seen. The skull and crossbones motif was a given, but he hoped to find a variation on the theme.

"Some are chapfallen and a bit too grim for me," said Rackham. "And I deplored Blackbeard's design."

"Wasn't there a captain who abandoned the skull?" I asked.

"Thomas Tew. Yes, he used an armed arm, that is, an arm holding a cutlass. I like the revolutionary spirit of it, but I also want my Roger to be jolly," he said, chuckling at his simple witticism. "I know I'm jolly when we're rogering."

I rolled my eyes. Was he testing the waters to see whether I was in the mood? Definitely not. I returned to the subject of the flag. "What about combining the two ideas? Swords and skulls with a grinning chap?"

Rackham pushed aside his charts and set to outlining the figures. He made the skull's teeth more prominent with a definite grin, bordering on an evil cackle or guffaw. He added a long fissure on the right side of the dome. I started to object at the lack of symmetry, but I was distracted by the two caterwauling felines in the corner near his hutch. The bigger one was chasing the smaller around the cabin and then ferreted it out through a porthole. When I looked back at the sketch, I decided the long gash was a good variation, smacking of mayhem and madness. He started to draw the crossed bones.

"How about crossed swords instead?"

Rackham paused. A breeze, laden with a blend of tar and oil, arced through the porthole. The men were caulking the seams and scuppers. "No crossbones?"

"Revolutionary, with a dash of good humor," I said.

"I like it well—impeccable taste for our noble skullduggery. Can you reproduce it with thread and needle?"

"Well, such women's work is the bane and bore I sought to escape, but I think I can make an exception for this piratical masterpiece." The feeling between us warmed. He touched my shoulder, and then pulled me against him for a lingering embrace.

"Thank you, Anne," he whispered.

* * * *

On our twelfth day at sea, the crew spied our first prize. The approach charged me (at least the first three or four hours), the battle disappointed me, the pillaging disillusioned me, and our treatment of the people shocked me. It looked like a merchant schooner, larger than ours, slow moving, and low in the water. Rackham ordered a full raising of the main and topsails, which sent us into a frenzy of activity.

We raised Dutch colors and waved and hailed as our sloop sped alongside them. Then Rackham commanded we run our new Jolly Roger up and fire a broadside across the vessel's bow. I had my brace of flintlocks set and readied two coconut grenades to ignite. The ship lowered its sails and gave up without firing a single shot. I threw one of the grappling hooks and secured it. Our crew made deft work of drawing the vessels close, even laying down a gangplank to walk across as if our boarding were a grand entrance. They looted the ship of all manner of supplies: lamps and oil, bolts of dyed fabric and leather, powdered wigs, and fashionable hats. We loaded up food, too—bottles of preserved vegetables and fruits; sacks of limes to aid against fevers; barrels of salt pork; bags of flour, sugar, salt, and arrowroot; and demijohns and calabashes of distilled liquors. We also found two goats and a dozen chickens, which availed us of fresh dairy. In the hold, we found boxes of gunpowder, extra weapons, and spare rigging. They had a box of musketoons and various carpentry tools, which we loaded onto the *Sweet Anne's Revenge*.

It was an efficient process until Carty, Corner, and Dobbin discovered a woman in hiding. By her screams, I had no doubt what they were doing to her. I walked into the cabin and found Rackham, Harwood, Fenwick, and Fetherston packing up silverware, plates, and glasses.

"Some of the men are raping a woman," I said to Rackham in a hushed tone.

Without hesitation he mumbled back, "Part of the spoils of a prize."

I began to say more but realized these ideas were long ingrained, even commonplace. It repulsed me. I knew I had been naïve of all that pirates do, considering only the romance and adventure. Certainly if we fought and robbed, rape could not be far from the equation. I weighed it from another angle. If the crew had fought rather than given up, perhaps the story would have had an entirely different ending.

As we pushed away from the ship, I stood amazed at the submissive faces of the robbed crew. They seemed to accept their lot without gripe, resigned to being hapless victims, begrimed and besmirched within and without.

"Why didn't they defend themselves?" I asked Rackham later.

"Pirate reputation precedes itself. Hoist the colors, fire a shot, and they cower like whelps. Yellow captains marshal spineless crews."

That night the crew overindulged in a feast of the spoils. Most were drunk and unconscious by the witching time of night. I spent the eventide with Rackham. He showed me how to set a course for Hispaniola, where he knew merchants who would purchase the booty. On the way, we would likely encounter more ships to plunder.

"We will become the thorn of Rodgers and the Spanish Main, forever written in the annals of pirate history," he said.

"I rather hope we encounter a bit more resistance next time."

"Easy prizes are not as exciting, nor as dangerous."

"But I want more risk," I said. "A test of mettle."

"I've seen enough to settle for a few easy catches."

The crew of the next vessel we attacked recoiled the same way as the first. But something unexpected happened this time. Four of the crew from the other ship asked to join us—Thomas Roose, Thomas Bourn, Jean Aouret and Benjamin Quick. Rackham looked them over, asked a few questions, and accepted them. But before they were allowed to join us in our sweet trade, Rackham told them they must either run the gauntlet around the sloop or haul themselves around the keel. They elected the gauntlet.

I had no clue what this meant, but Fetherston made swift work of handing each of us a paddle and lining us up about ten feet apart around the sloop and five feet from the railing. They started running and we were encouraged to give each a sound one as they passed. If they could not finish, they would be cast overboard to swim back to their plundered ship. I went for the legs, tripping Bourn and smacking him on the backside before he got up and scampered away. To Quick, I offered a shot right in the gut. He staggered back a step, and then dashed forward, ducking as I swung with a roundhouse. Roose endured a similar fate, but also passed the test. Arouet never appeared, opting to leap overboard and swim back to his ship. It was grand fun, and after the trio finished, we welcomed them to our band with bottles of rum.

Later that day we encountered another sloop flying the Yellow Jack, a symbol warning of an epidemic illness onboard. I asked Rackham if it might be a ploy, but he said it was not worth the risk. "Only a fool would take the chance."

"That's why we have our cats beat back the vermin: they carry disease. I have decided to name the cats—Dante and Milton. Dante is a hellcat, with those six-clawed paws that lay down the law on this ship. As Dante put it, 'gaudy pelt, all tremor and flow.' Now Milton is all purr and soft fur and rests in my lap when I read. But when she's hungry, the beast in her is set loose. Not unlike a lady I enjoy the acquaintance of."

I blew him a stealthy kiss. Rackham had such divergent directions of thought, finding the poetry in everything from felines and women to sailing and piracy.

My doubts about boarding the Yellow Jack quickly melted away a few days later when we came upon a ghost ship. It foundered along, its spars broken, its rigging slack, and its sails mere tatters flapping in the breeze. As we pulled alongside, the stench of death enveloped us. From the deck, we could see a couple of skeletons. Seabirds picked at the remnants of their decomposing flesh. Typhus, cholera, yellow fever, dengue fever, malaria, the bloody flux, and the plague claimed more pirate lives than guns, swords, and the gallows was Rackham's only comment.

"Blackbeard once grew so skittish about disease that he had three crew members thrown overboard because they showed signs of illness. He learned the trick from the slave ships. They did it so often that it is said schools of shark trailed the slavers from Africa to the Americas," he said.

"Could we not tow the ship into a harbor, quarantine it, and sell it?"

"And bring a curse upon us? We are a superstitious lot, you know."

Then he asked me if I had ever heard the story of the *Flying Dutchman.* I told him I had heard mention of it, but never the full story. According to Rackham, a Captain Van der Decken commanded the *Flying Dutchman.* Van der Decken, though not a pirate, was reputedly a cohort of Satan. One night he was attempting to round the Cape of Good Hope but a squall came upon the ship. Against the pleas of the crew to sail for safety, Van der Decken swore by Satan and by God that he would round the cape that very night even if he had to sail straight into the typhoon winds. No one had ever seen him again. Because of his oath, Van der Decken and his crew were condemned to sail forever against the winds in their phantom ship.

"The next storm we face, the crew will worry about seeing the *Flying Dutchman*—the death omen. Those who do often do not live to tell the tale," he said. "I have since heard claim that Blackbeard's ship has been sighted off the coast of Carolina. He searches for his lost treasure and his head. Another curse. So many curses out there to avoid."

I listened intently, but observed that Rackham did not tell the story with his usual light-hearted flourish and characteristic sarcastic tone. I said nothing more.

We arrived at Ocho Rios Bay and dropped anchor, and then unloaded our stores into cutters and oared ashore, where merchants were waiting. As Rackham negotiated prices, I decided to take a walk along the shore, and perhaps find a private place to bathe. My thoughts troubled me. I loved the high seas and our escapades, but the grotesque actions of the men and my killing of Throckmorton disturbed my sleep. I may not have participated in the rape, but my silence and tolerance, turning a blind eye and deaf ear to it, pierced me with knives of guilt. If

I had never left my husband and leaped aboard Rackham's ship, Throckmorton would still be breathing.

The magnitude of my desire for Rackham also bothered me in my still moments. My conscience was hardening, but I still had to concede that I had betrayed my husband. No matter how much I justified my actions, I had mutinied against our marital vows and shattered any trust he had in me. I tried praying, but I couldn't find any prayer that seemed to fit my circumstances. I recalled King Claudias' attempt to do the same in *Hamlet*: "My words fly up, my thoughts remain below/Words without thoughts, never to heaven go." My prayers merely bounced off the planks and slapped me in the face. After a spell, I wandered dejectedly into taverns until I found Rackham.

"Ahoy, like the prodigal, O'Malley returns to harbor. Fetch me more rum, barkeep, for my morose mate," said Rackham, puffing on a clay hornpipe. "Where have you been landlubbing?"

"Among the spires and cathedrals of our Lord's good creation."

"Ah, your melancholy madness skulks out of the shadows to haunt you? Your conscience is not sufficiently seared yet."

"Aye, but I gave the jackal a broadside and sent it off with its tail between its legs," I said. "The sea calls my soul to fair winds and easy tides. Here, I lose my sea legs and my soul feels tarred and feathered. When do we leave?"

"Poetic to the last," Rackham said. "Sit down and rest your weary ways."

As I sat down, the barkeep sauntered over with a pot of salmagundi and two bowls. Rackham spooned the stew into the bowls and then turned a couple pages in his book. "I was just reading. I believe Dryden knows your heart: 'Of all the tyrannies on human kind/The worst is that which persecutes the mind.'"

Rackham passed me a bowl of the stew, a conglomeration of sea turtle, fish, pork, duck, and beef. "And another from dear Dryden: 'Great wits are sure to madness near allied/And thin partitions do their bounds divide.'" He slurped his soup and chewed. "Most find haven on shore; you seem to only gain your deliverance from the sea. The land is your prison, the sea is your liberation."

"Then when can we depart?"

"The crew needs a few more days to drink up, lie with the lassies, and throw away their money. Patience is a virtue even among these scamps." Rackham gestured to the tavern.

"Who ye callin' a scamp?" roared the barkeep, tipping his hat and raising a glass.

"This festering, toxic grog and grub you pass off as rum and food dulls our brains and ladens our bodies with a multitude of ailments. And thus," Rackham raised his glass, "eat, drink, and be merry, me hearties, for tomorrow we die by poisoning."

"The more ye talk, the less I understand, Rack," shouted the barkeep.

I decided to return to the ship and spent the evening reading Rackham's copy of Exquemelin's work. The French writer had traveled the seas chronicling pirate practices. His writing jolted and yet intrigued me. I read about the French buccaneers Pierre Le Grand, the first to seize a Spanish galleon, and Francois Lolonois, who raided several galleons and sacked and burned to the ground Maracaibo, a Spanish stronghold. During that battle, he "drew his cutlass, and with it cut open the breast of one of those Spaniards, and pulling out his heart began to bite and gnaw it with his teeth, like a ravenous wolf…" I shuddered at the thought of such ruthless deeds, which struck me to be as violent, measure for measure, as Torquemada, Grand Inquisitor of the Spanish Inquisition, with their burnings at the stake, tortures with the Catherine Wheel and the rack, drawing and quartering, and brandings and dismemberment. Man, I reflected, if left to himself, slips into devilry and degenerates to sadism. He might be a beast above beasts, but he is capable of far greater perversity. Shakespeare may have had Hamlet claim a man was a piece of work, noble in reason, infinite in faculties, like an angel and god, but he was also utterly depraved and in need of saving.

As the ship bobbed softly with the gentle cadence of the current in the bay, my thoughts became religious. I remembered learning how Luther had turned Europe upside down and left many dissatisfied with the Church, and how he had spearheaded the genesis of the Protestant movement. Though my father had registered a Protestant in America, he stubbornly remained Irish Catholic in his heart, even though he seldom practiced what was preached in either church. "Had not St. Patrick eradicated all the snakes from Ireland?" he once asked me, trying to explain his unswerving allegiance to the Church. How could one turn his back on such a miracle? The flames of Protestantism didn't infiltrate our homeland so easily. But despite his loyalty, my father still had to pay additional indulgences to get all our names etched into the Book of Life, especially after his adultery and divorce and my illegitimacy.

I recalled once reading a forbidden pamphlet penned by Luther, which read, "had one ravished the Virgin Mary, or crucified Christ anew, the Pope would, for money, have pardoned him." That was one reason the Protestant movement appealed to me, for it changed such hypocritical rules. Revolting against and questioning the powers that betook courage, and I had heard of many a saint mercilessly tortured and burned at the stake for the cause of God. Such an extreme reaction to religious differences struck me as absurd.

As I mulled over these things, it was now clear my life had strayed far from God. I had been thinking little of Him or of His precepts, though at times I felt Him when I appreciated the beauty of His creation, but if I was to believe the Scriptures, or even Dante, my choices had made me fodder for the Lake of Fire—starting at the second level and swiftly plummeting to the bottom. What would it profit me to gain the world's booty and all the pleasures it promised, but forfeited my soul? I thought of Christ and His clear perception of humanity when He said, "For where your treasure is, there your heart is also." I fell asleep against the bulwark, my body garnered with guns and sword, my mind searching for peace in my soul.

Three days passed before the men returned, sallow faced, hung over, and grouchy. They whined about refitting the sloop and repairing the sheets and rigging. I helped Howell and Harwood pump water out of the bilge and caulk every seam.

"Look alive, ye scallywags," shouted Fetherston on topside. "A lazy back gets a hasty lash. Rack's orders."

Two days later we hoisted the sails and picked up a northerly trade wind, which snapped our canvas tight. We adjusted the rudder to luff the wind, raised the anchor, and slipped out of the port, past the dilapidated fortress the governor had let decay after His Majesty King George's ploy to offer pirate pardons had all but failed. Within a few hours our craft was beyond the sight of land.

While we were docked, Rackham had added six more men to our crew—Baker, Palmer, Earl, Howard, Cole, and Massaquehanna. Cole was a renegade slave from Carolina who had met Massaquehanna in the woods. Massaquehanna had been enslaved as well, by the Spanish. His Indian tribe, the Seminoles, had suffered much in vicious battles with Spanish *conquistadores*, and their prominence in Florida had been gravely reduced by disease. Massaquehanna stared with penetrating eyes and the most expressionless face I had ever seen. Several times I noticed him staring at me. I interpreted his gazes as potentially hazardous, so I kept a wary eye on his movements.

Both men had shaved heads and numerous tattoos on their faces, chests, and arms. They spoke little and had dangerous demeanors, but there was something about them I liked. Somehow, despite the cruelty and violence they had experienced, they possessed sensitivity in their eyes. I also admired the fact that though they had been slaves for a season, they were now unfettered from their shackles. A pirate ship was the perfect place for them because all the men were equalized by proof of their skill and bravery. I felt proud that they had joined our fellowship, and that Rackham treated them with respect.

Later in the day clouds formed on the horizon, boiling into black, ominous bubbles and hairy rolls. Fetherston ordered the hatches cinched, the sails lowered and secured, the ballast adjusted, and the chests and cannons tied down. I helped man one of the pumps to bail the seawater that had begun cresting over the decks while the crew waited for the squall to hit.

"Judgment of Heaven, by the powers," was whispered through the ranks. "The good Lord and King Triton have had enough of our wild oats."

When I heard this talk, I remarked to Harwood. "Perhaps we should draw straws, find the Jonah, throw him overboard and be done with this storm."

Harwood grimaced. "Then it'd be a ghost ship. Besides, my first name is Noah."

"The drop of water accepts no blame for the tidal wave," I said as the winds and rains grew stronger.

"A good word."

The waves rose and the sloop pitched, rising to the apex of a wave and then diving to the breach of the sea, where walls of water surrounded the craft and threatened to dash it to pieces. Lightning bolts streaked through the sky, followed by an electric crackling. I looked up and saw the bluish glow of St. Elmo's fire on our mast.

The waves dwarfed our ship and poured over the sides, swamping the deck. Torrents of water slanted into our faces. Quick was lifted off his feet by the wash and carried overboard, screaming and clawing at the deck before he disappeared into the hollow trough of the silver gray ocean. There was no saving him.

Our vessel bobbed like a cork. We manned the pumps, sucking water that sloshed the strakes and spitting it into the scuppers to drain back into the sea. The masts creaked and swayed. I waited for them to splinter and snap, but Fetherston had ordered that stabilizing lines be attached to them, which seemed to hold them for now.

Avalanche after avalanche of water lurched and crashed against the ship, canting it. I watched a second crewmember, a galley slave Rackham hoped would turn pirate, helping topside, lose his grip on a line and get washed over the railing. I wondered how much more the ship could take and how many more lives the sea would demand, but I felt no fear. In fact, if I was to die, a watery grave sounded more welcoming to me than a terra firma plot. But as quickly as it began, the storm started to abate. The whitecaps grew less dangerous.

Rackham emerged from his cabin. "Good work, mates. Fetherston, how many did we lose?"

"Two, sir."

"Indeed. Did anybody see the *Flying Dutchman*—or *The Queen Anne's Revenge* for that matter?"

No one answered.

"Very well. Let's get this ship ready for a prize. Fetherston, have the quartermaster instruct the galley to spread a big meal for the lot of you, with some demijohns of good rum."

The crew didn't cheer. They looked as mad as the vexed sea. I thought I knew why. Rackham had skulked in his quarters while his crew had risked their lives. The food and drink seemed a carrot to ease the bitterness, a lily-livered gesture to compensate for his yellow stripe. Yes, he was the captain, but some leadership had been in order while we faced the eye of the storm. I chose not to visit Rackham that night. Let him stew awhile and search his conscience, I thought.

CHAPTER XVIII

The next morning, I awakened to feverish shouts. "A sail! A sail!"

All hands rushed to the railing and searched for the prize. I came topside, as well, and squinted across the horizon. Little did I know, but this ship would bring great changes to my life.

"A Dutch sloop, riding low. Must be laden with goods, heading for England," Rackham said, pointing his spyglass toward the schooner. "She's got mounted guns. Lay on more sail and be ready for a fight, mates."

A cheer resounded across the deck. "Ain't had a good row in so long, me sword and pistol be vexed for blood," said Carty.

"Go aloft and determine the number of hands and guns," said Rackham.

"Appears to be a premium prize, Cap'n," said Harwood. He started climbing the ratlines to the masthead.

The ship was in full sail, heading for the open sea. Rackham idled on the quarterdeck, waiting for Harwood's reconnaissance of the Dutch schooner. A flock of gulls hovered over both ships, their shrill cries shrieking the air. The ocean, still turbulent from the storm, frothed and crested against the sides of the ship.

"Ten guns, twenty to thirty crew. No surrender, no quarter today, sir."

Rackham stared at the schooner. "We're outnumbered, but speed and experience give us the advantage. Men, prepare for a hot enterprise. *Caveat emptor.* Make peace with your god because some of us might not see the next day's sunrise. Ah, but what a way to unmoor from this life. Hoist the Jolly Roger and fire a warning shot."

The Dutchman cruised on, but it was only a matter of time. The chase lasted most of the day, but around 4 o'clock our smaller, speedier craft drew in close. We avoided a broadside from its very lethal guns. Harwood fired several shots from the swivel gun at the rudder, but with no effect. We maneuvered for position, raising and lowering our sails to luff and tack the winds. When we were perhaps fifty feet away, Rackham ordered the preparation of bottle and coconut grenades. By twilight Rackham managed a tacking strategy that drew us close to the Dutchman's stern, ramming it. We fired on the Dutchman with muskets and swivel guns and lobbed the grenades. As they exploded we heaved our grappling hooks. Rackham gave the command and I followed Fetherston, Harwood, Hood, Dobbin, Howell, Massaquehanna, and Cole to board the ship in two groups of four, one fore and one aft. Adrenalin raved under my skin. We climbed the ratlines to the spars and grabbed the lines, bracing to swing across. The remaining crew delivered a second barrage of grapeshot and grenades onto the vessel.

We waited for the concussions, and then swung across together and dropped onto the deck, pistols drawn. I knelt behind a barrel and spied for a shot. A musket shot tore away Dobbin's ear, but he kept firing. He discharged his musketoons and leaped for cover. Hood dropped forward onto the deck, a ball lodged in his throat. Fetherston, Cole, Dobbin, and Davis charged forward. I stood up and fired my pistols to cover them. I could hear the clash of cutlasses and the blast of pistols.

I drew my cutlass and charged the other direction with Massaquehanna and Harwood. I fenced with a sailor, parrying his thrust. I slashed and sliced open his right shoulder. He took a step back and feinted, and then charged forward. I evaded his blade but was bowled over when he stumbled. We clambered to the ground and wrestled for an opening to finish each other off. Chaos surrounded me. At any moment I expected a sword to be thrust in my back. The sailor reared back and punched me in the nose. My eyes watered and I could taste blood. I rolled away and drew my knife. He came at me, but I ended his charge with a knife throw that caught him squarely in the chest. Out of the corner of my eye I saw another mariner bolting toward me. I snatched up a sword and fended off his attack. Harwood flanked him. As he turned to avert his thrust, I grabbed his beard and yanked him off balance. Harwood finished him.

"Beards are a fatal flaw in battle," I panted, hiding behind a barrel to reload my gun.

"Aye," said Harwood. "That's why I shave."

I looked over at our ship and saw the second wave of pirates beginning their assault: Bourn, Earl, Palmer, Carty, Howard, Fenwick, and Baker. Rackham stood on the deck, raised a rifle, and fired. Two galley slaves busied themselves with reloading and handing a fresh rifle to him. Otherwise, he kept his distance from the fighting and smoke.

"Take out the rigging," I yelled.

Massaquehanna and Harwood nodded. Screaming like the crazed hooligans we were, we charged through the smoke, firing our pistols, tossing them aside, and grabbing loaded ones from our belts. I reached the mainmast and set to chopping at the yards. Harwood took a ball in the leg and keeled over but continued firing. As I cut lines, I saw Massaquehanna engaged in a swordfight with two men. I watched the sails billow up and flap wildly in the wind, drifting freely over the railing and into the ocean. I joined Massaquehanna and we cut down both men. Rackham shouted "grenades!" and we dove for cover. The shudder of one was so near it threw me into a cartwheel across the deck.

Pieces of glass and shot stitched my legs and peppered my arms. I clawed for cover and reloaded a couple guns I had found lying on the deck. Phantom figures battled in the smoke. Fires raged across the ship. At this moment I felt like I could be breathing hell's fumes, staring into the face of perdition's flames. I questioned whether this was my destiny. Would I dine on wormwood and wrath while trapped in brimstone? I had no last will and testament, and no legacy to leave. Only my blasphemies came to mind.

I strained to identify friend or foe. I saw Palmer battling one sailor and another one coming up behind him with a spike. I raised my pistols and shot at the Dutchman, but I missed and a second later I saw Palmer fall. I bit my lip and fought back my tears. I had failed him in his greatest moment of need. Rattled, I labored to reload my pistols. Across the deck I saw Roose's lifeless body. I heard calls of retreat, but I surmised they weren't from my side. I squirmed deeper among fallen timbers and rigging, cornering myself for a final contest. I would go down with my guns firing, not writhing against a noose while people watched.

The gunfire and explosions soon ceased, and the smoke receded in the breeze. I heard a cheer fly up even as I slipped into a semiconscious state. A figure loomed toward me. I lifted a shaky pistol. The figure ducked away. I fired wildly. The phantom took a wary step forward.

"A close call," Rackham said. "But we prevailed."

I shut my eyes and lost consciousness.

I awoke to the sting of a hot blade burrowing into my leg, extracting a slug of iron. I tensed and reached cautiously to feel my clothing, to see whether my secret had been revealed. Everything important was intact. Only Rackham, Massaquehanna, and Cole were working on me. Rackham laid a hand on my forehead and leaned over me. "It's all right. They knew anyway—from the first day they climbed aboard."

I stared at the Indian and the African, moving in an out of delirium. The tales of barbaric savages murdering and ravaging women and children in Carolina had scared me when I first landed in the New World so many years ago. I thought shamefully of the way I had treated the Africans subjugated on the plantation. But like Rackham, I had come to realize the foolishness of my old views. Massaquehanna and Cole had proven loyal, brave, wise, and cultured in their own ways.

Rackham told me of our success, the richness of the booty, and the pride we had gained in fighting like men.

"How many did we lose?"

Rackham frowned. "A Pyrrhic victory. We lost five—they lost nine, almost everyone of our crew was wounded in some way. We may have to indenture a few."

"I saw Palmer, Roose, and Hood fall. Who else?"

"Howard and Baker. A shame they couldn't divvy up their first prizes."

I could say nothing. I remembered Palmer. I had been a few seconds too late to save him.

The next morning, after the healthiest of our crew had unloaded the Dutchman, I overheard Rackham selecting some of the captured seaman to join us, with the hope they would eventually turn pirate and replace those we had lost in the fray.

We pushed off from the smoldering hulk, and then sailed a few leagues to an inlet passage on the coast of Cuba. The wounded pirates, including me, convalesced in our hammocks. Massaquehanna, Cole, Corner, and Howell watered our sloop, hunted for boar, and gathered bananas and coconuts.

The following day we performed a funeral of sorts for the five comrades we had lost.

Before tossing the dead overboard, we wrapped them in netting and chain, and Rackham read a requiem from his journal, a collection of quotes about death.

Rackham spoke of the silver cord being loosed and how though these loyal crewmembers had gone the way of all flesh, their passing was with a difference: they were free to the last.

He recited from the headstone of a Greek thief named Timon. "'Here am I laid, my life of misery done,/Ask not my name, I curse you every one.'"

We exchanged glances and smirked.

I liked Timon's insolent outlook and his defiant sentiments.

"And as Petrarch once said: 'A good death does honor to a whole life.' And I believe that Hood, Roose, Howard, Palmer, and Baker all died knowing they fought like true men."

I frowned at Rackham's interpretation of Petrarch, and his sugaring over our deeds to paint a noble portrait of men who had died merely trying to pillage a ship. There was no worthy causes in our actions. We fought for greed, not glory. They had died justly, not tragically.

"And now good men, we wish you a bold adventure, for indeed that is what death is—a journey into the undiscovered country from whence no traveler returns."

The crew murmured at the good words of death. Some raked their sleeves across their eyes. As I watched the funeral, I was surprised by the pirates' display of emotion and the deeper parts of their characters.

Rackham ended his eulogy with a quote from a Confucian sage: "'Empty your golden glasses to the dregs; life is dark, so is death.' Let's drink up, mates. Our kinsmen wouldn't want us gloomy for long."

The bodies were cast overboard, and the crew drifted away to drink. My wounds throbbed dully, with sharp jolts breaking through from time to time, causing me to wince and moan through the night. I drank heavily to shave the edge off my pain. The next day, Massaquehanna strung a hammock for me on deck. While I languished, I observed the five enslaved mariners holystoning and swabbing our deck.

My eyes kept returning to one man. He had his brown hair in a club, and his clothing was less soiled and worn than the others' garb. The man frequently glanced around the ship, then at sky, and he would close his eyes and take a deep breath. His face looked intelligent. I guessed he was a few years older than me, now nineteen. He started up a conversation with a man beside him. The intensity of his eyes and his animated expressions interested me. I longed to eavesdrop on the conversation. He said something to make the seaman laugh, and I was pleased to note he had nice teeth—a true rarity.

Later that evening while we supped on bowls of rice and fish, I saw him approach Rackham, who had been visiting me in my hammock.

"Permission to speak, sir?"

Rackham turned to appraise him. "Such deference? You must have been a military man."

"Aye, sir. I fought in the infantry and cavalry."

"But not the navy? What is your name again?"

"John Reade."

"What is your request?"

"I wish to hobnob with this pirate crew rather than be enslaved by it," he said with conviction. His stare was intense and steady.

Rackham slapped Reade on the shoulder. "So you wish to throw in with us gentlemen of fortune? I assume you can fight, but do you understand the risks that come with this sweet station of life? The danger of taking a prize? The noose if captured? The marooning if you cross me?"

Reade seemed steeled against these warnings. I liked his stony, sure expression. I also noticed a slight tick under his right eye. He paused. It suggested a keen mind that had surveyed the situation and reached the conclusion that pirating was a fine choice.

"As to hanging, sir, it seems no great hardship compared to the sludge and drudge of this life, for were it not for the gallows, every cowardly fellow would turn pirate and, willy-nilly, so infest the seas that men of courage would starve," said Reade.

Rackham smiled and turned to me. "What do you think of that fine answer?"

Before I could speak, Reade drove on. "If it was my choice, I would not have the punishment of piracy be anything less than death. The fear of the noose will keep us rogues honest by crook or hook," he said.

"A rare find," Rackham said.

"I've been a mariner long enough, working like a loyal dog for a pittance. Give me something above the muck and ruck of this peasant life. Pascal's view was—'Man's condition: Inconstancy, boredom, anxiety.' Perhaps the pirate life could disprove his melancholy sentiments," he said.

Rackham and I listened intently. When Reade finished, Rackham said, "Never in all my days have I heard such a fine bit of commentary on piracy from a man with no experience. Mr. O'Malley, you're my witness. Shall we give this chap a try?"

"Aye, time will tell if he fights as well as he speaks. After all, his crew surrendered. Where were you in the clash?" I said.

Reade stared at me without blinking, seeming to measure my words. "I saw the handwriting on the wall. Why forfeit my life in foolhardy fashion when the end result was obvious?"

I pointed a pistol at Reade. "We'll keep a sharp eye on you, understand?"

"That would probably be wise since I killed two of your crew in the battle. I believe it was Roose and Baker."

I cocked the gun. Reade did not flinch, saying nothing, but he slightly tilted his head and met my stare. Rackham placed his hand on mine and lowered the pistol.

"I will give you an answer in the morning," said Rackham.

"Thank you, sir." He turned and walked away, beginning to whistle.

"Try to get some rest, Anne," Rackham whispered. "I think you need it."

During the long night, peaceful sleep fought with my pulsing wounds. It rather surprised me that my thoughts inclined more often toward Reade than Rackham. I was growing increasingly burdened by Rackham's behavior, particularly after the battle. Yes, he was the captain, but his distance bothered me. Yes, his sharp shooting with the rifle had indubitably assisted us, but we needed every able swordfighter in that fight. Between the Throckmorton debacle, the storm, and this skirmish, I felt a few too many frustrations to contain. Reade, on the other hand, seemed intrepid and articulate. He intrigued me.

The next day, I finally felt well enough to limp twice around the deck. The seaboard breezes and the smell of palms and sand made me feel better. I came upon Reade untangling and repairing some rigging. I tarried a moment.

"Rackham speak with you?"

Reade looked up. "Yes, thank you. I have been accepted—provisionally. Whatever that means. How are your wounds?"

"Healing. Equestrian pursuits are a far cry from the nautical life."

"True. I started out as a foot soldier, but later joined the cavalry."

"And now you're getting your sea legs?"

Reade set aside the lines, stood up, and stretched. He leaned against the taffrail and gazed out on the bay. I stared at his solid, youthful face. He seemed to evoke vitality, and had a secretive sense that drew me.

"I was married. We set up an inn in the Netherlands—the Three Horses—and had a good business. We planned to start a family. But my spouse died, shot to death, and I killed her assailant." He hesitated, sliding his hands along the railing, appearing to study the grains of wood. He looked up. "After the funeral, I burned my inn to the ground. I was lost, empty—full of despair, I suppose. I wandered around the country and ended up in Holland. I needed a new start and the New World seemed like one. I didn't get far before your ship engaged us. Now I am here."

I resisted the desire to touch his shoulder and console his loss. His words stirred me. "How long were you married?"

Reade stayed his gaze on the sea. "Four months. We had some money between us. Before we settled down, we took a trip to Italy and Greece. My spouse loved sculptures and paintings. We saw some of the masterpieces of Michelangelo, Raphael, and Leonardo." Reade's voice grew animated, gesturing as he spoke. "She blushed at King David. I loved the fact it came from a piece of marble that every sculptor in Florence had rejected because of its flaw. Michelangelo transformed it into a crown jewel of Tuscany."

His knowledge and experience piqued me. "What else did you see there?"

"My spouse's favorite was *The Last Supper*. We read that after Leonardo finished it, he called one of his best friends to view the work before he unveiled it to the Sforza family and the Church. His friend praised the mural as his magnum opus, noting that the cup was exquisite, so perfect his eyes kept being drawn to it. Leonardo responded by painting over the cup, much to his friend's chagrin. Then he proclaimed, 'Nothing will detract from my Lord Jesus.'"

"A conviction to be respected."

Reade glanced my way. "My opinion as well. Now my favorite was the *Pietà* by Michelangelo. I was touched by Mary's sorrow at the loss of her beloved son," he said.

He looked out on the bay. "Those paintings and sculptures made me a believer in God. My mind has gone to them many times in my dark hours. But all that seems so far away now."

As I listened to his words, I looked deeply into his green eyes. I savored his voice and vision of art, something I had had very little experience with thus far.

"Not to offend, Reade, but you don't sound like a pirate. You would make a better teacher or preacher."

Reade grinned. "Aye. I suppose I don't. But something I treasured purely and honestly was taken from me. My dream was pilfered—murdered. That modest, sincere path was only a way of crushed hopes and cruel pain for me. I will no longer be a mark; rather I will make a mark on this globe. I plan to cut a new swath, and I will take whatever pleases me without regrets."

"At war with the whole stinking world?" I asked.

"Bloody right."

Chapter XIX

After nine days of recuperation, we prepared to disembark and sail back toward Florida to see what could be had in those waters. Rackham had learned that hostilities between Britain and Spain were rising. Spain was sending an invasion of men-of-war and nearly 2,000 soldiers to the Bahamas, where they would seize all the islands in the West Indies that had slipped from its grasp. Rodgers was receiving increased pressure to stamp out piracy and protect British merchants, but now he was being challenged with thwarting Spain's battle plans as well.

"Rodgers is fighting tooth and nail to retain his position," Rackham told the crew. "I say we assist as his privateer."

We looked at each other bewildered, and then back to Rackham.

"Begging your pardon, Rack," said Harwood. "I thought we despised the man. I thought he hung us out to dry."

"Indeed. He did."

We waited for an explanation, but Rackham let the silence linger.

"Then why would we privateer for his benefit?" Harwood finally asked.

"Because, Noah, we are better with the British in power than the Spanish. The British are hopelessly corrupt, easily bribed, and quite lazy. Afterward, Rodgers will have to be grateful for our humble support. And besides, those warships from Spain will have plenty of supply ships nearby. Those are sure to be easy targets, with bounty of booty to be had."

Rackham's dramatic approach soon convinced every crewmember to support him. He was masterful in his use of irony and logic. I had been waiting for the opportunity to speak candidly about his recent actions. I had overheard grumbling concerning Rackham's response to the last battle from Fetherston and Harwood, but his well-planned approach seemed to sufficiently lift him up again in the view of the others. Without saying it, his ideas showed the men that Rackham's brains were what kept our crew happy and prosperous, not his sword and musket. Men needed wise leaders who provided vision, and if those leaders were killed in the battle, the vision would perish with them.

That night I slipped into Rackham's cabin and found him writing in his captain's log. He tossed aside the journal and approached me with lusty bravado. I managed to temporarily set aside my misgivings. After all, it had been awhile, and I had amorous needs as well. I did not feel the need to deny myself just because I had problems to resolve with my man. We entwined our bodies, and our passions flowed for an hourglass. Afterward, we drank good port from goblets and enjoyed pieces of dried lamb and sugary biscuits. Rackham began to dream aloud about the plan to pillage the Spanish supply ships that lagged behind the galleons.

"The crew welcomed your plan. It seemed to raise morale," I said.

Rackham cocked his head toward me. "Raise morale?"

"After that hard battle for the Dutchman—nearly all of us were wounded and five were killed."

"I compensated every pirate for his wounds according to the articles of this ship," Rackham replied, his tone shifting. "And in terms of those slain, every one of us knows that piracy is a dangerous business rife with risks, Anne."

Partly because of his offense and defense and partly due to the throb in my legs, where my wounds were still healing, I impulsively counterattacked. I could not seem to control my nerves.

"Yes, but—"

"But?" Rackham stood up.

I unleashed the bile that had been festering in my gut. "Yes, but why didn't you join us in the fight? We were fighting with every drop of our blood, and you just watched us from the safety of the ship."

"I had a fine vantage point to fire the muskets on their crew. And I was risking just as much as you. If you failed, I would be next." Rackham began to pace, his fists clenched.

"If you wanted a sharpshooter, why didn't you keep Dobbin onboard? He's the best marksman we have. We needed your swordsmanship and leadership—"

"Leadership? I was directing the battle—"

"Directing the battle? Why didn't you lead us into the battle?"

Rackham turned away and stared out the cabin window into the darkness. He placed the palm of his right hand on the side of his head and sighed. My stomach was churning, my temples pounding. Rackham turned back to me slowly and folded his arms.

"Perhaps you are not happy here anymore?" he began. The tone of his voice had shifted to a calm, controlled monotone. His face was expressionless. "Perhaps you have forgotten what your role is in this privileged relationship we share."

Touch anyone in the fragile place at the wrong time, and it could spell the destruction of the relationship. His courage and leadership were a delicate membrane, not to be casually questioned. Some words can never be taken back. Even with my limited nineteen-year-old perspective, I realized my hasty, quick-tempered words had brought me to the precipice of our union and left me teetering on the edge.

"Perhaps you need to remember the secret we share and the precarious perch you sit on aboard this ship. How truly horrible it would be if it was revealed," he said without emotion. "Bridle your tongue if you know what's good for you."

"Jack, I..." I faltered, stunned. I felt stripped naked. The threatening pose he struck sent me reeling into a place I had not been for a long while: terror. Though I had questions, I was not ready to give up Rackham and the ways of the pirate life. The prospect of being repeatedly raped and then cast aside, even marooned, filled me with an unreasoning fear. Thus I did something I had promised myself I would never do, performed an act I would find repugnant in any other soul. My reaction left me ashamed and disgraced. I fell to my knees and pleaded for his forgiveness, weeping as I repeated my words, not for my sorrow but because of my fear of reprisal. Even as I spoke, I was disgusted with myself. I sobbed over my own cowardice, a set of manacles too strong for me to fracture.

Rackham lifted me up and held me. He patted me on the back and reassured me that all was forgiven and forgotten. He gave me a silk handkerchief to daub my eyes and wipe my nose. I thanked him for his understanding and left the cabin. I walked to the taffrail and stared out at the starry host. I fought the impulse to dive overboard and swim blindly away. My shame penetrated deeply. In this silent space I began to wonder whether perhaps rape was less demeaning than my pathetic display. I determined I would pursue a course of freedom from Rackham's shackles and the humiliation I would continually endure by letting his threat keep me locked away. I decided to never do what I had done again. Ever.

Chapter XX

A couple of days later we engaged three fishing boats and robbed them of their lines and food stores, and a portion of their sea turtle catch. It was a pitiful haul. Stealing from the rich I could justify, but pilfering from the impoverished seemed wretched. On another day we snuck up on a Portuguese brigantine at dawn, and then later that afternoon we gave chase to a French Guineaman in full sail. As we sped even with the vessel, they gave us an ill-timed broadside. We answered with a broadside of our own, which splintered one of their masts. Harwood, at the swivel gun, fired two more rounds at the weakened mast and it collapsed onto the deck, dashing men with falling spars, sheets, and riggings. We pulled alongside and softened the crew's fight with a fusillade of grapeshot and canister. Swinging across, we landed aboard their deck and clashed swords with only a few resisters.

It was a brief fight, but I noticed that Reade pounced into the hottest part of the skirmish. As we emptied the schooner's stores of goods, I overheard Reade bemoaning the lack of spine in the French, saying they had no stomach for the life and death struggle.

"I don't long for rapine and the ruin of my foes. I pine for the shank and flank of bloody battle with worthy nemeses to honor and respect," Reade said. "This is pell-mell piracy, and it gives me bitter bile."

Something about his spirit continued to draw me. His words were raw, yet roughshod poetic. I watched him often—the angular form of his body and the lean, tawny muscles of his arms. I liked his confidence and his hunger for action. I began to arrange my time over the next few days to work near Reade. We spoke of many things. I told Reade about my life as a boy in Cork, Ireland, our family's voyage to Charles Towne, and my decision to pursue the pirate life. I told him about Edward and how I missed his mirth, wisdom, and wit.

He told me of his military service. At sixteen, Reade had lied about his age and joined the military to escape the squalid conditions of life in London. While he experienced battle, most of his experience revolved around mundane exercises of marching and drilling. The pay was low, the food poor, the rules rigid, and the discipline austere. Everything Reade told me had a vague quality to it. I asked whether his name was an irony or a symbol. He concurred that he was inclined to the written word. As I listened to him, I watched the movements of his lips, the gentle lift of his cheekbones when he spoke, and the emerald glitter of his eyes. I liked the lilting cadence of the words that spilled from his mouth, edged with a splash of cockney accent.

I even watched him urinate off the ledge at the stern. His back was to me, but I observed the stream. My mind flitted around the improbable. Rackham, Cole, and Massaquehanna knew my gender. Could I dare reveal it to a fourth man and still hope to conceal my identity from the rest? The thought was foolhardy and I decided to pluck it from my mind. And yet whenever his presence brushed my eyes, my heart trilled.

Ever since our row, conversation between Rackham and I had remained strained, and our lovemaking was stale and mundane, absent of poetry and passion. When I asked him searching questions, his face grew stony and his attitude impatient. He reached for the bottle more frequently and his books less often. It did not help that the humidity and heat had grown worse, aggravating our tempers. Some of the crew wrestled with illness, which was marked by high fever, shaking chills, vomiting spells, and drumming headaches. It wore on the morale, so Rackham told Fetherston to find a quiet inlet off a remote island and lower anchor. Rackham's cure for our ailments was to order bowls of sangaree and ale passed around, but drunkenness only exacerbated his brooding and our symptoms.

During one of my boring rendezvous with Rackham, I let my mind drift to Reade. As I kissed Rackham, I became lost in a daydream—that his lips, his hands, his body were Reade's. I grew more passionate and nearly whispered his name but caught myself, remembered who I was with, and returned to our tiresome routine.

After a few days the crew was well enough to sail for Negril Point, off the coast of Jamaica, to make trades with our goods and procure medicines, ointments, potions, and hogsheads of spirits to imbibe. Rackham also had a list of fermented concoctions such as rum fustian, flipp, and sangaree. During our brief stay he received a parcel reporting on Rodgers' increase of royal men-of-war patrolling the West Indies for pirate ships and Spanish galleons. Rackham ordered late night watches as a precaution. The crew groaned when our beloved captain ordered all of us to sign up in pairs to keep each other awake during the long nights.

Some might call it pure luck, but I call it providence, for my name was paired with Reade's.

During our last watch, I asked Reade about his deceased spouse, hoping he would wax reminiscent again. He then related a story of legendary British romance that captured the breadth and depth of his love for his spouse.

* * * *

We were sitting against the mast repairing sails under candlelight during the late night watch. All was quiet. We shared a bottle of sangaree and snacked on fried dough glazed with sugar.

"Cromwell governed the British throne," Reade began, "and he was a taskmaster. He issued a fiat stating that any soldier missing curfew would be hanged the next day at the ringing of the curfew bell."

"Does make a statement with poetic justice," I said.

Reade drew the thread and needle through a sail and deftly tied a knot. "One drafted soldier was so smitten over his new bride of a mere week that he gambled and snuck out to taste the sweetness of her kiss."

"And a bit more I'm sure."

"And a fine time they were having until they were caught."

"I hope they let them finish?" I took a draught of the liquor.

"I don't know that for sure, but Cromwell decided to make an example of him and have him hanged the next night. The soldier's wife was frantic. She sought out Cromwell on bended knee and pleaded for his mercy. But Cromwell was as constant as the Northern Star."

"I believe that was Julius Caesar? I know my Shakespeare."

"Ensnared," Reade said with a grin. "A mere turn of phrase. Cromwell told the spouse that her husband's fate was sealed. So what does the wife do?"

I raised the bottle to Reade. "Find another fish in the deep blue sea?"

"A hopeless cynic, O'Malley. Where's your romantic spirit? The woman was so in love with her man, she climbed the bell tower of the cathedral and waited. Just as curfew approached, she leaped onto the clapper of the bell and clung to it like a viper. They began to ring the bell. It slammed her back and forth, but her body muffled the chime."

I shook my head. "Such agony and suffering for a man? And no guarantees her plan would even work?"

"'But love is blind and lovers cannot see the pretty follies that they themselves commit.' There's your Shakespeare. But I prefer Dryden: 'Love's a noble madness.'"

As I punctured the needle through the sheet, I caught the point against my wrist. I licked at the blood and grumbled a few curses, but was anxious to hear how the story would end. "What happened next?"

"Confused, they rang the bell harder. The pounding back and forth against the sides of the bell was too much for her. She started to lose her grip and she knew all was lost. So she screamed her husband's name one last time, hoping it would be the last voice he'd hear before he swung.

"Her cry echoed through the cathedral walls and right into the public square. Cromwell heard her and ordered the bell ringer to cease. He climbed the stairs and found her broken, bruised, and bleeding. And crusty, ornery old Cromwell was so moved by her loving sacrifice that he freed the soldier, proclaimed curfew would not ring that night, and ordered the soldier to carry his saintly wife home and tend her wounds because she had proven more brave than any of his soldiers."

I traced the edge of my bottle. "Ennobling tale."

"Aye, and whenever my mate and I were at odds, she'd ask me if I'd leap on a clapper of a bell to save her life." Reade's mirth drained from his face. "I always said, 'in a twinkling of an eye, my love.' Indeed, her death came to me like a thief in the night."

Reade paused, fighting tears. The only sounds were the creaking of the timbers and water lapping against the hull. He pushed the sail away, stood up, and wandered aimlessly across the deck.

I sighed and thought, "Oh, Reade, what treasure you are—through and through."

* * * *

I looked forward to our next watch. Hours before, I snuck overboard, waylaid a cutter, and rowed to shore. I followed a footpath to a fresh stream, bathed, and washed my clothes in the cool shadows of a freshwater pool. I shrugged off any thoughts of Rackham. His poetry and attentive ear now seemed like distant memories. We weren't married, and probably never would be. A sea rover's life was brief, as evanescent as the trade winds and currents. Make much of time, coy mistress, I told myself. One does not live for long. I delved into my imagination, seeing my lips pressed against Reade's and my body caught up in his embrace as my heart became hypnotized by his eloquence. I desired to heal his loneliness, to encourage him to rediscover the vast opportunities life had to offer. Returning to the ship, I found a few more of the crew shaking off the last vestiges of fever and making preparations to set sail the next day.

About an hourglass after the witching time of night, everybody had fallen asleep. Reade was at the stern relieving himself. I milled on the foredeck and drank from a bottle of rum, looking out at the infinity of stars, their glittering points opaque through the hazy mists. A southwesterly breeze chilled me. I listened to the gentle tapping of the rigging against the mast and the chirps and caws of nocturnal birds inland. Between my teeth I crunched mint leaves I had snatched from Rackham's cabin during our last meeting. I had been plotting a daring exploit. When I heard Reade's footfalls approach, I held my breath and took another drink, trying to quiet my nerves.

"'Ello, wot 'ave we 'ere?" Reade said, imitating a heavy accent. "Eez ye stewin' 'bout a bloody smuggler's watch? Wot say we swap shuteye so's to miss a buggerin' floggin' from the Rack Man?"

I laughed and joined his game. "Arrgghh, and shiver me timbers. Aye, Johnny boy, never 'ad a whippin', never 'ope to. Seen a one: fool's back wus like a side o' raw beef. Poor scurvy dawg, it put his tail danglin' b'tween his legs."

"Me druther swabbie the deck with me poxy tongue, sirrah."

"Aye, me druther scrape ye 'ull wit' me brittlin' teeth, milord."

"Knaves 'n' scamps 'n' scullions we be. O'Malley, kowtowing to yer glorious majesty."

"Just vermin 'n' maggots 'n' leeches, we be, payin' 'omage and givin' lip service to the powers that be."

We cackled and clasped hands. In the pale glow of a lantern, I studied Reade's leather jerkin and kerchief tied to his head. My stomach churned at the thought of revealing myself to him, and yet that was my scheme this night. We talked about Rackham's plan to set sail tomorrow and return to New Providence to trade for supplies and find more hands. On the way, Reade hoped to see some real action.

"Aye, me yen for a wild, fiery fray, O'Malley," he said.

"Give a toast to the Spanish Main and Barbary coast." I offered the bottle to Reade.

I shifted accent to my own. "It's a liberating life, the pirate way, but at times a lonely one, too."

"Aye, 'specially docked in a lonely cove and half the crew fighting a pox."

"But even in the high times, there's an emptiness in the soul that longs for love."

"I've heard New Providence can fulfill any desire a man may have."

"Skin-deep desires, but our passions pass and our souls languish." I took another drink and nudged a bit closer to Reade. The gleam of the lantern illumined his face. "I'm accused of excessive self-examination. I only share it with you because I see a kindness in your eyes. I hear soul-searching in your words."

Reade seemed to appraise me for several moments, and then turned his gaze back to the foggy line on the horizon. "We have shared some fine conversations, O'Malley. You are a good mate."

I lifted the bottle and swallowed several times. I offered the bottle to Reade but he refused it. "John, in this short span of time, I've grown fond of you."

Reade seemed to flinch at these words and shifted a bit.

I regretted moving so swiftly. There may be truth in wine, but there was foolishness in rum. Before I could soften my words, Reade stood up and said, "Now, look, O'Malley, you're a fine pirate, and I am honored to fight beside you, but let me be clear: my melancholy and loneliness are not so heavy that I would tack to the other side of human desire."

I bit at my lips. This wasn't going well. I grimaced at the confusion and foolishness of the whole plot I had conjured up. The hint-laced, gradual approach proved fruitless, a comedy of errors. I needed to be direct or this would never succeed.

"People aren't always what you pigeonhole them to be."

Reade sat back down. "Aye, when Rackham shanghaied me, he took me for a mere slave, but I tricked him in many ways."

Our conversation was headed nowhere near my intended goal. I emptied the bottle. Caprice possessed me. The spirit of liquor and the magic of the moonlight carried me over the threshold of reason. I stood up and turned away from Reade. I had already removed the linen wrap from around my breasts. Slowly unbuttoning my shirt to my waist, I ran my hands down the seams, pulling them slightly aside. I shifted toward the light of the lantern to illuminate my breasts.

I whispered, "Aye, John, tricked bow to stern."

Reade just stared at me. His eyes drifted downward and back up, and then snapped back to my bosom. I inhaled deeply, raised my shoulders, and arched my back. Reade blinked, stood up, and raised a hand to his mouth.

I stood and stepped toward Reade confidently.

Reade pointed and began to chuckle, not one of pleased surprise, but a laughter that embarrassed me.

I felt blood rush to my face as Reade leaned against the mast, now laughing uncontrollably.

I covered myself in shame and anger, fully sober. Not only did I feel spurned, but now my secret would spread like a woodland fire. "Shh…quit your raving!"

Reade raised his hand to calm my gall, but his shrill fit dragged on. He placed both hands over his mouth, trying to stifle himself.

"If you don't quit your snorting, so help me I'll cut your gullet out right now." I whipped out a knife and pointed it at Reade. Either him or me, I thought.

"Please, just another moment," Reade said, his voice softening.

Then he shocked me with the most unpredictable thing I could have imagined.

"A woman, too," Reade said, fumbling with her buttons, removing the fabric inside her shirt, and fully revealing her breasts. She raised her arms to the cool night sky. "Freedom. It does feel good to be a woman and enjoy the soft breezes on your breasts. Join me?"

I put away my knife and began to giggle at the sheer implausibility of it all. "My name's Mary Reade. Cute trick, one I've used myself in the military. Sorry I laughed. I just didn't conceive the possibility there could be another…"

"Nor I. My real name is Anne Bonney."

"The rumormongers said you were Rackham's dutiful cabin boy."

"A masquerade we've allowed, though as of late, I believe he sees me more as a Medusa than a mistress," I said.

"Grown weary of Rackham? He strikes me as a randy dandy."

"He is that. And I fear the weather is beginning to shift in our liaison. You were my only prospect on ship; however, I could sorely use a friend with common…"

"Experiences? Women disguised as men, deceiving a band of cutthroats?"

"I might add searching for true love, but otherwise that covers it."

Mary stretched out her hand. I took it and gave it a bit of a squeeze.

"Anne and Mary, piratesses of the high seas/Disguised by day, unveiled by night/Our lives like the untamed breeze,/Intrepid to danger like men we fight," Mary said, off the cuff.

"A poetic piratess. I've been dubbed a philosophic one."

"Calls for toast!" said Mary.

We lifted our bottles and clinked them together.

"To the wind and the sea/Where our spirits soar free!" Mary shouted.

"You could add bosoms to that," I said.

"Philosophical, you said? I'm intrigued. Please tell me all about your life up to this most ironic point."

We talked through the watch. First and foremost, I made Mary show me how she made her urination look like a man's. Mary showed me a tube bent in such a way as to funnel the urine and make it appear like a man from behind.

"I dreamed it up while in the infantry," she said.

I shared my story in detail and Mary asked many questions about my mother and father, Edward, and my husband James. It was so good to have female companionship. Later in the day we whispered more of our histories out of earshot from the crew while we mended sails and untangled lines. We also helped caulk the seams with pieces of mangrove and canvas. Our laughter turned a few heads. We ate together, and I set up my hammock next to Mary's that next night. I knew it would draw attention, but my frustration with Rackham propelled me to cast aside all caution. I caught Rackham leering at me with jealousy as he entered his quarters.

Mary's story fascinated me. Rackham's now bored me.

Chapter XXI

Mary told me her story while we holystoned the stern of the deck during the cool of morning tide.

Mary's mother had wedded a sailor who worked on whaling vessels. His voyages would keep him away for years at a time. They had a six-month-old son named Jacob when he set off on a new passage. Mary's mother grew lonely in Bristol waiting for her husband to return from the sea. She took a lover, and in her carelessness became pregnant. As each month passed, her anxiety grew, along with her belly.

"She birthed me, and one month later her husband's ship was reported lost in a squall. My mother hid me away when his parents came for the funeral. They promised to support their grandson with one crown a week," said Mary, scraping and sanding the planks.

They sent the funds religiously, she said, but when her half-brother, Jacob, contracted Rubella and died at two years of age, her mother's reason had slipped. Her lover left her in a lurch, and she feared being financially cut off by her in-laws, reduced to begging or whoring to pay bills and support Mary. Debtors' prison hung like the sword of Damocles over her head. One day she received a letter notifying her that her in-laws were intending to visit.

"Only fifteen months separated me from my dead brother, and my grandparents hadn't visited in five years," Mary said. "My mother dressed me as a boy, sheared my hair, and versed me on what to say and do. I'll never forget what she said when I asked her why I had to act like a boy. 'If you don't, we will be cast out of our home and into the gutter. We'll either freeze or starve to death. If you can't fool them, we'll die horrible deaths.'"

"A heavy burden to bear," I said.

"But my grandparents were duped by our little charade. After they left I thought I could go back to being what I am, but my mother sank deeper into despair. Other cavaliers warmed my mother's bed briefly and robbed her bit by bit of her money, her dignity, and her sanity.

"One day she burned all my girl clothes and forced me to wear my brother's. She said it was a man's world and that women were beasts of burden, ever cursed to be the recipients of man's folly, vice, and control. I would be a boy from that day forward. When I rebelled, she cowed me with a switch. Even at seven years of age, I could see she was on a path to bedlam."

As the years passed, Mary said she practiced speaking in a coarser voice and played among the boys. She learned to lash out in midsentence, kick for the crotch, gouge for the eyes, and handle a blade. Her mother continued to descend into a well of madness. During the ensuing years, Mary had to fend for herself and care for her unstable mother, who only seemed to descend further into a pit of despondency.

"One night in my twelfth year, my mother harangued and harassed me to the breaking point. I called her a raving lunatic, and she came at me with her belt. I decided then and there that I would take this no more. I grabbed her hair and slapped her again and again until she crumpled into a heap. I packed my belongings to the sound of her crazed railings and snuck out of the house and ran away."

Mary told me of an array of jobs she had worked before joining the British military. Her disguise intact, she worked as a footboy for a French aristocrat in London. But her ennui was so great she decided to slip away one day and enlist as a powder monkey on a royal man-of-war, hauling gunpowder and cannon balls to the sailors. She grew bored and traveled to Flanders, where she signed on with an infantry regiment. She learned to fight with blunderbuss, musket, bayonet, and sword.

On the battlefields, she saw so many men die that her loss of innocence became complete. The roar of cannon fire, the trilling screams of agony, the stifling smoke of gunpowder, the severed limbs, and the bodies piled high—all haunted her. She started out in the infantry but eventually took a position with the cavalry, even advanced to an officer, and slowly fell in love with her tent mate—John Reade.

Mary laughed as she told this part of the story. "One night I bared my breasts to him, but I daresay the result was a far cry different from the reaction I gave you the other night. The poor man was infernally relieved. He hesitantly admitted he had been attracted to me before I had revealed my gender, but was disturbed and repulsed by his feelings. Now he was game for immediate consummation."

"Typical man," I said.

"But I was a chaste woman with a treasure I would grant only to my beloved husband. I wouldn't let him bed me until he wedded me. We shocked the whole cavalry company. What I had done was against the law, but we had been through so much together that they accepted me with respect. They pooled together their money and bought me a wedding gown."

Her story was wonderful. I was proud of Mary and her bravery in the face of such adversity. I had never felt such a bond of friendship with another woman. Hers had been a gentleman's world among women. Talking with Mary made me feel larger than life itself, filled with an indescribable verve, and much less lonely. I wondered whether our veins pumped greatness similar to that of women such as Queen Anne and Queen Mary—women whose sensibilities had catapulted them to live boldly and prosper the coffers of their country. Though pragmatic souls, they were not without motherly sensitivity and romantic passion. They possessed the wit of a vixen, the vim of a maven, and the vigor of a monarch. Yes, I stood tall as I thought of them and felt fortunate to have found a friend to dream with and confide in.

The supper bell interrupted Mary's story. We considered skipping until we saw smoke emit from the sloop's stove and smelled an appetizing aroma. The cook, with the help of Thomas, had assembled a fine turtle stew. After filling our plates, we snuck down to a quiet place in the hold.

"I was a very merry Mary with my John. We purchased an inn near the castle of Breda in the Netherlands. It was such a beautiful place. It matched our new love. We planned to start a family." Mary shook her head and fell into a morose stupor. I laid a hand on her shoulder.

"A bloody aristocrat," she said, "stabled his horse and rented a room from us. At supper he invited me to his bed. I tried to shrug off his advances and let him down easily, but he was insulted and became rude. He grabbed at me and I pushed him away. John stepped in and suddenly they were at each other's throats. They screamed oaths and set up a duel. I was in shock and I pleaded with John to abandon this foolish spectacle, but a man's pride is as set as the sun rising every morning."

I pulled out my bandana and massaged my perspiring scalp. The midday humidity drained and drenched me. "This I know."

"As they took their ten paces, I was sure John's military training would decide this silly contest. They turned and fired. The aristocrat felled my husband with his shot. My John clutched his chest and dropped to the ground. As I ran to him, he said, 'So much love cut short before its proper time.' I was left reeling, holding my husband, rocking him like a child and trying to understand this futile waste of our lives. Then that damned aristocrat clapped me on the shoulder and began to tear at my dress.

"'I'll have you now, you slutty wench. Right beside your husband's ghostly gaze,' he said, grabbing my hair and yanking me to the ground." Mary's voice turned bitter. "I pulled a pistol from my dress and potted him in the gut. He fell down and stared at his wound. I dragged my husband's corpse into the inn and closed shop. Then I came back for that whimpering rapscallion. I made sure he suffered long into the night."

Mary fiddled with the pile of netting we reclined on. "I knew I'd be hanged for killing royalty. My dreams were murdered. I needed to escape my horror. So I burned the inn to the ground with my dear husband and that swine inside. I dressed in male clothing again and traveled to Bristol. I looked for my mother, but she was chained to a post in Bedlam, fit and seasoned for a ship of fools. I took on that Dutch schooner and sailed away from Europe for good, not knowing what lay ahead."

Mary stood up. "I couldn't imagine having dreams or hopes again. I was considering taking my own life when suddenly you attacked us. I was born and raised to fight, so I acted on instinct. But when I could see your crew would carry the day, I surrendered. I figured, why not see where this leads? So I took my fate into my own hands and joined your ship, to be a bane to rich merchants on the high seas and live as I bloody well please."

"And you got more than you bargained for?" I said.

"In spades." She considered. "You're helping me, Anne, giving me reason to lift myself out of my hammock and see what this day holds."

I reached out and she took my hand. "Pirate mates?"

Mary nodded. "This calls for an oath or a rite of some kind."

Before I could speak, we heard the hatch door open above us. The sound of boots tapping on the timbers and the sound of a sword pulled from a scabbard prompted us to rise and prepare for danger. Had we been overheard?

Rackham appeared from the dappled shadows, his face red and taut—somehow more handsome for it.

Chapter XXII

"Play me for the cuckold, will you?" Rackham pointed the sword at me. "You'll pay dearly, sweet. But first I must deal with this mate who dares give me horns." Rackham rent the air with his sword. "En garde."

Mary backed up, reached for her sword, and poised for Rackham's onslaught.

I stepped between them and raised my hands. "You don't know the circumstances, Jack."

"Know? I know you were quick to lift your skirts for me. Adultery is your way, but I'm not as understanding as your husband."

Mary and Rackham circled the cramped, dark hold. Rackham lunged and Mary parried the thrust, and then riposted. Their swords chimed and sparked in the shadows.

"Get out of the way, Anne," snapped Rackham. "I don't want to hurt you—yet."

"Jack, listen. Please."

The two clashed swords again. Rackham cut a bit of fabric from Mary's shirt. "The sharks will devour your corpse, and the crabs will gnaw at your bones tonight."

"Captain, I have no squabble with you," Mary said, continuing to move with Rackham. "But if you mean to force this to an end, I am game for you."

I could see the rage in Rackham's eyes, an intensity I had not seen in a great while. Oddly, it thrilled me. I had been transformed into an object of maddening jealousy, which made me feel wanton. All my waning infatuation was suddenly stoked afresh for him. I had to make them stop. I knew one would be dead soon.

"Jack, he's not a..."

"No, Anne." Mary said.

I turned to her. "It is the only way. I trust him."

"I don't," she hissed.

"Then trust me. We'll watch out for each other."

Mary said nothing. Rackham squinted at us and strained to hear our exchange, and then shook his head, cursed, and lunged forward. Mary dodged the attack and slashed, slicing a ribbon across his sleeve.

"Jack, he's a she. I mean, she's a woman too."

Rackham blinked, and then seemed to flinch. His mouth opened but no words came out. He backed up and lowered his blade a bit. "A woman?" He shook his head. "You lie." He raised the sword again and stepped forward.

I stepped toward him. "I've fooled many; why couldn't she?"

Rackham's eyes moved up and down Mary's body. He shook his head. "I fear I'm the doubting Thomas," he said, keeping the blade directed at her. "A bit of proof will be required."

I turned to Mary, searching her eyes.

"I'm not lowering my sword to get run through," she said, her teeth clenched. "Nor will I let my body be the object of his entertainment."

"Jack, she's my friend, and she can fight. She's proven that. Will you keep the secret? I've always been true to you. Please."

Rackham glanced back and forth between Mary and me. He lowered his sword slowly and opened the palm of his left hand. "A moot point if she's not a woman."

"Promise first," I said.

"No. Proof first."

I stepped to Mary's side and whispered, "Give me your sword. If he breaks my trust, hell will hath no fury."

Mary paused, staring at Rackham the entire time. She slowly handed her sword to me. She opened her shirt, loosened her bindings, and revealed herself for a quick moment.

Rackham shook his head and chuckled. He sat down on a barrel and leaned his sword against it. He then winked at me. "No, never seen a man look quite like that. Not one, but two Amazons onboard my ship. Truly remarkable."

"Now you promise to keep our secret. Let me tell you that one of us might be vulnerable, but the two of us will cut your crew in half."

"Female versions of Jonathon and David—Damon and Pythias. Touching. Perhaps she would visit me sometime while you are contending with your menses," he said playfully.

My blood boiled. I wanted nothing less than to run him through the loins and twist the blade over and over. But instead I arched my brow, crinkled my nose, and smiled. "Now, Jack, fidelity must be practiced if we are going to keep our passion a fiery foundry. And besides, tonight I have something new planned which will make you never want any other woman but me."

Rackham lifted his head and looked in my eyes, and then caught his breath and swallowed. Men, I thought: so simple in their desires, so easy to control. "Tonight it is. What's your real name?"

"Mary."

"After our wonderful queen. Bloody Mary, I suppose?"

"Aye. It may fit, piratically speaking."

"I'll expect you to fight and work like any man onboard. Presently, it's in my best interest since I'm abysmally short of hands."

I ambled toward Rackham, putting a bawdy sway in my walk. "Now, Jack, I request you wash up a bit before I visit your quarters later this evening."

Rackham was like a child before a plate of sweets. I would have to deal later with any designs he might be conjuring over Mary. He walked out and I glanced at Mary.

"You would have killed him, wouldn't you?"

I gave Mary the sword and she sheathed it. "I suppose if pressed to it. I still may have to, if he doesn't behave himself."

Mary reached up and squeezed my shoulder. "Nothing like taking a leap on the clapper of a bell, aye?"

"Aye, I would do it for you. Not sure about him."

"Well, he is just a man."

"Yes, if I married him, I would be marrying beneath me. Of course, all women do," I said.

"In truth."

I hugged Mary. The warmth of the moment filled my heart with a rush of emotion. Mine had been largely a world of men, where the tension of intimacy seemed to complicate matters. Edward had been like a caring father, but here, for the first time I stood beside a peer, a mate—a friend to count on. Jonathon and David? Damon and Pythias? I liked the allusions. I knew I would be the most loyal of friends. I pledged in my heart to support her in all things.

"Now, Mary, I do have a special favor to ask of you."

Mary's expression grew serious. "Anything."

"Well, you were married. I promised Jack a very special night. I need some new dalliance. Do you carry any secrets?"

"If memory serves, a few in those arts. We'll see if they are new for you." Mary sat down and giggled. "I haven't had a talk like this ever. Let's see…"

I plopped myself down and gave her my full attention.

Chapter XXIII

That night, flaunting a few new enchantments, Rackham and I reconciled our relationship, rekindled our passion, healed some wounds, and left a few others to fester. His jealousy over my affections and his willingness to lay his life on the line for me had reignited my desire for him. That night our phoenix emerged from its ashes.

Afterward, I answered some questions Rackham asked about Mary's life. I told him how grateful I was for a female friend, how we could understand each other so well.

"I know I do not deserve it, but I am thankful to God for this gift."

Rackham rubbed my shoulders. "And for me too?" His voice quivered with another kind of jealousy.

I controlled my voice to preserve his pride. "Needless to say."

He worked his fingers down my spine. "And that is all there is to this, right? A friendship."

Shutting my eyes and holding my breath for a moment, I tried to control my frustration. How deep did his insecurity go? There is so much a woman must keep hidden to preserve her man's tender illusions of irresistibility while at the same time protecting her own precarious security. I gritted my teeth to hold back the mockery and sarcasm caroming on the tip of my tongue. "Jack, it is sisterhood, not Sapphoism."

He laughed to cloak his insecurity. "Of course, my Anne. I was merely jesting."

I craned my neck. "But while we are on the matter, just what was your meaning, suggesting Mary visit you when I am contending with my menses?"

Rackham paused in his massage, and then patted me reassuringly on the back. "Another joke, a tease—pure and simple. Anne, please don't lose your sense of humor. It is one of the more attractive things about you."

Another smokescreen? I could see right through his cover-up and counterattack. He was testing the waters, hoping for an unexpected boon.

I decided to change the subject. "We will reach New Providence tomorrow?"

"In about two days if the weather holds," Rackham said, his voice tinged with relief. "It has been nearly ten months since we last moored there. Do you worry your husband will still be there a-spying?" He got up and poured himself a glass of claret.

"No. But it would be unsettling to see him." I tried to picture my jilted husband. I had trouble recalling his eyes, his face, or the sound of his voice. "I would hate to have to kill him."

"Well, now you will have two friends by your side."

* * * *

It took three weeks before our sloop reached Nassau harbor. First we came upon six men clinging to barrels on the sea. They were near death for lack of water, their faces blistered by the sun and their voices frail. Sharks circled them. We lowered a longboat and pulled them from the water. Two died that night, but the other four recovered. We learned that the mast of their sloop had been damaged in a storm. As they floundered, a British man-of-war had encountered them.

"They saw our captain, Robert Griffin, and knew him to be a pirate. Didn't even ask for our surrender. Asked us a couple questions, read us a verdict, and then just blew us out of the water and left us to die," said one of the survivors. His name was Alexander.

Between sips of water and slurps of soup, he said, "Twelve of us survived the cannonading. The sharks took half of our number. They had just finished off Mason when you came and rescued us."

The story had visible effect on Rackham. "No quarter offered?"

Alexander choked on the soup and wiped his chapped lips. "They said they had orders—to destroy or capture. They preferred destroying us. Said the noose was too good for the likes of us. You saved our bacon, captain. We're indebted."

Rackham walked away without further word.

Three of the pirates said they wished to join us. The other said he was done buccaneering and wanted only to be dropped off at New Providence. Alexander, Watkins, and Hoff joined our crew.

Two days later we spotted a Spanish merchant vessel. It proved a particularly harrowing experience. Harwood spotted it from the topgallant and issued the call. Rackham ordered us to lay on more sail. Our sloop heeled and we sped forward, slicing through the waves, briny wash blasting the deck. I remember looking back at Rackham, dressed in his calico waistcoat and a new black hat with a fresh plume. The wind whipped about his long brown hair that flowed below his shoulders. He was as suave as ever. He observed the small merchant galliot through his spyglass.

"No mounted guns. Her defense is her speed, but she's weighed down. We should catch her in a day, two at most."

"Raise a Portuguese flag?" asked Corner.

"No, the Spanish are skittish, and rightfully so with most of the world at war against them," said Rackham.

He ordered the gunners to lift the ports and fit the cannons out with balled chain and iron pieces. I helped fill hollowed-out coconuts with partridge shot and bits of lead. As the open water roughened, our bow pounded against the white combers and lurched over the swells. The winds whipped through the riggings, slapping them against the mast.

"Quartermaster, pass around the rum for a few swigs," Rackham yelled to Corner. "It appears a fine prize." He knelt on the bowsprit and patted the figurehead for luck. "All right, boys, let's look alive and fight with pride! Remember the cardinal rule: no prey, no pay, but a cut of the booty today!"

We marauders cheered and raised our weapons, hot for battle. Near the day's end, half the crew climbed the ratlines and sang a ditty: "Wind and sea and pirate booty/There's no sweeter life for me..."

As we drew alongside, we screamed vile threats and raised our swords. The galliot began to lower its sails.

"Give them a broadside for daring to run," shouted Rackham.

I looked over at Rackham, shocked at his order. Wouldn't such an act make them figure they had nothing to lose, that the die was cast, so why not fight to the end? Rackham's decision proved costly in blood.

Our gunners let hurl chain and ball. The blast snapped the smaller mast, and the falling lines tangled up the Spanish crew as they scrambled for positions amidst the chaos. In response, the Spaniards raised their guns and began firing on us. Mary and I, and four others, heaved grappling irons. Two fell short, but four hooked to the rails. When two of the galliot's crew tried to hack the lines, Dobbin potted both with a pair of muskets. We tugged at the ropes with all we had to draw the ships together. Led by Massaquehanna and Cole, several pirates crossed over by halyard. Gunfire erupted from the galliot. I saw two of our pirates scream and fall into the water like diving pelicans. One was Cole, the other Watkins, whom we had rescued. Such is this life.

"Drums and pipes!" Rackham yelled. Two of the galley crew, one of them Thomas, pounded out a beat. Two others blew horns. Rackham claimed it was a new way to bolster the confidence of his pirates and create terror in the ships we attacked.

The mariners on the galliot attempted to raise the sails on the second mast even as their crew began jettisoning crates and barrels to lighten the vessel.

"Missiles!" Rackham shouted. Mary and I gathered bows and arrows, set the arrows afire, and shot several at the sails, which bloomed into flame, fed by the swirling winds. Suddenly a keg of gunpowder exploded at the galliot's stern, where most of our men had boarded. The blast propelled them backward. Rackham ordered the second advance, and the rest of us leaped aboard the bow and fired a volley. We sought to box them in. The galliot's crew crouched behind the main mast, debating which direction to attack. They charged our way.

We saw musket flashes and instinctively ducked, but I was stunned to see Harwood and Fetherston fall, gripping at their wounds, gasping and writhing. Mary, Dobbin, Howell, Carty, and I advanced until we could see the glint of steel through the smoke. We engaged the Spaniards with our cutlasses, sparks flying as our swords met. I ran through a seaman and pushed him away, but at the same time saw Hoff being cut down by an enormous Spaniard with a sure sword.

I thought of our rescue of the castaway pirates. Perhaps their fates had already been sealed. We had merely delayed the inevitable for a few days.

The formidable Spaniard, his shoulders broad and his arms brawny, started for Mary. I screamed like a banshee and assaulted him. After matching swords twice, I knew I was in trouble. Each crash of our swords rattled my arm painfully, and the force of his blows pushed me backward. For the first time in all my battles, I realized I had engaged a superior fighter. My eyes darted about for help. I saw in his expressions an unwavering confidence. Every thrust I fended off weakened my arms. He was breaking me down, biding his time for the right opening to finish me off. I slashed wildly. He ducked and I bolted around the bulwark, keeping it between him and me. The concussion of explosions and eruptions of gunfire reverberated in my ears. The Spaniard stalked me around the wall. I struggled to keep my footing on the oily deck, which was strewn with debris.

"I will cut you to ribbons," I screamed. "And skin you to the bone!"

He merely pursued me without a word, and suddenly he sliced me in the leg. I cried out and stumbled, trying to block his sword, but he still managed a slight slit across my belly. I started to topple, knowing this would be my last breath before I felt the hot steel pierce me.

A few weeks ago I would have welcomed death, but it seemed I now had more reason to live. And though I did not feel I had the right, I cried out to God for more time. Just as the Spaniard moved in for the coup de grace, Mary appeared out of the smoke and barreled into him. The two began to battle, slashing and hacking. On one knee, struggling to draw a full breath, I braced myself for an opportunity.

As they shifted and feinted, thrust and parried, the Spaniard finally drew near enough that I lunged forward and swung at the calf of his right leg, slicing at his tendons. He shouted and staggered, but regained his balance and battled on, keeping me in his periphery. Through the haze, I spotted a musket spout and then saw a bloody rupture gush from the Spaniard's throat. He stiffened, dropped his sword, and crumpled to the deck. I looked back through the smoke and saw Rackham lowering his musket. After the tough Spaniard fell, the spirit dissolved from the rest of the Spanish.

I drooped to the deck, but Mary caught me up in her arms.

"Are you badly wounded?"

"No, just dizzy and thirsty."

The fighting had stopped. Massaquehanna and Corner stretched long timbers across the two vessels to form a gangway. Rackham walked across the planks with a regal air, his musket still in hand. The pirates had already begun yanking back the tarpaulin and grating on the hatches, busting open crates and barrels, looking for valuables, and cramming loot into rucksacks.

"Attend to the wounded first, you bloody rogues," Rackham shouted.

Mary gave me a slug of rum. I watched Fetherston and Harwood slowly get up and hobble around the deck, but Alexander remained still. All three, I thought. There's no beating destiny.

Massaquehanna leaned over the railing and stared at the frothy waters. He began to chant. It was a Seminole death song to honor Cole, his brother in chains. I could not understand his language, but the depth of sorrow flowing off his lips was unmistakable. As he chanted, he cut himself in the palm and let his blood drip into the ocean.

Mary bandaged my wounds, and slowly I felt my strength return.

"Thank you. He was more than my match."

"I believe mine, too," said Mary. "A shame we couldn't have saved him for our crew. He was a brave man."

Rackham strolled along the deck, studying the rigging and sails. "Excellent work, my hearties." He stopped at Mary and me and knelt down. "How are you holding up?"

"I'll survive."

He looked at me with warm, concerned eyes.

"Thank you," I said. "I suppose you're not such a bad shot in a tight spot, aye?"

"Indeed. Join me in the captain's quarters?"

We accepted the honor. Mary helped me up and we entered. Dobbin, Corner, and Carty had the Spanish captain bound and gagged. A trickle of blood dribbled from his nose, and disheveled gray hair hung down over his beefy face. Rackham strolled around the room, looking over the charts and compass.

He approached the captain. Rackham rested a blade under the captain's chin and lifted his head. He nodded at Dobbin and he yanked the gag out of the captain's mouth. "Foolish to run, and more foolish to fight," Rackham said, "but I don't condemn the attempt. Any caches of silver and gold hidden away?"

The captain glowered back without a word.

Rackham shook his head. "Another bloody hero for King Philip, I see?" Rackham let the blade cut a bit into the captain's flesh. "What's the point, Captain? This isn't a hero's quest. It's only commerce. Why endanger the life of your crew and yourself? Give us the silver and we won't scuttle your ship and strand you in longboats."

The captain grit his teeth. "Your scum won't pollute these waters much longer. I'd rather see you in hell than give you one damned piece of eight." He hawked and spat at Rackham.

I stepped forward and smacked the captain across the face with my pistol. "How dare you insult our captain! Let me mark him?"

The Spanish captain snapped back, "You're nothing but a bedeviled son of a whore!"

I unsheathed my cutlass. A man bolted suddenly from a hidden panel in the cabin, yelled, and fired a pair of muskets at Rackham. One ball struck a desk, and the other split the plume on Rackham's hat. It happened with such speed that nobody moved. When we realized none of us were hurt, we raised our guns and pointed at the now unarmed man enshrouded in smoke. He dropped his guns, cursed his poor aim, closed his eyes, and raised his arms as if crucified—prepared to die.

"Wait," Rackham said.

"Let's kill them both, Rack. String them from the yardarm," Dobbin growled.

"Yes, it must be done," said Rackham, "But let's not deprive ourselves of a bit of fun and frolic." He pointed at the slight man who had leaped from the panel, who looked more like a teacher than a sailor or soldier. "Still, I like your spirit. Suicide missions in the name of honor...they just move my bedeviled soul." He walked up to the man who still had his arms raised, though his eyes were now cracked open. "You are a hardy soul, standing there, waiting to be pummeled with shot, bravely accepting your inevitable demise."

"Permission to hang them from the halyard," said Dobbin. "Or do you wish to tie them to the mast and give them a lashing first, sir?"

Rackham circled the two prisoners, staging a fugitive air of dignity. "No, I believe the savages of the New World have made me appreciate the beautiful rarity of true bravery. The captain we'll maroon for his folly, but a keelhauling is in order for this suicidal mercenary."

Rackham watched with amusement when the man flinched at the sentence. "And if you survive the barnacled hull and the sharks, we'll talk again of your bravery." He headed toward the door. "Carty, Corner, tear the ship apart until you find the silver and gold."

The pain seething in my leg and gut had me feeling mean. I raised my blade to the sailor's face. "Methinks your appearance too comely," I said, laying the blade against his right cheek. He stared back at me without expression.

"My, we are as brave as a chivalrous knight of Camelot, but we'll soon look homely. What's your name, sir?"

"Thomas Deane."

"What is an Englishman doing on a Spanish vessel?" I said.

"Tutor for the new governor's children."

"You picked the wrong side, Mr. Deane, and to misquote the Good Book, the handwriting is on your wall, so set your house in order," I said.

We dragged Deane on deck and bound his legs, shoving him to the bowsprit. "Give him some time to stew on it," said Rackham. "You may want to make peace with your God, Mr. Deane."

We left Deane to stew alone.

Our crew set about plundering the galliot. Massaquehanna, now finished with his Seminole ritual, paced back and forth across the deck, surveying the Spaniards who had surrendered. He slung his tomahawk over his shoulder and studied each carefully.

Mary and I sat down beside Rackham, who was leaning against the anchor hawse. Massaquehanna's shirt was off, and we looked at the tattoos on his arms. Feathers and circles speckled his chest and lightning bolts snaked up his back.

"Massaquehanna, are those decorations or declarations?" Rackham asked.

He lowered the tomahawk, but his eyes continued to sweep across the prisoners. "Battles I have fought. Men I have killed," Massaquehanna said.

"Ah, yes, bravery in battle. The savage virtue. Tell me, I have heard it said of one of the tribes that before the young men are allowed to join a war party, they must cluster tightly around their peers and shoot arrows straight into the air, and then stare into the sky and wait for them to come back down. If they flinch or duck, they are proven cowardly and are unprepared for the ravages of battle. Is that a true custom?"

Massaquehanna nodded his head, and then raised his tomahawk and bashed it over the head of one of the sailors. He stiffened and then buckled to the deck. Wordlessly, Massaquehanna hefted his tomahawk once more and ended the man's life. We stared in shock at the Indian's sudden action.

"Cole's spirit just told me who claimed his life," Massaquehanna said.

Rackham resumed as if nothing had happened. "But haven't some of your youth been killed by this tradition?"

Massaquehanna nodded again. "But their souls strengthen us for the fight; the memory of their bravery is powerful medicine."

Carty gave a holler from the hold. He emerged with a chest. "Enough silver to retire on, Rack," he said.

After looking at the chest of coins, Rackham's mood lifted. He decided to set the captain free and we pushed off, but not before allowing two volunteers to join with us. We also kept Deane. We waited for the galliot to grow quite small in the distance before Rackham called for Deane to be brought topside.

"The time for your keelhauling has come, Mr. Deane," Rackham said, gulping from a demijohn of ale and handing it to me.

Deane stood stoically, whispering "'The Lord is my Shepherd, I shall not want/He maketh me to lie down in green pastures…'"

"I fear the waters will not be still, but they will be deep," I said.

"'Out of the depths, I will cry to You, O Lord, hear my voice,'" Deane quoted.

"Fitting," I said.

The pirates began to cheer as they lifted Deane unto the taffrail at the bow. They let him teeter a moment to consider the waves.

Rackham called to him. "So begins your wet, dark odyssey, Mr. Deane. If you meet any souls on our hull, tell them good luck and that I hope their wet clothes will cool the tongues of perdition's damned for a spell."

"You'll all swing from a noose soon!" Deane shouted.

"Indeed, but pray tell, don't give up the ghost so soon. I've seen a man survive this piratical pastime. Godspeed to you."

Rackham waved his hand and we pushed him overboard. Dobbin slowly pulled the rope along the side of the ship and provided commentary. "Oh, I felt him bounce against the hull. Aye, I believe he may be caught. Captain, the hull needs a good careening. Wait, I feel him struggling. No, no, he's free again."

We followed Dobbin until he reached the end of the ship. Then we pulled on the line until the still body of Deane rose just above the water. We waited for signs of life. Deane jerked, coughed water, and heaved for breath. As he flailed at the rope, spinning himself in tightening circles, we gave him a cheer and hauled him back on deck.

"A first for the *William*...that is, the *Sweet Anne's Revenge*," yelled Fetherston, slapping Deane on the back. "Marvelous. We'll make you an honorary buccaneer, whether you like it or not."

"But someone will have to teach him how to shoot," Rackham shouted. The crew laughed and untied him. Deane slumped and spurted out saltwater.

"You're right fortunate to be breathing, mate," I said to him.

Mary, who had been quiet through this entire ritual, patted him gently on the back. "Damned courageous of you."

"Fetherston, what's the status of the swag on this venture?" Rackham asked, removing his hat and with a disgusted look plucking the broken plume.

"Garment cloth, silk, papyrus, tobacco rolls and ribbon mostly, sir: plateware, tobacco, pimento, foodstuffs, and grog, too. And of course the chest of silver. The men are pleased."

Rackham nodded. "Best advice my old friend Blackbeard ever gave: rogues will not plot mutiny when there's ample liquor onboard and sharp prizes to be won. Keep the company hot, damned hot, and all will go well."

"Well quoted, sir," said Fetherston.

"Now we can arrive at New Providence in royal style. We finally have some serious trading to do."

But before we reached our destination, I had a second brush with death. At dusk, as we sailed windward, our vessel encountered a cool breeze and strong currents with enormous swells. Waves crashed across our decks, but there was really nothing too alarming about it. The wind tasted brackish, though, and the rawness of the humid air disfavored my gut. I vomited once over the edge. Just then a sharp wind gust suddenly snapped the rigging on our mainsail. Our spare was tattered; it needed to be saved.

I jumped on the portside ratline and began clamoring up toward a spar. Others joined me. Between the hot action of the day and my ill stomach, I began to feel dizzy. The wind whipped at me, and I started to lose my grip. I cried out to Massaquehanna, who climbed only a short distance from me, but my voice was swallowed by the wind. I lost my grip and fell backward, weightless. There was a moment of dreamy peace, and then the impact and brisk blast of water jolted me awake. I flailed among the white-crested combers, trying to catch my breath.

Our sloop pitched and raced ahead, leaving me bobbing in its wake. I started to scream, but then turned to prayer. A passage of Scripture surfaced in my thoughts: "All Your breakers and Your waves have swept over me…" Was this my hour? Was I ready to meet God? What would I say to Him? I yearned to repent, but the thought rang hollow. It would be a game, and I knew God searched hearts and sifted words. As the ship grew smaller, I felt the last ounces of my strength slip away. The sounds of the ocean filling my ears beckoned me to deep sleep.

I whispered one last phrase to God, "Please, let me have more time." My eyes closed, and I slipped under the water and felt weightless again.

Something firmly grasped my wrist and my body heaved upward. I had the impression I was ascending heavenward and I gurgled out, "Thank you, Lord, for hearing me."

Dropped onto hard planks, I suddenly felt hard shoves against my stomach and chest, trying to force out the water I had swallowed. I reeled forward, vomiting and coughing and choking for a clear breath. I opened my eyes and saw Massaquehanna and Mary staring at me. I wanted to laugh at the contrast—Massaquehanna's stony expression and Mary's anguished face, but then I lost consciousness.

Chapter XXIV

As we entered New Providence harbor, the saffron sun was rising above the horizon, changing hues and painting the sky roseate and amber. I stood amidships with Mary and Fetherston. It was March of 1720. In three months I would turn twenty. Two near-death experiences the day before had left me philosophic. I knew my prodigality, and I remembered vividly my prayer, but I wasn't sure where to go from here. I wanted God's peace, His favor, and His approval, but I wondered what sanctuary I could find at this point. Could I legitimize my present course? Or did I have to give up all trappings of piracy to be right with the Almighty? A Christian pirate—a paradox or a mere contradiction? Yet my heart still beat for adventure and the freedom to live any way I saw fit. As my conscience seesawed, Fetherston described Nassau Island and New Providence harbor to Mary and me. I tried to distract my thoughts and listened for something new I might learn about this place where my pirate story began.

"The British conquered it but then left because the reefs are too shallow for their men-of-war. It's ideal for the shallow hulls of our sloops, so we took it right back a couple of years later. Then that scalawag Rodgers tried to stamp us out again. He laid siege to this place and trapped about a thousand pirates. Some he hanged, but most he pardoned for privateer work. Then he sailed for Jamaica, and now this place is once again a haven for us rogues—a refuge for rest and reparations, randy recreations, and rum-fueled revelries." He laughed and slapped the palms of his hands repeatedly against the rails.

He pointed out the high coral peaks that surrounded the bay, providing fine lookout posts to warn of approaching enemies or to alert pirates of a tasty prize heading for Cuba, Hispaniola, or Jamaica. Food and fresh water were abundant. Between the fish and sea turtles off the coast and the wild boar, fowl, and fruit inland, the island supported all manner of beauties and beasts.

"Ah, New Providence: a lair of prostitutes and pirates. No laws, no morals. The pirate doesn't dream he will die and go to heaven; he dreams to return to New Providence," mused Rackham, meandering toward us.

All in the eye of the beholder, I thought.

We lowered the main and mizzen sails, released the hawser line, and dropped anchor. The crew lowered our cutters by pulley, and we rowed ashore. A kind of nervousness roiled in my belly. Rackham ordered shifts on the watch, just in case Captain Haman was still marooned here. Rackham, Fetherston, Harwood, Mary, and I walked along the white sand beach, which was sprinkled with pungent tropical flowers. We reached the trading posts, where Mary and I stood back and watched Rackham haggle and hawk deals for food stores, tobacco, liquor, rigging, and canvas sheets. He offered the lace, silk, velvet, oil, skins, and fishing nets we had robbed from merchant ships and fishing boats over the past months. There were a few more permanent buildings on the island since the last time I was here, some constructed against the coral outcroppings and shaded by palms.

Afterward we entered a tavern and found an empty table and chairs. "Glasses of stout and an assortment of cakes," Rackham called.

A motley group of pirates in search of a crew glanced our way. Like us, each carried braces of guns and swords. Each had his own grisly assortment of burns, scars, and tattoos; few of them were completely intact. Most were missing an eye, an ear, an arm, or a leg. Their hair hung in greasy tails and locks or was stuffed under sea-worn hats and bandanas. The place, dimly lit by lanterns, reeked of sweat, bad breath, and mildew. Prostitutes roamed the room. I could hear above us the sounds of bumps, groans, and shame-sharpened laughter—a territory of pleasure for pay. A young woman wearing a tattered dress approached our table with bawdy, inviting movements. She bent over, face to face with Rackham, her breasts amply exposed.

"Greetings, Captain; have a go, my love?"

Rackham grinned. "Haven't seen you before, lass. What's your name?"

"They call me Dulcinea, milord." She reached down and squeezed Rackham's knee, offering a seductive look.

My face flushed. I could feel Mary's glance. Rackham was doing nothing to discourage this whore, so I reached over, grabbed the back of her hair, and pulled Dulcinea toward me. "Listen, you poxy doxie, Captain Rackham doesn't want diseases from a sordid nag like you. Go find another Don Quixote."

I shoved her backward, and she fell on her backside. A lewd chorus of laughter and cheers arose from the men in the tavern. She picked herself up and limped away to the back room while some men applauded the scene.

Fetherston looked away, embarrassed by my open display of territorialism. Rackham patted me on the back. "Are we jealous, O'Malley?"

"No, Captain, just protective of my leader," I said. "Would hate to see you under the grip of burning sensations, oozing pustules, festering sores, and fiery fevers while we engage a royal warship in battle."

"Vividly put. Just the trifling thought of it gives me a tremor. God in His wise judgment didn't condemn casual fornication merely to be curmudgeonly. He wants to safeguard our constitutions lest we rot away limb by limb," Rackham said. "And yet the temptations are so great, and giving in to it is so very simple."

"If those men over there are any indication of what resides on this island, I would say you have poor gleanings to find more crew," Fetherston remarked.

"My first thought as well."

"John and I will wander through the other taverns and look at the prospects," I said, looking to Mary.

"A fine idea. I am going to visit with the new lackey of Rodgers and see whether there has been any progress on our clemency now that we have pillaged a few Spanish ships. See you back at the ship," he said.

We left Fetherston, Harwood, and Rackham and sauntered outside.

"Quaint place," said Mary.

"A cesspool where the dregs of this world congregate."

We passed through several taverns and mentally registered a few potentials. I asked Mary to inquire of a tavern keeper about James. She returned to tell me that he had left the island several months ago on a British man-of-war. I relaxed, glad I would not have to confront him but curious about what had become of him. I simply could not clear my conscience of our rift.

I took Mary on a brief tour of the island, showing her the falls. No one was in sight, so we threw off our clothes, hid them among the vines, and sprang into the pool. We paddled through the falls and cradled ourselves in the cleft of a mossy rock.

"It has been so long since I have been able to bathe and relax. This is truly splendid," Mary said.

"I have not been this clean in months, either."

"My body can finally breathe. Those wraps are rough on the breasts. By the way, how did your special night go with Rackham?"

I colored a bit.

"You don't have to be embarrassed."

"All right. It was marvelous. And I must duly give you thanks for your lessons in love. They served me well." I looked away, lingering in another place and time. "It had been awhile."

Mary didn't say anything. I caught myself.

"I'm sorry. You must miss your husband a great deal."

Mary swirled the water with her fingers. "Yes, desperately."

"And the intimacy, too, I'm sure?"

"Immensely. But not enough to offer myself to any of the milksops infesting this so-called pirate's paradise."

I sensed a slight wavering in her voice as if she had more to say. "Except?"

Mary stopped swirling the water, considering for a few seconds, but then raised a dismissing hand. "Nothing, never mind."

I poked Mary in the ribs. "I can hear it in your voice; there is someone. Oh, please, I've never talked with another friend like this. Tell me. He must be onboard our sloop, then." I splashed her.

"Hey!" She splashed back.

"Tell me who you fancy or I will dunk you. No, let me guess? Let's see, Harwood? Fetherston? How about Massaquehanna? He is one strapping, manly Indian." I raised my brows and made my voice sultry. "Am I warm?"

Mary shook her head. "No, they are brutes—illiterate and facile. My attractions reside first and foremost with a man's inner nobility. Trust, loyalty, compassion, mental maturity—those are the qualities that spark my soul and my body. Then and only then do I evaluate the exterior blessings of the man."

"Call me petty, but I confess I have an equal weakness for both," I said.

"And does Jack have both?" Mary asked suggestively.

"At times he lacks one, but seldom the other."

Mary reflected. "Duncan used to bathe me and lavish me with kisses from head to toe, but not before he wooed me and swooned me with poetry."

"Reminds me of my James. That is one of the things Rackham lacks. A bit too quick to the finish for my taste, the other night notwithstanding. But you still haven't told me: who interests you?"

"Well, I'm sort of embarrassed, because he..."

"Don't worry, I won't laugh. They're just men, after all."

"All beneath us. True." Mary bridled a moment, and then leaned closer to me as if she feared someone else would hear. "It's Thomas Deane."

"Who?"

"I know, I know. He's not even a pirate, but I cannot help it. I like him. He knows what he wants and knows what he believes. He tried to kill Rackham to save his captain, and he survived a keelhauling. He's never buckled under the pressure and profanity of the pirates. He's enslaved but he's free in mind and spirit."

"He's a bit slight in stature on this vessel, reduced to washing dishes and swabbing decks," I said.

"He's a man of letters and that's a stratum worthy of my affinities. He was teaching the captain's children English and French literature, and I find his body not altogether displeasing."

"True. He is handsome in an un-roguish, un-scoundrelish sort of way. A teacher of English? That would explain his eloquence and book knowledge."

We fell silent. I let my hand crawl underneath the surface of the sand, so cool and silky to the touch, and watched a fish slip away into the turbulence of the falls. I gathered up a handful of the sand and watched the grains slip through my fingers.

"So, any plans? The burden of initiation falls on you, Mary. I believe I showed you how to properly reveal yourself."

Mary punched me playfully in the arm. "That was my trick long before you conceived of it."

We plumbed the intricacies of the problem and plotted potential approaches for a couple of hours, savoring our talk and knowing we would have to conceal it from the others onboard ship.

Chapter XXV

On the sloop the next morning, Rackham parceled out shares of the money he had received in trade. Harwood, Fetherston, Davis, Fenwick, and Howell received slightly larger cuts because of the wounds they had incurred in our last battle. Mary and I elected to stay on the ship while the rest went into town to carouse away their ill-gotten gains. Before I could suggest anything to do, Mary decided to wander down to the galley and strike up a conversation with Deane, the professor.

"Don't forget to quote some Shakespeare," I said, fending off my disappointment. "Try *Twelfth Night.*"

Mary smacked me on the bottom as she passed me.

I went into Rackham's cabin to read. The two cats flanked me, Dante grooming himself and Milton purring and kneading his paws against my leg. In the quiet my mind flitted to the faces of my past—to my mother, so weakened by her fears and insecurities; to my father, so savvy in law and commerce and yet dense in his convictions and bound by his appetites; to Edward, prone to overdrinking, and yet a man of devotion and character; and to James, my first love, lost so quickly to his timidity and dishonesty.

I started to write about each in my journal, but then I had an impulse to write Edward a letter. I told him how much I missed him, and I shared, without sugaring over the details, all I had chosen to do. I described Rackham, Mary, and the pirates, the battles we had fought, and my conflicted thoughts concerning sea roving. I marveled at how one choice could irreparably change us and lead us down corridors of destiny we could never have imagined. Granted, I had both regret and gratitude. I embraced both freely, though the guilt vexed me more severely than my accomplishments. With pride, I wrote of my bravery and my ability to stand and fight any man. I closed by telling him I loved him dearly and hoped for a time to reunite with him. I sealed the letter and later learned of a merchant vessel heading for Cuba. From there the letter would hopefully reach Charles Towne.

Rackham returned later in the day. He was in a dark, brooding mood. Despite our crew's contributions to the English cause against the Spanish, a commissioner had informed him that Rodgers remained immovable in his decision to give no further pardons to pirates.

"He said pirates could not be trusted. I have half a mind to sail into Port Royal and give him a taste of pirate vengeance," he said. "The good news is we do have more crew signed on. One of them is a man named Frederick Lowther, son of Captain George Lowther, who worked in cahoots with Captain Edward Low. But the captains had a falling out, and Low marooned Lowther's son on the Leeward Islands. He seems like a good man, but knowing how Low operates, we should keep an eye on him."

"What do you mean?"

"Low is a brutal, savage miscreant loyal to Satan and his minions," he said. "He gives piracy a bad name. From what I've heard, he is even crueler than Blackbeard."

Rackham said that whenever Low captured a ship, he made sure to leave with one of the captain's ears, which he cut off himself. He kept a collection in a leather pouch. He once took a Portuguese brigantine, and when he heard the captain had tossed a sack of moidores overboard, Low responded by tying up the captain, cutting off his lips and broiling them before his eyes. He then forced the captain to eat them only to finally murder him and the rest of the crew and scuttle the ship.

Shaking my head at such macabre details, I asked, "Have you ever seen him?"

"No, he roves more southward, and also prowls the shores of West Africa. If our ships ever cross paths, I would attack him outright. He is a sadist who tortures for pleasure and kills on a whim."

The next morning I awoke with the same kind of illness I had felt the previous day at sea. After throwing up my breakfast of dried sea turtle and biscuit, I was struck with a revelation. I was six weeks past my menstruation, I felt anemic, and my appetite was paltry. I was with child. Was this the reason God had spared me? To save the life of my illegitimate child? The thought of motherhood did not please me; it made me cringe to contemplate pushing a child out of my body. Motherhood itself appeared to me to be nothing more than prison bars and manacles. I couldn't see myself consigned to domestic life, grubbing to feed my baby while Rackham sailed the seas in search of action. I knew this was a consequence of my adultery, just as I knew I owed my life to an act of adultery. Once again my conscience pestered me.

I told Mary first. Her response was guarded congratulations. She could see I was not pleased about this development. We talked about my options: abort the baby, carry the baby and give it away, or keep the baby and change my entire life. I decided to stay behind on the island and at least deliver my baby.

I approached Rackham with uneasiness. I could not predict his response. He spoke with gentleness and support, but I could sense detachment already taking hold in his heart. I expected it, but it saddened and angered me nonetheless. It was agreed I would remain at New Providence. In the meantime, Rackham and the crew would not be leaving for several more weeks because we were going to beach the sloop and careen the barnacles off its hull. He also told Corner to rename our vessel *Destiny*.

While I felt a twinge of sorrow to see my tribute painted over, I did like the sentiments of the new name. I was not showing yet, so I joined in the work. Rackham tried to forbid me, for example, by sending me into town under the pretense of finding supplies and seeking out any new information that might concern us. But I would have nothing of his controlling ways, and I refused to be nudged out of the crew's circle.

I found the morning sickness was becoming intolerable without a bowl of salmagundi, which always seemed to stave off the nausea. One morning, as I was scraping and sanding the stanchions, Mary came up with a calabash of water and a damp cloth. "You are sweating so much in this heat, and I know you're vomiting. You need to keep drinking, or you'll get sunstroke."

I thanked her and took a swallow of brackish-tasting water. A surge of nausea climbed up my diaphragm and I spewed it right back out. I drank some more. "I find after purging, it is easier to keep down whatever I eat or drink the second time."

"Then I will bring you twice as much. And how are you coping with this willy-nilly pregnancy?"

"It leaves me higgledy-piggledy," I said, mimicking her style.

She bumped me with her hip. "Keep at it. You are getting better at my claptrap and cruel gruel." She reached up and took hold of the keelson and looked at me levelly. "Your Coventry is inevitable. Let me stay with you here until you have the child. You shouldn't be alone, especially in this den of thieves and savages."

This proposal caught me by surprise. It seemed such an immense offer. The reality was that we might never see Rackham and his ship again. To forfeit the freedom of the ship for the domesticity of pregnancy and motherhood was too great a sacrifice for her to make on my account. I started to refuse but she raised a hand and waved me off.

"You need someone to help. Without me, you would make a mess of everything."

I punched her in the arm. She punched me back. "And besides, I'd miss you."

I fought back my tears. The idea of friendship had always appealed to me, but I had never made a close friend in my youth. With Edward I had always had a father-daughter love, and with James and Jack it was passion, but with Mary, this feeling stretched my heart into a place I had never ventured. Sacrifices for family and lover were *de rigueur* and *noblesse oblige*, but sacrifices for a friend seemed noble and pure.

"I would miss you, too."

Later that night I told Rackham my plan—to stay in New Providence with Mary until I had my baby. He seemed more relieved than anything. His restlessness and discomfort hurt me. Either the burden of progeny weighed on him, or the future lack of romance at sea wearied him, but he raised a smokescreen by explaining that Rodger's marauding men-of-war had been sent out from Port Royal and were prowling the waters. It was unwise to stay in one location for too long.

Rackham set us up in a fine room and left us generous funds to cover our costs. When the day came, I watched the sloop from my bedroom window as it coasted out of the horn of the bay and slowly disappear on the horizon. I was livid. Was it really that dangerous for him to stay here? Did he have to turn tail and run at the first whisper of a man-of-war? Or was I placing unreasonable expectations on him? He was the father of our child, but I had to admit that he never once had said his goal was to marry me, settle somewhere, and raise a child. Part of me wanted to tame him, but the other part of me knew I would be appalled if I did break him. Can the leopard ever change his spots?

Mary and I spent the days promenading around town, exploring the island, sharpening our fighting skills, reading to each other, and playing card games. I asked around about Annabelle, but no one seemed to know what had happened to her. She had just disappeared out of the blue.

One day, after a bath, we treated each other to a thorough pampering. I brushed Mary's raven hair, which shimmered in the light. I also touched up the brows over her glimmering chestnut eyes. Her skin was darker than mine, olive in color, and her pearly teeth were straighter than mine. Her slender figure was accentuated with supple hips and willowy breasts. When she cast aside her male clothing, dressed in a flattering frock, and applied a bit of powder and rouge, I thought her exceedingly more alluring than I. Ironically, after Mary spoiled me, she remarked, "I wish I had your flaming red hair and morocco skin. You are much more beautiful than I." It was a sweet time.

As I ate breakfast one morning, I realized my bouts with nausea had passed. I also began to feel what I thought were distinct kicks. I asked Mary to feel my belly. She flinched and giggled when it happened. "That was a kick," she said.

On an agreed-upon day, I transformed back to a woman, but Mary kept her disguise, acting as my loyal husband. My belly was protruding, and my pants were becoming too snug. For the next few weeks Mary escorted me, my arm locked in hers, around town. We roamed the remote parts of the island and took swims. One day we came upon a little settlement of wattle huts. Out of curiosity, we walked through it but saw no one. A pungent odor hung in the air; I crinkled my nose and peered into one of the huts. Then we heard a rustling among the palms.

"Go away!" a woman's voice called. "You don't belong here."

I glanced at Mary. She put her hand on her sword.

"We mean you no harm," I said.

"Nor do we, so leave now." Her voice sounded familiar to me.

"Are you in danger?" I asked. "Perhaps we could help you."

"No one can help us. Now be gone with you!"

I stepped toward the voice. The woman thrashed about the foliage, moving sluggishly and unnaturally. I swept back some branches of a palm. She was a leper. I took a step back, covered my mouth, and held my breath. Oozing sores covered much of her face, and one of her ears was so swollen it hung like a flap over her shoulder. Her left hand looked like talons. The fingers on her right hand had rotted away. She had only a thumb. The rest of her body was covered in rags. As she tried to move away her legs gave out and she tumbled to the ground. She covered her face and began to cry.

It was Annabelle.

"Stop gawking at me. I am not a monster. It's leprosy."

"Annabelle? It's me, Anne."

"I know. I could see you through the trees. I just didn't want you to see me this way," she said, burrowing deeper into the bushes.

"Are you here by yourself?"

"There's more of us. We go fast, but there's always new ones to replace us."

"Oh, Annabelle, can I do anything?"

"Some food, a few bottles of rum. Anne, this is my lot. I am making peace with it. It won't be long now."

We talked a bit more and left. I told Mary about my friend. The cruelty of the disease left me squeamish, made my skin prickle and crawl. I had heard of leprosy, read about it in the Bible, but seeing the torments of it up close gave me a shock. I knew it was highly contagious, and I fought my fears. When we reached town, we purchased food, rum, and clothes. We took the goods back, leaving them beside a hut. Annabelle did not appear, but she thanked us from a distance. I promised to return in a few days with more. As we left, I couldn't help but notice they had picked a pristine place to spend their last days.

Despite Mary's warnings, I wended my way back though the jungle a few days later with more supplies. Mary never left my side. I did accept some of Mary's precautionary measures and wore a scarf around my mouth, keeping my distance. After Annabelle quaffed a few slugs of liquor, she forgot her ailment for a while, and her old feisty spirit returned.

"Well, did you ever become a pirate?"

"A pregnant one," I said.

"And he left you high and dry in a family way?" Her voice was gritty, and each breath sounded like the scrape of holystone on timbers.

"That about sums it up."

"Why's your friend skulking about dressed like a man?" she asked.

I turned around and looked at Mary, who raised her hands and shrugged her shoulders.

"Quite a sight. A knocked up piratess with a wench disguised as a man who is acting like your husband. I'll grant you this, it is original." She started to chuckle, which turned into a hacking fit. She spat. "There's another tooth. Just five left."

I took a step back, torn between two urges. I wanted to minister to Annabelle's needs and return some of kindness she had showed me, but the ravages of this disease made me want to bolt from her presence. It was such a sad and gruesome end for a woman so full of spunk: hopeless and helpless.

"Preacher came by. Told us God sent this leprosy to awaken us. Doused us with holy water and told us God would give us new bodies in the heavenly realm, if we repented of our sin. Thought about running up and biting him and smearing my pus on his body, but I'm all out of rage. Just resting easy, waiting for my final hour, trying to get right with good Lord," Annabelle said.

I started to weep, held out my hands and walked blindly toward her. "Oh, Annabelle, I'm so sorry…"

"Anne, don't!" Mary said.

"Yes, what the hell do you think you're doing!" Annabelle shouted. "I don't want you around here blubbering and whimpering over me! It ain't doing me a bit of good. Best wishes, Anne. Now leave and don't come back here!"

Her words were a slap across my face. I turned and ran. Mary caught up to me and grabbed my arm. I cried on her shoulder, trying to express the sorrow and horror I felt for Annabelle.

"She is brave and marvelous woman," Mary said. "I wish I had met her sooner. Next time control yourself."

"But she told me never to come back."

Mary released our hug, held my shoulders, and stared into my eyes. "She wants your company; she just doesn't want your pity."

We decided to go back, so I spent some time preparing myself for the shock. I steeled my emotions, planned a few safe subjects to talk about, and even picked up a few coarse jokes and anecdotes to share. But when we reached the colony, another leper said Annabelle had died.

Some regrets we carry all our lives.

CHAPTER XXVI

As the baby in me grew, I found my mind wandering back to my younger days.

Though I had not thought about her much in quite some time, I started contemplating my mother's life more thoroughly. The similarities of our lives were uncanny. We were both unmarried women with illegitimate children, lovers who lived elsewhere, and foggy futures; it all left me unhinged. While I loved my mother, I had been frustrated by what I had determined was her inherent weakness and inability to adapt. But as I reminisced about her years of faithfully rearing me, I perceived her character much more clearly.

Beyond domestic matters, she had taught me to read and patiently answered all my questions. She had given me the gospel and a belief in God. Though I had chosen rebellion and fallen out of God's good graces, a day did not pass without me considering a prodigal daughter's return to Edward. She had taught me to be a woman.

My scars and the angers of the past melted into grief as I pictured my mother in the timely stages of my life. Too often I had called her loyal acts of patience and gentleness clear examples of feebleness and frailty. I had deemed her sacrifices and her longsuffering nature pathetic rather than recognizing the loving displays of a mother for her child. I could not recall a cruelty she had committed against me; I, on the other hand, had judged her by what she did not or could not do. I placed my hands on belly, feeling my child, who had started moving in my womb, and I felt a sense of shame for the ingratitude and the condemnation I had heaped upon my mother over the years. My blindness so upset me that I began to weep uncontrollably.

When I shared my remorse with Mary, she began to cry for her lost mother as well, who was perhaps still alive in Bedlam.

A week later I experienced spasms of joy and worry. My child was kicking more frequently; the feeling of life thriving within me elated me, but a few days later I noticed spots of blood and felt cramps coming and going around my abdomen. Mary set down the clothes she was making for the baby and escorted me to a physician and apothecary, if he could be called either of those. He said my diet had been poor, and he sold us an assortment of extracts and herbs to be boiled for teas.

Mary was the portrait of utmost seriousness and servitude. She prepared the medicines and served me, and then went out and came back with vegetables and fish. She would not let me rise except to go to the bathroom. Her actions heartened me. I found my Bible and devoted myself to meditation and prayer, hoping God would hear our cries for my child.

Two days later it was over.

I miscarried my child, carrying it only five months in my womb. Mary was there to help me as I delivered my baby—stillborn. As Mary cut the umbilical cord and carefully washed my baby with a warm, damp cloth, I watched her tears flow freely down her face. Her sense of loss touched me.

"It's a girl," she said.

I looked away, feeling ashamed. My womb had been too feeble to protect my daughter. My body had betrayed my own child, abandoning her during the most vulnerable of times. My mother, whom I had always considered frail, had carried me nine months and then raised me for thirteen years. I could handle the responsibility, but five months...Remorse and guilt enveloped me.

Mary was always there. She swaddled the baby and brought her to me. My daughter looked so peaceful, but as I touched her forehead with my lips, her skin was cold to the touch. Mary eased me against her chest, and I spent most the night sobbing, pleading for my mother and the Lord to forgive me, seeing my loss as just retribution for my sins. It was the darkest night of my life. If not for Mary, I would have taken my life as my body had taken my baby's.

The next morning, thinking of King David's response to the loss of Bathsheba's child, I arose stoically, took a long drink of rum, washed myself, and suggested to Mary we take a long walk along the shoreline, though I was still weary from the delivery.

"I'll never be able to have a child, will I?"

Mary put her right arm around me. "Anne, I know this is difficult and you believe God is punishing you, but miscarriages are common. Ask any mother on this island, and I wager she has experienced one or knows someone who has."

I shook my head. "No, I have done wrong and God has judged me. No more mercy. I am in prison and He has slammed shut the doors."

Mary walked along, saying nothing.

I stopped and leaned against a palm tree. "I know the truth and therefore I am even more accountable. All my marauding, pirating, and adulterating has been weighed, and now God is settling His accounts with me."

Mary sat down on the remnants of a broken hogshead, pulled out a knife, and started whittling on a shard of wood.

I was infuriated. I was pouring out my soul, and she seemed preoccupied with carving on a stick. "Well, say something!"

She continued her work. She spat out of the side of her mouth and said, "You sound awfully prodigal, but are you ready to be a prodigal?"

"What the hell is that supposed to mean?" I stepped forward and braced to hit her, my fists clenched.

Mary seemed unconcerned or unwilling to prepare for an attack. She finally looked up at me. "Look, are you sorry for what you do, or are you just sorry about the consequences? Make a choice—repent or rebel. Turn or burn. It's a simple question. Are you going to be penitent or a pirate?"

In spite of my fury, I could not help but feel a minor release of the tension in my veins. "A Christian with piratical moorings?"

Mary laughed. "Try a pirate with Christian trappings and plenty of harum-scarum choices. Some truths don't set us free, Anne, because we don't want to follow them."

"Pascal's wager," I mumbled.

"What is that?"

"Betting your life on whether there is a God—the infinite versus nothing. It's one of the few things my father told me about, or I suppose one of the few times I listened to him."

Mary pulled at her fingers, cracking several knuckles. "An intriguing gamble with the highest of stakes."

I sighed, plopped down beside Mary, and swore in several ways, over and over. Mary hewed on the piece of wood, occasionally praising me for a particularly creative selection of epithets. I thought about the prodigal son, wondering whether while he resided among the pigs, before he began starving, if he kept telling himself things would start looking up again. Why is it that true repentance seems to come only when one has reached the very bottom of the well or is grasping the last strands of one's rope? A new way of life? I just wasn't ready to jettison this one yet.

Mary and I returned to our room and decided to name my daughter Maryann, or Mara for short. We took the name from the book of Ruth. Naomi, after losing her children, had changed her name to Mara, which means bitterness. We baptized Mara and asked God for His mercy on her soul. We trudged to a place we had picked and buried her beside a palm tree near the falls. Mary placed some stones as a memorial, and I carved my daughter's name and the date of her death, July 17th, 1720, into the bark.

"Thank you, Mary," I said after a long silence, "for all that you've done for me."

Mary wiped her eyes.

"I feel such sorrow, so cast into a gloom, but somehow I'm still more pirate than prodigal. As long as it includes you, the pirate life is still for me," I said.

"Well, do we wait for Rack to come back, or do we find another crew to join?"

"I do confess I still have some weakness for the rogue," I said, plucking off an orchid nestled among the cresses and ferns. I scented it and stuck the stem behind my right ear. "And if memory serves, don't you have amorous interests onboard as well, a one Mr. Thomas Deane, professor of literature and stowaway slave?"

"You see right through me."

Chapter XXVII

Two months later, Rackham's sloop threaded through the narrows of New Providence and entered the bay. Hope for new adventures set off an excited sensation through me, but when I noticed the dilapidated condition of our vessel and its sails, I realized it had endured either a storm or battle. It no longer glided, but rather seemed to hobble along lamely. The crew pulled it along the quay and strode down the pier solemnly. There were no cheers, no prizes to auction, and no booty to celebrate with. Rackham was as subdued as the rest.

I was disguised once again as a man. Rackham's eyes fell on my belly, and his face seemed to wither away.

Over a bowl of punch and a pot of stew, Rackham listened to me tell about my loss, nodding over each detail but averting his gaze from mine, staring mostly into his bowl. I felt distant from him, emotionally aloof, and yet his reaction revealed an emotion—grief—I had never seen in him before. He spoke of a fierce hurricane off the coast of Jamaica that had nearly staved the ship to cinders, and he had also learned that Charles Vane, his former pirate captain, had lost his ship and crew in the storm. A short time later they had received word that Vane had been turned in and arrested and was awaiting trial at Port Royal.

"He'll be strung up in a gibbet soon. Rodgers is no longer pardoning us gentlemen of fortune, only hanging us now," said Rackham.

I could sense foreboding in his voice, a realization that his days were indeed numbered. "A quick drop and a sudden stop is our destiny, Anne. I am experiencing the awareness of my certain and swift mortality." He took a long, deep drink from his tankard and sang a solemn shanty:

Drain, drain the bowl, each fearless soul,
Let the world wag as it will;
Let the heavens growl, let the devil howl,
Drain, drain the deep bowl and fill.

That night I coupled with him to lift his spirits. It had been a long time, and I found it exceedingly sweet. I thought briefly of the prodigal son among the pigs. I wasn't starving—not yet.

The next morning Rackham awoke in lighter spirits. As we lounged in bed, his tongue loosened, and he bragged about his time with Captain Charles Vane.

"It was May 1718. Blackbeard was six months beheaded, and I was now Vane's quartermaster. We were right here, enjoying the spoils of a few prizes we had taken, when suddenly Rodgers sailed into the bay with two men-of-war, demanding that all pirates surrender. Well, we slipped our cables, set fire to the prize we had towed into the harbor, and sailed out as boldly as could be with our Jolly Roger flying. We even fired a shot at one of the men-of-war as we left. Guts and backbone." Rackham's eyes widened and flickered with the memory and the glory of his gall.

I rested an elbow on the bed and set my fist against my chin, reveling in his storytelling bravado.

"Every vessel we took, Vane ordered it to be set ablaze to shroud the evidence. We were rich with prizes, and the crew was feeling invincible, ready to flaunt and strut against any vessel in the Spanish Main, be it merchant or man-of-war." He drank some wine and leaned over and kissed me, as if this was part of his storytelling routine.

"By this time we had sailed up the New England coastline," Rackham continued, his reverie straying off into a story of another infamous sea rover, Captain Samuel Bellamy. He had apprenticed under Blackbeard and Benjamin Hornigold, harassing vessels along the Spanish Main between 1715 and 1717.

"You'll appreciate this: his sloop was named the *Mary Anne*."

Bellamy had plundered a square-rigged ship, and his delusions of greatness rose. He gave the sloop to his quartermaster Paul Williams, and he took over the *Sultana*. He later captured a British slaver called the *Whydah*, and because it was even bigger, he suggested a trade with the slaver's captain. The captain wisely accepted, and Bellamy fitted out his new ship with twenty-eight guns. They sailed north along the Atlantic coastline, pillaging vessels and growing wealthy, but in May of 1717, Bellamy's ship ran aground off Massachusetts during a heavy fog. The surf obliterated the vessel, and almost 150 pirates perished, Bellamy included. Williams returned and salvaged what he could before setting out on his own. He took only two prizes before stopping at Cape Cod to resupply, where he was arrested, tried, and hanged with his crew.

"Pirates don't last long in the trade, do they?" I rested my elbows against a pillow and cradled my chin in my palms to prop up my head.

"It's rare. Most of us will surely hang high. We want too much and don't know when to stop. The sweet trade's engrained in our heads and engulfed in our guts." Rackham paused and grimaced. He blinked, forced a smile, and took a drink. "But back to my story of Captain Vane. We found no prizes for nearly a month. The crew was restless. Finally, we glassed a ship, gave it chase, and hurled a broadside. But it hoisted French colors and showed her guns.

"Vane wanted nothing of it; I was compelled to speak. It was my chance in the sun, a way to make a name of Rackham. I proclaimed that though it had more guns and men, we could still board her and the best boys would carry the day. The crew cheered my speech. It was a glorious moment. Vane said the plan was too rash and ordered us to trim the sails and make off as fast as we could."

Rackham took another drink and then lifted himself out of bed and began to dress. He looked off, reliving a scene from another place and time. "We obeyed him, and since our brigantine had the heels, we cleared off. But the next day, the pirates put it to a vote and branded Vane a bloody coward. They then turned the ship over to me. We had a small escort sloop with us. We put Vane and those loyal to him on it and set off on our own sweet journey into the Caribbean. We renamed the ship the *Vanity*—couldn't resist the irony."

It was the old Rackham, back in form, a portrait of a braggadocio.

"What is your plan now Captain Calico Jack Rackham?"

The phrase pleased him. "After a morning tumble with you, my fair Anne, I will assess the damage to this sloop. I am afraid she is done for, and with Rodgers' ships skulking about, I am certain we'll need a new plan."

"I have a plan as well."

He turned to me, eyebrows raised, intrigued.

"I have been thinking for awhile, and I believe it is time to end our pretense. Mary and I want the crew to know who and what we are..."

"But Anne..."

"And," I raised my hand to muzzle him. "And I believe it is time to legitimize this immoral affair with a marital vow—a pirate wedding, a first for the history books."

My spunk swept him up and put him into good humor and a daring spirit. "I do want my crew and the world to know that Anne Bonney is my wife and the toughest female pirate on the seas."

"Or I could bare all as fair Lady Godiva did, but in protest of these unjust and superstitious laws against women aboard pirate ships."

"No, I believe courageous St. Joan of Arc, armored, sword in hand, leading the charge, and forcing social change, suits you much better. Of course, the virginal saint, devoted to all things pure, doesn't quite fit you, aye?"

"More the pleasure, Jack. One more thing…" I said as he approached me.

"My, we do press when we have the advantage. Anything, my love."

"Mary is also planning a wedding with Thomas Deane."

"The professorial bilge rat, galley slave, and deck swabber?"

"There is no accounting for one's taste and preference. The heart makes its own choices, and we are defenseless against it."

"Our desperado of letters and scruples?" Rackham said, shaking his head. "And when might this be happening?"

"Perhaps as we speak."

CHAPTER XXVIII

Later that day Mary steeled her nerves and cornered Deane in the galley while he performed some of his ongoing duties—peeling potatoes, shelling peas, slicing fruit, gutting fish, and butchering hogs. They spoke of various literary subjects for a season, and then Mary carefully repeated the technique we both once tried—a slight, scintillating peak of our womanhood.

As Mary told it, Deane, at first, pretended not to notice. "So I grew bold," Mary said. "I told him, 'No, Thomas, your eyes are not playing tricks on you, and your mind is not imagining things. I am a woman—every ounce of me—and I find every ounce of you titillating. Pun duly intended.'"

"How did he react?" I said, poking her in the ribs. "I so wish I had been there."

"Relieved, amazed, and enthralled." Mary ticked off each detail with her fingers. "He sheepishly confessed I had been on his mind for quite some time, though not without a little disturbance to his own masculine identity. Our chemistry is a mystery," said Mary. Her eyes flashed with wanton pride.

"What then?"

Mary giggled. "Let's just say even a refined and educated man is still a man. He hungrily sought my affection immediately, but I held off, though I must admit he was so irresistible I almost relinquished my principles."

"You're a regular pilgrim. Not even a kiss to seal your hopes and offer him a taste of the delights to come?"

"Well, yes, a kiss. Of course a kiss or two."

"Or three or four?"

She arched her brows and stretched her back. "That would depend on how you interpret the duration of a kiss. They occurred at various times while I shared my life story with him. He is a most passionate man."

"Then perhaps moving up our marriage dates is necessary, lest temptation overtake you. After all, we must keep the Scripture in mind, since we are pirates with Christian trappings."

"Which Scripture is that? Do not fornicate? Flee youthful lusts?"

"Better to marry than to burn."

"In hell?"

"No, with uncontrollable passion."

"Well then for both our souls' sakes, let us act with haste. I am past smoldering and starting to rage into one lusty conflagration."

"Let's make a pact. I will deny myself as well until the weddings are performed. Agreed?"

Mary clasped my hand. "A bargain it is. And if Jack is anything like you describe him, that ought to speed up the process."

We decided the next day we would unveil our gender to the crew. We planned the time, considered the reactions, and prepared for the risks, and then clasped hands and vowed to always be within earshot in the coming weeks in case of trouble. Mary spoke with Thomas, and I conversed with Jack. That night we could not sleep so we traded the watch with Carty and Dobbin and spent the night as sentinels.

I watched the crawling sea under the light of the moon. It was a beautiful, living beast with countless hidden secrets. Though I had sailed it now for a couple of years, I still loved its raw energy and untamable spirit. The winds and currents could be harnessed but never controlled. How did that verse go that I had had to memorize in catechism? "The wind bloweth where it wishes, and you hear the sound of it, but cannot tell where it cometh from or where it goeth. So is everyone who is borne of the Spirit." The sea was as mysterious, incomparable, and unattainable as God Himself.

We gazed up at the starry host and shared the never-ending amazement that ensnared our imaginations when gazing upon the constellations and the shooting stars. The dazzling concept of the infinite filled us with awe, made us feel infinitesimal, and gave us perspective on our little dramas.

"How do you think tomorrow will go?" I asked.

"Men respect strength, pure and simple. We'll be fine." She pointed at me. "After all, you have the spirit of Grace O'Malley, the Irish pirate who visited Queen Elizabeth. And I do believe I possess the spirit of Queen Boadicea."

"Boadicea?"

Mary appeared chagrined. "You've never learned of the warrior queen of Britain? It is a shame how Irish pedagogues deprive the youth of the most important stories of our history."

"Aye, I am a living, educational travesty," I agreed.

She got up. "I'll be right back." She returned with a book and read to me Boadicea's story.

Julius Caesar had started an invasion of Britain in 55 BC, but it wasn't until AD 43 that the Roman Emperor Claudias effectively conquered the island. One people, the Icenis, were still free, but when their king, Prasutagus, died, the Romans ignored their treaty and invaded, plundering the Iceni houses, arresting Queen Boadicea, and ordering her stripped and scourged.

"They left, foolishly believing they had subjugated her and the people of her land. They were gravely mistaken."

I leaned forward. "What did she do?"

"She rallied her people, raised an army, and started a rebellion, marching on towns and capturing back what Rome had occupied. They even seized what is today London and St. Albans. The Romans called her the Killer Queen for her brutal successes."

"I like the sobriquet. Hell hath no fury like a woman scorned or scourged."

Mary turned a page in the book. "According to the Tacitus, 'She was very tall. Her eyes seemed to stab you. Her voice was harsh and loud. Her thick, reddish brown hair hung down below her waist. She always wore a golden torc around her neck and a flowing tartan cloak fastened with a brooch.'"

"A woman warrior with style to boot," I said. "I do believe I am ready for a little fashionable styling myself."

"Amen."

Mary read that the Romans were forced to backtrack and contend with Boadicea and her Iceni hordes. Under Governor Suetonius' command, the Romans sent an army of 10,000 against the Iceni fighters.

"They have recorded in this book her speech to the army before they went into battle."

"Read it."

"'This is not the first time that the Britons have been led to battle by a woman, but now I do not come to boast the pride of a long line of ancestry. I take the field to assert the cause of public liberty, and to seek revenge for my body seamed with ignominious stripes, and my two daughters ravished. From the pride of the Romans nothing is sacred; all are subject to violation; the old endure the scourge, and the virgins are deflowered. But the vindictive gods are now at hand.... On this spot we must either conquer, or die with glory. Though a woman, my resolution is fixed: the men, if they please, may survive with infamy and live in bondage'"

"Fitting words from a brave woman. What happened?"

"Unfortunately, the Roman army proved better prepared and more experienced. They vanquished the Iceni soldiers and slaughtered thousands of them. They captured Boadicea. Rather than undergo another flogging, followed by an execution, she drank poison in prison and died."

I took a drink from a bottle of rum. "While I don't much care for the ending, I would be proud to have the spirit of Boadicea coursing through my veins," I said.

"We do, Anne. And tomorrow we will prove it to the rabble on this ship."

In the morning we lingered in our hammocks while the rest of the crew went topside, straining to refit and repair our vessel.

Rackham finally came down and checked on us. We applied a few touches of makeup, let our hair down, and fitted our shirts to emphasize our bosoms in a modest but definite way, still wearing our pants loosely. We held our breaths as Rackham climbed onto the deck and called the crew to assemble near the mast. In his typical eloquence, he spoke of our pirate adventures, of the bonding of our spirits in battle, of the losses we suffered which served to forge our souls, and of the unbreakable level of respect we had for one another. He proclaimed that while all of humanity possesses personal secrets, which all of us should honor, there were some confidences that deserved being revealed for the benefit of the crew.

"So I confess to you freely a secret I have kept too long from those I trust most on earth. I share it now, believing pirates to be most progressive and democratic in our philosophy. Anne and Mary, the time has come!"

We climbed topside, locked arms, and presented ourselves. The response was pure silence. Our free hands cautiously rested on our cutlasses and cocked musketoons. After a full minute of nothing but creaking timbers and the whisper of the sheets, Rackham launched into a diatribe over the pathetic pirate tendency toward foolish superstitions about women onboard a ship. Had we been bad luck thus far? Had we not proved ourselves time and again in the hottest of battles?

"Pirates have always been a step ahead of the masses. We are enlightened. Consider Charlotte de Berry. She disguised herself as a man in the English Navy. When captured by the Moors, the captain discovered her gender and raped her, a knavish decision to make against so strong-willed a woman. She snuck into his cabin that night and beheaded him, and then led a mutiny and turned the crew into a band of cutthroats in her charge. A caveat to consider," Rackham proclaimed.

Rackham waxed grandiloquent on the famous Alvilda the Goth, who revolted against a forced marriage to Prince Alf of Sweden. She pulled together an all-woman crew and began harrying vessels in the Baltic seas. They had proved such a plague that Prince Alf himself armed a ship and routed Alvilda's crew. After his victory, Alvilda ironically reversed her decision and deigned to accept Alf's marriage proposal because he had won her admiration by his deeds of courage.

"As shipmates who have counted on each other in battle, I warrant you that Mary Reade and Anne Bonney are deserving of your respect," Rackham said.

While Rackham spoke, I scanned the faces of the crew. I could tell we had won over the majority. The only one who exhibited clear disdain was Lowther. After Rackham finished, the men, starting with Fetherston and Harwood, stepped forward with outstretched hands, giving us the right hand of fellowship. Massaquehanna, though stone faced, hugged me.

"Let us give toast to Mary and Anne for their bravery," Rackham announced.

A demijohn was passed around, and we all took a hearty swig.

"And I have another earthshaking announcement. We are going to have a wedding—no two weddings—on deck tomorrow. Anne and I will be wed, and Mary and Thomas Deane will also tie the knot of marriage—in piratical fashion," said Rackham.

Whether or not they thought it through I cannot say, but the crew cheered this news as well, and the demijohn went around a couple more times. Howell pulled out his fiddle and began to play a melodious tune. Spontaneous dancing commenced. It was marvelous to feel part of this group, which seemed like family. I glanced over at Mary, who looked quite pleased. We sported and capered around the deck in a spirit of free celebration. The only snag I sensed was Lowther; he was nowhere to be seen.

As I gamboled with Rackham, I pressed my cheek against his and I said softly, "Thank you, Jack. That was marvelously done."

"Indeed. It went better than I hoped."

"You could make doomsday sound like a wondrous journey. It is a gift."

"Never thought of it that way," said Rackham, and he twirled me about. It was a superb night. I felt as though I was taking steps toward a more favorable place in God's eyes. Surely he would reward me, wouldn't he?

The following day Rackham went ashore and brought back a baker and a chef to prepare the finest delicacies the island had to offer. He rented two rooms, hired a tailor to mend and alter two old wedding dresses, and enlisted a couple of musicians to play flute and fiddle; he even found a backslidden Jesuit priest to perform the ceremonies. We also paid a fair sum to the priest to write up a document of annulment for me.

We had a full day of preparations for this historic event. Mary and I were consumed with giddiness and giggles. My only sadness was that Edward would not be here with me. I would have asked him to walk me down to Jack, but I wondered now whether I would ever see him again.

At sunset, the musicians began to play. We climbed on deck and the crew applauded us. Rackham was dressed to the hilt, sporting a calico waistjacket, a white blouse, black pantaloons, polished boots with silver buckles, and a new hat with fresh plumes that covered a freshly powdered periwig. Caught up in the spirit of the moment, Rackham offered from his own collection whatever Deane would like to wear.

For Mary and I, our frocks were a combination of French lace, Ruche muslin, and Chinese silk with satin petticoats. I had never seen Mary look so svelte and beautiful; we had spent a long time curling her hair and applying makeup, which looked wonderful thanks to my mother's lessons. Rackham gave us jewelry as well—earrings, bracelets, and necklaces "stolen from filthy rich aristocrats."

We stood on deck, the Jolly Roger flapping wildly and the boat gently swaying, and said our wedding vows according to the Book of Ruth: "Your people will be my people, your God will be my God…" What followed was a memorable piratical party with every kind of food and drink to glut ourselves upon. There was plenty of festive music, lively dancing, and bawdy shanties to keep us entertained. Howell regaled us with "The Sailor's Hornpipe" and "Drunken Sailor." A few eager doxies were ferried across at the behest of the crew. After a reasonable amount of time, we were lowered by pulley to cutters and conveyed back to the island for our honeymoon night. It felt freeing to be officially married and now clear of the stain of adultery.

For the next couple of days we luxuriated in our new marriage. I enjoyed hearing Mary's tales about the proper Mr. Deane, who had abandoned all prudishness on the wedding night. "He is a fine man," she said. "When we reach Cuba or Jamaica, we are planning to jump the ship and begin a legitimate life."

Mary's words stung me; my stomach fell. I had not foreseen that love and marriage could so quickly separate us. With much angst, I grappled with the thought of losing Mary. Our husbands were dissimilar in nearly every aspect. There was no hope of them being friends. I felt lost, suddenly empty.

About this time Rackham received a parcel, and I received a letter from Edward. Rackham had information that Governor Rodgers was sending two men-of-war, burgeoned with guns and soldiers, toward New Providence. Though our sloop still needed repairs, Rackham set a course for Cuba. I did not know it then, but this would be my last view of Nassau, where so much had happened over the past eighteen months.

Our time was short indeed.

In our haste to set sail, I had forgotten to open Edward's letter, so I found a quiet place, broke the seal, and read. As I expected, he evinced pleasant surprise on hearing from me. He told me I was in his prayers, and that he tended my mother's grave weekly. He hoped to see me again soon. Without going into details, he wrote that my father had fallen on hard times, broken down by his excessive drinking and physical afflictions, and now was inclined toward moral and philosophic reflection. He was gentler. Edward said when he mentioned my letter, my father wanted to know every detail and often wiped his eyes as he listened to Edward recount my words.

"He sends his love and hopes harmony and comfort will be your constant companions in the name of the Lord," Edward wrote. "Anne, you and your mother were ornaments that decorated this house. Bereft of your spirit and presence, it is lonely and morose. We long to be reunited with you. Godspeed, Edward."

I read over these lines several times, puzzled by my father's change of heart and saddened by Edward's somber words. I wondered what catalyst had sparked my father's supposed transformation. Edward was as sweet and caring as ever. Frankly, I was full of doubt about my father. I tucked the letter away and began to meditate upon a reply. Many things now hung heavily on my heart—escaping Rodgers' ships, parting from Mary, and now Edward's letter. I wished Edward were here to listen.

Standing tall as a woman onboard a pirate ship and marrying Calico Jack Rackham now seemed dull and drained of excitement, as if it was only a dream I had had a long time ago.

Chapter XXIX

We tacked against the northerly winds, the vessel groaning and the sheets straining under the duress of their unrelenting force. Because I hadn't tried it for a long while, I stretched myself out onto the bowsprit and let the winds whip my red hair about as I stared down at the brisk swath the hull cut through the sizzling waters. My thoughts drifted back to my first voyage across the Atlantic, when I was twelve.

In the distance I saw the flukes of a whale and its geyser spout. Oh, to take a ride on the hump of that noble leviathan of the sea! I had heard of whaling but couldn't imagine killing such an agile and swift behemoth. I am not sure why, but I always felt harming whales or dolphins seemed more cruel at heart than injuring humans. Whales and dolphins possessed so much personality, playfulness, and purpose. Just then Deane dumped a full bucket of fish heads and offal over the side. I peered over and saw sharks appear from the depths, churn up the waters, and feed in a blood frenzy. It was a harrowing thought to imagine falling overboard into the middle of a shark soiree.

My reverie was interrupted by a cry from Fetherston, who had sighted a Portuguese schooner. We gave chase for half a day. As our sloop overtook them, we hoisted our Jolly Roger, lifted our gun ports, and fired a shot across the Portuguese's bow. The ship lowered its sails and allowed us to board without a fight. It proved a good catch. While the crew looted it, Mary and I kept our guns trained on the Portuguese sailors we had sitting in a cluster on the foredeck. Screams of some horror below punched holes in the gossamer thread of our harmony with the other pirates. We listened to the unmistakable sounds of rape coming from the galley. This brutality fell in sharp relief with the bliss we had experienced a mere week before, muting the levity and felicity of marriage we had felt and darkening our feelings for those we called friends.

I indignantly marched into the captain's quarters, where Rackham was perusing the captured vessel's books and charts. "Jack, this must stop."

"What must stop?"

We stood silently, hearing the piercing screams and pleas of the women and the pirates' taunts and laughs. Rackham shook his head. "Anne, we have already exhausted this subject."

"No, Jack, now it is different. You have two women among your crew, and rape is abhorrent to us. It's among the lowest, most beastly of crimes of men. We cannot and will not tolerate it on this ship."

"Do you think this is a crew of ministers and marble saints? Awaken, Anne. We're pirates, men who have made a pact with the Devil to get what we can out of this life before the axe falls and grinds off our heads. We are a crew in weal and woe."

A fuming rage broiled hotter within me. I was debating with the deaf and dumb, pitting my wits against the blind and foolish. "If you won't do anything about it, Mary and I will!"

"Careful, Anne. You are outnumbered and not indispensable in their eyes," Rackham cautioned. "At best their lust will turn on you."

"I will not stand by without intervening, Jack. I would rather commit my soul to the deep."

"Choose your fate."

I swore under my breath, and then dashed to Mary and whispered a plan. We looked to Massaquehanna. He seemed to understand and pulled his tomahawk from his belt. The three of us entered the galley and witnessed the crew taking their turns with the women. It was nauseating to see one frightened woman being ravaged, despite her pleas for mercy. A second woman merely acquiesced to their brutality without fight, seeming to transport her mind and heart outside her body.

I clapped my right hand on Lowther's shoulder and yanked him off one of the women. He roared obscenities, but Massaquehanna cuffed him to the floor. Mary and I drew swords. Carty backed away from the other woman.

"Ladies, you are safe. Cover up and leave immediately," I shouted.

Dobbin, Earl, Carty, Lowther, and Fenwick stared at us bitterly, debating what to do next. The women wrapped themselves in their clothing and ran up the ladder.

"What the hell is this?" Lowther yelled, hitching up his trousers.

"There will no longer be acts of rape on this ship—or any other," I said.

"Says who?" Lowther roared.

"We do," Mary said. "Unless of course you wish to rape each other. Far be it from us to interrupt sodomy."

I could tell by their expressions that the pirates had taken measure of Massaquehanna, Mary, and I and decided to choose a different time and tact to fight what they considered an unprecedented outrage, but Lowther remained under the delusion that the others would join him to fight us right then and there.

"Come on, boys, let's teach these doxies a lesson in respect," Lowther rasped, starting to pull out his broadsword.

"Don't be foolish. I would hate to emasculate you with that little sword of yours," Mary said.

Lowther hesitated. He glanced over his shoulder and saw his support was folding. "What kind of men are you, backing down from two wenches and an Injun?"

Dobbin and Carty started to back away. Earl and Fenwick looked down.

I backhanded Lowther. "His name is Massaquehanna."

Lowther pulled the sword halfway out of its scabbard, but then relented and shoved it back in. He cursed and spat. "This isn't a pirate ship. It is a ship of bloody fools and spineless, castrated choir boys." He backed away. "Where are the real pirates? This is not over. The devil rot you!"

"Oh, I eagerly await our next meeting," Mary shouted as he headed up the ladder.

I turned back to the others and saw in their faces that we had crossed a line. It could not go unaddressed if the men wished to retain their dignity. I had counted on that, which was why I was grateful Massaquehanna had joined our humanitarian alliance. We also needed Rackham's allegiance in this matter, however, if we hoped to create lasting change. Meanwhile, we three would stick close together and post guard around the hourglass for each other. When Deane heard of our little revolution, he, too, pledged to do whatever necessary to protect us as well as his beloved Mary.

Chapter XXX

During the next week I kept my distance from Rackham, but our crew was bustling and buzzing, taking one prize after another. Our conquests rewarded us well. We scoured the inlets and small harbors around the northern parts of Jamaica, taking several fishing vessels, although once again I objected to robbing the poor fishermen of their nets and tackle. We caught two sloops anchored at Dry Harbor Bay. We raced in, fired a shot, and watched as their crews leaped overboard and ran ashore. We plundered those vessels of their stores, including livestock.

We then took a schooner captained by Thomas Spenlow in Ocho Bay, and it was there I killed my fourth man. While we searched the vessel for treasures, we found a mariner hiding in the hold near the ballast. When Howell, Mary, and I approached, he fired from the shadows and wounded Howell in the shoulder. I aimed in the direction of the muzzle flash and fired. There was no return shot, only silence. We stepped gingerly forward and found the man with a ball lodged in his windpipe.

"Impressive shot," said Mary. "Remind me not to duel with you."

The man's eyes were open wide, and the last scrapes of breath were sighing from his frame. I saw the spirits of Throckmorton and the other two men I had slain in his eyes. They stared at me, accusing me, reminding me they would not be groping for heaven or hell if I had stayed put in Charles Towne or had remained faithful to my husband. My choices continued to ripple through the lives and deaths of others. Was my life just random shards thrown together, or was there a mosaic—a design? I had broken every single one of the Ten Commandments many times over and still my heart beat for worldly freedom. But my conscience, though seared and hardened, seldom allowed me to enjoy any of my sins for long. I leaned down and closed his eyes. I thought of Christ's words: "Live by the sword, die by the sword." I knew my time would soon arrive.

We held the schooner for two days, and when we finally decided to release the captain and his crew and depart, Spenlow shouted at us across the waters, "Your day of judgment is coming! Justice will one day be served! I will see to it!"

Harwood responded by firing the swivel gun at the schooner. When Spenlow ducked we all laughed and mocked him.

"Rack, perhaps so close to Port Royal, we should scuttle Spenlow's ship?" Fetherston said.

"What about their crew?" Rackham asked.

"Drop them off on an island."

"Maroon them? We're pirates, not murderers."

"Their tongues will hang us one day."

Rackham crossed his arms and contemplated. "No, let's not forget our souls," he said. He walked slowly to his cabin, his head down, and stepped in. His pensive words bewildered me. He had been so cavalier about the sexual assault on the women a few days ago, and now he was pondering his soul.

Later that evening, Rackham surfaced from his cabin, clearly intoxicated. He said that with so many spoils we could enjoy a hiatus from the sweet trade. We dropped anchor at Point Negril, went ashore, and toted our provisions to a sandy area for our celebration. We also needed to replenish our water, so we spent the better half of a day rowing our barrels ashore, rolling them up the beach, and filling them from a spring. We then ferried the barrels back and used block and tackle to hoist them into our sloop.

Later that day ten Englishmen who were a-turtling in two small piraguas hailed us. Rackham offered hospitality and requested their company, particularly when he learned that two of them played instruments. It was a festive evening. I reclined against Rackham and saw Mary leaning against Thomas. It was a calm night with clear skies, and the tropical zephyrs were pleasant. Some of the pirates sang songs around a bonfire, while others busied themselves with gnawing on the bones of a roasted goat and scooping up beans from their platters, shoveling them into their mouths.

I noticed Lowther sitting by himself, a permanent scowl etched on his face. He was brooding—plotting something. He methodically sharpened his sword with a whetstone, his eyes mesmerized by the embers of the fire. Nobody had said anything about our stopping the rapes, almost as if it had never happened, but

Lowther appeared to be a serious hitch in bringing about change among the crew. His face was like sharp stones in my shoes.

I shifted my attention to Mary and Deane. He scrawled in a journal while Mary rested her eyes. "What are you writing about, Tom?"

"My experiences with a band of pirates," he replied without pausing from his writing.

"Rife with the lurid terrors of our tribe, I suppose?"

He stopped and looked at me. "I am more intrigued by the pirate philosophy and perspective as well as the personalities of this tribe of sea thieves. You run an interesting brand of democracy here. My book will be more like a travelogue along the lines of Daniel Defoe."

"I don't know the name."

"He just published a book called *Robinson Crusoe*. I was reading it when your crew kidnapped me," he said.

Rackham paused and looked into the fire. "That's right; we did shanghai you. I think the crew has nearly forgotten that incident."

"I haven't."

"You are making the best of it, though. Quite admirable. So tell me, what was that book about?"

Deane frowned, considering for a moment whether to tell Rackham. "I was not able to finish. But it was about a man who sought fortune on the seas."

"A pirate?"

"Not quite. But he was captured by Moorish pirates and enslaved."

"Touches close to the bone," I said to Deane.

"True. Crusoe managed to escape and eventually wound up running a Brazilian tobacco plantation. He prospered again through slave labor."

"That brushes near to my home," I said.

Deane set his journal aside and shifted his body on the log he was leaning against. Mary stirred briefly but then settled back into the shelter of his chest. "He became a brutal man. His heart hardened, he abandoned his faith, and he abused his slaves. While embarking on a profitable slave gathering voyage, his vessel was shipwrecked, and he was the sole survivor on an uninhabited island, though he did have guns to hunt with."

"Sounds like a marooning," Rackham interjected. He leaned forward, taking an interest in the story.

"He salvaged what he could from the ship, built a shelter, and subsisted on sea life, wild goats, and tobacco-steeped rum. His life was lonely. One day he fell ill and hallucinated that an angel of the Lord appeared to him, warning him to repent. He awoke and remembered God's grace and salvation. He was grateful for the extra time God had granted him to change his ways," Deane said.

"Another prodigal story with a moral—I should have known," Rackham said, taking a drink, now weary of listening.

"Go on," I said.

"After many attempts at constructing boats and trying to escape the island, he finally gave up and accepted his fate, but then he sees a set of human footprints."

"His rescuers?"

"No, turned out to be cannibals. He heard gunshots on the other side of the island and went to investigate, only to find a vessel run aground and a scene of human carnage. All the people had been killed and consumed in a vast cannibal feast. He saw the partially eaten bodies of men and women, and a few skeletons."

I noticed that not only was Rackham riveted again to the story, but nearly the rest of the crew were as well. "Cannibals? What happened next?" he asked.

"He set up a fortress, stockpiled his guns, and stayed vigilant throughout the night. The next day he saw about thirty cannibals with two remaining men. Crusoe saw the cannibals kill one man with a spear and prepare to finish the other, but the man broke free and ran in his direction. Two of the cannibals gave chase. Crusoe picked up a rifle and killed the first one, wounded the second. The fleeing man turned back and finished off the wounded cannibal with a rock. Then he reached Crusoe's protective lair. That's when the cannibals attacked in full force, with spears." Deane paused.

"Zounds, tell us what happened next?" Rackham demanded.

I caught a hint of a smile on Deane's face. "I cannot tell. That was the spot I reached when you attacked our ship and abducted me."

Thus followed a series of questions about the book. Predictably, Rackham shouted with exasperation. "By thunder, I must have this book!"

As the party split up and everyone maneuvered to their respective places of slumber, I walked over to Deane and whispered in his ear, "Ingenious mode of torment."

He gave me a mock look of shock. "Anne, whatever do you mean by casting aspersions on my character?" He winked, and it made me think of Edward.

"I laud and applaud you. May I hear more later as a reward for suspecting?"

"The pleasure would be all mine."

The following morning, Mary and I meandered into the forest of palms and mangroves. We talked idly and playfully about Deane's little cruelty and eventually found a secluded pool. We stripped and bathed. It was the sort of peaceful time I had come to count on with Mary, a break from the primitive nature of the men and the violence of our piracy. It had now been nearly a year and a half since I had donned male clothing and set out on a life of piracy. So much had happened, and now my thoughts turned toward a future egress. Too much of this freebooting existence had disturbed my thoughts, robbed me of peace. Edward's letter, my lost child, my failed marriage, my father's apparent change, and the possibility of Deane and Mary leaving the ship all solidified my decision to search for a way out and hopefully still be close to her.

When we wandered back, we saw Deane clumsily wielding a sword, practicing thrusts, ripostes, and parries on a palm tree. His every move looked gangly and clumsy.

"Look at my husband trying to impress me again," Mary said, loud enough for Deane to hear. "You already have my complete admiration, Tom."

Deane turned toward her, his face grim and angry. He said nothing, merely wheeled around and awkwardly slashed at the fronds and cresses.

I glanced at Mary and saw concern spreading across her face.

"Thomas, what's the matter?"

CHAPTER XXXI

"I am preparing for a duel," he said, singeing the air with a sword swipe.

I saw unmistakable anxiety on Mary's face. Her dark eyes jittered back and forth between her new husband and the island surroundings. "Tell me what has happened?" She kept her voice calm and controlled, but I could sense her apprehension.

He didn't reply, instead stroking his sword awkwardly at palmetto fronds.

Mary carefully reached out and held his shoulders, and then pressed the side of her face against his back. He sighed and his trembling frame began to relax. It was a poignant sight. "Please, love, tell me."

"I cannot just stand by and allow him to say such things."

"Who? What things?" Mary asked in a tender voice.

"Lowther. He said...he called you..."

"What, what did he say?"

"I can't say. It is shameful and vulgar and an absolute lie I will not allow him to get away with," he said.

Mary turned Thomas around and cupped his face in her hands. She looked directly into his eyes. "Now, listen to me, my love. Lowther is a crazy, wicked man and everything he says is a lie, but we need to find another way to..."

Deane flinched and pulled away. "You want me to back down? What kind of man do you think I am?"

"You are the bravest, strongest man I have ever known," Mary said. "But you are not a pirate or a swordsman."

"But I have been practicing..."

"Thomas, he will kill you!"

"Then show me how to gain back our honor! Mary, he claimed you insulted him; he called you a whore, and then he slapped me across the face and demanded to know whether I was man enough to settle this dispute fair and square. What was I supposed to do?"

Mary's mind reeled. She shut her eyes, covered her head with her arms, and shuddered. The dilemma and its inevitable result muddled her thinking. There was no easy way out of this. Thomas returned to his awkward practice.

I said, "When is the duel, and where is it to be held?"

He looked toward me, perhaps registering just now that I had witnessed their entire discourse. "At noon, over there between those trees." He pointed with his sword.

"Where is Lowther getting ready?"

Again he used a sword to direct us toward a general area. "Mary, I will start helping Tom, but we need our swords. Go get them. Now!"

Mary lowered her arms to her sides, deliberating my instructions. I could see several of the pirates slouched around the fire, chatting about the duel. I also noticed Massaquehanna, Fetherston, and Harwood standing together near the shore. I nodded to Mary and absentmindedly gave Deane instructions while I watched Mary race over to the three at the shore. Massaquehanna handed her his sword and guided her in a direction among the palms. She ran in that direction. The trio gazed at each other and moved quickly in the same direction. I could not miss this moment.

"Excellent, Tom. You are improving. Keep practicing your ripostes. I will be right back."

I moved nonchalantly at first, but soon quickened my pace. When I reached the edge of the palms, I sprinted toward the sounds of the dispute. I reached a clearing and saw Mary talking with Lowther. Massaquehanna, Fetherston, and Harwood stood off at a distance.

"I am asking you, please, to withdraw the challenge," Mary said.

"Go straight to bloody hell," Lowther croaked. "Both of you offended me, and by the articles set down in Rackham's ship, I have the right to unsoil my honor."

"It is not a fair fight!"

"If your man knew when to keep his mouth shut, we wouldn't be having this pleasant little chat."

"Then I challenge you right now!"

Lowther spat. "Agreed. Right after I give your husband a castrati voice, and then run him through." He looked at his timepiece and smiled. "'Bout that time."

I wanted to rush forward and slay him right there, but Mary stepped in front of him with a sword drawn. "A fat, spineless hog, a yellow-bellied lap dog, a diseased-ridden goat..."

Lowther cackled. "Give me your best, wench."

"I wasn't talking about you. I was wondering what animal your mother had relations with to have you for a whelp."

Lowther's face steeled.

"When I pulled you off that woman and got a look at you, I wasn't sure if it was hog, dog, or goat, or perhaps a rotting, poxy combination of all three."

Then a truly unusual thing occurred. Massaquehanna began to laugh with gusto. I had never heard him laugh before. It was full of mockery. Fetherston and Harwood parroted him, projecting a robust laugh that crescendoed across the island.

It was too much for Lowther. He yanked his sword from its sheathe and bellowed, "I will slice you into pieces, you filthy whore."

"My pleasure, you Merry-Andrew."

Mary drew her sword. They circled once, and then Lowther lunged and they clashed swords. She parried each thrust, but he drove her backward with vicious slashes. As she neared a tree, Mary feinted to the right, and then riposted. They locked swords and stared at each other. He spat in her face. She blinked once and pulled back her sword just enough so he stumbled forward. She hammered him in the head with the sword's pommel. He staggered a step, cursed shrilly, and charged forward. They engaged several more times, fending off each other's onslaughts.

"Mary!" Deane shouted. He had heard the commotion and come toward it.

Mary glanced to her right, and it was almost the end of her. Lowther tried to capitalize on the distraction with a fierce attack, driving Mary aft in defense.

"After I gut and skewer your harlot, I'll chop you up!" Lowther rasped. He let hurl a hoarse scream and charged at Mary again, hacking and slashing.

She kept sidestepping and deflecting each blow. It seemed that for every five sword strokes he meted out, Mary offered only one in return. But I could see her ploy—wear him down. Soon Lowther's breath became labored, and his thrusts became slower and more predictable, and then the moment came. He wheezed, swallowed hard, and seemed to grasp that his energy was flagging, that the time was now to finish the fight or he would be the vulnerable one. He feinted twice and pretended to stumble, hoping Mary would lunge forward, but she read the ruse. She took a half step forward and screamed like a banshee, but then shifted sideways. Lowther reared upward and plunged ahead, leaving his abdomen unguarded. Mary drove home her blade to the hilt.

Lowther quivered all over and his eyes widened. He struggled to draw a breath. Mary was right up against him, so all he could do was beat weakly against her back with the side of his sword.

"Thank you, Lowther. I have never enjoyed killing anyone so much." She jerked the blade up and down a couple of times. He gurgled and his eyes fluttered. She spat in his face and then pushed him away. He flopped to the sand, palpitated for a few seconds, and then lay still.

Massaquehanna applauded. "Some men…just need killing," he said in his stilted manner. He looked to Fetherston and Harwood. "A square fight?"

They hesitated for a moment, looked at Lowther's body, and nodded.

Mary wiped her sword blade off of Lowther's shirt.

"It was my fight, Mary. Our honor to defend," Deane said. He struggled to contain the emotion in his voice.

"Thomas, my love, your honor needed no defending. This maggoty cockroach was not worthy to cross swords with you. I merely, but gladly, stepped on him for you," Mary said tenderly, walking toward her husband and reaching out to him.

I watched him glance toward the three men, who then looked away. There simply wasn't a reasonable way to convince a husband he needed to be protected against a thug by his wife. It cut right to the core of his masculine pride.

"I just couldn't stand by and watch the love of my life killed. It happened to me once. I could not let it happen twice," Mary said. "Please, hear me. I did it for us." She looked down and kicked at a root, and then wiped her eyes.

"That was not your decision to make," Deane responded, but his voice sounded more sad than bitter. He walked away.

Massaquehanna, Fetherston, and Harwood drifted off in the other direction.

I stepped toward Mary and touched her shoulder. She grabbed me and sobbed against my chest. I could feel the ache of her deep sorrow. The intensity of her loyalty and love and her unswerving drive to avert loss left me speechless. While greater love may hath no one than this, to lay down his life for his friends, I saw in Mary that great love may also demand we fight to the death to preserve it. To experience passion that strongly left me envious. I had never felt such an impulse when I thought about James or Jack. Edward had fought to save me, and I knew Mary would fight and die for me. I searched my heart and was relieved to see I would leap into the flames of perdition for Mary.

"Give him time. He will come around," I said. I tried a joke. "No doubt you will find ways to help him forget and bolster his pride."

Through her tears Mary laughed. “True. I have cast my siren spell.”

“That spell even fooled me for awhile.”

Our conversation was interrupted by a cannonade in the bay. For a moment my stomach churned as I squinted against the glare of the sun and peered out to sea, fearing a man-of-war. But it was a sloop, and its crew called to our vessel, inquiring about trade. We made our way to the shore. I looked back one last time at Lowther’s still form.

Life seemed to be getting cheaper by the day.

CHAPTER XXXII

Later that night, after the sloop had departed, we enjoyed another party with the crew and the ten English turtle hunters from the piraguas. We roasted wild boar, boiled potatoes, stewed salmagundi, fried bananas, and mixed bowls of punch onboard our sloop. Nothing was said of Lowther, though everyone knew the story. The men told ribald stories, played poker, cast dice, sang tunes, danced merrily, and drank heartily.

At one point, Corner the quartermaster set in motion a mock trial. He put a wig on Carty and draped black cloth around him. "Ye' be the judge, Sir Farty Carty."

The pirates hooted. Corner sauntered over importantly and then grabbed Fetherston by the jowls and squeezed. "And this here ugly mug, what heinous crimes do ye charge him with?"

"Rape and rapine!" Harwood bellowed.

"Rape?" Fetherston stood up and shouted. "It was they who begged and pleaded; they wanted to know what a real man was like!"

The pirates hollered and laughed.

"Quiet in the courtroom or I will have you castrated, drawn, quartered, hanged, flogged, and gagged—in that order," Carty yelled and burst into laughter.

"How 'bout killin', stealin', and maimin'?" Dobbin croaked.

"Ooh, the big ones," said Corner. "First witness?"

Harwood raised his stump and stepped forward. "Look what he done to me!"

As the crew continued their trial, I bristled at the jokes they made about rape. I marched up to Rackham and said my piece, but Rackham was preoccupied—aloof and introspective. I nuzzled under his right arm.

"What torments your mind tonight?" I asked.

He said nothing, merely stared in a trance off the portside bow into the darkness, oblivious to the activity onboard. He took a long pull from a bottle of liquor. I searched the features of his face and plainly saw some fearful resolution. He seemed to be counting his days, preparing for the inevitable.

I hugged him tightly, wanting to strengthen him for a final battle of glory against the British men-of-war we heard were scouting for us.

"Captain Howell Davis is dead," he said. "We met at New Providence once with Blackbeard and Vane."

"Yes, I recall."

"A fine Welsh pirate—a colorful man with charm and wit and elegance. He started with Captain Edward England and later consorted with Black Bart. They liked to harass the slave traders along the Gold Coast to Portuguese Guinea. Took some of those Africans back. Some joined as pirates."

"What happened?"

"The captain of that sloop that departed earlier today told me he was ambushed by militia on Principe. He tried to pass himself off as a privateer. He was always sly with his schemes and ruses, but not this time. They killed him. At least Black Bart gave the island a good drubbing before pushing off."

"Well, he's not as smart as you," I said.

"He was smarter." Rackham's voice was morose, resigned. "Blackbeard, Bellamy, Vane, Bonnet, Worley, Griffin, and now Davis—all fine pirate captains and all now dead within just a few years. Our numbers grow thin. The winds and currents are shifting, Anne. We've sold our soul to the devil, and now he's demanding his due. I see his spawn swarming our vessel, smelling blood and licking their chops at the pending feast of our souls,"

His despair went deep, bordering on bedlam. He took another long drink. I swung from sympathy and pity for this man I loved to rage and revulsion for his cowardice. He did not sound like Blackbeard, defiantly making his last stand. He resembled Stede Bonnet, the captain I had seen whimper and plead just before he swung from the derrick in White Point, Charles Towne.

"So let us embrace our paganism—eat, drink, and be merry, for tomorrow we die," he said, unhooking himself from my arms and stumbling off toward his cabin to finish off his consciousness with another bottle of port.

I glanced toward the pirates. The trial had broken up, and now they turned to gaming. In their soused states, they began to turn violent. The poker game was interrupted by accusations and counteraccusations of cheating, and a brawl ensued. I watched Harwood and Fetherston team up to beat one of the Englishmen unconscious. When Dobbin and Carty objected to the relentless beating, they turned on them and more scraps broke out. Massaquehanna managed to break up the fights with an axe handle, but most of the men had already slipped into drunken, snoring oblivion. I walked up to Mary, who had also been drinking steadily, and sat beside her. I took the bottle and took a swallow, relishing the burn down my gullet.

"How's Thomas?"

"Still giving me the silent treatment," she said.

As Mary prattled on about Deane's fine qualities, I could not help but catch the whispered words shared between Earl and Fenwick as they hunkered over a demijohn and leaned against the mast. They plotted that once we passed out they would have their way with us, teach us a lesson and put us back in our places. As they chuckled, my frustration exploded. Were we among men or beasts? Was this civilization or savagery, liberation or slavery? What did those pirate articles we had signed really mean? Weren't they about respect and understanding?

I spied an oar, snatched it up, and moved quickly. Before either could defend themselves, I jabbed Fenwick in the gut, and then swung the oar and bashed Earl across the face. As Fenwick gasped for air I finished him off with a swipe to the temple. For good measure I gave each a sharp kick and a good mashing with my heel where it mattered most to them and least to me.

Mary watched me with detached interest. I tossed the oar aside and plopped down next to her. "What was that about?"

"Plotting revenge against us. Thought I'd beat them to the punch."

"Feel better?"

"Much."

"Reason and logic do seem to have broken down here."

"On the contrary, I think it logical they will reason that being more careful around us would be a prudent course," I said.

"Aptly put."

I looked up through the ratlines, rigging, and spars to the obscured stars. "I am lonely tonight, Mary. And I fear our adventure is drawing to an end."

"I feel miserable, too."

"Are we too late to make a fresh start of it—too late to begin the prodigal's journey? We could slink off into the forest there and disappear. Begin a new life and blot out the old one."

Mary looked down and nudged at an empty hogshead. "I can't leave Thomas."

"Wouldn't he be pleased with such an idea? We could hold him down, tie him up, and kidnap him. He would come around after awhile."

Mary bit her lips and sighed. "I want to wait for him. Perhaps in another day or two we can all make our move. Anne?"

Her voice had changed. "What?"

"I'm with Thomas' child."

I reached out and held her. "I might be with child again, too. I missed my last menstruation."

We were quiet for a long time, listening to the jungle sounds waft across the inlet. "We won't leave without Thomas," I said.

"What about Jack?"

"I think Jack is beyond my reach anymore. Fear and liquor have him in their clutches."

"Piracy, marriage, and motherhood make poor bedfellows," Mary said.

"A whole new set of values has been dropped into our laps," I said.

We leaned against each other and dozed for a while. Then we stirred, helped each other up, and climbed into our hammocks.

The next morning Dobbin suggested target practice with a cannon on a cluster of palm trees. I joined in loading cannonball, carrying gunpowder from the ship's magazine, priming the fuse, and using the rammer and swabber. He helped me aim and I was pleased when my round sheered off the top of a tree. I rather enjoyed the smell of burning gunpowder and feeling the quaver of the cannon's recoil along the deck.

The fun would not last.

CHAPTER XXXIII

Harwood sighted a sail entering the bay. Rackham glassed its progress.

"A large sloop flying royal colors—heavily armed," Rackham noted. "Fetherston, have the crew put the shoulder to the capstan and raise the anchor."

The crew set to feverish work, weighing anchor and hoisting the main and topgallant sheets. The man-of-war drew a bead on us, trying to cut off our escape and bottle us in. Rackham ordered a tacking and we slipped by, keeping too far away for an effective broadside.

The sloop hailed us. "Captain Jonathon Barnet, commissioned by the Governor of Jamaica to take all pirates in these waters! Identify yourselves!"

"Jack Rackham from Cuba!" Rackham replied.

"Surrender or we will destroy your ship and all that are in it!"

"If you can catch us!" shouted Harwood.

"You will find our surrender coming out of the muzzle of our guns, Captain!" Rackham shouted.

Dobbin, Carty, Bourn, Corner, and Fenwick screamed profanities and taunted the vessel by exposing themselves and clapping their behinds. I heard a shot fired from a swivel gun and turned to see Howell shaking his fist at our sudden enemy. Our crew laughed and mocked theirs.

"Raise our Jolly Roger for good measure!" Rackham ordered.

The pock-faced English captain of the piraguas rushed up. "Captain Rackham, can we disembark? My men and I wish to retrieve our boats and our turtle stores on the isle."

"A bit late for regrets. It is time to cut your losses while we hedge our bets."

The Englishman glared at Rackham. "We didn't bargain for any of this!"

"It is what it is. You're now guilty by association."

He shook his head and moved feebly to his crew, who crouched below the railing at the bow. They looked grim.

Though we were faster, Barnet managed to keep us in sight. We spent the remainder of the day fleeing, slowly gaining distance on Barnet's sloop. Being hunted was a new experience. I would have preferred a straight fight. I hinted to Fetherston that we put fight or flight to a vote.

"I say we stand tall and fight them. Let the best ship win the day," I whispered, hoping to inspire Fetherston to take the lead. He said he would bring it up, but he never did.

I wandered over to Mary and shared my burden. "What do you expect? These men are pirates out to save their own necks, not revolutionaries sacrificing their lives for a worthy cause. See the handwriting on the wall, Anne, not what you wish was on it."

Without a word, I walked to the whetstone and honed my cutlass. Later, I cleaned my muskets and loaded them. After that, I sat down on a barrel in the stern and watched the pursuing sloop. I thought about the words of judgment on King Belshazzar's wall: *Mene Mene, Tekel, Upharsin*—measured, weighed, and found wanting. Yes, our time was at hand.

After nightfall, Rackham ordered all of our lights extinguished so we wouldn't jeopardize our position. He picked a bay and we cruised into it under the glimmer of the stars. We waited in quiet for several hours to see whether we had given Barnet the slip or would be forced to levy a night battle.

After four hourglasses, some of the pirates began drinking again, congratulating themselves on their cunning flight, their navigation skills, and their speed at raising and trimming the sheets. I overheard Rackham talking to Fetherston of Madagascar, another pirate lair in the Indian Ocean, where Black Bart had sailed after Howell Davis' demise. It was an old and secure haven for such pirate captains of the past such as Kidd, Culliford, Tew, Halsey, White, and North. It was still well fortified enough to fend off even the best men-of-war of Britain, France, and Spain.

I sat beside Mary and rested against her, feeling the beat of her heart.

"Let's make our move tomorrow morning," she whispered.

As I looked out at the starry host, I felt enticed by "dewy-feathered sleep," as Milton once penned.

We never got our chance.

Chapter XXXIV

We jerked awake to the deafening concussion of a cannonade punching holes in our sails and splintering our mast. I stood up in the now-glowing darkness and beheld Barnet's sloop, brightly lit and casting dim light on our ship. All its guns were showing, primed and ready. An instant later, I saw gunpowder flashes followed by smoke plumes and the jarring impact of the cannonballs against our timbers. Dozens of red-coated soldiers stood at the gunwales with muskets trained on our sloop.

"All is ready, Captain Barnett. We await your order!" shouted a gunner from the ship.

"Demast them. Pour it on. Keep firing at will!" the captain shouted from the poopdeck.

I wheeled around and surveyed the deck. Nearly everyone was just stirring awake, but they were still drunk. Massaquehanna stood by the mast and let loose a Seminole battlecry, trying to arouse us to war. He raised his tomahawk with one hand and a musket with the other. I started to call to him, but my voice was lost in a thunderous torrent of cannon blasts. The pounding of the balls catapulting into our vessel jounced me off my feet. I looked up and saw a cascade of wood splinters and iron shrapnel raining down from the topmast. I covered my head and felt hot pieces of iron burning through my clothes. I brushed the smoldering metals, and then heard the crack of our mast and watched it start to totter. I saw Massaquehanna, wounded and still crying out, struggling to free himself from a tangle of rigging. I screamed as the beam fell and crushed him, and then he cried out no more. I tried to grasp the meaning of this moment, but there was no time.

I heard others on deck groaning and calling for help. Across the way I could hear the British reloading. There was a period of silence while Captain Barnet assessed our response.

After shoving aside broken spars and frayed rigging, I looked toward Mary. She brushed away cinders and dust from her face. "Hopelessly outnumbered, right?"

"Aye."

"Why swing in shame when we could choose our time in a whirl of gunfire with laughter on our lips," Mary said.

"Boadicea."

We leaped up and fired our pistols. I saw two soldiers cry out and go down. We fired our reserve musketoons and then dove below the gunwale. A deluge of musket fire followed, splintering the taffrail and deck. As we reloaded, I finally saw activity. Fetherston, clearly drunk, pitched an unlit coconut grenade at Barnet's sloop, and then ducked behind the shards of our mast. The rest of the pirates were running about helter-skelter, searching for weapons. We rose again, fired twice, and then crouched down, scrambling toward the mounted swivel gun at the stern. Whenever we found a loaded gun, we stood up and discharged it.

Another broadside battered our sloop, pitching me forward. I looked up and saw that the swivel gun had been destroyed. Our ship began to canter to the starboard side. None of our guns below deck were ready. Mary and I jumped up and fired our pistols again into a wave of redcoats. They massed in such tight ranks it was easy to wound them, but their sheer numbers were overwhelming. We dropped to the deck just as they greeted us with a massive volley of gunfire. I looked toward the cabin door and saw Rackham emerge, his clothes wrinkled and unbuttoned, a bottle of wine in one hand and a sword in the other. His face looked stunned, his eyes wide. I scanned the deck and could see that actually only Massaquehanna and one of the English turtle hunters were dead. Everyone else cowered. No one was returning fire.

I could hear the sound of grappling hooks bouncing onto our planks. The British crew dragged the hooks along by rope until they caught hold of the timbers. I peered over and saw Captain Barnet's men tugging at the coils and drawing the two vessels together. It was difficult to load our guns in the glimmering dark. Just as I finished priming my second pistol, I witnessed a shocking sight. Led by Rackham's cry, the entire crew scampered and crawled to the hold, vanishing below deck. It felt like I had consumed a scalding cannonball that burned down my throat and boiled in my gut. My temples pounding, I felt suddenly dizzy. It made no sense. The dastards were merely delaying the inevitable if they wouldn't fight, accepting the authority of judges and rulers, which pointed to bound hands, a few steps up the derrick, humiliation from the crowd, a hemp noose snug around the neck, a chance to confess, and "a quick drop and a sudden stop," as Rackham once put it.

"Cowards! Traitors!" Mary shouted. "You'll swing from the gallows anyway! Why not fight? Why give them the satisfaction?"

"It's over, isn't it?" I said.

She stopped yelling and looked at me. Sweat and grime soiled her face. Her raven hair was matted to one side. A trickle of blood ran from one ear. "Afraid so, Anne."

"Then let's give our real enemies a taste of the hell that awaits them."

I charged across the deck, Mary following me. We stayed low to avoid the soldiers' scattered musket fire. We reached the doors of the hold and flung them open. Below, the pirates and the turtle hunters sat in the shadows, hunkered down.

"Quarter! Mercy!" they shouted from the hold, expecting to see British soldiers with guns trained on them.

"You gutless, spineless cowards!" I screamed. "I thought you were men—real pirates!"

And then I did what I had never thought myself capable of doing. My outrage and shock were so great; I acted on primal impulse. I emptied my guns on my fellow pirates, men I had sailed with and fought alongside these past two years. Their turning tail and running like rabbits felt like betrayal, desertion. In the face of such a marooning, only silence and violence pulsed through me. I caught Fenwick in the thigh and Dobbin in the shoulder; they clambered to the timbers and held their wounds. They cursed and pleaded with me for mercy. Mary unloaded her guns, too. More high-pitched screams followed.

"Anne, have you lost your mind!" Rackham cried.

My body functioned like clockwork, made to act without a mind. I looked down and saw a musketoon on the deck. I picked it up, swore at them, and fired again into the crowd of pirates. Harwood grasped his ear and squealed.

Suddenly we heard the footfalls of the British soldiers behind us. I stiffened back and braced for capture. I dropped the guns, stretched my arms outward, closed my eyes, and raised my face upward. This final attack on my men had emptied me of all resistance, draining the aggression and mortifying my nature. Sorrow spidered its way throughout my being. Soldiers grabbed me roughly from behind and lifted me off the ground. A scream came hurtling from deep within my throat—a scream of rage and horror, of guilt and bitterness, of regret and loss.

I did not stop screaming until they gagged my mouth and clapped irons on my arms and legs. I watched stupefied as Mary fought the soldiers, throwing elbows, spitting and scratching at their faces. One of the soldiers bashed her in the temple with the butt end of his musket, and I saw Mary crumple to the deck.

They dragged me to their sloop. I cast a backward glance and saw the pirates emerging from the hold with their hands raised high. I stumbled at the gangway and fell to my knees. I felt strong arms grasp my shoulders and pull me back up. I looked into the face of the soldier who had lifted me up. My head swirled and I gasped for breath.

It was James.

We stared dumbfounded at each other.

"Anne?"

For the first time in quite a while, my face flushed and my tongue was still. My ego skewered and my dignity seared, I struggled to find words to mask my sudden shame.

"Is it you then?" he asked. "Bring me a taper!"

"Yes," I said and looked away.

He paused, chewing at the inside of his mouth. I could sense his eyes scan my body, my face, and my eyes. I felt naked.

One of the soldiers asked, "You two know each other?"

"This is what it's come to?" he asked, seeming to choose his words.

I straightened myself and stared at him.

The other soldiers sensed something significant occurring. One whispered, "Do you need your privacy with her, sir?"

Like a bucket of icy water dousing a sleeping man, his tongue awakened. "So this is it? You're now a lowly, pathetic whore living on a ship of spineless rogues? Keeping them happy?"

His self-righteousness lashed my pride. My tongue roused from its slumber.

"Who are you to dare judge me!" I screamed. "A snitch, a lackey, and a slave to Rodgers! You're not a man; you're a cringing mouse. And if memory serves, not much bigger than a mouse down south." I smirked and let my eyes fall below his belt to make sure the other soldiers grasped my meaning.

"You back-stabbing, adulterous whore…"

"You expected faithfulness from me when you are nothing but a trembling, lying, conniving weasel with no backbone. I was ashamed of you, you pitiful, hen-hearted…"

"Why did you abandon me so quickly?" His voice had abruptly changed. I heard heartache and confusion, no longer accusation. "Didn't our vows before God mean anything to you? Did you ever love me?"

His softened, questioning tone unsettled me. I did not know how to respond so I spat on the deck and looked back at him defiantly, but he had already begun walking away, issuing orders. I wanted to chase him down, wrap my hands around his neck, and stifle the breath out of his sanctimonious voice and gouge out his judgmental eyes with my nails.

"Place her in the galley with this other woman. Make sure they have fresh straw and water. Treat them with consideration."

I squinted at James' uniform, and seeing the epaulets I realized he was now an officer for the British Royal Navy. And I was in his custody.

CHAPTER XXXV

The voyage to St. Jago de la Vega took only a handful of hours. The British towed our barely seaworthy sloop into the port and anchored along the quay. We were lined up and escorted in shackles to the prison. I noticed that not only the pirates, but also the nine English turtle hunters from the piragua and our galley slaves, including Deane, were all taken to the prison. I could see Rackham at the front of the pack, his clothes dirty and wrinkled, trying to walk with dignity even in the face of public jeers. People lined up on both sides of us, a kind of gauntlet, and heaved gobs of filth at us. A couple of drunken men chanted, "Pirate trollops! Buccaneer strumpets!"

When the soldiers said nothing, the pair grew emboldened. They ran up to Mary and me and grabbed at our breasts. Our hands were trussed from behind so all we could do was swear and spit at them. A soldier intervened, and as they drew away, he slapped me on the behind and laughed.

We passed the gallows, where I saw two pirates hanging in gibbets; they were covered in tar to preserve their bodies and keep the birds from pecking away at their gory flesh. Mary and I were led down a dark corridor to a steamy, fetid dungeon that smelled of sweat, urine, excrement, and death and locked in a separate cell from the men. On the brick walls were etched names and dates of prisoners, some quotes and drawings. Skull and crossbones, gallows and a noose, dated headstones, a few nude women in provocative scenes—all covered the walls and low ceiling. I read the classic phrases I had learned as a pirate: "No prey, no pay," "The sweet trade," "A merry life and a short one," and then a more solemn one—"Father, forgive me. I knew not what I did."

All manner of insects crawled over me during the night hours. I could hear rats scratching nests in the straw. Mary, still loopy and droopy from the blow she had received the day before, fell asleep frequently. Withering in the humidity, I tried to keep her cool with a damp cloth. I saved my gruel and bread for her. After a day passed she started to perk up, though she complained of an excruciating headache. An official presented himself and read from a document from the Court of Admiralty informing us of our trial date. He clarified our ages, places of birth, and most recent abode. I was surprised to learn that Mary was twenty-seven, seven years older than me. We were to be prosecuted as pirates, marauders of the sea. The trial would commence in two weeks as the British tribunal was still in the middle of Captain Charles Vane's trial. After the official left I slumped next to Mary, sitting on a pile of mildewed straw.

"A far cry from the winds and the sea," I said, glancing around the cell.

"Aye. We are facing a dim and grim end."

"Should have jumped ship when we had the chance."

"Couldn't leave my man—my fatal flaw," Mary said. "By the way, what was that row you had with the officer?"

I plucked at a piece of straw and began snapping off little pieces of it. "He was my first husband, James."

Mary chuckled and shook her head. "You are the queen of chance encounters. And?"

I stared absently at the far wall. "He seems different now."

"In a good way?"

"I think so. Stronger, more confident maybe—grown up."

"Anne, I feel miserable. My head is throbbing and I have morning sickness."

"Stale bread, stagnate water, and cruel gruel, along with a wallop on the head—quite the combination," I said.

Mary bent forward and retched on the ground. I rubbed her back and shoulders. When she was finished, she wiped her mouth and lay down. I soaked a piece of cloth in the water, wrung it slightly, and draped it around her perspiring neck. Once I heard the rhythmic breathing of her sleep, I picked myself up and paced around the cell. I, too, was pregnant. Would I live to see my child? Would my body carry this one to birth, or would I reject it again?

I whispered a long prayer, asking God to forgive me and to give this baby a chance to live. Stopping at the barred window, I looked out at the silvery bay. I closed my eyes and breathed the remnant sea breezes that drifted to these prison bars.

Starting with my earliest memory, I let my attention slowly meander through the mental portraits, the memorable events of my life, in the recesses of my mind. As one thought flowed and rose, it crested for a moment, and then slid down only to be followed by another. I did not rush through my past; I had time.

I committed myself to spending the coming days letting my brain mull over every remembrance I had, substantial or inane, turning each one over with care, considering its meaning. I remembered reading of Socrates in prison, defying the powers that be, bravely awaiting the bowl of hemlock. Obviously I was no Greek philosopher, but I took his words to heart with what was left of my existence: "The unexamined life is not worth living."

The days passed slowly. Mary's fever and cough worsened. The dampness and stench of our cell and the inedible food and briny water did not help her condition, but my pleas for help fell on deaf ears.

The day of our trial finally came. The guards rustled us from our beds of straw and clapped our feet and hands in irons. Dressed like scarecrows, unwashed for a fortnight, and smelling like cattle, we were led to the court. I asked whether we would be given any opportunity to change and bathe, but the guards did not answer.

As I walked in I saw officials of the Court of Admiralty assembled. Sir Nicholas Lawes presided. The guards seated us. On the other side of the courtroom I saw my fellow pirates and heard their names recited aloud: John Rackham, mariner, late master and commander of a certain pirate sloop; George Fetherston, late navigator of said sloop; Richard Corner, quartermaster; and John Davies, John Howell, Thomas Bourn, Noah Harwood, James Dobbin, Patrick Carty, Thomas Earl, and John Fenwick. The nine English turtle hunters were also present, as well as the half-dozen galley crew, including Deane.

After a lengthy and tiresome recitation of Sir Lawes' official commissions from the British Parliament, the court officials proceeded to read the charges against us. I listened vacantly—"did piratically, feloniously, and in an hostile manner attack, engage...set upon, shoot at, and take merchant sloops...in corporeal fear of their lives."

"How do you plead?" Sir Lawes asked.

Rackham arose, and with a show of his former bluster and bluff, proclaimed, "Not guilty, Your Honor. We are privateers fighting for freedom, and therefore, we are at war with all nations who enslave and waylay their people with heavy taxes and subjugate them with absurd and unjust laws. We believe you, not us, are the real criminals of humanity..."

The judge banged his gavel and ordered Rackham to cease and desist unless he wanted to be gagged. "Keep your decorum in mind! We know you are the lynchpin to this piratical endeavor, but your rodomontade and vainglory will accomplish little in this honorable court. Need I remind you we hanged your former captain, Charles Vane, at Port Royal just yesterday?" Sir Lawes added.

Rackham grimaced. He seemed to consider another verbal affront, but instead he sat down. I could see that even this vaunting display was weary and half-hearted, a feeble attempt at representing his crew and his life with grist and impudence, a last stand mustered against the impending certitude of death. For all my prison cell introspection and prayers to God, I could not shake off the bitterness I harbored in my heart against Rackham's last act as a pirate captain—leading a surrender of his ship and his men.

The court called Captain Thomas Spenlow to testify. Our crew exchanged stunned looks. Fetherston shook his head. Dressed to make an impression, Spenlow stepped proudly to the docket and sat himself down with a dose of panache. He smiled broadly at us. I fantasized knocking out his teeth one by one with a belaying pin and then slicing out his haughty tongue. Trumpeting in a grandiose tone, he described, in minute detail, how his schooner was fired upon, boarded, and looted of its stores, and how he and his crew had been incarcerated and tormented for two days before we set them free. Other than the exaggerations of his torment, I had to grant that Spenlow kept to the facts in the case, though he varnished his account with a bit too much florid language. By the look on the commissioners' faces, the incriminating testimony struck home. Once dismissed, Spenlow arose with noble mummery and walked slowly for the door.

"Sniveling little weasel. Should of cut your testicles and made you eat them," Harwood rasped.

Spenlow froze, wheeled, and pointed. "I will gladly be present to witness your performance of the fancy dance on the air."

Harwood struggled to rise, but two guards pushed him back down and crammed a wad of cloth into his mouth.

Spenlow turned to Sir Lawes. "Your Honor, may I suggest each of these cutthroats be given the canto from Dante's *Inferno* about thieves. It's quite vivid. It will give them something to cogitate upon while they're eternally roasting in Satan's dominion."

"That will be enough, Captain Spenlow."

He flashed us another smile and left the courtroom.

A second witness, James Spatchears, provided the specifics concerning the action between our band of pirates and Captain Barnet's man-of-war.

Eventually, Rackham was allowed to speak. He attempted the privateer argument, claiming that every ship we had taken either failed to properly identify itself or was clearly an enemy of Britain. Even though he didn't possess official papers, Rodgers and Britain had benefited from our actions. He then tried to save those we had enslaved to work in the galley and the English turtle hunters, Mary and me, and even the two galley cats: Dante and Milton.

Sir Lawes ignored Rackham's plea for the nine Englishmen or us. He did spend some time clarifying with Fetherston and Corner about the men of our galley. To abbreviate the whole laborious process, he finally set them all free, including Deane. I glanced at Mary and saw her clench a fist in triumph.

Ordering the pirates to rise, Sir Lawes declared: "Based on the testimony given, I find you guilty as pirates. You are condemned to hanging until you die. May God have mercy on your souls."

I looked at my pirate friends. They expressed no emotion, except Howell, our fiddler, who put his face in his hands. He had been the most sensitive of the pack. I thought he deserved Fiddler's Green rather than Inferno. Upon hearing his sentence, Rackham set his stubbled jaw. He blinked once and I could see the vein in his forehead bulge. He glanced toward me, forcing an unruly grin. My thoughts flailed. Rackham had led the crew in a crazed race to the hold, which I found pathetic. On the other hand, I carried his child in my womb and wanted to be proud of that fact. I turned away, feeling forlorn.

"Due to the unusual circumstances of this case, we will hold separate trials for the nine Englishmen who were aboard the pirate ship when it was captured by Captain Barnet, and another trial will be held for these two women who have been accused of piracy—Anne Bonney and Mary Reade." Sir Lawes closed a book and left the bench.

Back in our pestilential cell, Mary and I slipped into a pensive silence. Each of us shuffled aimlessly, distracted by our diverse thoughts—our fellow pirates and their fates, our upcoming trial, our babies starting to move within us, and what future, if any, we could wish for. Just as I was about to comment on Deane's freedom, a guard marched up to the bars.

"Anne Bonney?" the guard asked.

I turned toward him.

"Before his execution, Captain Rackham has requested a final meeting with you. The judge has granted his last wish. You are asked to make an appearance in Rackham's cell immediately," he said.

Mary and I exchanged glances as the guard opened the jail door. As I was escorted to Rackham's chamber, I ignored the guard's lewd comments about my relationship with Rackham. He appeared to like the ring of "piratical prostitute." My mind focused instead on the last words I would say to my second husband. What was the point in mincing words, covering the truth in the name of kindness, and carrying lies to the grave? Honesty would be my one and only course from here on out, I told myself.

We stopped in front of a set of bars. From the shadows, Rackham emerged like an eel from its lair. With tears in his eyes, he reached out for me through the bars, but I was too far away and I did not move toward him.

"A little privacy if you will," I said to the guard.

He debated whether to ignore my request, yearning to hear the details of our last chat, but finally he drew away.

"Anne, I wanted with my last breaths to express my love to you, and tell you I have only beautiful memories of you. You will be all that is in my mind as I stand at the gallows. You will be my final and sweetest thought as the chute collapses and I drop…"

I cut him off. During my days of introspection, I had looked intently upon my pirate story and my days with Calico Jack Rackham. I had seen too much posturing and cockiness and too little bravery and valor. He was a tightly wrapped package of pride and show, but without courage and principle. There was nothing honorable in us; we were only sea raiders. From guiding the marionette strings on Throckmorton to ducking opportunity and responsibility in every real battle we had confronted, Rackham had taken the safe passage each time. He had deserted me with child and then abandoned his crew in the hour of their greatest need—and for what? A few more days of life decaying in a jail cell? A chance to give Rodgers the fulfillment of watching us die in ignominy? I would live upon no more lies. So I spoke.

"Jack, what unmanned you? No. No more," I stammered, and then regained my composure and slowly raised my hands. "I have only one thing to say: if you had fought like a man, or even a woman for that matter, you need not have been hanged like a dog." I turned and started to walk away.

"Anne, don't end it like this. I'm begging you!"

As I started away, I could hear Rackham's pleas echoing down the corridor. It left me cold, indifferent. "Lord, have mercy on him—because I can't," I whispered under my breath.

As I entered our cell, Mary asked, "Well?"

I heard our prison door slam shut and the key drive the bolt home. "Cowardice, not death, did us part," I said.

"Grudges—just another set of chains and prison bars you'll feel weighing you down even after he's gone," Mary said.

"That milksop didn't deserve..." I continued.

I hesitated, searching for a suitable response. I walked to the furthest corner in our cell, kneeled down, and pressed my face against my legs, battling a storm of anguish.

The next day, November 16, 1720, Captain Calico Jack Rackham, Navigator George Fetherston, Quartermaster Richard Corner, Gunner John Davies, and Fiddle player John Howell were led to Gallows Point at Port Royal, Jamaica, read their crimes aloud for the benefit of the eyewitnesses, and hanged. I was told Rackham's body was tarred and hung from a gibbet as a warning to any who considered piracy as a career. A guard told me they had all faced their last moments coolly.

The following day the remaining six pirates of our band were strung up in Kingston.

Only my memories of each man survived.

And now all I had was my friend Mary and my baby.

CHAPTER XXXVI

The guards started eyeing us more, making lascivious remarks to us, and promising a visit real soon.

"You're welcome to us," Mary said. "That is if you don't mind a dose of the clap. I understand the burning sensation is ecstatic for men."

"There's other means," one of the guards taunted.

Mary picked up a hard clay plate, smiled, and chomped down hard on it, cracking off a piece. "Enter at your own risk."

The guard spat and moved away.

Mary clasped my hand and gave me a nod. "Never dissevered, forever together. Aye, Anne?"

"Until we fertilize the earth."

A clergyman visited us shortly after all our fellow pirates had been executed. By then both of us were feeling our bellies swell. He spoke of repentance and grace and offered to lead us in the sinner's prayer. The worm of bitterness was still wriggling around my heart, so I made it clear I wanted nothing to do with his "hypocrisies and distortions."

He was an obese old man with a threadbare suit and an old wig. His paunch rolled over his belt like a sack of groats. His nose was bulbous and his cheeks puffy. With his rheumy eyes he gave me a stare that seemed to snarl. I wanted to leap up and bash him in the nose, but I controlled myself. I did not want to be separated from Mary and consigned to a solitary cell. He pointed a beefy finger at me.

"Have you ever seen a leper, miss?" he snapped.

"Yes, I have."

"Grotesque, wasn't he?"

"She! She was a friend of mine!"

"Do you know why her body rotted and dripped away?" Each word he uttered sprayed sprinkles of saliva at me. "Her nerves were dead, so her limbs decayed a little each day. Lepers can't feel. Touching a pillow or a burning coal—it is all the same to them."

I thought of Annabelle slowly wasting away, trying her best to keep her spirits up. "What the hell is your point?"

"Your heart is leprous! Virtue or vice—it's all the same to you. Meanwhile your conscience drips and rots away. So much wicked pride before facing your demise—'tis a pity truly."

"May a leprous pox form on your sagging, blubbery body! I don't have much to lose, so be careful what you spew from that putrid maw," I shouted and turned away.

"Spiritual leprosy," he mumbled.

After that display, I assumed Mary would share my attitude and send him packing, but she asked him to stay. They spent an hour talking in a quiet, cordial tone. He had a Bible open and led her in prayer several times. He gave Mary the Bible and threw me a disparaging glance as he left.

We spent the next few days talking and reading to each other. Mary tried reading from an epistle or two, but I suggested we try the colorful stories in Genesis, Exodus, Samuel, Kings, and Judges. Because the mood seemed appropriate, we also delved into the bizarre images in the Book of Revelations.

Once, as I thumbed through the pages, I noticed a passage from Micah underscored in ink. I read it aloud: "He hath shown thee, O man, what is good; and what doth the Lord require of thee, but to do justly, and to love mercy, and to walk humbly with thy God?"

"Well, it's a good thing that's only addressed to men," Mary said wryly, "not exactly living models of it, are we?"

"Edward used to tell me it's never too late to be reconciled to God, but I don't think I'm ready."

"I suppose it is by God's grace we've been granted more time than our comrades had," Mary said. "Perhaps it is time to read for the message instead of the stories."

Another time Mary surprised me in her supplication to thank the Lord for the rats and insects and stench of our prison cell. I began to think her mind was slipping. After she had finished her prayer, I asked her what she meant.

"Don't you see? We are chained, unarmed, and outnumbered. This infested cell and our unkempt appearance protects us against rape from those beasts."

Mary had a way of seeing reality that never ceased to make me wonder. At one point in Acts we stumbled on the story of Paul in prison. He sang hymns late into the night and then an earthquake tore down the walls. We gave it a try. Nothing gained, nothing lost. We also spent some time on the woman at the well and thought about the thirst that had driven us to piracy. During this time, Mary continued to struggle with a nagging cough and fever.

Our trial started Monday, November 25. To put it succinctly, it followed a similar path to the trial of Rackham and the men. The charges were identical, but the witnesses more numerous. The court had a difficult time accepting that we were bona fide female pirates, but every testimony matched the prior one: we had been willing and active members of Rackham's pack of sea rovers. The only differences revolved around whether we had donned male versus female clothing. Otherwise, Mary and I proved every bit as roguish, brutish, and profligate as the men, renowned for our vulgarity, aggression, and larceny. I felt detached, as if I were watching actors on a stage, or having a vivid dream one remembers after awaking.

Told to stand, we arose, our arms linked, our free hands resting upon our stomachs. "In your perpetration of piracy, the court finds you guilty as charged, finding that you did piratically and feloniously victimize innocent seafarers, robbing and tormenting them," Sir Lawes said.

I squeezed Mary's arm. She leaned slightly against me.

"You, Mary Reade and Anne Bonney, are to go hence to the place of execution, where you shall be severally hanged by the neck until you are severally dead. And may God in his infinite mercy be merciful to both of your souls."

He paused and gave us a grim stare. "Do you wish to say anything?"

Mary and I looked at each other and played the only card we held.

In unison we said, "We plead our bellies."

A hush of silence fell upon the room as the judge and commissioners grasped the import of our words.

"You are both quick with child?" Sir Lawes clarified.

We said nothing.

"Pirates and prostitutes? You probably don't even know who the fathers are!" he shouted indignantly. "Do you have no shame?"

His moral outrage, preached like the brusque old parson, struck me as comical. His shaggy eyebrows quivered, and spittle bubbled off his lips as he yelled. Was I incorrigibly callused? Or was it simply that he was an ornery old man grousing out his self-righteousness? Whatever the reason, I thought it hilarious. I started to laugh. Mary joined me.

"You make a mockery of your whoredom and turpitude, you poxy, pregnant bed sluts?"

Our laughter was suddenly interrupted, or rather stunned to surprise, by a most remarkable event. From the back of the courtroom, Mary's husband marched forward to the bench and yelled, "I'll not have you disgrace my wife." He lunged over the bench and slapped Sir Lawes across his glib old face, causing his periwig to slide askew on his bald skull and his jowls to wiggle. Those in the courtroom fell into convulsing laughter. "I demand a duel to restore the dignity of my respectable spouse."

Three guards pounced on Deane and tackled him to the floor. He continued to shout, but his words were muffled. I looked over at Mary and saw an enormous smile spreading across her face. She whistled loudly and applauded. I joined her.

As Deane was dragged from the court, he reached out toward Mary and shouted. "I love you, Mary! I will wait for you!"

"I love you too, Thomas Deane! I will always be true!" Mary hollered back.

As Sir Lawes attempted to regain his composure and the order in his courtroom, Mary nudged me. "A fine man. I do know how to pick them, don't I?"

"Without a doubt, Mary."

"A shame I couldn't finagle a little private time with him. He deserves all my appreciation, and I have much to give," she said, arching her brows.

"I'm sure you do, you little doxy," I said.

After some hurried discussion between the commissioners, we heard the predictable sentence. Because it was against British law to execute a pregnant woman, we would be allowed to live until we gave birth, and then we would be hanged. Custody of our babies would be granted to family, if we had any, or they would be sent to an orphanage. First a physician would examine us to make sure we were indeed with child.

We now had about five months before we faced the gallows.

As we were marched back to our cell, I looked askance and mumbled to Mary. "And now we've become a cautionary tale for parents to tell their children."

"Or a good bedtime story. Do you think kids would hear our duly unruly story and learn what not to do?"

"Do they ever?" I asked.

A couple of days later we were placed in a better cell with beds and blankets and given a greater amount of sustenance more regularly. We received new dresses and were allowed to bathe frequently. Our days passed peaceably, except for Mary's chronic cough and fever. A physician gave her medicines and herbs for grippe, malaria, dengue, and yellow fever, but they had little effect. I worried about her whenever she slept, as she seemed to suffer more during the nights.

One day we received the jolting news that the nine English turtle hunters had been convicted of piratical intent and associating with and assisting Rackham's pirate vessel. On February 17, 1721, they were put to death at Gallows Point. The draconian injustice of it all refueled my fury against the British government. I found myself taking issue with God, not just about the Englishmen's demise, but also about Mary and her unborn child's waning health. Did God care? Was He fair?

After Deane was flogged and released for his assault on the judge, he was allowed visits with Mary. I would sit in the corner of our cell, trying to give them privacy, but honestly I enjoyed watching them cuddle and whisper into each other's ears, making the most of their last moments together. Their little acts of affection and the endearing terms they whispered warmed me. They had decided that Deane would raise their child in the Americas, where he could find work as a professor of letters at a college.

About this time my life's course took another unpredictable tack: James came to visit me. He stepped up to the bars, dressed in his formal regalia, cleared his throat, and called to me. The past two years had given him a more rugged look. He had a few more creases on his tanned face and a scar imprinted on his forehead down to the bridge of his nose. He was somehow more handsome for the marks. He stood tall in his brushed uniform, giving him an air of assurance. The military hat, the gold buttons, and the epaulets filled me with a mixture of disdain, curiosity, and pride. I wanted to ask him questions and learn about his odyssey, but all kind words stuck in my throat, overpowered by my ego and an impulse to insult him with shame-sharpened words.

"What the hell do you want now? Curious for the spicy details? Looking to slake your lust on a pregnant woman, you perverted swine? Or do you have a damned self-righteous sermon to preach?"

He sighed and fixed his eyes on mine. "None of those, Anne."

"Then what? Spit it out, you little mouse. Your uniform doesn't impress me one bit. Did you think you could flaunt your rank, be the little cock of the walk, and I would bow to you?"

Mary gave me a frown, which inflamed me even more. I felt this creeping sense that James had not come to hurt me, but that only prickled my nerves more. There was no knife or gun in his hands, though, and no hidden agenda in his tone.

"Anne, after your capture and incarceration, I knew you would face a court of law..."

"And?"

He paused, trying to find words.

"Out with it. I don't have all day!" I railed.

"I sent a letter to your father and your Uncle Edward."

"Who gave you the right to do that? Were you trying to humiliate me more? Well I congratulate your efforts, but they won't work. I don't care..."

"I told them you were with child."

"You bastard! Who do you think you are? How dare you stick your nose into my family's affairs? To the devil with you!" I turned away and let fly a string of profanities.

"Anne, I know you hate me. But your child needs a better home than an orphanage. I am offering to you...I would be willing to take your baby to Edward and your father in Charles Towne, if it is your wish."

I stared at the wall, trembling, trying to control my rage and yet trying to think over his kind and noble offer. I craned my head toward Mary. She gestured to her throat and swallowed, and then pointed to my belly. I knew her meaning. I closed my eyes, inhaled deeply, and then exhaled loudly. I turned back to James.

"James, forgive my cruel outburst. I jumped to conclusions that were wrong."

"I understand. The stress must be taxing," he said.

I wanted to launch into another diatribe; how could he know what it is like to walk in my shoes? Shoving my emotions aside, I forced myself to focus on his intent. I swallowed hard and asked, "Has my father responded?"

"Yes. He expressed great concern for your situation. Without hesitation he has asked to care for your child. He seems like a different man—more considerate." James passed a letter to me through bars. I accepted it and stuck it into a pocket of my dress.

"I will have a messenger alert me when you go into labor. I have purchased the services of a midwife to assist in your delivery and a wet nurse to care for the child."

I stared at him, realizing my teeth were clenched and grinding. "Why are you doing this for me, James?"

He glanced down and kicked at the prison bars a couple of times. He looked up and met my stare. "Memories of the time we cared about each other...There's still something within me for you. And this could be a way to make our peace...before the end."

I could muster no response so I merely nodded.

"I will take my leave now, but I will remain in touch," he said. He started away, his boots clicking the cobbled floor.

"James?"

He stopped and glanced over his shoulder.

"Thank you."

"You're welcome, Anne." He disappeared down the corridor.

I stood at the bars, still in shock, my emotions in turmoil. I thought for a long time about James, Edward, and my father.

"That was thoughtful," Mary said after a time.

"Yes, I suppose it was."

"He's nothing like I imagined him, like you described him."

I traced the edge of an iron bar with my finger and felt my baby kick in my womb. "He's changed. All of us have. He's a man now." I leaned against the wall and slid down beside Mary. I caressed my belly.

"He looks downright manly in that uniform," Mary said. Before I could comment, she was overcome with a coughing fit. I patted her on the back. She hacked and spat on the floor. Her mucous was a combination of yellowy phlegm and frothy blood.

"Damn doctors and their purgatives and blood lettings. Don't do a bit of good," Mary said. "A black plague on their pride."

I rested my hand on the back of her neck. It was clammy. I offered up a quick prayer for her healing. I would send thousands more to God in the next month.

Chapter XXXVII

Mary's illness worsened. She struggled to sleep, lurching up several times each night to cough uncontrollably and spew foul discharges. It was difficult for her to keep food down. She was now nearly six months along in her pregnancy. As her abdomen bulged, her strength drained, and she grew listless. The stifling humidity only magnified her discomforts. The doctors had raised their hands in surrender. I didn't want to accept the obvious; she would not reach her delivery date, or her scheduled execution for that matter.

I tried to make her as comfortable as possible. For hours she laid in my lap, slipping in and out of delirium, murmuring undecipherable phrases, sweating, and shivering.

As I stroked her hair, I read passages of Scripture aloud. She seemed to rest more peacefully when I did this. Images of my mother loomed out of the recesses of my mind. As a child, I had viewed my mother's illness as a mental and physical weakness. Now, as I contended with this infirmity in Mary, my friend, whom I saw as strong in every way possible, I felt confused. I imagined my mother's spirit, hovering near me, supporting me during my pregnancies. Another dose of shame surged around my heart. I whispered an apology to her for my restlessness and for my haste in leaving her presence when she had been ill.

Jealousy prickled me as well. I didn't easily give Mary's husband his allotted time to tend to her needs. I fought back the impulse to tell him Mary was too sick to see him. Such pettiness shocked me, but I also knew it was my constant concern and deep love for her that propelled my emotions.

Thomas struck a spirited and hopeful posture during his visits, but when Mary dropped off to sleep, he broke down and wept over her, rocking her gently in his arms and kissing her forehead lightly over and over. I had never seen such grief and misery in a man. His love moved me, and yet wounded me. I had never known such love with a man. When his visiting time was through, I hugged him and assured him she was in my safekeeping.

"I knew I was going to lose her, but I always thought I would have our child to preserve her memory," he said, "someone who would remind me of her and who would want to hear her story."

I cried with him. After he left, Mary stirred to sudden alertness and called to me. I knelt beside her.

"He's a good man. His heart will heal, and he'll eventually find another," she said. "Not that any other woman could possibly give him the thrills I have afforded him."

"Certainly not," I said, holding tightly to this moment of lucidity in her.

"Anne, I can feel it in my chest. Death is posting guard right outside those bars there." She coughed weakly. "Last word and testament time."

I brushed back the hair from her moist forehead.

"You are a fine woman, and you've been a grand friend," she began. "You gave me back my reason, my hope. It has been an adventure, a pleasure, and a privilege. And..." She pointed at me. "I will be waiting for you, with my baby in my arms, right in front of the pearly gates, proclaiming to heaven and earth at the top of my voice, 'Here is my Anne, the one I have been patiently waiting for: my good friend, former pirate, and prodigal pal. By God's grace, she belongs right here.' And we will walk arm in arm, and I will show you all around, never dissevered and reunited for forever."

I smiled and wiped my eyes. "I will miss you every day of my life, and I will long for our reunion in my every waking moment."

"Hmm. Not bad at all for a couple pregnant pirate-prostitutes on death row."

I kissed her on the cheek. "I love you, Mary. Could I ever hope to have another friend like you?"

"No. But I give you permission to try in vain. A shame we don't have a drink to toast ourselves: 'To the wind and the sea/Where our spirits soar free.' Now would you do me a favor?"

"Anything."

"Would you blow lightly on my face and neck and tickle my arms and legs with a feather. It cools me."

I spent most of the night soothing her fever.

Just as the first rays of light peeked through the prison bars, Mary slipped into unconsciousness. I held her until she breathed her last. It felt like my heart stopped with hers. How could I face my last hours without her? I thought of her baby slowly dying within her. I could not imagine a more peaceful place for her child's life to end than in the comfort of her womb.

I could not bring myself to notify the guards of her death. I kept waiting for her to wake up, but later that morning they knew something was wrong. The guards had to pry her from me, and I watched as they wrapped Mary in a blanket and carried her and her child out. Thomas made arrangements for her burial. I was not allowed to attend, but I did not offer a complaint. We had already said our good-byes. Turning to David's song for his dead friend, Jonathan, I began to read aloud, changing the second-to-last verse in tribute of Mary: "I am distressed for you, my *sister Mary.* You have been very pleasant. Your love to me was more wonderful, passing the love of *men.*"

I sat in a corner of my cell and spent the day thinking of other places and times, giving honor to Mary for all she had been to me. My every thought celebrated her image and character, and recalled her words and ways. Now completely alone, it felt like the walls were closing in on me, and I was cast into the deepest gloom I had ever known. My mind reeled with such sorrow, a prison of my soul.

I had only two things left to do: give birth and be strung up. I despaired, my soul at the bottom of the darkest pit, starving for a glimmer of light.

Toward evening my reverie was broken by a visit from James. It surprised me how happy I felt to see him again. Since our last meeting, my heart had been thawing toward him.

"I wanted to see how you were," he said. "I am sorry you lost your friend."

"Thank you. Maybe it was better this way. We talked and she died in my arms."

"A harsh blessing. It must be lonely here now."

"Ghosts from my past are my only company. I do have my memories and a Bible," I said.

"I just wanted to say...well, if you wish. I would be here for you."

The last rays of the day's sun cast a glare between us. I squinted through the light at him. "James, I have been thinking a great deal in here. I know I don't deserve it, but I want to ask if you would forgive me...for betraying you and abandoning you. I must have hurt you tremendously."

He kept his gaze steady on mine. "It did, Anne, more than you can ever know." He paused. "I'm sorry for my lies."

I glanced down, feeling the weight of our sorrow smothering me. "We were young."

He took my hands.

I shook my head. "I kept trying to minimize my regrets, but I have only seemed to multiply them. Could you save me from one worry that weighs heavily on me?"

"What is that?"

"Take my baby to Father and Edward."

"I will."

We slipped into a lingering silence.

"Well, if I knew we were going to bare our souls and repent of our wrongs, I would have cleaned up the place and dressed up for the event," I said with a smirk.

James laughed. "I always loved your quick wit."

"Get arrested and join me. You'll get your fill of it."

"Would I have to turn pirate?"

"It's the only life." We snickered together. "James, could you stay for a spell?"

"Yes, Anne."

I sat down on the floor. He started to reach for a barrel, but changed his mind and sat down beside me on the stones, with only the bars between us.

"You'll get your uniform dirty."

He shrugged his shoulders. "His Majesty's Royal Navy keeps me well supplied."

The rest of the evening we shared our stories. I told him of my pirate life and my amazing encounter with Mary. He found our breast-baring experience particularly amusing. James told me that shortly after my disappearance, he had been in such despair that he joined the navy. The first year had been a combination of harsh restrictions and severe punishments. He was strapped to the mast, stripped, and flogged twice, but his hard work paid off in time. He was trained as a gunner and learned sword fighting. His vessel was commissioned as a privateer, with orders to plunder enemy ships from France and Spain as well as destroy or detain any pirates they encountered.

"I once saved the bosun's life. That's where I got this scar." He traced it from his forehead down to his nose. "Nearly died. After my recovery they rewarded me with an officer's rank for my valor and meritorious service to the crown."

James described how Governor Rodgers had assigned him to Captain Barnet's vessel for the purpose of snuffing out piracy around Jamaica. "We captured the pirate, Vane, and then went after Rackham. That's obviously how we met again."

"Mary said I was the queen of chance encounters."

We talked well into the night. I expressed my initial captivation and ensuing disillusionment with the pirate life. There was Rackham, the pirates, Mary, and my miscarriage—all lost to me, and now my death was inching ever closer. Though it was bittersweet, we reminisced about our brief life together and the subsequent separation. While I had many regrets, I could not lie to James and claim I did not have some fond memories of my pirate life as well. I could see my words did not please James, but being so close to death, I felt more lies would only diminish what little dignity I still possessed. When he finally left, I thanked him for his attentive ear and kind heart. Then I crouched in a corner and wept.

The next two months passed agonizingly slowly. I looked forward only to James' twice weekly visits. Otherwise, I fought the insects and rats, read the Bible and John Bunyan's *Pilgrim's Progress*, and considered my provisional life. Each verse and chapter of the Scripture gave me a growing sense of comfort and peace.

James had brought me the leather-bound version of Bunyan's allegory on his next visit. "He wrote it during the twelve years he was stuck in an English prison. It's soulful," he said.

"What was his crime?"

"Preaching without a license."

"I was hoping you would say privateering without a license. Twelve years?" I opened the book. There were drawings with the text. "Thank you, James."

I read it voraciously, identifying with such characters as Obstinate, Hypocrisy, and especially Ignorance. The City of Destruction, the Slough of Despond, the Valley of Humiliation, and the trial in Vanity Fair were vivid settings. I thought of Charles Towne, New Providence, and Port Royal. I had indeed dwelt in each of those places for a season, and had been led astray by Flatterer of the Delectable Mountains and the Country of Conceit. Now I was locked away in Doubting Castle under the charge of Giant Despair and his wife Diffidence. When Pilgrim reached the Celestial City, I closed the book. It was a dream I could not imagine.

Chapter XXXVIII

The day of life and death arrived. My distended belly ached, and I had not been able to find a comfortable way to sit, stand, or lie down for the past few days. Finally my water broke. I called to the guards frantically and repeatedly, all the while trying to rest on the clean set of blankets James had brought me. I waited for the midwife to come and ease my fears and pangs. A couple of hours passed. My agony was excruciating and my loneliness miserable. Finally James walked up, and when he discovered that the midwife had failed to show up, he railed at the guards and demanded to be let into my cell. He adjusted the blankets and pillowed my head with his naval coat. He softly patted my face with a moist cloth.

"I am so sorry you've been alone all this time. If I had known..."

I gritted my teeth and fought the impulse to curse at him. "I'm glad you're here with me now," I said. The pain was so sharp I struggled to catch my breath between each word I spoke.

I do not know how long I languished in labor. It felt like an eternity times two. I envisioned my mother floating above me, fanning me with her angelic wings and offering me words of comfort and strength. James stayed with me the whole time, whispering encouraging words. These sometimes refreshed me, but more often they enraged me. With James' arms around me, I could smell him, and the memory of our intimacy took me back to our days together. I wanted to linger in those fond thoughts, but my searing contractions were coming one on top of another.

It embarrassed me some to have James hunkered down between my legs to help in the delivery, but the compulsion to push overwhelmed that passing concern. My energy was spent, and I cried out to James that I no longer had the power to go on. I began to sob.

James looked up. "I can see the top of your baby's head!"

I took a deep breath, squeezed my eyes shut, leaned forward, and started to scream and push at the same time. Then it was over. My baby had entered the world. The rest of my life could now be measured by the hourglass.

It was James who first held my baby, James who smiled and told me the child was a girl, James who cut the umbilical cord, James who washed my wailing daughter and disposed of the afterbirth, and James who swaddled the infant and rested her in my arms. He did all of this with confidence, yet gentleness.

"Do you have a name for her?"

"Mary," I whispered. "She is precious." I began to weep because I knew I had no more than one day before I would be separated from my daughter for the rest of her life.

Nursing my daughter and then snuggling her against my heart as she slept infused me with a love I had never known. I spent the night plotting an escape, thinking of ways to persuade James to assist my daughter and me to freedom. But even as I tried to stand, my body refused to obey my commands.

The next morning I awoke with a start. I looked around the cell. James was not there. I called to the guards but no one answered. Then I heard the sound of footfalls. An official approached and held up a parchment.

"Anne Bonney. I have an official document from Sir Woodes Rodgers, governor of Jamaica under the aegis of our British Majesty."

The time had come. I cuddled my daughter close to me and kissed her forehead, her nose, her cheeks, her lips.

"Your sentence of death by execution…"

I stopped listening and began speaking to Mary, my daughter. "I will be waiting for you right at the pearly gates with your Aunt Mary and her daughter…"

"…has been pardoned…"

"…proclaiming to heaven and earth at the top of my voice, 'Here is my daughter, Mary, the one I have been patiently waiting for…'"

"…and you will be set free after…"

Then the word "pardoned" suddenly registered with me. I snapped my head upward, looking with shock at the official. James appeared from around the corner, then Edward, and then my father, who leaned on a cane. Unsteadily, he hobbled toward the bars. I was in a state of complete confusion.

"Here to rescue you once again, my Anne," Edward said with wink and a smile.

"I am stunned, too," James said. "They arrived a couple days ago, but I did not know about it until less than an hour ago."

"We had a few matters of commerce and law to negotiate with the governor," my father said. The smile on his face amazed me. His hair was sprinkled with gray and his face looked haggard and gaunt, but his eyes were softer than I had ever remembered.

"Father?"

"Yes, Anne, I know. So much to talk about, but suffice it to say, I am finally here for you," he said.

I fought back my tears. "But how is it I am free?"

"A ransom," Edward said.

"Your debt is paid in full," my father added. "Your condemnation is lifted once and for all."

The periwigged official cleared his throat. His tone was pompous, his manner impatient. "I have not yet finished reading the document of Governor Rodgers." He cleared his throat and began to read. "You are still required to pay the penalty for your first crime."

"First crime?"

"Nearly two years ago you were charged with adultery, abandoning your husband, defying British law, and escaping arrest and justice. You are duly ordered to the public square, where you will be stripped and flogged."

The three men in my life froze.

"I request the immediate opportunity to speak with Governor Rodgers on this issue," my father said.

The official rolled up the parchment. "Governor Rodgers made it clear that this punishment is unpardonable," he said. "There will be no considerations heard for a lesser sentence. You will be remanded to the public square at St. Jago de la Vega at 3:00 PM today to serve your sentence: Moses' Law—forty lashes, save one. Afterward, you will be set free on your own recognizance."

"I demand to speak with the governor! This is an outrage!" James shouted.

The official turned to James and smiled. "An interesting response, since it is your signature on the initial charges and your signature agreeing to the punishment." The official clicked his heels, wheeled about, and exited with artificial dignity.

"The bastard. Rodgers is struggling to save himself from debtors' prison in London. He was recently recalled to Britain," James said. "Everyone knows he is financially broken from failed investments and speculations. He blames the pirates for his downfall. This is a ploy to squeeze more money out of you." He pointed to my father.

"I gave him virtually everything I brought. I will have to offer a promissory note."

"If he can't get more money then he would like to exact a bit of revenge?" Edward asked.

James nodded. "Sounds like Rodgers, the leech."

My father assured me he would use every means possible to secure my pardon, and James echoed his words. As James assisted my father down the corridor, I could hear them planning strategies for my release. Only Edward remained with me. He looked exactly as I had remembered him.

"It is so good to see you, Anne. You've grown into a beautiful woman, and a mother, I see," he said. His tone was warm and good-humored as always.

"I missed our talks," I said.

"I missed your spirit."

"Edward, are you disappointed in me?" I wiped my eyes.

"Anne, this is a homecoming." He reached out and took my free hand and squeezed it. "We're going to kill the calf that's been fattening ever since you left us."

I showed him my daughter and told him my story. When I told him about killing Throckmorton, he controlled his shock pretty well, though after telling him the grisly details of my two years as a pirate, Edward was visibly jolted.

He told me he was married now, and detailed how he had helped my father through his emotional and physical collapse after a slave revolt on his plantation. Father had been beaten so badly he had spent the next two months bedridden. Only Edward and members of a church visited him and assisted in his convalescence. During this time he had experienced a spiritual revival in his heart.

"During our voyage here, he spoke of it as a rescue and ransom mission. He kept mumbling the text: "He gave Himself a ransom for all."

The guards interrupted our conversation. They unlocked the jail door, read the sentence again, and led me out of the prison into the street. Edward helped me walk because I still felt weak from my delivery. We reached the square and I saw the whipping post. A small price to pay for your sins, I thought. An adulterer, a murderer, a pirate, and a thief—I deserved the very fires of hell. A good thrashing seemed an endurable price to pay. I handed little Mary to Edward and grabbed his shoulder to step up to the whipping post, mustering my inner resolve and dignity. A guard shoved me to the ground. I kneeled and he grabbed my wrists roughly and tied them to the splintered wood, and then I felt the back of my dress torn down to reveal my shoulders and back. I could hear a crowd beginning to gather behind me, jeering at me as they listened to the charges read aloud. James came dashing frantically around the corner of a building.

"Anne, I'm sorry. He refused to see us. We can't save you from this," James said.

"There he is—watching," James said, pointing up to a balcony.

I looked over my shoulder and saw Governor Rodgers emerge from a pair of French doors onto a balcony of his mansion. His hands clasped behind his back, and I thought he acted smug and stern.

The crowd grew louder. I felt something cold, wet, and soft strike me on the back. It started to ooze down my spine. More rotten fruit and balls of mud pelted my back. Tears welled up into my eyes, but the sickness in my stomach as I anticipated the first lash left me feeling resolved. It would be over soon.

"I ask you to relinquish the charges," James shouted to the governor. "Since I made the initial complaint, I now appeal to your sense of propriety to withdraw the charges."

I craned my head to see his response. Governor Rodgers shook his head. When James began to plead further, he merely raised a hand to quiet him.

Several guards walked among the crowd, and they kept an eye on James. One soldier unleashed his whip and snapped it in the air—a bit of anticipation for me.

James planted himself between the soldier and me.

"Since you have refused my request," James shouted. "I humbly request that her punishment fall on me." James yanked off his jacket and stripped off his shirt. He turned to the crowd.

They sneered and heckled him. "Let the pirate whore be whipped!" one screamed. James fell to his knees, with his arms raised, appealing now to both Rodgers and the mob. "She has just given birth. Have mercy on her," he pleaded. "Let me stand in her place!"

"I like the idea. Let's see how this officer of Royal Britain can handle a whipping for his little harlot!" someone yelled from the crowd.

The tide started to turn. They began to cheer for James' flogging. I tried to protest against James' offer, but the raucous crowd drowned out my words.

Rodgers paused, pacing the veranda, caught between public opinion and personal vengeance. Finally he raised his hands. "If the people wish it, then let it be so, but the piratess must stay tied to the post. Choose your course."

The throng applauded and pelted us with more rotten fruit, muck, and animal feces.

I could feel James' arms wrap around mine. His warm chest pressed against my back, his body completely covering me. His knees rested against my heels.

"James, no. I deserve every bit of this," I said.

"Anne, you have been ransomed and pardoned of your crimes."

"But you shouldn't be scourged."

"I condemned you. I will take your stripes to save you."

"James, go away. I will take the beating I am due."

"You can't endure it. This is my choice."

The flogging began. I heard the crack and James's arms tautened, his chest quivered, and his knees stiffened. With each whiplash, I felt his chest heave. My ears were filled with the roar of the crowd. I wanted to scream and rail at them with curses, but I could see this wouldn't help James. I began to recite Psalm 23 and the Lord's Prayer over and over. The flogging seemed to go on interminably.

A remnant of Scripture entered my mind and I began to weep. "By His stripes we are healed." I whispered to God a plea for His forgiveness and thought about all He had endured for the salvation of His sheep gone astray. My starving was complete, and my prodigal soul yearned to return to the Lord.

I could feel James' tears drop on my neck and drops of his blood and sweat spatter on my sides. I moved my head and could see Edward holding little Mary and my father hunched over beside him. Tears flowed down their faces. All this suffering for a stubborn-minded, rebellious, fool-headed young woman, I thought. It made no sense at all.

Love and forgiveness never do.

It was finally finished. The soldiers lifted James and carried him to a bench. Edward cut my cords, and I hobbled over to James and held his head against my chest. I was crying and blubbering repeated apologies. He put his hand to my lips and shook his head for me to quiet. I held him for a few minutes and then I whispered, "I'm going to take care of you."

I spent the entire night going back and forth between breastfeeding my daughter and tenderly dressing the wounds on James' back, wetting his face and neck with a cool cloth, and fanning him. I would not let Edward or my father help me. It was a night unlike any other I had experienced, and I was distressed and grateful for it. I was so full of love for both James and little Mary.

Chapter XXXIX

One week later, I stood at the bowsprit of the *Phoenix*, a merchant schooner cruising for the Carolinas. With little Mary in my arms, James by my side, Edward and my father somewhere on deck, and the Caribbean breezes tossing my hair about, I looked out onto the sea in deep reflection. I was heading back to the home where my mother lay buried. My friend, Mary, was buried in Jamaica. The pirate crew shared a common, unmarked grave in Kingston. Jack Rackham continued to sway on a gibbet in Port Royal. Governor Rodgers had been recalled to London to face a debtor's prison. Though we had made inquiries, Thomas Deane's whereabouts remained a mystery.

The year was now 1721. I had been a pirate for two years. Divine design granted me a daughter to rear, and my body had not rejected her. I was grateful for this blessing. Now I looked on the horizon and realized once again I had choices. What was it I wanted? And for what purpose had I been rescued from the hangman's noose?

As I gazed up at the blue sky, sprinkled with streaks of feathery clouds, I felt first and foremost that I wanted to know the Lord of the Heavens, in a way I had never felt before.

I also wished to reacquaint myself with Edward, my mentor and protector. And I wished for a friendship with my much-changed father. As I glanced at the sure face of James, standing in his uniform, I now hoped to revive my first love and reignite our passion. But would he have me back? Forgiveness is one thing, but forgetting is not possible. To leave one's scars behind and start anew is truly noble. I had always striven to keep control over all matters of my life, but I realized the possibility of reconciling with James resided outside the realm of my control. I felt powerless to win back his love.

I looked up at the clear blue sky, listening to the rippling of the sheets in the wind and the sizzle of the foam along the hull. The sun began to canter toward the horizon. All my old love for the sea rushed through me. I decided that despite where life would direct me, I would have to live near the ocean.

I heard the captain shout to his crew to keep a wary lookout for pirates. I grinned at the irony. I wondered what I would do if we were attacked by a band of cutthroat marauders. There are too many priceless treasures onboard this ship to lower my sails, I thought. A fight to the bitter end would be my one and only course.

"James?"

"Yes, Anne?"

"Could you ever imagine trying again?"

"Trying what?"

I looked into his eyes. "Love."

He smiled, drew his right arm around me, and pulled me against him. "I could."

When I had been imprisoned, I thought I had lost everything, but now it seemed God was renewing many things for me. He had brought back the loves of my life, which I had turned away from—a blessing beyond belief. If Mary were here, my world would be complete.

A sweet scent suddenly came up in the breeze. I turned. There was a presence, imagined or real, but it didn't matter. I lifted my hand as if to toast and whispered, "To the wind and the sea/Where our spirits soar free, Mary."

978-1-58348-467-8
1-58348-467-1

CPSIA information can be obtained at www.ICGtesting.com
Printed in the USA
BVOW04s1825151214

379497BV00001B/38/A